The Iron Triangle

Joe Rhinehart

ISBN: 1-4196-8026-9
ISBN-13: 9781419680267

And it came to pass in the morning, that David wrote a letter to Joab... saying, Set ye Uriah in the forefront of the hottest battle, and retire ye from him, that he may be smitten, and die ... And the men of the city went out, and fought with Joab; and there fell some of the people... and Uriah the Hittite died also.

Samuel II

Sir, I hope the bastards surround us; then we'll know where they are.

Sergeant Arch Bigwitch
the Iron Triangle, 1966

ACKNOWLEDGEMENTS

This is a work of fiction and any resemblance between characters and events in this story and real persons and historical events is purely coincidental. The First Battalion 202nd Infantry is also fictitious; however, the other battalions of the 1st Infantry Division mentioned herein are indeed real.

To Colonel James A. Franklin, *the finest Infantryman I have known, and* **to Bill Hawkins***, without whose help this book would never have been published.*

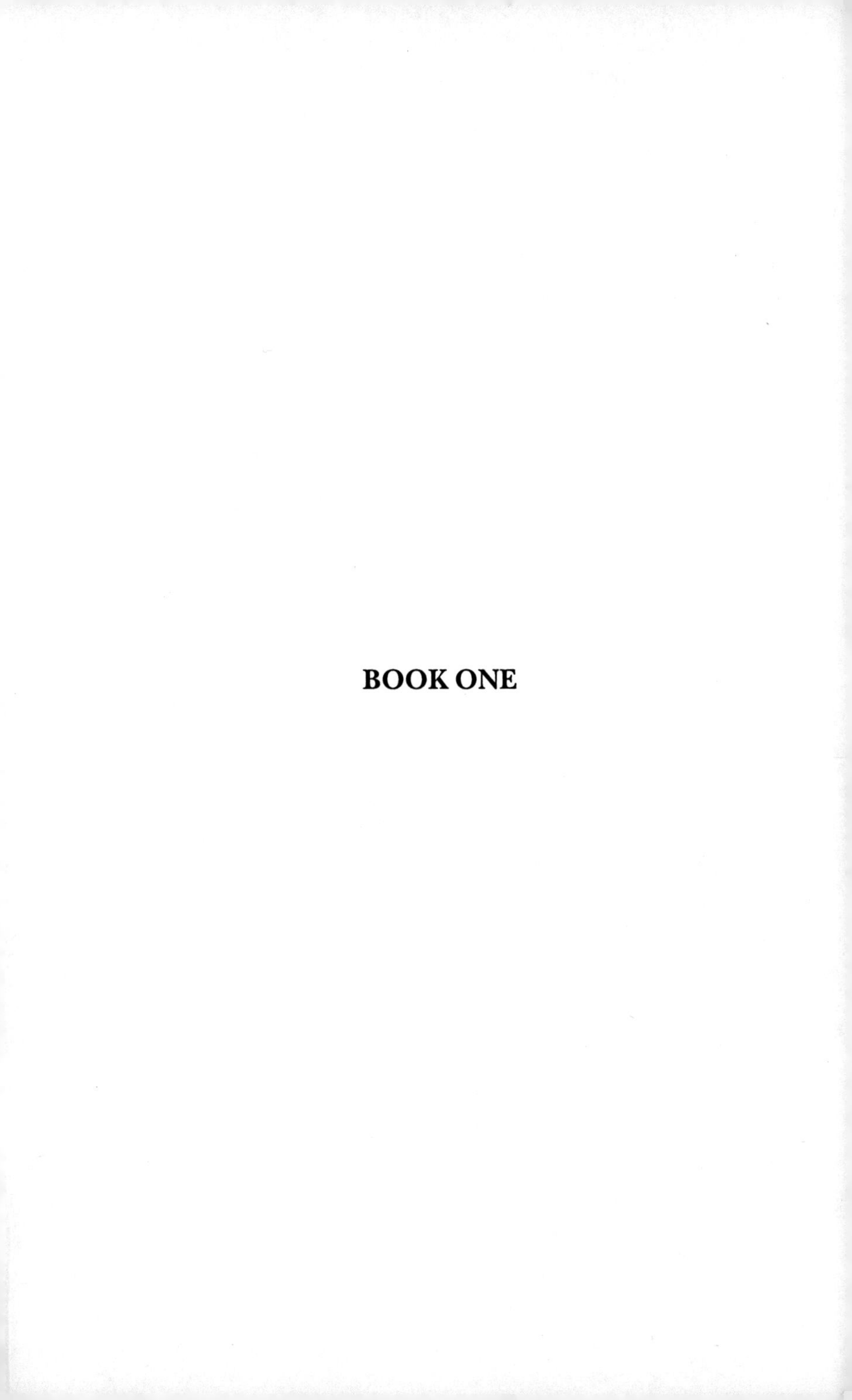

BOOK ONE

CHAPTER 1

The snow came early, and the autumn hues in the hills and mountains quickly gave way to the cold, harsh reality of the Korean winter. Chains clanked against metal fenders, as the U.S. Army vehicles broke through the slush in a seemingly endless fight against the elements.

"Damn the cold," muttered Lieutenant James Worthington, as he watched his soldiers marching in light winter clothing to be changed to thermal gear when they stopped.

The news that winter held snippets of the growing war in Vietnam, but Worthington was more worried about keeping pace with his Korean counterparts, and getting back to base and the warm confines of the Officer's Club. The Brigade Club was a dimly lit drab wood and stone building at Camp Casey at the edge of the town of Tongduchon. It was dry, clean, and warm inside and stocked with plenty of alcohol.

"Hey Aggie, your skirt's too short," Worthington teased one of the Korean waitresses. They were dressed in short red skirts and blouses showing nice brown legs that Worthington thought looked even nicer as his time in Korea grew longer.

Along the Demilitarized Zone separating South and North Korea the situation was tense; from time to time small North Korean infiltration teams were detected and killed as they tried to cross to the South. The DMZ is four kilometers wide, and North Koreans control the northern two kilometer strip, and the South Koreans and Americans control an equal strip to the south.

A wailing siren blasted Worthington out of bed and a deep sleep.

"Another Goddamned monthly alert," he yelled, as he rallied his sleepy troops in a mad rush to be ready to move out in full combat gear in the two hour limit allowed by some Division Colonel's relentless clock. Units had to load all kitchens, supplies, and ammunition, but never seemed to have enough trucks, or some fool had misplaced the key to the ammunition dump, or vehicles wouldn't start in the icy cold. Somehow we rolled past the gates in the allotted two hours, but the inspecting generals and colonels weren't satisfied. That night back in the general's mess, the officers raised martinis in hand and laughed about how the exercise had gone.

"One of these days it will be the big one. We'll be facing commies and we won't think this is so funny," Worthington muttered.

That was the reality of life in Korea. It was tense every day, and no more than ten percent of the men could be on leave at any one time. We lived with the pressure. And it shaped us.

But we learned to cope; discovered most little secrets about decreasing preparation time and reduced most fumbling and confusion to practical motion. Combat packs stayed tightly packed and strapped for movement, and when we went to bed at night we laid out our clothes and gear so that when the screeching blast of the siren came we knew where things were. We could function, even though we had gone to bed drunk two hours before. When we reached that point of experience we didn't worry anymore, and though we cursed the siren when it blew, we knew we would not fail, that our platoon would not fail and that everyone could move out within two hours.

My platoon quartered in a quonset hut along with several hundred others, in the long narrow valley established as Camp Casey, following the armistice in 1953. The wind howled between the steep bald ridges overlooking Camp Casey and down the valley and through the cracks of the old quonset structures. The men slept in sleeping bags laid out on mattresses on double-deck steel cots. The platoon lieutenants slept in an identical, but separate quonset hut across the road from the men. That hut was known, less than affectionately, as "Combat Alley," and usually just called "the Alley." The mess hall was located near the men, and despite stories about army food, meals were not bad. I ate there in the mornings and in the officer's club otherwise.

My platoon was full strength and consisted of three rifle squads. The platoon-sergeant was a Korean War veteran and a good leader. With him assisting, my job was made easier. There were times in garrison when he didn't need or want me around. He felt that my job was to lead the platoon tactically in the field and leave leadership in garrison to him.

We trained hard that November. There were routine problems; one or two bad soldiers and a Korean augmentee with English trouble. Overall, my men were hard physically and proficient at their jobs as December came.

CHAPTER 2

Major William David Ricksley had played end on the Army football team at West Point during his cadet days. That, and just being a West Point graduate, seemed the high points of his life. Although, according to rumor, he'd never played in a varsity game and had been a bench-warmer for four years, his days on the West Point team were his favorite subject. His straight black hair was combed back; his lips were thin, a sort of purple color and didn't meet exactly where they should have. A part of the upper lip hung over the lower lip in a crooked way and gave the appearance of a sardonic smile, even when he had no intention of smiling. His nose had been broken during Plebe boxing. He was proud of that and often spoke of it in the way that some men brag about the Purple Heart from past combat operations. At one time or another, in the officers club bar, we had all heard how it had been broken four times and that there was not much cartilage left.

Ricksley had served a tour in the British Army as an exchange officer and was self-impressed by that highlight in his career. He affected a phony British accent, and in the field wore a scarf around his neck that flowed behind him when he stood up in an open moving vehicle. He performed frequently to achieve that specifically desired "Lawrence of Arabia" effect. As he went about his duties as the operations and training officer of the battalion, he paused from time to time to pull reflectively on his Meerschaum pipe, ever conscious of both the image he tried to create and of those who observed him. He tried to do this in a casual manner, but the conscious effort was precisely the thing that betrayed his intentions. Natural accents are one thing but affected accents are hypocritical, and the phoniness disgusted me. Ricksley wasn't British but he tried to be and obviously could never succeed.

Ricksley had decided early in his career as an army officer that the sure way to success, which for him meant a rapid advancement through the ranks up to general officer, was to please the officer he worked for. As his rater, that officer held full power to advance or arrest his career. He constantly sought to please and comfort his boss in even the smallest of situations. "Would the Colonel care for a cigar?" Or, "I've had your driver bring your jeep to the door of the club, Sir." In the battalion area he sought the battalion commander's company on and off duty and drank with him at the club as often as possible. His career was advancing well indeed and absolutely in accordance with his time schedule.

More than anything, Ricksley was known to the officers equal and junior to him as a "rank bully." A rank bully could be described best as a man who uses his rank, power, or position the same way a strong bully uses his strength. Thus, rank becomes strength, because rank provides security against retaliation against its owner; it has the force of law behind it. Because of the Uniform Code of Military Justice, the law in the American military, no retaliation is possible without risking confinement, loss of pay and allowances, and an abrupt end to one's military career, no matter how many years or how much sweat and blood one has invested. "Lieutenant, I'll shoot your kneecaps off," or "I'll rip your face off" were two of his favorite verbal bashings. Junior officers frequently gave briefings in the battalion, usually to their senior officers. Ricksley's favorite type of bullying was to dress down an officer giving a briefing in front of his peers. "Captain, if you don't know what you're talking about, get the hell out of this briefing room." Or, "Lieutenant, you're a fool and a disgrace to the battalion." Few had been spared this embarrassment, and it had served to cast a cloud of gloom over the officers of the battalion. While we hated it, we learned to live with it.

Ricksley's smile was a little more twisted than usual as he approached us at the bar of the club that evening.

"Worthington, when are you finally going to get your act in order?"

I didn't know what he was talking about, and my mind raced in anticipation of expected chastisement and its accompanying embarrassment.

"Sir, what are you referring to?"

"That disaster of a rifle range you ran this morning. The report says your sergeant reported to the inspecting officer late and very sloppily. The police of brass looked like amateur hour." He waited for my reaction, and I felt relieved because I knew he had the wrong officer.

"Sir, we weren't on the range today, nor were we inspected."

Suddenly Ricksley was confused, and as suddenly his confusion turned to anger. He had obviously misread the report. He quickly turned to Tom McCarter and gritted the question to him.

"Did you run that company rifle range this morning, Lieutenant?"

"Yes Sir, I did."

"Then say so, damn it. No guts? Where in the hell did you get your commission? Out of a cereal box?"

McCarter's face was red with anger but clearly he was in a losing situation.

"We will do better next time, Sir."

"McCarter, you may be running out of next times." Ricksley wheeled and bolted into the dining room as if he could spare no more of his valuable time.

"That son-of-a-bitch. He sent that asshole of a sergeant who works for him out to the range this morning, and he turned in a bad report because he wasn't treated like an officer." Tom was visibly shaken and angry.

"Hey, Tom baby," I cajoled. "Don't worry about that guy. He's that way to everyone. Don't give it a thought."

But it was only after several more drinks that Tom began to feel better.

Tom McCarter was one of our company platoon leaders, and where my platoon succeeded, his platoon did as well or better. To say that we didn't compete would be a lie. He was a slender, blond officer from Pennsylvania, and the girls in the clubs in Seoul thought he was a double for Steve McQueen. Now Ricksley had made one more enemy.

Nolan Broyles, the other platoon leader in the company, joined us and ordered a martini. He was Irish, a short and pleasant parachutist who had served a tour in an airborne division before he was commissioned. He was very proud that he was "airborne" and referred to those who weren't as "leg." "He's a leg" or "He's a dirty leg," he usually remarked, half in jest, but he also used that expression when he was angry.

"There's a basketball game in the fieldhouse tonight," Nolan told us.

"Yeah, it's a woman's basketball game," Tom said without enthusiasm.

"But it's an American university team playing some Korean bank team, and afterwards they're coming to the club." Tom decided to go, and they prodded me to come along.

I was tired from training the previous night, but after another drink I decided to go. There was precious little else to do at Camp Casey. We left Choe the bartender a tip and stepped outside into air that was clear and cold with the stars hanging sparsely in the early evening sky. The outline of the long, high ridge bordering the south side of Camp Casey was distinct, and the line of the crest looked like the form of a woman lying on her back and looking up. We caught the post bus, crowded with soldiers on their way to Tongduchon and a night of fast girls and slow booze. Nolan yelled at the driver to let us off at the fieldhouse, where we pushed through the crowd. Some of the troops on the bus were from our company, and they spoke to us as we got off.

The fieldhouse was packed and a thick haze of cigarette smoke hung over the noisy crowd of soldiers. Korean girls signed on post by their soldier friends, watched the game with the troops. The soldiers were black, white and brown, and Korean augmentees. KATUSA' s as they were called, were mixed in with our units. They served for three years; good soldiers with high IQ's who had been hand-picked for this program. "KATUSA" was an acronym for "Korean Augmentation to United States Army."

The Korean team was very good and three of the starting five were members of the Korean National Team. They were fast and well conditioned and their shooting and defense were solid. At halftime they led the Stanford girls by ten points, and they widened the margin in the third quarter, much to the delight of the Koreans. The center was a tall graceful girl who couldn't have been more than nineteen, and her shooting was deadly. She preferred shooting from the inside but she had the ability to pull up during a drive and score on a one-handed jump shot. Her name listed on the program was Hae Ja Kim, and the mimeographed program said she was twenty-one and from Ha Nam Dong in Seoul.

After the Koreans won the game, we stopped across the street at the Aviation Battalion officers club for a drink. The bar was crowded with loud helicopter pilots in their flight suits. One warrant officer pilot looked at the three of us and whispered to the captain next to him. "Dog-tag check!" the latter bellowed; the bar hushed, and everyone pulled their dog-tags out and displayed them to the crowd. Nolan didn't have his, and by the house rule of the club he had to buy a round of drinks for everyone at the bar. He was angry but it was a rule posted in large letters behind the bar, so he had to pay. I lent him the ten dollars he was short.

Then the aviators tried to throw him over the bar. Nolan punched the first one to touch him, and blood trickled from the aviator's nose. I knew the battle was about to begin. We started backing for the door, shoulder to shoulder, but the rush of aviators caught us, and we had to punch, kick and wrestle our way out the front door of the club. A large warrant officer with a handlebar moustache slugged me in the side of the head, and I went tumbling on my back out into the gravel. I kicked a tall captain in the groin as I got up, and he doubled over. Nolan heaved a fist-sized stone through the open front door, and it smashed the large mirror, emblazoned with the battalion motto. The gravel lot was a battlefield, and we were starting to get our asses kicked when suddenly the aviators scattered and ran. Like keystone cops the MP's roared in with lights flashing. We ran through the alley past the club, up the hill behind it and came out through an old Korean graveyard. We made it back through the barracks to the battalion area, stopped in the Alley and cleaned up. The soap and water burned my cut lip, and we joked about "the battle of aviator's gulch." I cleaned up the best I could and changed clothes. My head ached and throbbed; I wondered if that warrant officer had hit me with a hammer.

"Hey James, what were you doing down on your ass in that gravel?" Broyles laughed.

"Goddamnit, you didn't exactly cover yourself with glory, Broyles! You should'a spent more time on that warrant officer and less time breaking mirrors!"

"I could have whipped them by myself if the MP's hadn't showed!" Tom yelled.

"Yeah, laying there on your back you could have whipped them! Strangest fighting position I've ever seen," Broyles responded.

CHAPTER 3

I left them arguing over whether we had won the fight or not and went out the door of the Alley, into the brigade officers club. I ordered a beer. My head ached a bit, but after a short while it felt better, and I went into the dining room where the players from the basketball game were being entertained. The officers flocked around them, and the Stanford coach was overly concerned about the prospects for her team members. The Korean team was the object of at least as much attention, and the center Hae Ja Kim sat at a table sipping a bottle of coca cola with two teammates.

The officers mingled with the girls. I tentatively sat down at the table with Hae Ja Kim and the other two Koreans and introduced myself to them in Korean. They replied in English which was better than my Korean. They wouldn't drink anything but coke, so I filled the awkward moment by ordering another beer. I was interested in Kim. Her hair was shoulder length and luxurious, and her facial features were fine. She was an incredibly attractive girl. She laughed easily, and I hardly noticed the other girls as we talked.

"You played a fine game tonight," I began.

"No, but anyway we won," she laughed. Her teeth were straight and white, and while her lips were not thin they were heavy in a pretty way. I suddenly became aware of an unexplainable, uneasy feeling, as if something extremely important was about to happen.

Two lieutenants that I didn't know pushed in and sat down at our table and began talking to Kim's friends. The band started in the lounge. I invited Kim to dance, and we went into the dim light of the lounge and held each other, moving in unison to the slow music. The next song was a rock and roll arrangement, and we danced to that facing each other. Her laughing eyes said she was having a good time, so we danced to two more fast tunes before we sat down at a table in the lounge, perspiring and laughing. She finally let down her guard and drank a beer with me as we talked. As we talked I tried to pin down the cause of my emotional attraction to her.

"Where did you go to school?"

"I graduated from Seoul High School," she glanced shyly across the bustling room.

"But didn't you want to go to a university?"

"Yes, but I was selected for the National Basketball Team and given a job at this bank so I would play for the bank team and be available for the national team. And where are you from, James?"

"I come from a small town in the mountains of western North Carolina," I said.

"And are you a graduate of West Point?"

"No, I'm afraid not. I went to Officer's Candidate School. That's why I look a little older than the average lieutenant."

"You are probably Irish or German," she said.

"And why would you draw that conclusion?" I asked, mildly surprised at the forwardness of her statement.

"Because you have a kind of blondish red hair and brown eyes. Isn't that what you Americans refer to as strawberry blond?"

"I suppose. Will you continue to work at the bank when your career as a player ends?" I was curious because I had heard stories about the exploitation of Korean athletes.

"I don't know. I may have to move on to something else."

"So there it was," I thought. "She was being used, and like others in the same situation would continue to be used until she was thirty years old and would then lose both her position on the team and her job in the bank to another nineteen year old basketball flash." But she didn't seem unhappy about her situation.

"I must go," she suddenly murmured.

"Can I see you in Seoul tomorrow?" I blurted.

"Yes," as she moved away from the table, looking back over her shoulder.

"I'll meet you at the lounge of the Crest Hotel at five," I spoke a little too loudly.

"I'll be there at five." She turned to leave with the bank team.

I nursed another beer and thought of Kim for awhile. The club closed, and I went home to the Alley through the cold clear night. I entered my room and undressed slowly; my head had begun to throb again. My ribs on the left side were bruised and sore, and I could vaguely remember a glancing kick there as I tried to get up from the gravel in the parking lot at the Aviation Club. "Crazy-assed aviators," I thought as I lay down on my bunk and pulled the brown army blanket over me.

That night I dreamed of dancing and holding a tall Korean girl who was not Kim, and woke in the middle of the night, sore, my head aching, and knew I would have trouble going back to sleep. I lay and thought of Hae Ja Kim and was puzzled and surprised, because tonight was the first time I had known she existed. I finally fell asleep before daylight and woke as the Korean dawn crept through the small window over my bed.

I showered, shaved and went across to the mess hall and met Tom and Nolan there with the company commander, Captain Laird. Laird was a good man to work for, and tried to take care of us. Like the rest of us, he suffered under the poor leadership and the lack of judgment of Ricksley and Lieutenant-Colonel Ziegler, the battalion commander.

Lieutenant-Colonel Weldon Ziegler was a confused commander. His priorities were wrong, and he didn't seem to be able to understand what was really important for the battalion to accomplish. He was what was known in the officer's corps as a "rock painter" – a commander interested only in cosmetics. How things looked, not how well the soldiers were trained or how prepared they were, mentally and physically, to fight a war, seemed to be his primary concern. In important decisions he acquiesced to Ricksley, and Ricksley was eager to gain the extra authority.

We ate breakfast, drank coffee and discussed the inspection we had planned for the morning. Captain Laird picked Tom's platoon for his personal inspection. My inspection was uneventful, and I finished and went to the club at noon. I ate lunch there and then went to the Alley.

I took a hot shower, dressed, and caught the post bus to the transfer point to Seoul. I sat next to a black soldier who had a transistor radio on his lap. We pulled out of the terminal, passed through the gate and turned south on the highway to Seoul.

The rice fields south of Tongduchon were all stubble, and piles of rice straw lay in bundles alongside the paddy dikes. Where there was water, it had frozen to ice between the stubble. The pines were green but everything else was a light brown. The bald mountains rose to the left and paralleled the highway; on the right paddy, fields of stubble stretched out and met the banks of the shallow river in the middle distance. Beyond the river, more brown hills rose in the far distance.

The bus hurried down the highway, passing American and Korean military vehicles, gravel and sand trucks, bicycles, and an occasional ox cart. We met a Korean Army artillery battalion moving north to fire on St. Barbara Range.

The bus turned right into Camp Mosier, where a sign said that this had been the site of an important mobile army surgical hospital (MASH) during the Korean War. We picked up three soldiers, turned back onto the highway and headed south again.

The bus neared Euijongbu, turned right off the highway again and went around to Camp Red Cloud. Some soldiers got off; others got on, and the bus went back on the highway and on into Seoul, where the traffic was thick, and the bus was slowed by the congestion. We stopped at Itaewon, and I got off with the black soldier with the radio. He went up the first alley past the bus and disappeared into the maze of pawnshops and bars.

CHAPTER 4

I walked up the street to the Han Hotel and hailed a cab for the Naija Hotel. The taxi went past Yongsan, then turned right and weaved in and out of traffic up the busy main street around Seoul's Old South Gate, past the Koguryo Hotel and City Hall and up past the statue of a famous Korean warrior, looking fierce in his armor, and into the wide concourse that was Se Jong Ro. We turned left at the entrance to the palace and reached the Naija, where I went into the hotel bar.

A large afternoon crowd drank and talked in the lounge. I sat at the bar and drank a beer. The Naija Hotel was known for its food, and if one wanted to impress a Korean friend it was a good place to go for dinner. The service was good but the dining room was always crowded, and if you had no reservation, on weekend nights you couldn't get in. I finished my drink and left. At the door to the dining room a Korean in a black tuxedo waited with the reservation book.

"We're booked full for the evening," he said without smiling.

I slipped ten dollars in MPC (military script used instead of green dollars) under his reservation book and told him, "For two at eight."

"Name, please."

"Worthington, James."

"Two for eight. It's OK."

"Thanks." I reserved a room for the night at the front desk, and took a cab to the Crest Hotel on the other side of town.

The most prominent landmark in Seoul is Nam San, meaning "south mountain." It rises high in the middle of the city and is topped with a tower. To get around the city you must cross Nam San or go around it. The Crest is located on the southeastern slope of Nam San; a tall plush hotel with well-to-do clientele, and there is a cocktail lounge and dining room near the top. I took a table by the window in the lounge and waited for Kim.

The window looked out over the south slopes of Nam San and after that the Han River, and one could see the two way traffic streaming along north and south of the Han River, parallel to the river. Beyond the river to the south the paddy fields flanked a north-south highway, and in the far distance the blue mountains rose. In the early evening the lights twinkled around the crests of some of the peaks, indicating the location of an air defense site, a communications station, or some other military compound. I sipped my drink and watched and waited.

It was nearly 1800 when she arrived. As she sat down at the table she apologized for being late. It was something or other about her job and her boss at the bank and having to recount drawer money because of a small change discrepancy. She was more beautiful than I remembered. She ordered some exotic looking pink fruit-punch drink. We sat and watched the darkness and the lights of Itaewon and the traffic along the Han River and talked about unimportant things. Later a Korean girl started singing, who was quite good. We left, took the elevator to the first floor and out to catch a cab.

We circled up and around Nam San, and I held her hand and sat close to her. We wound down Nam San, up the street and circled around Nam Dae Mun, the old south gate to the city, and up past the warrior's statue. The traffic was bumper to bumper. We passed the Korean guard at the gate and went into the hotel.

A Korean in black trousers, maroon jacket, and bow tie seated us at a table recessed in a small alcove. The room was dark except for the flickering candles that burned on the tables. We had privacy on three sides and could see the tables in front of us and the customers passing in or out of the dining room. We ate an appetizer and then the main course.

"Do you come to Seoul often?" she asked.

"No, perhaps once a month."

"Do you like Seoul?"

"Yes, very much, and more than ever tonight." I was mildly surprised at my own words and didn't know exactly why I had said that.

She smiled, "Is that so?"

"Of course."

"Have you travelled out of Korea much?" I asked.

"Yes. We have been to Japan to play three times and to Singapore once."

"And did you like Japan?"

"Singapore was much better, but Japan was OK because we beat them every time!" She laughed. "James, you seem to like sports very much. Did you play team sports in school?"

"Yes, I played football, soccer, and of course baseball in high school and even at an earlier age. I say 'of course baseball' because most Americans play at least a little baseball."

"And were you good?"

"Not particularly. Average I suppose, except for baseball. I really loved the game. I was a catcher; I chose that position because the catcher seemed to be more a part of the action, the strategy, than say an outfielder."

"Americans have so many opportunities!" she smiled.

"And how do you like working at the bank?"

"I hate it," she said simply without any explanation. I didn't pursue the subject.

We talked of small things and finished eating. After dinner we went into the cocktail lounge, had a drink, and left.

"Where to, Sir?" The cab driver asked in Korean.

"To the Eighth Army South Post Gate in Yongsan," I replied in Korean. It was cold and the driver opened the cab's front windows a half inch to melt the fog inside his windshield. In the Eighth Army Officers Club we got a table in the back lounge. The band was loud and not very good but we danced and talked.

"How tall are you, James?"

I was comfortably taller than Kim; perhaps two or three inches taller, but I was amused at her question. Obviously a girl that tall would be concerned with such things. "I'm six feet one inch."

She seemed delighted. "Oh, that is just right!" she beamed.

"Just right for what?" I joked.

She seemed mildly embarrassed. "No, a girl of my height has to think of those things," she smiled shyly.

I was sorry we had to leave soon because of the curfew. Everyone had to be off the streets by midnight, and starting around 2200, the rush for cabs began. Drivers started charging double fares and doing other things to take advantage of the curfew. At the gate we got a cab for her, and I kissed her lightly on the lips. She pushed me away and said good-night.

"May I call you tomorrow?"

"Yes, please do."

Kim waved through the rear glass of the cab. My breath caught in my throat; I couldn't help it. So quick, so unexpected, and why?

I caught a taxi for the Naija and stopped for a nightcap.

"Who was your lady friend, sir?" the bartender asked.

"A basketball player," I told him.

"Yes, I've seen her on television many times. She's very good." He seemed to show a slight resentment toward me, an American, taking a Korean girl of Kim's social status and public image to the Naija. I had the feeling that if I had gone there with some whore I picked up in Itaewon things would have been quite normal. But Kim was a national team athlete and in a way, she belonged to all Korean people. So I could feel the barman's disappointment at her coming here with me. Anyway, I didn't care, so I left the bar and picked up my key at the front desk and went upstairs to my room.

The room was too hot, but the heat couldn't be controlled because the thermostat was broken. I opened a window wide and let the cold night air cool me. I wrote a couple of letters, and tried to sleep but I kept thinking of Kim. I hadn't intended to get involved at all with anyone ever again, but I realized that I was becoming involved, and that if I wanted to stop it I would have to do it now. I finally fell asleep sometime after midnight.

I awoke with a headache the next morning. After a hot shower I went across to the lobby and bought the American newspaper, the Stars and Stripes, and a copy of the Korean Herald and read them as I ate. The news was about Vietnam and control of the government there and how the war against the guerrillas in the countryside was going. North Korea was protesting that

South Korean positions in the DMZ near Munsan had fired on North Korean positions. On the sports page of the Stars and Stripes there was an article on Paul “Bear” Bryant of Alabama. The writer said he was, or would become, the greatest football coach ever. The Korean Herald had a picture of President Park, (Chung Hee), cutting the ribbon at an opening ceremony dedicating a new recreation center in a small town north of Seoul.

Later I called Kim. We met at Seoul Station and took the bus out to Inchon. We walked along the deserted beach and didn’t say much. It was cold, and wind off the Yellow Sea began to cut, so we took a cab up to MacArthur Park and walked around. We stopped at the statue of General MacArthur. He stared majestically out over Inchon, to the point where he’d stood on the ship’s deck and watched the amphibious assault that morning in 1950. He had planned and executed the operation against the counsel of his subordinates. His forces had hit the beach here, knifed inland, and completely cut off and defeated the North Koreans. Subsequently, he drove their remnants all the way back up the peninsula to the Yalu River. I thought about how that would have unified the country under a free flag if the Chinese had not entered the war.

“My father fought here,” Kim said. “He was also an Infantryman, and he was much like you in some ways.”

“How do you mean?” I asked.

“Well, he was a patriot and he hated communism. His father was still in North Korea and too old and sick to make the trip south when my family fled from the North.”

“Yes,” I said.

“And you are a patriot, aren’t you?”

I had never thought of myself as a patriot but I had the feeling I was being put on the defensive rather than congratulated. "Perhaps."

"My father died near Wonju, in February of 1951, during the allied offensive," she said simply. I felt she was asking me to draw some conclusion, but I was aware that I was resisting being led in that direction.

We went to the Neptune Hotel in Inchon. At the bar we had a drink and then went into the game room and I played blackjack. She enjoyed the game, but couldn't play because she was Korean, and it was against the law for Koreans to gamble. I won fifty dollars and quit, but I had the feeling the dealer was a little angry because she hadn't intended that I quit ahead.

Outside it was colder; the sky was slate gray, and tiny specks of blue snow fell intermittently. We took the bus for Seoul. The old man who sat across from us wanted to speak English with me. He said he had been a KATUSA in the American Seventh Division during the war and was wounded five times. He pulled up the leg of his trousers, showing the ugly shrapnel wounds had turned to ragged scars across his bony shin and calf. His English was good, and he was eager to practice. Kim had bought a bag of tangerines from a vendor, and we shared them with the war veteran. He seemed very grateful as he munched reflectively on the tangerine and talked of great struggles against desperate odds, then finally went to sleep.

From Seoul Station we went over to the Bando Hotel and sat in the lounge and listened to the music. A man played piano while a girl sang popular songs and I held Kim's hand. I knew I was more committed to this relationship than I intended but I had no strong urge to do anything about it. Later, we ate, then left for Yongsan.

I kissed her as we parted at Yongsan; she waved as the taxi merged into traffic and disappeared.

I took the bus to Camp Casey and went on up to the club, where I found Tom. His right eye was shadowed with a deep purple wreath. We talked and laughed about the fracas at the Aviation Club. Someone started the dice up, and we played "horse" for the next drink. Ricksley joined the game. I knew he had heard about our trip to the Aviation Club. He lost the roll and bought the round. As he paid Choe, he looked at Tom and made some remark about its being a good thing that Tom didn't have to pay, because he would need the money to pay for the mirror at the Aviation Club. I knew we would hear more about that the next morning.

CHAPTER 5

The wailing screech of the siren pierced the night air, my feet hit the floor and I flipped on the light switch and started pulling on my field pants. It was 0400; I ran across to the platoon quonset and the platoon-sergeant gave me a count. The count was right, and the men had begun to draw weapons. I ran around to the orderly room, told Captain Laird we had a number of men who would be ready to move in another fifteen minutes.

"Good. It looks as if we will move," Laird said. The other platoon leaders were there. "Issue four C-ration meals to the men. I'll be back in a few minutes." He ran out the door in the direction of battalion headquarters.

I went back to the platoon area, the troops finished drawing weapons and squad leaders broke out C-rations. We were ready to move, and I had the men wait in the quonset hut sitting on their bunks. Captain Laird returned from battalion, and Tom, Nolan, the Weapons Platoon Sergeant, and I were waiting for him in the orderly room. We were short two lieutenants in the company, so the Weapons Platoon was commanded by the platoon-sergeant, a strong leader. If any platoon could get along without an officer it was the Weapons Platoon. Laird spread his map on a table and issued instructions. The division alert would be followed by the deployment of several units. Our battalion would conduct an airmobile assault to seize the high ground in an area northeast of Munsan, just south of the DMZ. The scenario called for us to block there, as part of an effort to stop a North Korean penetration into the area. Our company would lift out first, and my platoon was to seize the high ground around the sharp top of a peak on the company right. Tom's platoon would be on the left, and Nolan's platoon would be seven hundred meters back, in reserve.

We lifted off from on top of a ridge line just south of Camp Casey. The helicopters raced forward, nosed down, then picked up altitude and flew in formation to the northwest. I recognized the ground we flew over and knew the mountains we were going to assault very well. The helicopters hovered in; we slipped out of the doors, flattened on the ground, and waited, and took up hasty positions after the empty helicopters picked up and left.

We had landed on a ridge line, and the ground my platoon was to occupy was a short distance ahead. We moved forward rapidly, but cautiously, and took the hill according to our plan. We posted security, positioned machine-guns and started to dig foxholes. I located myself in the center, a little behind and above the line of foxholes, for control purposes. As the men dug in, I sent out a small patrol to our front, about one kilometer, to see if there were any enemy there. They made contact with the simulated enemy in about fifteen minutes and were given credit for killing ten of them. The umpire for the exercise, waiting with the enemy force, was favorably impressed by the action from our side. In the action a "prisoner" was taken, and we evacuated him under guard by helicopter. In the scenario he gave away information which led to an advantage for our side.

Around noon we ate a C-ration, washed down with canteen water, and waited for something to happen. Ricksley came by to inspect at 1300 and seemed reasonably pleased with our company's performance. The exercise ended at 1600 hours, when we climbed onto two and one-half ton cargo trucks, (the troops called them "deuce and a halves") and rode the two hours distance back to Camp Casey.

At the platoon dismount point the extra C-rations were collected by the supply sergeant. The men cleaned weapons in the platoon area and turned them in to the arms room.

I showered and changed clothes and went to the orderly room. Captain Laird was on the phone. I could tell he wasn't listening to something he wanted to hear. He said good-bye and slammed the receiver down.

"That rotten son-of-a-bitch Ricksley! He turned in a bad report on Broyles' platoon because the men were digging without steel pots. Colonel Ziegler wants to see me and Broyles at battalion," he said.

"Should we stand pat, Sir?" I asked.

"No, let the men go. I'll let you know how we came out later, at the club."

"OK, Sir." I went into the club, and to my surprise Ziegler and Ricksley were already at the bar. I wondered how Ziegler would see Laird and Nolan. Ziegler was flushed and happy and I knew the alert had gone well overall; otherwise he would have stayed in his quarters and sulked.

"Worthington, one hell of a job today," he beamed. "Your quick action on sending out that patrol, and the quick evacuation of that prisoner pleased the brigade commander and the commanding general."

I thanked him but assured him that we had done nothing other than the routine. I felt pretty good about the day's work anyway, but one glance at Ricksley's twisted smile and I snapped back to reality.

"Sir, Lieutenant Worthington specializes in brawling with aviators," he said. His sarcastic smile was at its best.

"Yes, what about that incident, Worthington? The commanding general wants me to explain tonight," Ziegler said.

"Sir, we were in the Aviation Club Friday night after the basketball game, and the aviators tried to throw us over the bar. We chose not to be thrown over," I said simply.

"Well, as a minimum, that mirror will have to be paid for, and the commander over there is mad as hell and wants an apology," he said.

I was angry. "How much is their goddamned mirror?" I asked.

"Two hundred dollars," he said.

"OK, Sir, we'll pay for their mirror, but I'll be damned if I apologize to them."

Ricksley saw his chance. "Lieutenant, you'll do what you're told to do. Don't be telling the battalion commander what you will do and what you will not do," he said.

Ziegler changed the subject, but I knew the issue was not dead. I left to find Tom and Nolan and Captain Laird so that I could keep them from walking into the same thing I had. They were crossing the street as I left the club. I explained to Laird why Ziegler had not been in, and I suggested we go over to Camp Hovey club for dinner. Laird declined and went inside to see Ziegler. The rest of us went to Hovey, where I filled them in on where the Aviation Club incident stood. After a few beers everything was OK, and we returned to Casey and the Alley and turned in. It had been a long day.

I had barely dozed off when the telephone rang. It was from the company charge of quarters. He rang to tell me that two of my soldiers were in military police custody for a curfew violation. I had to go get them out or they'd have to remain in jail overnight. I took the duty vehicle and picked them up at MP Headquarters. I finally got back to sleep around 0200. At 0530 the alarm clock started another day.

CHAPTER 6

On Friday, we went over to the Aviation Battalion and paid for the mirror, and that's all we had to do. Ziegler had gone to bat for us at division for a change, but nevertheless we had to pay for the mirror. After paying, we walked by the Aviation Club and decided to go in and order a drink. The amazed crowd of aviators turned as one. The situation was tense. I saw the tall captain that I had kicked stand up, so I told Nolan and Tom to get ready. The captain and the rest of the aviators looked considerably more sober than last Friday night. The tall captain said, "Hey, I think we owe these guys a drink!" Everyone got up, and they were talking about the great airmobile we had had on the Monday morning alert. They apparently had received accolades for the exercise and wanted to share them with us since we were the battalion they airmobiled.

"Pass the hat!" the tall captain yelled, and they filled an aviator's hat with bills and threw it on the bar and counted it. It came to two hundred and thirty two dollars. "Here's two hundred dollars for the mirror, and the rest is for a drink," he said. We were a little overcome by all this, but nevertheless, we took the money and the drinks. After that there was much backslapping and comparing of wounds from the previous fight. We finally got out of the Aviators Club at 2300, having been made "honorary aviators" and associate members of the Aviation Club. On the bus back to the Alley I thought about the evening's events; we had somehow passed some initiation rite and were now accepted.

The next morning Captain Laird inspected my platoon. There were some minor discrepancies, and one soldier had a dirty rifle. He was one of the problem troops. From the first day I saw him, I thought he'd end up busted out of the army for unsuitability. I inspected his weapon after Captain Laird handed it to me. The bore was badly carboned up as was the chamber. I told my platoon-sergeant to pull his pass for the week and to have him ready for rifle inspection every morning at work call. I would restore his pass after he learned to clean his weapon.

Following the inspection I stopped by the orderly room and called Kim in Seoul, but I couldn't get through. When I finally got the Yongsan operator, she asked me for a control number. I gave her my name and rank, but she still insisted that she would not ring a Seoul number without a control number. I hung up and called again a few minutes later. A different operator answered and put my call straight through.

"Yovo se yo," (hello) the voice at the other end answered the telephone.

"May I speak to Miss Hae Ja Kim, please."

"Yes, just a moment, please."

"Kim, it's James, how are you?"

"I'm fine, thank you. Why haven't you called? You must have been very busy."

"Yes, we've been pretty busy. I have to stay up here this weekend. Could you meet me in Tongduchon?"

"Yes, I think so. But I have an appointment, tonight. Tomorrow is all right."

"Then meet me tomorrow at eleven a.m. at the arch at the south end of Tongduchon, and dress for a picnic. There's a small hotel there called the Lee Inn. I'll be in the lounge," I said.

"The Lee Inn at eleven in the morning. OK, I'll be there."

I went over to the club and ate. Choe talked about the trip he had taken the previous weekend. He had driven one of the club vehicles he said. Sometimes he drove his friend's car but gasoline was very expensive. He talked on, and I half listened and could not understand why Kim was unable to come to Tongduchon today. If she had a date of course I wouldn't know the person. Why couldn't she have a date? I'd just met her and certainly had no claim on her time. I thought that after tomorrow I should break it off completely or just not call her again. That would really be better for the both of us. I wasn't sure if she felt as I did. Before I was sure, or before she reached that point, I could bring the matter to a halt and get back to my safe, if solitary, life. Someone slapped me on the back; Tom McCarter.

"Hey, why do you have to wake a guy up like that? Couldn't you just say hello?" He was the best friend I had.

"Jimmy-boy, what are you moping around about? You look like a sick cat. Let's go have a drink. That damned Nolan went to Seoul, and I've got the duty at brigade headquarters tonight."

"Well what the hell. You don't need to go to Seoul, anyway. I saw you talking to Miss Pak at the Hovey club the other night!" I lied.

"Hey, you want a punch in the mouth?"

"Well, if it isn't any more than you gave those aviators last week, go ahead!"

Tom eased a tap to my chin, and I slapped him on the back. We drank a beer and talked about the company, and politics, and basketball. When we talked about basketball I thought of Kim.

"What are you doing tomorrow, Tom?" I asked.

"No plans, sport. What do you have in mind?"

"Get a date, and let's take some charcoal and meat and beer and pop and go up on the Han Tan River and have a picnic."

"OK. You buying?" he laughed.

"Yeah. Give me ten bucks."

The next morning we left Camp Casey with two large rucksacks full of picnic supplies. We each carried another knapsack in our hands. At the Lee Inn we took a table and leaned the rucksacks and knapsacks against our chairs and ordered a drink. Soon Miss Pak arrived, and I was kind of surprised because of my joke the day before, and now here she was. Tom looked at me and laughed. It was a typical McCarter joke, and he chuckled at my surprised look.

But she was a live wire, this one, laughing and joking. Apparently she had heard all about the Aviation Club incident. She pretended to be an aviator with a handlebar mustache and kicked the hell out of an imaginary form on the ground. We had a good laugh. The picnic was off to a great start.

Kim showed up and we introduced Miss Pak to her. They immediately liked each other although there was a difference in their backgrounds. It was not too obvious, but noticeable by the conversation. In spite of this, they got along well. We picked up the rucksacks, the girls got the knapsacks, and we went out onto the street and waited for a cab. The sun was warm but the December chill reminded everyone that we were a little crazy to be picnicking now. We were dressed for the weather and headstrong enough to do it. We hailed a cab, loaded the gear in the trunk, piled in, and off we went up the highway toward Yonchon. South of Yonchon we turned up a gravel road, past the small villages and a Korean Army compound. We crossed a stream which had ice on its fringes. After the cab dragged bottom a few times we told the driver to stop and we got out. I tipped him well, he smiled, then asked when we would be leaving. I told him about 1700, knowing that we would be seeing him then.

We left the gravel road and followed a small trail which led down to the river. The river was shallow there. We walked across on stones and parked our gear on a gravel and sand bar on the other side. It was tucked up tight against a rock cliff and protected from the wind on two sides. We dragged some dead stumps and branches from the woods downstream, where the rock cliff ended and the trees started, and made a fire to keep warm and fired up the charcoal to cook. Soon we began a game of tag, running back and forth on the spit like children. We were warm, as the heat from the burning stumps reflected off the granite face of the cliff. Later we threw the wire grill over the charcoal and placed the slices of beef and a few pieces of chicken on it. We stood close together near the fire. There was no wind down on the tiny spit of a river beach. We drank beer, Kim drank pop, and soon we began to eat charcoaled beef on buns. We had music on Tom's transistor radio.

After awhile we started skipping rocks over the surface of the water. Miss Pak narrowly missed Tom's head as she attempted to skip a stone, and Tom looked at me. "Do you think I'm safe?"

I laughed, "Probably not, but your head is flint anyway, so don't worry!"

After a while Kim and I walked up the spit and around the bend in the river. I held her tight and kissed her. She trembled slightly. We held each other, and I knew that I'd missed my last chance at an easy out. Too soon the shadows began to lengthen, so we went back to the fire. The four of us put out the fires, packed, and hiked back up to the road. Our cab was waiting, and we took it back to Tongduchon. Tom and Pak got out at Camp Casey. We passed through Tongduchon, went on south to Euijongbu and got out at a Korean hotel. We went into the hotel bar and sat in a booth. We were the only ones in the bar. We held each other; the blood pounded in my ears. I needed her more than I had wanted to.

"Kim, let's take a room."

"I can't stay tonight."

"Then we'll leave in a couple of hours."

She lowered her head. We registered at the desk and went upstairs to a tiny room.

"Let's take a bath together." We stripped and stood together in the hot shower, holding each other tightly. I carried her directly from the shower to the bed, and we loved each other without restraint.

"James, I must go home."

We dressed and went outside into the cold darkness, where we parted. At Tongduchon I entered Camp Casey and went straight to the Alley. In my room I tried to read, but I kept thinking of Kim. The thought of her sparkling smile through pouting pink lips parting to reveal white straight teeth came back to me. The smell of her, clean without anything artificial as we brushed cheeks; her radiant black hair touching my face as we kissed; I couldn't get my mind off of all things Kim. The warmth of Kim pressed against me and the feel of her unfettered breasts, high and firm, against me as we held each other, haunted me and left little room for other thoughts.

Where were we headed in this relationship? Many Americans had married Koreans, and it was not unusual to see them in significant numbers on military posts and bases throughout the world. And what of the racial problems that people in mixed marriages encounter? That was certainly a consideration, but not an insurmountable obstacle, judging from the number of successful marriages of this type that I was personally familiar with.

What affect would having a Korean wife have on ones career as an officer? I could imagine the snobbery of the old biddies in the officers' wives clubs as they rudely rejected any attempt by a Korean wife to be a part of their "closed" organizations. To an officer who was totally career oriented, like Ricksley for example, this would be important. "Well it doesn't make a tinker's damn to me," I said aloud.

As for Kim's side of this, she well knew that for an upper-middle class Korean to be seen with a foreigner, particularly an American military member, was to become an outcast to that strata of Korean society. First of all, she would be judged by Koreans on sight to be a bar hostess from some Korean town or village adjacent to a U.S. post or base. That sort of impression could not easily be overcome. Those who became acquainted with her would soon learn that nothing could be further from the truth, but few would be socially involved with her to the extent necessary to erase this impression. In other words, there was a clear sacrifice to be made if Kim were to marry an American. She would have to decide what she really wanted from life and proceed accordingly; all this, of course, assuming that she was totally cold and calculating in her approach to the problem. It never works that way though — two people slip from infatuation into a far more serious relationship, and emotional control and common sense are no longer competing factors.

There were no easy answers. I guessed that there probably never were. It would be difficult if not impossible to remain firmly in control of the situation when there were so many uncontrollable factors to consider.

I tried to read a Hopkins poem, but after going over it several times, I decided that it was stretching it attempting to imagine Christ as a kestrel. I picked up a Faulkner novel, mentally got tangled up in the wisteria, plodded through the fecund mellow earth of Mississippi and went to sleep wondering who was cousin to whom.

CHAPTER 7

The next morning I rolled out of bed and went to physical training, PT as the troops called it. We did PT every day unless it was raining or the temperature dropped below zero. I took my place in the rear of the company formation. We did calisthenics; then formed into a company column of fours and went on a run. I felt good and perspired even though it was cold and dark. A cloud of breaths hung over the mass of soldiers as we ran, and our feet pounded out the even cadence. A tall black sergeant sang out Jody cadence; "I got a girl in San Antone," we replied "I got a girl in San Antone." He sang "She won't leave my money alone," and we replied in cadence, and he continued.

I showered and dressed, and we formed the company after breakfast. We slung rifles, and marched out in cadence for a day's firing on the rifle range.

Captain Laird ran the range, and his voice came over the loudspeaker, "Is there anyone down range?" Pause and repeat, "Is there anyone down range?" Pause and a third time, "Is there anyone down range?" Then "Firers, watch your lanes; commence firing!" The rifles cracked, the rounds snapped in the cold air and knocked down the silhouettes, or churned the frozen earth around them, or sailed over them into the face of the mountain behind them.

We ate a C-ration meal at noon so that we didn't have to break, and the soldiers ate as they completed firing. I sat on a bench, ate my turkey loaf meal, and looked down the valley to the road. A jeep raced up the road with the dust boiling behind it, and Major Ricksley arrived. Lieutenant McCarter called attention, and the men eating or not on the firing line stood. Tom saluted, and reported to Ricksley. Ricksley poked around and couldn't find anything wrong in particular, but finally a half smile crept onto his face. He marched to the base of the tower and ordered Captain Laird to give a cease fire and report.

"Cease fire, cease fire, cease fire. Lock and clear all weapons," Laird commanded, then told the men to keep weapons pointed up, down range and to wait. He came down out of the tower and reported to Ricksley, who, without bothering to take him out of earshot of the troops commenced to dress him down for feeding a C-ration meal in garrison.

"... no regard for these men ...," and "... not taking care of these soldiers ..." and "Colonel Ziegler will want to see you about this!" Ricksley shouted.

Laird looked him in the eye and angrily replied "These are my troops, and I command them, Sir. It was my decision to feed a C-ration, in the interest of time. Otherwise we couldn't have completed firing the entire company in one day. I'll be glad to explain that to Colonel Ziegler."

"You can add insubordination to your troubles also, Laird. We will see how you squirm out of this one!" He wheeled, mounted his jeep and went back down the road in a cloud of dust.

We left the range at 1600. Everyone had fired qualification, and the troops had shot well. I had a feeling of satisfaction in knowing that the job had been done. The weak firers were identified and could be sent through extra marksmanship training. When we arrived at the company area, Captain Laird dismissed the troops. The First Sergeant told him that Colonel Ziegler wanted to see him right away. Captain Laird moved toward battalion headquarters with a calm and resolute stride. Precisely at that moment I decided that Laird was a good man. He had guts, and I knew that when they decided to kill him, they could only do it once, because he wasn't afraid.

I left the platoon-sergeant to supervise the cleaning of weapons, while I went to the Alley, showered, changed clothes and went on to the club. Tom and Nolan came in and we played "horse" with the leather dice cup. I went out first. Nolan and Tom tied with three sixes each, and on one flop Nolan threw two deuces. He gave up and started to pay for the beer but Tom threw two aces, lost and grudgingly paid.

"Look up your backside Broyles, and see if the horseshoe fits!"

"Just buy the beer and shut up, McCarter!"

Captain Laird came into the club and joined us at the bar. We bought him a beer.

"How'd you come out, Sir?" I asked.

"OK." he said. "Ziegler agreed with me for a change, and old Ricksley about died. Watch out for him in the next few days."

"Hey, let's drink to a happy ending!" Nolan yelled.

We tipped glasses and drank our Budweiser, but I knew it wasn't over. When you get into a biting contest with a cobra, you can't win. It was good to be tired and drinking with good men and good friends.

I switched to scotch somewhere during the evening, and ended up alone at the bar with Choe. He wanted to take a trip in his friend's car the following weekend. The more scotch I drank the better the idea sounded.

"Where will we go, Choe-si?"

"Let's go to Kang Nung," he said.

"But it's out of season," I said.

"But we can still get good seafood and the night spots are fine," he argued. "Let's leave Saturday afternoon and come back Sunday evening."

"I'll get some wine and have sandwiches made up."

"Miss Kang will go with me. Who will you take?"

I hesitated. "Maybe someone will meet me there Sunday morning."

"Hey, you sound like the chaplain now!"

"Yeah, Chaplain Worthington, a man of the cloth! Let's drink to it!"

Choe slipped back into the kitchen and drank scotch.

I left late and read myself to sleep.

CHAPTER 8

Choe picked me up on Saturday afternoon, and I put the sacks of wine and sandwiches in the back seat. We went through the Casey main gate, and headed south along the highway, the main street of Tongduchon. Near the Lee Inn we stopped, and Choe went into the compound there. He came out with Miss Kang a few minutes later. I got in the back seat with the food and wine and Choe turned the car down the highway, south toward Seoul.

It was a cold clear December afternoon; the sky was high and blue. Traffic on the highway consisted of Korean Army trucks, a few American military vehicles, and many taxis racing in either direction. The traffic in Euijongbu slowed us for a short time but soon we were into Miari and northern Seoul. The traffic was bumper-to-bumper. Choe drove like he was in a tank, forcing his way in and out of the line of vehicles, bluffing buses, almost daring vehicles to sideswipe us.

"Hey, Choe! Are you trying to fly?" I asked.

"In Korea, the driver with the most guts wins!"

"Yeah, but that won't put him back together after a head-on collision," I said.

"Not to worry, Lieutenant! You're in good hands."

"I'm glad I have the wine back here. At least I can embalm myself and save the morticians the trouble." It was cheap, but good.

We crossed the Han River, continued south down the highway in the left lane. We passed many cargo trucks with their canvas covers lashed down over loads of produce, machine parts, military equipment, lumber, and anything else an industrializing nation needs to transport. Choe slowed to the speed limit, to enjoy the landscape. Soon, we turned off to the left and travelled east on the highway to Kang Nung.

Miss Kang sat close to Choe, laughing at something he said. I opened one of the paper sacks and handed sandwiches to Miss Kang. She ate and fed Choe. We laughed a lot and enjoyed being together. I poured some red wine into two paper cups and handed them to Miss Kang. The car was warm, and we had music on the radio. The ground began to rise, and there were more curves in the road as we went up the mountain. After two cups of wine I cut Choe off so we could get to Kang Nung in one piece. Miss Kang and I continued to sip the wine. Occasionally, we saw black and white patrol cars on the side of the highway but we weren't speeding. We kept the cups out of sight as we passed them.

We passed the cutoff to Wonju and continued up and over the mountains. The road was very crooked, then it straightened a little and finally we reached Kang Nung. It was the off season; most hotels were closed, and the ones that were open offered rooms at reduced rates. We found a nice place with clean rooms on the beach.

I showered and changed and walked down to the beach. The cold wind blew off the sea and felt good. The sand was damp and hard packed. I walked down the beach, went into another hotel, found the bar and had a drink. The bartender said that they had a seafood buffet all day Sunday and guaranteed that we could not possibly eat all the seafood they offered. I decided we could at least try, and made a mental note that we could go there for brunch tomorrow no matter how we felt.

I checked out another hotel. They had a band coming that night. The bartender said that space was almost impossible to get, but he would save us a table. I thanked him, gave him a tip and went back up the beach to our hotel. The sandwiches were in Choe's room but one bottle of wine was left in my room, so I started to work on it. I hadn't realized that the wine on an empty stomach could creep up on me and soon I fell asleep in my room. I finally awoke to Choe's pounding on my door.

I let them in, and we sat and drank wine, then went down the beach to the hotel with the band. We had good seafood for dinner, with a bottle of wine. We sat and listened to the band, and Choe danced with Kang. I danced with Kang once, then asked a Korean girl, who sat at a table with two other girls, to dance to a fast tune. She was shy; we spoke in Korean as her English wasn't good. I danced with her once again, then Choe suggested we go across the street to a night club; he was getting drunk. Kang began to scold him, making him angry.

As we crossed the street Choe staggered badly. I attempted to lend him an arm but he only got irritated. In the night club we drank scotch. Kang was visibly worried and not having a good time; finally they quarreled loudly. The waiter in the night club spoke to me about the condition of my chingu (friend). He was getting worse and more abusive of Miss Kang. He knocked over a glass of scotch and made a mess on the table. He argued with the waiter and finally I persuaded him to leave. We crossed the street and went back up to the rooms. Choe kicked open the door to his room, fell face down on the bed, and passed out. Kang apologized and was visibly embarrassed. I told her that Choe was my friend, and there was no need to apologize. I made an excuse about going out for an evening newspaper. She was taking Choe's shoes off as I left.

I walked back down the beach and wondered why in the hell I had decided to go to Kang Nung with Choe, because he always got this way and spoiled things in the end. I stopped at the hotel where we had eaten, went into an upstairs bar, drank some scotch and felt sorry for Miss Kang.

Kim was due to arrive the next morning by bus. I couldn't think of anything else and walked down to the sea to watch the waves lap the shore. The words of Arnold's "Dover Beach" came to mind. After a while I went back up the beach and went to bed. I tried to read but I'd had too much scotch, and kept rereading the same paragraph, so I gave it up and went to sleep.

The next morning I walked down past the bus stop to a place on the corner that sold newspapers and picked up a copy of the Korean Herald. A cold wind blew, so I went into a small tabang, a Korean tea room, which also served coffee, and drank black coffee and read the paper. I went back up to the hotel. Choe and Kang had not left their room, so I went out and walked along the beach and passed the time until Kim's bus was due.

Kim arrived and we went down the street to the hotel that had the Sunday seafood buffet. We sat by the window and looked out at the gray cold sea. Kim was beautiful, dressed in a brown sweater and slacks with a beige wool winter coat and scarf. The bus ride had been chilly and she wanted coffee to warm her.

"How long was the ride?" I asked.

"Too long," she laughed. "The bus was not well heated, and my feet and legs really got cold."

"In the next life we will have a space bus and I'll whisk you away to wherever you want to go," I said.

"Oh, there's a next life, probably, but not one of those Buddhist next lives, I should think," she said.

"Well, I don't know but I guess we all have to hope for something."

"Yes, but aren't you oversimplifying it?" she asked.

"Well, maybe. Anyway, let's talk about the here and now!"

"OK. Where are your friends Choe and Kang?" she asked.

Just then they came in; I stood and introduced them in my best formal Korean.

"Not bad, James, but don't be so damned formal!" Choe laughed.

The girls laughed, and the day was off to a good start. We ordered seafood and it just kept coming.

"Kim, drink some white wine!" Choe offered.

"OK. Just a little."

We all touched glasses, said "Tipsida," and drank wine. It was good.

In the early afternoon we went back to the hotel. Kim was surprised at the cleanliness of the rooms. I made some joke about staying another night, and she blushed and laughed. I kissed her and we stood, taking each other's clothes off, and lay across the bed; I took her gently at first and then again with total abandon until we lay satisfied and exhausted in each others arms. Before I really wanted to we dressed, I packed my AWOL bag, and we went out into the winter afternoon.

We put the overnight things into the car and took the wine and blankets down to the beach. We sat down in the chilly afternoon sun and drank wine and talked.

Soon Choe was drunk again, so Kim and I walked down the beach and turned into a pine woods, out of sight of Choe and Kang. We sat and talked, then made love under the blanket. She realized that she was in over her head too. I remember whispering a little prayer for us.

As the shadows lengthened, we kissed and walked back up the beach to rejoin Choe and Kang. We sat with them and laughed, and Choe told a dirty joke which Kim pretended not to understand. Apparently Kang had heard it before, so she just scolded Choe for telling it. Finally we loaded the blankets into the car, left Kang Nung and crossed the mountains, then rolled into Seoul in the darkness and dropped Kim off at Ha Nam Dong. We got back into Tongduchon late. I went to bed in the Alley and slept until 0530 and another PT Monday morning at Camp Casey.

CHAPTER 9

The division went on a half-day schedule the week before Christmas and stayed on that schedule through New Year's Day. I wondered if the North Koreans were also on a half-day schedule. There were many games, tournaments and contests and a little mandatory military training.

One night we went to the Hovey gymnasium to a boxing smoker. The fight card listed twelve three-round bouts between our battalion and one of the Hovey Infantry battalions. It was an interesting evening; the small gym was filled with smoke, crammed full of troops and officers, but the place was stuffy and too warm from their body heat. The excitement ran high, and the din of the troops rooting for their units peaked at the main event. This final match pitted well-known heavyweights who had fought to a bloody draw at the last smoker. Our battalion heavyweight was from our company, a tall black soldier with a lot of reach and good speed. The other heavyweight was a short chunky black kid; he hit like a sack of rocks, was a great body puncher and liked to fight close in. From the first bell, it was clear that they came to mutilate each other; the jabbing was sharp, and the hooking and uppercutting was vicious. They didn't clinch through the first two rounds. Our soldier bled from the nose and he had opened a cut over the other man's eye. Midway through the last round the rangy kid from our company really connected; a solid left hook to the head, followed with a right cross, which put his opponent's lights out. As Tom, Nolan and I left the gym, the trainers were still working with him.

We stopped at the Hovey club to have a drink, and the club soon filled with officers from the brigade. Since they had lost the smoker they weren't much interested in talking about it; however, Nolan made a few sharp remarks that weren't appreciated, and pretty soon it was apparent that we were working our way toward another Aviation Club situation. Finally, I bought a round and made a toast.

"Here's to the Infantry; to the Hovey Infantry, the Casey Infantry, and all the Infantry!" Since everyone present was Infantry, that was probably the safest toast ever made in the Hovey club. The peace restored temporarily, we drank up. I called a post taxi, and we went back to Casey and into our own club.

Captain Laird stood at the bar with Lieutenant-Colonel Ziegler and Major Ricksley; they were discussing something. We went to the other end of the bar and ordered. The club was packed; an all-girl Korean group called The Daisy Show was entertaining. They were on break but soon came back out, picked up their instruments and began a popular American song. They were good, and the officers loved them. There was a base guitarist, a lead guitarist, a drummer, an organist, two other guitarists, and they all sang well. They sung in English, but you could tell that they had memorized the words by listening to the records, and therefore probably didn't know what the words meant. But that was OK. They were probably the best group we had ever had in the club. The show ended at 2200 so that the band could get back to Seoul and home before curfew.

We barraged Choe with requests to keep them overnight and close the club at 2400, and passed the hat to collect the money to pay them for the extra two hours. They were glad to stay, and we had a great evening.

The holiday schedule continued; the troops really enjoyed the half-day schedule, and the sporting events were popular. Kim came up on Christmas Day to eat turkey dinner with me in the club. After dinner we danced and talked. We laughed about our trip to Kang Nung when she stopped by the bar to speak with Choe. That evening Kim wanted to take a bus back to Seoul because it was cheaper, though it took longer. I wanted her to stay as long as possible so I offered to pay for a cab. I kissed her in the shadows of a building next to the cab stand. As she left she waved through the cab's rear window. I went back to the Alley to read, and finally switched off the light after midnight.

On New Year's Eve I met Kim in Seoul. She was wearing a blue cho-gori, the traditional formal dress for Korean ladies, and I couldn't remember her ever being so beautiful. I had reservations for the New Year's Eve party at the Naija Hotel. It was loud and crowded, and at midnight, people popped corks from champagne bottles and drank and blew horns and made a terrific din with rattles and other noisemakers, then threw confetti all over everything and everyone. Total strangers were kissing each other. We welcomed the New Year in fine fashion, but behind the laughter we wondered where we were going with this thing. What would the New Year bring? I thought about the increasing involvement of the United States in the war in Vietnam. At first I felt that I shouldn't make any serious plans until I knew a little more about the future. I finally rejected that; our future was now; the uncertainties of now would always be uncertainties; and that's life, probably.

That night Kim drank champagne. She was red-faced, as most orientals get when they drink, and her heart beat rapidly. I took her upstairs to my room and put her to bed. The next morning we awoke clinging to each other. We made love until we lay exhausted, caressing each other as the morning light grew brighter through the windows and thin curtains. The future, with all its uncertainties and pitfalls and hostilities wasn't frightening at this moment. I was very much aware of the potential responsibility facing me, and hoped silently that I would be able to see the thing through. I wanted a conclusion that would not hurt anyone; not leave anyone hanging and cut off with no return to the last safe plateau of previous existence. But there was an unexplainable dull tugging; a nagging sort of ill feeling that wouldn't go away.

CHAPTER 10

Mid-January there was a special alert, called by the corps headquarters at Euijongbu. It began in the bitter cold of the January night. Lieutenant-Colonel Ziegler was called to division headquarters and was gone about three hours. Soon after he left for division, he called Major Ricksley and told him that we'd be moving north and to get the battalion ready. We were to participate in an exercise as part of a Korean regiment; the thing was expected to last from four days to a week.

We made the time limit and were prepared to roll. The troops ate a hot meal while we waited for Ziegler to return. I saw his jeep lights swing around as he turned into battalion headquarters, then Captain Laird returned and issued the order which Ziegler had initially given the battalion. We were to move to an assembly area up on the Han Tan River north bank and be prepared for further operations.

Shortly after daylight we closed into the assembly area and began to dig foxholes in the frozen ground, camouflaging vehicles and tents. Wooden tent pegs splintered as troops tried to drive them into the ice hard ground; they cursed as they worked. That morning we received liaison personnel from the Korean regiment we were to be attached to, and by noon we received an order to occupy the combat outpost line in front of the regiment. Our battalion passed lines on foot through the two forward Korean battalions, moved to a ridgeline about one kilometer and a half in front of them and then spread laterally along the high ground, there to form the COP, Combat Outpost Line. The COP was a high bushy ridgeline covered with scrub-oak and pine, and we could see far up the valley from there. That night we patrolled in front of the COP; a full moon bathed the cold landscape in an incredibly bright light. My platoon made contact with an "enemy" force just after midnight; I judged it to be a battalion by its weapons and numbers. We surprised them as they moved through a dry streambed, where we had established a hasty ambush. We exploded simulators which represented claymore antipersonnel mines and hand grenades, and the night flashed with the explosions and the cracks of blank rifle ammunition. I reported the action, and we rapidly made our way back to the COP, and took up our position there.

At daylight the "enemy" forces to the front began probing, and finally the battalion was withdrawn back through the FEBA (Forward Edge of the Battle Area) where our regiment main defense was dug in. Using fighter bombers and all available artillery, the regiment slowed the enemy. We limited their success to a small breakthrough in the area of the Korean battalion to the right of the front. As the reserve battalion in the defense, we were ordered to counterattack to destroy the enemy forces that had forced the break in the forward wall of the defense. We passed through the Korean battalion that had been driven back and hit the enemy element from the flank. Apparently it went well, so the umpires assessed casualties to the "enemy" and made them withdraw. We then pulled back to our reserve position after the Korean battalion again moved forward and reconstituted their defense. As the Korean troops moved through us they looked like a strong and well trained Infantry unit.

That night, the regiment attacked with the two forward Korean battalions. At first light, our battalion passed through the Korean battalions that had made the night attack and continued the offensive. We seized our initial objectives shortly after daylight and were ordered to continue the attack. We attacked the rest of that day and through the night. The exercise ended the following day, just before noon. We had captured large numbers of "prisoners." Now they had to be returned to their units.

At the termination of the exercise we accounted for all men and equipment and moved back down the highway to Camp Casey in a long column of military vehicles. I was dog-tired and couldn't really remember getting any sleep over the past four days except a catnap here and there. At Casey the first order of business was the cleaning of weapons, then the other gear and the vehicles. I cleaned my rifle, then went over it a second time, with emphasis on the bore, applied a light coat of oil to the weapon and turned it in. At the company orderly room there was a note that I'd had a telephone call from Seoul. I slipped into the company commander's office and called Kim. She hadn't heard from me in a week, so she was worried. I explained about the alert and asked her if she was free the following day, Sunday. I could not leave overnight this weekend but I could get away Sunday morning.

"I have a special place to show you, James. Can you make it by nine o'clock?"

"Yes, I'll be there. Take care."

"Good-bye."

After that I took a hot shower; the water was steaming, and I was pleasantly drowsy; my aching muscles relaxed. I stopped back by the company; the weapons were all turned in. In the arms room I had the armorer open one of my weapons racks, pulled out a weapon from the middle of the rack and checked it over, finally looking down the bore in the light of the overhead bulb. That weapon was clean, so I picked two more at random; they were also clean. I went across to the club.

Tom and Nolan sat at a table in the lounge, so I joined them. We were happy tired, the way I remembered after a particularly hard football game our team had won. The battalion, and our company in particular, had done well on the alert and the exercise that followed. At the "flash" critique held on the spot before the units left the field, the Korean regimental commander had been unusually generous in his praise of our battalion's performance. The Korean regimental headquarters had done a commendable job of overcoming the language barrier — in fact, there was no language barrier. Every regimental order had been given in Han Gul, the Korean language, and in English, and the soldiers they sent us as liaison were all fluent in English and understood each mission very well. I wondered why we never bothered to send officers to the Korean language school before they went to Korea?

The waitress brought beer, but after the third one I fell asleep in the chair. I left the club and slept soundly until my alarm went off the next morning.

I met Kim near Seoul Station. I had no idea what she had in mind for the day but knew I would enjoy whatever it was. She was dressed in a gray suit and heels, which made her look even taller.

In a cab we went northeast for a few blocks, turned into a narrow alley that went up a hill and got out in front of another alley. We walked up the small street, which soon widened and we confronted a small crowd of people talking in front of a red brick Methodist church. It was a small church with wooden pews on both sides of the aisle which led down to the altar. Directly at the end of the aisle, behind and higher than the altar, was the pulpit.

The Moksa Nim (Korean minister) led the congregation in hymns familiar to me but in Han Gul. The words at times did not seem to fit the music but it had a very pleasant sound, anyway. He read scripture, and two small girls passed the collection plates; then he preached his sermon. I had a sort of hopeless feeling which I couldn't then or later, explain. My palms were damp; my breath came strangely and my memory wandered back to my childhood and its Sunday mornings in a little stone church, nestled among the hills near home. I was strongly aware of Kim's presence beside me, but felt an urge to flee out the church door and run down the steps, out of this time, this situation. Kim squeezed my hand tightly, and I turned to look into her face, but she was staring passively at the pulpit. She acknowledged my attention only by the hint of a smile at the corner of her mouth.

I recognized a phrase that the Moksa Nim uttered in Han Gul, "You shall run and not be weary, walk and not be tired." And then, "I will lift up mine eyes unto the hills, from whence cometh my strength ...."

"My God," I thought, "the Lord must have been an Infantryman!" Then I was all right, and laughed to myself, but I was a little ashamed that I was taking serious moments so lightly. I raised my head and looked at the tattered coat of an old Korean man in front of me. A baby started crying in the rear of the church, and an old man with a dirty beard, shabby blue trousers and a set of crutches coughed nastily at the end of our pew. I was returned to reality.

"And may the Lord bless you and keep you...and give you peace. Amen."

We filed out of the church. I knew we had been too far up front because we were the last out. Everyone was gathered outside, and of course I would have to talk to acquaintances and relatives, but suddenly I realized there were none, or at least no one was talking to us. It wasn't what I had anticipated at all; we found it very easy to leave. I glanced at Kim, and thought I saw the gleam of tears but she turned her head. Later in the cab I thought that maybe I'd been wrong, there were no tears, and I wondered why my imagination had wandered to sad things because she was quite lively and gay as we made plans for the afternoon and evening.

The cab turned east, paralleled the north bank of the Han and then wound its way up a hill to Walker Hill Hotel. We had a drink at the bar and ate a sandwich, then went into the game room. I played blackjack and lost, but won most of it back at the dice table. We passed time in the lounge and I thought how really beautiful Kim was.

"James, what if you have to leave Korea?"

"Nothing like that will happen soon."

"Yes, but I think your country will soon be involved in Vietnam in a much greater way than now. The Korean papers tell of this every day."

"Maybe I won't be sent."

"James, please don't go to that war." It was a simple innocent request spoken earnestly, as if all I had to do was just refuse to go.

"No such thing will happen. Let's talk about something else."

"James, do you think we can be this happy always?"

A line I had read somewhere about living for the moment came to mind. "Yes, we will be even happier."

She smiled. It was OK, for we knew we had something very special, and it was our secret from the world. But I could not see what was ahead and knew only that I wasn't afraid, that I would take it as it came. At that moment, I thought perhaps she felt the same way.

Kim had gotten tickets to a dinner theater across the hall from the lounge, The Nelly Kim Show.

"Are you hungry?" she asked.

"Starved."

"Me too!" she laughed. "Let's order."

We ordered drinks and prime rib and a bottle of burgundy. The show began, traditional Korean music and dancing. A woman played the kayagum, a long stringed instrument which lay on the floor, and then a troupe of girls in white costumes, with capes and sashes, did a Korean fan dance, and the wide stage with left and right wings was bathed in the brilliantly colored lighting effects. Then the troupe played traditional Korean flat drums in red wooden frames; the drum was suspended in the frame, edge down, and the sticks clacked in unison alternately against the wooden frames and the drum heads. The girls twisted and turned as they tattooed the rhythm with the sticks.

Then Nelly Kim came on in a white gown, beautiful as always, and her husky voice was as ever intriguing. She worked her way through song after song, to the long ovations of an obviously appreciative audience. There were American songs, Korean songs, and she was especially good in the Italian songs. One had the feeling that she was aware of each person in the audience individually. Kim and I sat quite near the stage, so we were sure that at one time she was giving us personal attention as she belted out the lyrics of a song about young lovers. At the end she was given several standing ovations and responded by singing three extra songs. When you watched Nelly Kim perform you understood the meaning of the word charisma. I had never seen any performer so sensitive to audience appreciation, and the more appreciation she was shown the better she got. At the end of the final song we too were exhausted, and that was Nelly Kim.

It was so late that we had to hurry to beat the curfew, so we parted at the front of the Walker Hill Hotel. I kissed Kim and found a cab driver who would take me back to Tongduchon for double the meter fare. It had been worth it.

CHAPTER 11

Winter dragged on and the alerts came, and there were training inspections, boxing smokers, clashes with Ricksley, and rare occasional chances to see Kim. And then winter began to loosen its grip, and the men no longer had to wear thermal boots at the halt. Field jacket liners were shucked out of the jackets and left in the quonset huts, trigger finger mittens were replaced by gloves, and pile caps were gratefully discarded. Trees began to bud and the more aggressive farmers began to plow, and men followed the red oxen that strained against the curved single yoke and pulled the crude plow, to try to start conditioning the harsh land for the planting and short growing season. Water was scarce in Korea; it had to be hoarded. Every little trickle of a spring was diked and piped and canalled into the fields for the rice which would be planted later on.

Captain Laird had grown in the job, a solid company commander with a good tactical head and good leadership principles. He was from Virginia and had been commissioned at his small university, in the Reserve Officer Training Corps (ROTC) program. His father was a respectable farmer who had made some money and invested wisely. He was proud of his Army son who commanded a company in Korea. The father had gone into the landing at Normandy in World War II as a young soldier, had fought through France and been evacuated, seriously wounded, and was recovering in a general hospital in the United States when the war ended. David Laird was proud of his father and wanted to do well in the military to please him; he should have done so.

In early April the battalion received a call on a Monday morning at 0500 and was told we were to undergo our Annual General Inspection, better known as IG Inspection, beginning that morning at 0900 and continuing all day each day through Wednesday. Short of combat an IG Inspection is probably the most comprehensive test any military unit can be put through. The IG Inspection Team travelled on a bus — it took a bus to haul them because there were so many of them. Each member was an expert in his own particular area: vehicle maintenance, small arms, crew served weapons, signal equipment, supply, or whatever. The inspection weighs heavily on everyone in the unit, because it covers every piece of equipment, every job, every aspect of what the men and officers in the unit do as soldiers, and all of this is done thoroughly. In our division, as an officer in particular, you didn't want to fail an IG Inspection because it most certainly would be reflected in writing in your efficiency report. In addition, depending on how bad the failure was, you could be relieved from the command or staff position you had occupied as an officer. Being relieved for an officer in the United States Army quite simply spelled the end to that officer's career, whether he had invested his flesh and blood and twenty-five years or was a new lieutenant. It was the "chop."

An Infantry battalion has five companies: three rifle companies lettered A, B, and C; a combat support company; and a headquarters company. If three companies failed in any one area of the inspection then the battalion failed in that area. The battalion would fail the inspection if it failed four or more areas of inspection, or if it failed two or more of the most critical three areas of weapons, vehicle, and signal maintenance, or the "shoot, scoot, and communicate" areas.

The first day of the inspection, my company's wheeled vehicles were inspected in the morning, and of the eleven vehicles inspected six failed with very serious deficiencies, failing the company in that area. That afternoon we also failed signal maintenance because the vehicle mounted radios were inoperable. The fault for these two failures lay mainly with the Weapons Platoon Sergeant, who was in charge of vehicle maintenance, but ultimately Captain Laird was responsible as the company commander. Unfortunately for Lieutenant-Colonel Ziegler, two other companies failed the same two areas of wheeled vehicle and signal maintenance over the period of the next two days, and at the inspection critique on Wednesday evening, the commanding general relieved Ziegler of command, in addition to Captain Moss, the battalion motor officer, and Lieutenant James, the battalion signal platoon leader.

The battalion executive officer, Major Blair, had rotated back to the States a month before the inspection without being replaced, so the ranking man in the battalion was Major Ricksley. He took over as battalion commander for the time it would take to get another lieutenant-colonel suitable for command to take over the battalion.

Our company had failed the inspection, but Captain Laird escaped relief because others took the brunt of responsibility for the failures. Tom, Nolan, and I had done very well in our respective areas of responsibility, and as officer in charge of small arms I had received a "commendable" in that area. But we were very concerned for Captain Laird, rather than being worried about our individual fates. As we walked out of the theater where the critique was held, Ricksley stopped Laird at the door.

"Laird, you have two weeks to get that mess straight or I'll relieve you," he said. They were not out of earshot, and of course we heard. Laird said nothing and rejoined us as we went back to the company area. "My God," I thought, "Ricksley is actually the battalion commander."

One week later, on Rodriquez Range, northeast of Camp Casey, Ricksley relieved Laird on the range. Our 81 millimeter mortar section was firing and had failed to post a range guard at a road leading into the impact area. Posting this guard was necessary to stop people from entering the range on that access road. Someone, Korean or American, could enter the range and be killed or wounded during firing. So Captain Laird's career was finished; he would be kicked out after "pass overs" for promotion which would surely result because of the relief. Again, as in the IG Inspection, the Weapons Platoon Sergeant was at fault, and even though he was inspecting training on another range at Camp Casey, Laird was ultimately responsible, and Ricksley took him in a helicopter to Rodriquez Range, showed him the problem, and relieved him of command. He was gone in three days, transferred to a battalion at Camp Howze to the west of Camp Casey, to finish out the month and a half he had left on the tour.

I talked to him at length in the club the night before he left, and I have seen bitter men but he was blood-hate bitter. He sincerely believed that the relief came as a result of the clash on the rifle range, months before, when Lieutenant-Colonel Ziegler had backed Laird rather than Ricksley in their disagreement. He had no intention of voluntarily leaving the Army. He was still a professional, and he thought that somehow he could overcome this and still serve and be of value to his country. He told me very plainly that Ricksley wasn't worth killing but that it was a beautiful thought, anyway — Ricksley lying out in the sun with his throat cut and his life's blood draining out on the ground. Somehow I agreed that made a rather pleasant mental picture. He left for Camp Howze the next morning, and I knew I'd probably never see him again.

CHAPTER 12

The battalion was visibly shaken with the relief of Ziegler, Laird, Moss, and James. No unit undergoes that kind of trauma without commensurate morale damage. The battalion was down. I tried hard to keep my troops keen for training and preparedness but it was much tougher than before. A senior captain named Jenkins had come down from the division staff and taken over the company. He wasn't a bad officer, but no Captain Laird, when it came to commanding a rifle company.

Ricksley scurried about frantically, trying to hold things together but there were serious problems. I kept my platoon in the field and on the range as much as possible. I found that in the leadership vacuum that existed I could pretty much do as I chose.

Near the end of April there was a battalion training holiday on Friday and a division training holiday on Monday, so I was able to string together a four day weekend. Kim and I were on the train for Pusan early Friday morning. Kim carried a paper sack of sandwiches which she had made up, and I had brought along a couple of bottles of cheap burgundy from the club. We both carried small overnight bags.

We were soon passing Suwon and later Taejon. There was an obscure marker beside the tracks at Taejon telling about General Dean knocking out a North Korean tank near that spot in the Korean War. Task Force Smith had fought back through here in the first days of that war; what a pitiful response to such an act of aggression. To reply to a North Korean sneak attack of at least eight divisions, a single U.S. battalion task force was sent initially. One would have had a far better chance at the Alamo. As we ate sandwiches and drank the wine I explained the Task Force Smith debacle to Kim, and how the tiny force was overrun, defeated and the survivors had fled.

Beside the tracks the rice fields were flooded, seed beds reluctantly yielded the tightly packed bright green rice shoots to be transplanted to the paddies. All was in readiness for the planting, and the farmers and their families waited in anticipation of their own war which was about to begin. They waited for that backbreaking centuries-old race against time that Korean farmers must battle: get the rice into the ground, hope it grows well if the rain and the sun and the wind cooperate, then harvest it rapidly before the vicious winter gripped the earth and the winds roared out of Siberia. And then there were the cabbages and the peppers and other vegetables used to make kimchi, which along with rice were the staples of the Korean diet. All of that had to go well, and after the harvest, the careful preparation and the fermentation. If lucky, one was able to eat new rice and kimchi, sitting on the floor of his snug and warm charcoal heated home as nature destroyed the less diligent. Even the system of heating the mud stuccoed cottages was dangerous and required hard work and constant attention. Charcoal and twigs and wood and whatever else would burn were utilized. The heat produced was forced through flumes running under the floors of the house, and if the system permitted leaks, the family perished by the silent death of carbon monoxide poisoning in the night as they slept. The cottage roofs were now mostly tile, because President Park Chung Hee had established a government program to roof every house in Korea, replacing the centuries old custom of roofing the cottages with rice straw. Occasionally you would see a rice straw roof here and there, housing some stubborn high-spirited old farmer who insisted on clinging to the old ways. The ridge beams of the roofs were curved with the ends pointing almost skyward, so the evil spirits would strike the ridge of the roof, be deflected away from the house and be sent flying helter-skelter throughout the universe. In front of the doors to the dwellings some sort of fence or barricade was also necessary for the same reason, since apparently Korean evil spirits only travelled in straight lines. I thought it strange that these agents of the most incredible sicknesses and ill luck could be so easily defeated and cast aside.

We reached Pusan Station about noon and headed to Beach Hotel at Haeundae where we had reservations. The taxi climbed a suddenly steep hill, left the crowded streets, careened down the other side of the hill and twisted around a deep curve which rounded a narrow finger of the ocean, made a run along the little peninsula and up the hill to deposit us in front of the hotel.

Our room was on the fifth floor. The view from the window was north, and Chosun Beach could be seen, with its narrow yellow strand lapped by the blue ocean. Further up the beach, away from the hotel, the houses and shores of Haeundae met the beach. Nearer, a small park touched the beach, the pigeons fluttered about, and an old man sold tidbits to be fed to the pigeons. On the ocean side was a low rock cliff, perhaps ten meters high, which gave way to large boulders extending down into the water.

We showered, finished the sandwiches and wine, then went down and walked along the patches of sand and across the large flat smooth boulders. Old women sold seashells, peanuts, beer, and soft drinks at various spots amongst the rocks. At one point we encountered an old lady with a tubfull of eels in water. We picked an eel and sat on the old woman's low folding chairs, watching as she filleted the still wiggling eel into small slices, which we dipped into soy sauce and ate raw. The tanned, wrinkled old woman squatted beside the tub and asked as many questions of Kim as she could possibly manage. The eel was tough and tasteless, but with the help of soy sauce and the beer I was able to enjoy it after a few slices. The old woman's face was leather brown but her eyes were still clear and black and flashed as she talked. In the time it took us to finish the eel, she had managed to tell us her life story, as well as question us pointedly about ours. We heard how she had come here from up north in the countryside when the North Koreans came and killed her entire family. She settled here and made her living selling eels and had no desire to leave.

We left her, walked over the boulders, and up the steps, to the sidewalk. At the little park we bought a packet of seeds and fed them to the pigeon sitting in my hand, beating its wings for balance, as it pecked at the seeds I held. Kim laughed and made some foolish remark about me and the pigeon. As she smiled in the warm sunshine, I thought she was very beautiful.

We walked on up the sidewalk and looked out across the water to the small fishing boats on the horizon. Along the sidewalk were small booths selling seafood; covered against the weather with blue striped oil cloth. Later we walked through the streets of the little beach village and stopped at a restaurant with a wooden sign in Han Gul which said “Kalbi Chip” or literally “Rib House.” Kim explained that this Kalbi Chip was President Park’s favorite spot in Pusan and Haeundae, and he always came here for barbecued ribs when visiting the area. The attendant brought the barbecue, regulated the fire and cut the red meat from the bones with scissors and placed it on the grill. We ate barbecued rib meat and ordered more after the first plate was gone.

Outside, the shadows began to lengthen and soon it grew dark. It was chilly, and we wore jackets as we walked back to the hotel. There was a night club in the basement where we took a table in the corner. The band was good, and we danced until late, then went outside and walked to the water’s edge. We looked out at the vastness of ocean and stood holding each other tightly in the cold night air. I kissed her.

The sea breeze was cold as we walked back to the hotel.

The next morning it was raining, and we slept late. The dining room was crowded, and we sat at a table with a Korean couple obviously on their honeymoon.

“Are you from America?” the man directed his question at me.

“Yes, I’m here in the military.”

“Yes, we appreciate your efforts,” he said sincerely, in his broken English. His new bride smiled as she and Kim talked in Han Gul. They were from Wonju, and they had come here on their honeymoon because his mother and father had honeymooned here when they were married.

“Are you here on your honeymoon also?” the lady asked.

"No." Kims' cheeks flushed a deep crimson, and I got a little angry but the subject was dropped; they were quite pleasant after all.

After lunch we went over to Haileah Compound in the city. The post was quite small, and, we could walk across it easily in thirty minutes. The rain stopped. We went to the post gymnasium and found that we could sign out gym clothes and a basketball, so we shot baskets for the better part of an hour. Kim was incredibly good, and I could not believe the smoothness and accuracy of her long jump shots. Every shot was the same — released high over her forehead with a lot of backspin and a high looping trajectory. It rippled the net and backed up from the spin as it hit the gym floor. We showered and dressed and went across the compound to the officers club.

We sat in the lounge and talked.

"Who taught you to put that high arc on your shot?" I asked.

"Oh James, that's just common sense!" she laughed. "But I can't use that anymore."

"What do you mean?" I asked.

"James, I quit the team just after that game at Camp Casey," she said.

"But why?" I asked. I suddenly began to feel guilty, and wondered if I had had anything to do with her decision to quit. I had a sort of letdown feeling, as if I had destroyed something important that could never be replaced.

"Don't look so serious, James! I really feel very happy about quitting."

"Was I the reason for your quitting?"

"No, I made the decision before I met you. They were using me, and I had already decided that I'd had enough. Then a friend of mine who had played for ten years was cut from the squad and lost her job at the bank. She had helped me a lot when I joined the team, and I respected her. She had lost a couple of steps on the fast break, and her shooting wasn't as sharp as it had been, and they just terminated her. That was the thing that made up my mind."

I felt better. "But you're still working at the bank."

"Yes, but that's because there's no one to replace me, and I've been doing a good job, according to the manager. But I still dislike the bank."

"But why didn't you tell me?"

"Because you would have thought it was your fault and felt badly. Anyway, I've told you now!" she laughed. There wasn't a hint of sadness in her voice, so I decided that maybe it wasn't so bad after all.

We ate dinner there, then left for the hotel. It was raining again and Kim sat close to me in the cab. I put my arm around her and held her; the cab's heater was warm, and the click-clack of the windshield wipers made me drowsy. We stopped for a drink at the lounge, where we sat and talked. I thought I knew what I should do in regard to the future, but I was unsure. Being in the military complicated everything; I liked the army, and the Infantry in particular. I put it out of my mind, we had another drink and went upstairs to our room.

"James?" We lay there in the darkness.

"Yes?"

"What will happen to us? I'm so afraid," she said. I could feel her trembling beside me.

"Kim, everything will be fine. Please don't worry." That seemed to help. I held her and kissed her till the trembling stopped. Her arms relaxed; she breathed deeply and I knew she was asleep.

The next day was Sunday and the weather was clear and sunny. We left the hotel and went over to the United Nations Memorial Cemetery. We walked through the graveyard, reading the tombstones of the dead of the sixteen-nation United Nations force that had repulsed the North Koreans and the Chinese and allowed South Korea to remain free. Almost no Americans were buried there because the American dead had been returned to the United States. Very prominent were the graves of the soldiers from Turkey. Shortly, I had had all I could handle of the place and its beautiful, peaceful and eternal sadness. I wasn't in the mood for that kind of thing.

We left the cemetery and travelled south to Taejungdae; there the high rocky cliffs fell straight down into the ocean. You could look over the guard rail from the top of the cliff and see the ocean far below. The fishing boats and scenic tour boats looked tiny in the distance. I thought that probably it would be easy to parachute into the water there because there would be plenty of time for the chute to open. The observation point was crowded with tourists and honeymooners. Everyone had a camera and snapped away at everything they saw. We held hands and looked down at the rocky crags and twisted pines growing from the cracks in the rugged granite faces and the green ocean far below. Eventually, we went back into the city, and to the Beach Hotel.

That night we ate in the hotel dining room and sat in the lounge afterward, listening to the vocalist sing popular American and Korean songs. I got rather drunk and we went to bed late.

Monday morning we caught a train to Seoul. We slept during the trip, but it wasn't a restful sleep, and at Seoul

I wondered if I had been asleep at all or just sitting with my eyes closed. From Seoul Station we went together as far as Miari.

"James, please call me. I know you are busy, but please call."

"Yes, I'll call. Good night, Kim."

"Good night, James."

I left for Tongduchon, where I caught the bus to the battalion area.

"Hey Tom, look, we got a new officer!" Nolan yelled at Tom as I went into the Alley.

"Welcome to Camp Casey, home of the Infantry!" Tom yelled down the hall.

I threw my bag down on the floor in the corner, as Tom and Nolan came into my room. "I hope you finished the war while I was away!" I said.

"New officer! This calls for a celebration; break out the beer!" Nolan said.

We sat on my chair, my bunk, and my footlocker and drank beer. We talked, and I told them about Pusan, and they both swore they were going to Pusan right away.

"Ricksley's about to drive the troops and everyone else around here crazy," Tom said. "He has been in town every night. A regular one man police force. Every soldier from the battalion who even looks as if he's had a drink has been run back to post. The man's gone berserk!"

"Anyone from the company?" I asked.

"Yes. He got two of your men last night. I went over to battalion to pick them up when he called, and they'd had a couple of beers but were far from drunk," Tom said. I guessed my next round with Ricksley was upcoming in the morning.

"To hell with Ricksley," I said. "I'll never forgive him for relieving Captain Laird."

"Yeah, the son-of-a-bitch has rotten judgment. He doesn't know a good officer from a bad one because he himself isn't worth a damn," Nolan said.

"To hell with him! Let's have another drink."

"Get your bottle, Tom," Nolan said. Tom went across the hall and brought back a bottle of scotch, and we sat and drank scotch with water. That mad dog Ricksley — no telling what his next move would be.

Soon we were feeling the effects of the scotch, and turned to happier thoughts. We ended up finishing Tom's bottle and got to bed late. I resolved not to flinch no matter what came, for the thought struck me that a person could run around scared all the time, with the pressure we had to put up with, and it wasn't worth it. If you didn't flinch they could only kill you one time. Someone had to stand up to Ricksley, for the sake of the troops if for nothing else.

CHAPTER 13

As things turned out I never heard of the incident again. Apparently he had played policeman with so many troops that long weekend that he couldn't possibly follow up on every incident. Later I learned that the pressure on him from the brigade commander and the division commander had occupied all his time. He had been given specific instructions on what to do to get the battalion back into shape to pass the IG reinspection. The reinspection would also be "no notice," so the emphasis on maintenance was his primary concern, and therefore ours, also.

For the next few weeks, the entire battalion had maintenance for days on end when everyone in the battalion worked on vehicles, signal equipment, weapons, and other types of gear. As a result, training started to slack off. One afternoon I was down in the motor pool, along with everyone else, when General Banson, the brigadier general in charge of training, drove up to the motor pool gate in his jeep and got out. Ricksley ran across the motor pool and reported to him. Ricksley had been up under a truck on the grease rack, and his nose and fatigue shirt were smudged with grease.

"Major, you look like hell!" Banson stated matter of factly.

"Sir, I was inspecting a truck," Ricksley said.

"Well that's all very well, but what in the hell else have you done lately? When do you think you might get around to doing some training?" he asked angrily.

Ricksley was crimson and having trouble getting his breath. He sputtered something about taking the battalion to the field the following week, but quite clearly General Banson was not satisfied. He turned and walked out of the motor pool gate and out of hearing of the assembled men. Ricksley followed behind him with the stride of a convicted felon approaching the steps to the gallows. They stopped across the road, the general turned squarely to face Ricksley. He raised his hand and pointed his finger in Ricksley's face, and we could only imagine what he was saying. Tom came across to where I stood and propped his foot up on the bumper of a jeep.

"Takes an ass chewing badly!"

"Yes. I would have thought he would come back with something about being told to do this," I said.

"He's probably doing that now."

Finally it was over and Banson got into his jeep and roared back down the road toward division headquarters. Thirty minutes later the sergeant-major's jeep came tearing down the road in a cloud of dust. The sergeant-major jumped out of the vehicle before it stopped rolling and ran urgently across the motor pool to where Major Ricksley was standing.

"Sir, we've been alerted for the IG reinspection! The IG team will arrive any minute now!" the sergeant-major told Ricksley.

It was like a bad soap opera. I turned and looked up the road and there came the olive drab bus with the white top and sign on its grill which read "Inspector General Inspection Team." It wasn't hard to imagine the plot. General Banson had gone back to division headquarters, checked on what the IG was doing, and told him to get his ass over to the battalion and get the reinspection over with, so the battalion would get out and do some training.

Ricksley was positively overwhelmed by the afternoon's events; reduced to a pale, shaking, pathetic figure. As the IG team set about the reinspection, Ricksley raced around from one area being inspected to another, panic stricken, asking questions about how the inspection was going. It became apparent early on that the standards had changed somewhat. The inspectors even smiled occasionally. I watched the inspection of a vehicle mounted radio, which appeared to me to be in worse shape than during the initial IG Inspection, and I knew it had not been worked on in this recent flurry of maintenance activity. The inspector quickly turned a few knobs, mashed the "push-to-talk" switch, and passed the radio. Suddenly the fog lifted. "So that's the way it works," I thought. I gained an insight into how things really were in the army — it was quite simply a matter of priorities, and one just had to learn what the priorities actually were at any critical time. Clearly, they shifted, turned, doubled back, and moved on again very rapidly. For example, I guessed that probably General Banson had told the IG to do the reinspection now and to pass the battalion and get it over with. But the cruel irony of the thing came home when I thought of Captain Laird, his career destroyed, faced with two or three more years in the army at most, and then kicked out in the middle of his life, to find a new profession, to make a new start, somehow. It was quite clear to all of us that he was relieved because of the failure on the IG inspection and not because of the incident on Rodriquez Range. Worse, he had been relieved because of his clash with Ricksley on the range for feeding the C-ration meal rather than a hot meal. The range incident on Rodriquez Range was merely a convenience for Ricksley – he had already decided to relieve Laird and had been waiting for any excuse when the range incident occurred and provided a plausible reason to drop the ax. A line of rather grim graffiti on the latrine wall in the Alley read "Captain Laird died for your sins!" And he had.

The inspection was over in less than two hours, and the battalion passed with a high score. General Banson showed up at the outbrief and made a speech about this favorable outcome to things being the result of hard work and dedicated effort, and now it was time to move on to other things. Banson patted Ricksley on the back and made remarks about his turning this disaster of a battalion around and molding it into a solid fighting machine. Ricksley beamed and drank in the praise and then talked about the new training program that he was on the verge of launching. Banson was pleased, Ricksley was pleased, the IG was pleased, and the curtain rang down on this hypocritical little scene. That night in the club I drank a silent toast to Captain Laird, a better man, and a better officer, than anyone of the three of them.

The next day was Saturday, and Nolan went to Seoul. Tom and I stayed in the battalion, but Kim came up that night on the bus, and I met her in the Lee Inn lounge. We sat for a while and talked, and we were very happy to see each other, to hold hands, to be together. Our relationship shielded us from the pressures of our other lives, and no matter what happened we had each other, at least for the time being. After a while we left the Lee Inn and went down into the west side of Tongduchon to a small Korean restaurant which served sashimi, raw slices of ocean fish. We sat and ate sashimi dipped in soy sauce.

Later we went up to the club at Casey where we met Tom in the lounge. The three of us sat together and enjoyed the band that Choe had brought in from Seoul.

Major Ricksley was at the bar, quite drunk, celebrating his escape in one piece from the IG reinspection and the threat of being relieved that the possibility of failure carried with it. He had been particularly impressed with our company's success on the reinspection, and he spotted us at the table and came over. Tom and I stood up, and I introduced him to Kim. He sat down at the table, uninvited, and proceeded to pass out compliments to us on our success in the reinspection. Then he really noticed Kim for the first time; he paused mid-sentence and did not have the presence of mind to understand that he was staring. He came to himself and attempted small talk with Kim.

"Miss Pak, where are you from?"

"I'm sorry, my name is Kim," she said.

"Oh, I'm sorry, Kim and Pak are both so common that I confused the two," he said. I found this an extraordinary feat in view of the fact that I had just told him her name.

"My home is Seoul," Kim said.

"And are you visiting Camp Casey for the first time?" his twisted smile was at its best.

"No, I've been here before."

"Well, please do come again. I would like to show you around the post."

Kim smiled and nodded politely without answering.

"You're very tall. You must be an athlete," he insisted.

"Yes, I played basketball."

"Now, I remember!" he said. "You were on the team that beat our post team here during the winter."

"Yes," Kim said.

I was losing my patience as he was obviously drunk and not in total control of his faculties.

I got up. "Excuse me, Major. We are leaving now." I took Kim's hand and she stood up. Ricksley showed surprise and irritation.

"Hey, stick around. I may want to dance with her later."

"No thank you," I said, as I stopped and turned to look at him.

Tom got up and reached for my arm, "I have to be going too," he said.

We walked out of the club together, and I felt that punching Ricksley would be a less than appropriate response. In the cool air I gradually dismissed the irritant and realized I was grateful that it had not gone any further.

Tom went back to the Alley, and Kim and I went to Tongduchon. I kissed her and waved as she left for Seoul.

CHAPTER 14

Following the IG reinspection we trained hard. In a few weeks the troops were back in good condition after the letdown they'd suffered during the intensive preparation for the reinspection. They were shooting well on the ranges, and we were doing twenty-five mile road marches with loaded packs three times a month. These usually started at 1800, so there was added advantage of having the troops become familiar with the area around Camp Casey at night. With the tension on the Korean peninsula that had long existed, war could start at any time. We would probably end up leaving, under pressure, in the middle of the night.

The weather was warm, without being hot. The rice was planted, and one could almost see the tiny shoots growing as we passed the fields in training. All of the paddies were flooded, and the farmers worked hard to keep water in them. Trees were starting to become green and wild flowers blossomed on the hillsides. Magpies strutted about in their shiny black and white plumage, and partridges and pheasants crossed the trails in front of us or burst explosively from under the startled Infantrymen's feet.

As we crossed the shallow creeks and streams we passed by Korean women hand-washing clothes in the stream beds, soaping and rinsing and rubbing the clothes out against flat rocks in the water. They smiled now but I'd seen them at the same task in the harsh winter, when they had to break the ice to get at the water. The American Infantrymen paused to reflect on the washer and dryer their mothers used to accomplish the same task and were not unimpressed with the hard life in a harsh land that was the lot of the Korean people. Along with that thought came an intelligent insight into the toughness of the race that had toiled so for centuries on end, clawing a living out of this rocky peninsula. Koreans were tough-minded, tough-bodied, intelligent, aggressive, yet warm and friendly people who loved music, art, and poetry. They loved the United States of America. Every child was taught in school about how the Americans had come from a wonderful land far away; had bled and died and been successful in saving their country from Communist aggression. And they were taught that before that, the same great people had crushed the hated Japanese, driven them from the peninsula in total defeat and ended the thirty-six year occupation of the land. It had been an occupation during which cruel oppression was the rule, including an attempt to stamp out the very language of the Korean people. We saw many signs of their love for us as we marched and trained.

On the south bank of the Im Jin River, near Freedom Bridge just north of Munsan, there's a large statue of a small man. He is poised there in a most majestic pose for such a common fellow from Missouri. The bespectacled figure stands, head erect, countenance stern, right hand raised, with index finger pointing upward, making a point, caught in mid-sentence for all time, all men, good and bad, to see. The school children by the tens of thousands visit that spot every spring and summer. If they listen carefully enough, and concentrate hard enough, they will perhaps hear a faint utterance from the statue, which will sound something like "The buck stops here!" Harry S. Truman is a hero in Korea.

We trained, and then trained more to become proficient with our weapons and tough in our bodies and minds so that if we were called upon to stand and fight beside the Koreans to save their country we would be able to do so. Ricksley was intolerable, but we had resigned ourselves to the fact that we were badly led. Realizing that this was the case, the obvious question was what should we do about it? The equally obvious answer was that we all had to do our best to make things work out, in spite of Ricksley.

Kim had told me that her father was killed near Wonju in the counter-offensive in February of 1951. On another day we talked about this, and she told me that he had died on 14 February, 1951 at a small crossroads village called Chipyong Ni. I recognized the name of the village. We'd studied the Battle of Chipyong Ni in OCS as an example of how to fight when surrounded, in what was known as a perimeter defense. This is nothing more than fighting out of a circle of foxholes with artillery, mortars, the element headquarters and any other supporting forces inside of the protective circle of foxholes, which were occupied by the riflemen and machine-gunners who formed the cutting edge of the defense. The Battle of Chipyong Ni had been fought for three days and two nights, the 13th, 14th, and 15th of February, 1951. I knew by the dates and name of the place that Kim's father had died in that battle. We located the small village on a road map. I got the military maps of that area and checked out material from the library at Camp Casey on the history of the battle and studied it until I thought I had some appreciation of that colossal struggle.

One warm Sunday morning I left early and met Kim at Seoul Station, where we caught a train to Chipyong Ni. I'd packed a rucksack with food and had thrown in some wine and Cokes. The train ran eastward along the north bank of the Han River, passed the point where the Han split into the North Han and the South Han River, crossed the North Han over the railroad bridge, went through the low hills between the higher mountains, stopped at Yangpyong, and finally deposited us at the village of Chipyong Ni.

The mid-morning sun was bright and warm and the sky was high and clear blue as we stepped off the train and looked out on the little village of one hundred buildings or so. Two dirt roads divided the village into quadrants. One of the roads ran north-south through the village and the other ran east-west, and the place where they crossed formed the center of the village. The few shops and businesses were located around this cross. There were dwelling houses, and in the southwest quarter of the village there was a school building with a grassless schoolyard, soccer goals at each end. A small monument next to the road told of the great battle fought at Chipyong Ni. Small boys kicked a worn-out soccer ball across the yard, happily oblivious to the struggle that had taken place here. A Korean Army ordnance battalion headquarters was located on the low rise just south of the school, and the area around the military installation was posted with "Keep Out" signs in Han Gul. Ammunition bunkers could be seen throughout the area. The ordnance battalion was there to operate the ammunition storage facilities. I knew I should let the Korean Army personnel there know that we wanted to walk around the battlefield and have a look at the old positions.

We walked to the gate in front of the battalion headquarters, and Kim told the gate guard that we wanted to walk over the battlefield and that we were requesting permission to do so. I showed him my army identification card. He rang a field phone and conversed with someone on the other end of the line. Soon a Korean lieutenant arrived at the gate and escorted us to the battalion headquarters. We were taken in, seated on a couch and served coffee. A Major Lee, the battalion executive officer, sat down with us, and we told him why we were there. Obviously this outpost saw very few foreigners this far out in the countryside, and Major Lee was anxious to practice his English. He was very impressed that Kim's father had died in the battle and took us outside to point out different parts of the battlefield to us. He asked me where we would like to start, and I picked a high hill just north of the village, in the center of the defenders' fighting circle. I thought that from that vantage point we could probably see most of the battlefield. Major Lee assigned a jeep and driver to us. The driver took us out the gate and up the road to the north, past the school and the crossroads in the center of the village, and over the bridge that spanned a small stream on the north side of the village, up to the foot of the hill. The trip took about five minutes. We thanked the driver, who turned and drove back down the road.

Kim and I took a small trail off the road and started to walk up a finger of a ridgeline. We immediately came upon an unexpected monument, partially hidden there in the pines. It was on the side of the ridgeline, a stiletto shaped stone monument set in concrete and standing upright, pointing at the sky. A metal plate with an inscription told how the U.S. 23rd Infantry Regiment, a force of about four thousand five hundred men, had withstood the savage attacks of Chinese from at least four identified divisions. The story on the plaque was in English and Han Gul. The English had obviously been written by a Korean and not proofed by a native English speaker. I remember the phrase describing the attacking Chinese which read in part "... surging as hungry wolves ..." Nevertheless, tears came to my eyes, and I saw Kim dab at her eyes with a handkerchief. The effect of the not too perfect English was stronger than if an American had written it.

After a while we climbed the hill, winding our way upward through scrub oak and pine and occasionally crossing piles of granite. At the top, the hill flattened out and a small shrine was there. I took the map of the library account of the battle from my rucksack and matched it to the terrain surrounding the hill. Then I pointed out where the three American battalions of the 23rd Infantry Regiment had defended and where the attached French Battalion had dug in and fought. We sat down on a poncho liner, took the food and drink from the rucksack and had lunch.

"I wonder where my father was in the battle," Kim said.

"I'm sure he fought with one of the American battalions," I said. "In fact, there were fewer than seventy killed on the United Nations side, and most of them died on the south side, with the 2nd battalion of the 23rd Infantry Regiment." I pointed to the area on the south side of the perimeter, on the east side of the road, where the Chinese had succeeded in breaching the perimeter, but had been unable to reinforce and pour through the gap.

"Can we go down there later?" she asked.

"Yes, of course," I said. She seemed very thoughtful about the prospects of perhaps walking on the ground where her father had perished.

The sun was high and we were alone. I held her and kissed her and the world belonged to us at that moment. She pulled away but held my hand and sat on the poncho liner looking at me in an innocent, pleading, loving sort of way. I took her hand, "Let's go down to that spot and see what we can find." We walked down the hill, pausing again at the monument, and then reached the road and walked south. We passed the school and the entrance to the ordnance battalion headquarters and then went under the little railroad bridge, where we reached the cut where a small hill rose on either side of the road. There we turned left off the road, went up the hill and crossed to the side which would have been facing the attacking Chinese. There, just where they should have been, were the old decayed, filled-in foxholes, where the 2nd Battalion of the 23rd had defended. We walked along the line of foxholes and a chill ran up my spine. I could imagine Lieutenant Magee running back and forth between the positions under assault by the Chinese, coordinating the defense as the attackers slithered on their bellies through the snow in the gloom of night. I felt like I was in church. We talked in hushed tones; I was very aware of where I stepped. As we moved along the foxhole line we encountered some large granite boulders, forward of the perimeter. The sides of the rocks that had faced the Chinese attackers were scarred and pockmarked where the fusillade of rifle and machine-gun bullets had struck. At one point, a bullet had penetrated a crack in the stone, and was lodged there as a rusty reminder of the struggle. The battle accounts and their accompanying sketches were not perfect and greatly lacked detail; nevertheless, I was able thought about the battle. We talked about it, and I was impressed that he knew many of the battle's details.

An old man sitting in the corner drinking his tea hobbled over to our table and told us he had helped bury the Chinese dead in a mass grave in the hills south of town. He spoke of the many days the task had taken, and then told me that the Chinese had buried many of their own dead in the hills and valleys around Chipyong Ni. Sometimes, even now, farmers discovered Chinese remains as they cultivated the earth, constructed houses, or dug for any reason. He reached into his pants pocket and produced a single U.S. Army "dog tag." The tag bore the name "Ferguson," and was pierced through the center, probably by shrapnel. The man's serial number told us that he was a regular army enlisted man, rather than a draftee, the difference being that a draftee's serial number was prefaced by "US" and a regular's was not.

"Did you know this man?" he asked me.

I started to smile, but I saw that the old man was serious. "No, but I'll try to find out who he was." That seemed to please him, and he shoved the tag back into his pocket.

We had thoroughly enjoyed their company, and I felt as if we had been interviewed, by the news media, but I knew it was only because they saw Americans so rarely and because of the innate Korean curiosity. We left the tabang, walked up to the station and turned and waved to them. We left for Seoul, and parted there. I barely made it to Camp Casey before curfew.

CHAPTER 15

The war in Vietnam had taken a new turn. Almost daily, the news carried details of the American troop buildup. The 173rd Airborne Brigade was there, and elements of the 1st Infantry Division had arrived from Fort Riley, Kansas. Almost simultaneous with the arrival of the 1st Infantry Division, the lead elements of the 1st Cavalry Division arrived, and there were already Marines there. These units were thrown into combat as they arrived. A few officers and men from our division volunteered for duty in Vietnam, and at first only a few were sent. Then more and more of the volunteers began to receive their orders for Vietnam. The tour in Korea was normally thirteen months, and those who volunteered finished their tours in Korea, then were sent straight to Vietnam.

Kim was increasingly apprehensive about the prospect of my volunteering to go to Vietnam, and the decision weighed heavily on me, as the news of the fighting became the constant topic of discussion in the club and around the battalion. My dilemma was quite simple – there was a war, I was a soldier who expected to go sooner or later. And there was Kim; I desperately hated to leave her, and I knew that with the war growing rather than winding down, Kim and I could not possibly make any serious plans for the future. So that was it. I hated the position I found myself in. I couldn't take the initiative, make a quick decision, and carry it out because it wasn't that simple. Finally I realized that my tour in Korea was up in September, and that I had better get the paperwork in to volunteer for Vietnam or it would be too late. I went by the S-1 section and volunteered.

I didn't know how to tell Kim. She had pleaded with me not to go until they sent me, but she had known that it would never turn out like that. Finally, I told her on a Sunday afternoon in July.

We returned from the field on Saturday, grimy and dog-tired. I slipped into the company commander's office and called Kim, and we decided to meet at Munsan at the bus station the next morning. The following morning I took the early bus from Camp Casey to Camp Howze. At Howze I caught a Korean bus for Munsan. At the bus station I looked around, but Kim wasn't there yet. I crossed the street to a tabang and drank coffee, and after a while the next bus arrived, and Kim got off. I crossed the street and met her.

"What, no rucksack! What will we eat today?" she laughed.

"Hi! How was the trip?"

"Fine, and everything is so beautiful and green; you've ordered up a perfect day for us!" she replied. She was quite happy to see me, and I knew it wouldn't be easy to tell her. Suddenly, nothing seemed easy anymore, and I decided not to tell her until late afternoon. We crossed the street to the tabang and sat at the table I'd taken earlier.

"I've missed you so much! How was the field trip?"

"Not bad except for a bad decision or two by our good friend Ricksley."

"What kind of bad decisions?"

"Tactical decisions on how to attack a strong enemy force, dug in and waiting." I didn't want to discuss it because it was dull, mundane, and would be uninteresting to her.

But she insisted. "And?" she asked.

"He wanted to attack in the day time, and the route he chose was not even a flank attack but rather a frontal assault. We should have done it at night, and we could have hit them from behind."

"But he seemed like such a nice man." She hadn't understood the tactics, and I was sorry I had bored her. We had never talked about Ricksley.

"Yes." We left and walked out into the sunshine. Happily, Ricksley seemed a thousand miles away. We took a cab north toward Freedom Bridge, through two or three tiny villages. Within minutes we saw the small park on the left and the statue of President Truman. Just beyond that was Im Jin Gak, or Im Jin House, which was a large tourist restaurant which had good roast rib Korean style. We passed Im Jin Gak and immediately arrived at the south end of Freedom Bridge. This bridge spans the Im Jin River with wooden planking and is wide enough for one-way traffic only. The Korean and American MP's at either end of the bridge controlled the traffic, alternately letting it flow from the north and south sides. The MP saluted and waved us on across the bridge. On the right, in the muddy waters of the river, were the concrete pilings of an old bridge, destroyed during the war. On the other side the taxi wound through the low hills along the two-lane paved road, passed Camp Greaves on the right, on around the curves until we passed Camp Liberty Bell and reached the main gate of Camp Kittyhawk.

At Kittyhawk we went through the gate and walked up some steps, crossed the top of the hill and entered to determine with a fair amount of certainty where the defenders had fought and where their artillery, mortars, and other supporting weapons had been located. We doubled back up the hill, above the saddle where hand-to-hand fighting had occurred. At the high point of the hill, we stood and looked out to the south over the rice fields, down the dirt road from the direction that Colonel Marcel Crombez had brought his tank force to assist the 23rd. That had been on the last day of the battle. On the afternoon of 15 February, 1951, Crombez had hit the Chinese from the rear and the battle turned into a complete rout, with the Chinese fleeing in all directions as all weapons were brought to bear on them. The wind stirred through the trees. Kim shivered, and I recalled Homer's description of "... the ringing plains of windy Troy ...," I thought it sad that no poet had ever properly sung the account of this Homeric struggle.

We walked back down the hill to the road, where the jeep and driver waited to pick us up. We got in, and he took us back up the road past the battalion headquarters and schoolhouse and stopped the jeep just beyond the crossroads. Major Lee met us there, along with four other officers; we were then introduced to the battalion staff. Following the introductions, Major Lee invited us into a tabang located at the crossroads. The beaming waitress told us there was tea, coffee, or beer, and presently she came out with a tray full of drinks, complete with peanuts and potato chips. It was early summer but there was a strange looking stove in the center of the room. I was told that it burned sawdust exclusively. Of course, it was not necessary now but I was assured that in the dead of January it would run one out of the room if the barmaid heaped too much sawdust into it. The S-1 of the battalion, a Captain Kim, wanted to know what I the club called "The Monastery." We took a table and ordered sandwiches.

Camp Kittyhawk was the base for the Joint Security Area (JSA) personnel who policed Panmunjom inside the DMZ. These hand-picked South Korean and American soldiers had the job of policing the daily activities, as well as other special meetings, and the talks between North Koreans, Chinese and the United Nations. They worked in and around all of the buildings in Panmunjom, Communist and United Nations. Daily they confronted the North Korean contingent of guards, also handpicked and skilled in martial arts. When not on duty, the Americans and South Koreans at Panmunjom lived at Kittyhawk.

We finished the sandwiches and boarded an already loaded bus that took us back out the gate of Kittyhawk, and up the road to the DMZ. On the other side we were waved through a south barrier fence by American guards. After a short distance, we crossed a small hill. As we started down the other side we went under an overhead sign shaped like an arc, which marked the south tape of the DMZ. We entered the DMZ at that point, passed a South Korean guard post and soon after passed American Guard Posts Collier and Ouellette. These posts are named for two American heroes from the Korean War. Inside the DMZ it was green, peaceful and the clear stream flowing beside the road was home to schools of minnows and small fish. Pheasants could be seen walking around like domestic chickens would on a farm in the United States. Between the road and Guard Post Ouellette there was a pond profuse with water plants. Wading birds stood in the water, and here and there wild ducks dotted the surface. The DMZ, and this pond in particular, was one of the last habitats of the beautiful and rare Siberian crane. Here, where men were at a silent war, nature was at a silent peace. Rare species of small animals could also be seen, ranging from the small deer of Asia to a rare breed of wild cat, simply called salkwangi, or wild cat, by the Koreans. One could catch fleeting glimpses of them while on patrol on moonlit nights. As we passed Ouellette we topped a small rise and then went down the low incline and into Panmunjom. A JSA officer gave us a guided tour of Panmunjom. He pointed out the Bridge Of No Return where prisoners from both sides in the Korean War had crossed during repatriation, following the signing of the armistice in 1953. The bridge was so named because many of the North Korean prisoners chose to stay in the south, and all prisoners were told that once they crossed the bridge there was no possible chance to return.

The North Korean guards paraded and postured, watching us through binoculars, although we were no more than twenty yards from them. They were dressed in brown uniforms with brown "saucer" caps and high black boots. It was easy to see that the uniform was modeled after those of the Soviet Army. We looked through the window at the table where the talks were held; it sat squarely astride the Military Demarcation Line (MDL), a thin line exactly in the center of the DMZ and exactly lengthwise down the center of the table. We reboarded the bus, returned to Kittyhawk, and took a cab back across Freedom Bridge, and then on across the highway to Im Jin Gak. We walked into the restaurant and were seated in a small room with a table on which sat the barbecue grill. We ordered the house specialty, beef ribs and beer.

"James, have you been in the DMZ often?" Kim asked.

"No. We were here two months last year and I ran patrols throughout the American sector. That's why I know the area," I said.

"And did you see North Koreans?" she asked.

"No, just a lot of deer and pheasants."

"It's a beautiful, deathly quiet place, isn't it?" she said.

"Yes, a bit like being in church, or perhaps a graveyard." I had never been able to explain the feeling that I had inside the DMZ. It was a four kilometer wide strip of land running all the way across the Korean peninsula, and it wasn't really demilitarized at all. Both sides maintained fortified guard posts throughout their respective sides of this buffer zone. The fragile peace was mostly preserved except when North Korean infiltrators committed acts of violence or were killed before they could do so. Since the armistice, over two hundred people had been killed in these small, deadly clashes. In the DMZ I felt that the strange, long hush of the death-like solitude was like a vacuum. The two great land armies faced each other over that silent four kilometers, watching, waiting and biding time while trying to find out more about each other.

And there were other activities-the North Koreans were believed to have dug deep and sophisticated tunnels all the way under the DMZ. With a little imagination one could envision multiple tunnels all across the front. These would permit North Korean troops to avoid the main South Korean defenses by going under them and surfacing to their rear. They'd successfully bypass the Im Jin River and other major obstacles, as well as the first line of troops. For this purpose, the North Koreans had developed an elite ranger commando force of suicide "throw away" troops. Their leader was their president Kim Il Sung. Some leader. Some cause. The most closed society in the world, totally brain-washed for years; ready to slaughter, maim and hold back peace and prosperity in the name of Kim Il Sung –that was North Korea. At night, when every Korean laid his head on his pillow, on the charcoal heated floor of his home, his last conscious thought was probably the threat of war hanging over the peninsula. And Koreans know war. The ones too young to have experienced the North Korean invasion of 1950 know all about it from many sources; numbers of absent uncles, aunts, and grandparents, killed as the war swept up and down the peninsula. Seoul was overrun three times during the war.

"A penny for your thoughts," Kim brought me back to the present.

"I'm sorry," I said. The problem facing me nagged at me, and I finally knew I had to stand up to it, but I made up my mind to tell Kim after we ate. The kalbi was good but my mind was hardly on it. After the food we sat in silence.

"What is it James? Do you have something to tell me?" Kim asked quietly.

"Yes. Kim, I will leave for Vietnam in September."

"Yes, James, I knew." Her head was bowed as she cried softly. I felt totally helpless, and there was no reason to talk about it. It was done, and the hurt could not be helped. I held her hand and after a while she looked at me and tried to smile.

Outside the weather had changed. It was cloudy now. When we left Im Jin Gak it had started to rain. I watched her bus leave; she waved through the window, but her smile was forced, and I knew that things could never be the same again. I took a cab across to Tongduchon, feeling low as hell all the way.

CHAPTER 16

Nolan Broyles left the battalion on the first day of August. He was on his way to Vietnam. We gave him a proper send-off. I wish his homecoming had been as cordial. He was in a body bag, dead, and on his way home within a week. We got the word by reading the casualty list in the dispatches. He was killed, along with two of his soldiers, when they tripped a booby-trapped artillery round. I learned later that he had died instantly. Small comfort. Nolan had been one of the finest men I'd ever known. The day following the news of his death, we gathered in Camp Casey's Stone Chapel for a memorial service. There were three, and now there were two.

The following week at commander's call, Ricksley addressed the battalion in the theater. During his talk he tried to touch on tactics, a subject that I thought was totally alien to him, based upon his past performance in the field. Then he took a "lessons learned" approach to the subject. He described the incident in which Nolan was killed as a bad example; he explained that Nolan and his two soldiers were walking too closely together; that they had tried to go through a hedgerow at a break, a natural place for a booby-trap. "So don't bunch up, and break through hedgerows rather than going through existing openings!" he shouted.

I have never been as angry as I was at that moment. I knew I was going to do something stupid, but I had completely lost control before I got to my feet. Later I could not remember what I had said, and Tom had to tell me.

"You son-of-a-bitch! Nolan Broyles is not a number, not a piece on your war game board. He was a member of this battalion!" The realization that I had overstepped the mark slowly came to me; then I heard Ricksley say something.

"Captain Jenkins, take Lieutenant Worthington out of the theater. I'll see him this afternoon."

Tom and Captain Jenkins had me by the arms, one on each side, and we left the theater through the side doors.

"Sir, I'm OK. I'll go back to the orderly room and wait," I said.

"OK," Jenkins replied, not knowing what else to do.

Tom and I walked back over to the company area. He was trying to console me, to calm me down, but it wasn't necessary. I had said what I thought needed to be said, and I felt fine. The thought struck me that if I had killed him I would probably have felt even better. I sat down in Captain Jenkins' office, and Tom went back to the theater.

In half an hour Jenkins and Tom returned to Jenkins' office. "Your're the luckiest officer alive," Jenkins gave me a strange smile.

"Sir, I meant what I said. How could that rotten bastard use Nolan as a negative example to the troops. He's barely in the ground, and his so-called friends from the battallion he loved so well are making a negative example of him."

"James, of course you're right, but I would not have done it the way you did. Fortunately, the division chief of staff was sitting in the back of the theater, and he totally agreed with you. We overheard his conversation with Ricksley. You don't even have to talk to Ricksley about the matter. The chief told Ricksley that he was lucky he wasn't relieved on the spot for incredibly bad judgment. He also warned Ricksley against writing a bad report on you when you leave."

"Are you saying that's the end of it, then?"

"Well, I hope so. If Ricksley goes to the commanding general with the incident, then you could still be in trouble. I doubt that he will, because he knows very well that the commanding general will back his own chief of staff."

I knew I'd probably never hear of the matter again. Ricksley was too career oriented and gutless to try to take on the chief of staff. He was an expert in the guidance of his own personal career, the most important thing in his life, above morals, the men, and anything else. He was like the good mariner, knowing where the rocks and shoals lurked beneath the surface of the water, and he steered clear of them if it meant going a mile or more out to sea to do so. Still, I understood very well that I now had enemies in high places, and I knew that, with my remaining time in Korea, my ship could still run aground.

After the incident I was sort of a folk hero around the division. Officers I had never seen before greeted me with a smile, and the troops in the battalion whispered to each other as I passed them in the battalion area. I really didn't like it much, and would have been very glad to put the whole thing behind me. I felt very uncomfortable when the subject came up, and often wondered what the big deal was. After thinking it through I realized that people need a hero. It may be a natural psychological urge, but if they don't have one they'll create one. That's why the stories of deeds great and small get blown completely out of proportion, so that when the story finds its way back to one of the participants he can hardly recognize it. There seems to be a natural tendency to exaggerate and make the hero larger than life. Once the "legend" begins, it takes on the strange aura of something almost supernatural or magical, because that's part of the formula for satisfying this human urge. Certainly in cases like mine, there was the vicarious aspect. Secretly, many had always wanted to do something like this, and through my experience, were able to do so in some small way. I have actually known old soldiers to become confused, and to tell each other's war stories! And there was always a hero in the war stories. I must have met a thousand soldiers who claimed to have fought with Patton, side by side; the foxhole they occupied would have been the size of four football fields laid end to end. A few weeks after the affair I overheard two captains at the bar in the Eighth Army club in Yongsan discussing it. One of them swore to the other that this brash lieutenant had dragged his battalion commander off the stage of the theater and punched him senseless! People need a hero.

The week following the incident in the theater, Major Ricksley received the word that he had been selected for promotion to lieutenant-colonel below the zone, in other words, ahead of his contemporaries. The irony of the whole thing was more than I could handle. There was a brigade officers' call that evening in the club to celebrate Ricksley's good fortune, but Tom and I went down to the Aviation Club to toss a few down to ease the pain. The bar was quiet at the Aviation Club. Most of the aviators were in the field taking a training test.

"Good old Jim; you won't go over there and get yourself dinged, will you?" Tom asked. He had volunteered for

Vietnam, but his time to rotate was sometime around October.

"No problem, they wouldn't dare shoot me," I said.

We played horse for a round, and I lost on three straight rolls. After that we rolled for several more rounds. We were drinking scotch.

"Here's to Nolan Broyles, the finest lieutenant in the Army," Tom said. We touched glasses and drank to Nolan.

"I really miss him. He was a fine one."

"Yeah, I'll never forget him out there in the gravel that night last winter," Tom said. We smiled at the memory, and then it was OK.

"What will you get for a rotation date?" I asked.

"I'll probably leave mid-October."

"I'll write and let you know what unit I'm in and maybe you can join me."

"OK."

Finally we gave it up and caught the bus to the Alley. The mood just was not there. I took a hot shower and read. I read a paper from home; it was just one long obituary. I put out the light and went to sleep. Thirty minutes later the charge of quarters called, woke me and informed me that one of my soldiers was in jail for being drunk and disorderly. I took the duty vehicle to the MP Headquarters, picked the soldier up and took him to the barracks.

As I left the barracks and crossed back over to the Alley, Ricksley stumbled out of the club across the street and saw me. "Lieutenant, get over here. I want to talk to you," he said.

"Yes, Sir," I went across and saluted him.

"Too good to celebrate my promotion, Lieutenant?"

"Sir, I don't care for you or your promotion."

"Lieutenant, I'm going to get you. You can mark that down in your little black book. I'm going to nail you." He was drunk, his face flushed with alcohol and anger.

"Will that be all, Sir?" I asked quietly.

"You're damned right, that's all. I'm going to get you." He stumbled off toward his quarters.

I went back to the Alley, had a beer and reflected on the leadership in the battalion. Some leadership. This time I slept until the alarm went off the next morning.

CHAPTER 17

The last weekend in August I met Kim in Seoul at the Japanese restaurant in the Koguryo Hotel. One of Choe's friends was the manager, and I had met him in Tongduchon. He had invited me to come down and try the Japanese cuisine. We were cordially received and seated at a nice table by the window. It was delicious. I liked the red strips of raw tuna the best. Outside the window we could see City Hall, and running to the northwest was the road to Munsan and the DMZ. You could reach the DMZ in about an hour from that spot in central Seoul. It was a bit sobering to think that the North Koreans were just about an hour away from the capital by ground transportation.

Kim really enjoyed herself. She loved Japanese food as much as she disliked the Japanese people. Following the meal we had an after-dinner drink, then the manager came out, waved us off with a smile and told us the meal was complimentary. We shook hands and he asked me to remember him to Choe. He had a drink with us downstairs at the main bar. Afterwards we took a cab for the Naija Hotel.

At the Naija we sat down at a table near the stage. The Korean duet was good that evening, and we danced on the tiny floor several times. After that we took a cab across

Nam San to the Crest Hotel and sat in the lounge. Miss Lee was belting out a Korean song when we arrived, and she flashed her beautiful smile at us. Kim really liked her personally, and at her first break she came over and had a drink with us.

"Why so thoughtful tonight, Kim?" Lee asked.

"Oh, nothing. This one is going to leave me soon," pointing a thumb at me. Lee didn't quite know how to answer.

"It's only temporary," I said.

Kim looked at me in a way I'd never seen before.

"Do you really believe that, James?"

"Kim, of course I believe it."

"Then what shall we do about Nolan?" she asked.

"Pray for him."

"And shall we pray for you too, James?" The words cut like a razor, I didn't answer and Lee tried to get things back on track.

"I'm finishing early tonight. Let's go to a cabaret," she said.

"OK," Kim was drinking scotch. For the first time I saw her drink scotch, and I thought that perhaps she had already had too much.

We left the Crest with Lee, took a cab down the mountain to Itaewan and went into a cabaret. The place was packed. I slipped a won bill to one of the waitresses, who promptly seated us at a table with three Korean girls. We danced quite a bit, and were sweating profusely when we finally left. It was very late, and I had serious doubts about the possibility of catching a cab. Finally Lee got a cab going up towards Miari where she lived. Kim and I gave up, walked down through Itaewan to the Han Hotel and went downstairs to the night club there. We had to pay a cover charge at the door; the place was packed. We squeezed into a table on the balcony and ordered. Kim sobered with the dancing.

"Oh James, please come back," she said. It wasn't getting any easier, but then I hadn't expected it to. There was no hint of bitterness about the situation we found ourselves in. It seemed that we had no control over the roles we were playing. The forces that controlled our destinies seemed to be far removed, obscure, and impossible to predict or understand in any significant way. We couldn't express anger at the futility of our situation because there was nothing tangible to focus our anger upon. We reluctantly accepted it. The future could only be taken one small step at a time. The next step was only two weeks from now, when I would board the airplane at Kimpo. We didn't speak about it again that evening.

The night club at the Han stayed open through curfew, so many people who were caught without a way home before curfew ended up there. They had to stay there, trapped a little like animals, until 0400 in the morning when the curfew lifted. If I were going to be trapped I couldn't think of a nicer way to do it than with Kim. We danced through the night; talking wasn't much use now, and when we tried it only deepened the gloom that we were attempting to put behind us.

At 0400 the night club emptied onto the street in front of the Han; the flood of taxis was there to meet the crowd, and Seoul officially came back to life once again. I had the duty at brigade headquarters from Sunday afternoon until Monday morning, so we parted there, and I waved as the green cab went out of sight down the street. I crossed to the other side and caught a cab for Tongduchon. I slept most of the way; the driver woke me as we went under the arch at the south end of Tongduchon and passed the Lee Inn.

In the Alley I showered and went to bed. I got up at 1130, cleaned up, and went across to the club. Tom was there and we ate lunch together.

"So you have the honors today," he said.

"Yes. I'd rather take a beating than to have the duty at brigade," I said.

"Well, keep the coffee hot, and you'll make it OK!" he said.

After lunch I went up to brigade headquarters and relieved the lieutenant on duty. I had a Master Sergeant for my duty NCO, and a PFC as the driver. That afternoon I received a long distance telephone call from the States, from a brother of one of the soldiers in our battalion. His mother had died of a heart attack, and the soldier was urgently requested to return home for the funeral.

"Have you gone to the Red Cross to have them telegraph the Red Cross here, verifying the emergency leave?" I asked.

"No, I didn't know that was necessary."

"Yes, get in touch with the Red Cross now, and have them telegraph the Red Cross at Kimpo Air Force Base Army ATCO (Air Traffic Coordinating Office) as well as the Red Cross here. I'll get him ready to go and send him on down to Kimpo. He can pick up the emergency leave orders there," I said.

"OK, I'll do that now. Thank you very much," and he hung up.

I called battalion and had them get in touch with the soldier. He was in the field with his company, so it took two hours to get him back to Camp Casey. His company had everything packed and ready for him. He showered and changed into a class A uniform, and I put him in the duty vehicle and sent him to Kimpo. I explained everything over the telephone to the sergeant on duty at Army ATCO at Kimpo. He booked the man on a flight departing that night, the first flight leaving for the States. Within two hours the Red Cross at Casey called; they had received verification from the Red Cross office in the soldier's home town that this was a bona fide emergency leave. I called Kimpo and the sergeant told me that they had received the verification also, so there was no problem.

I'd just settled back in the chair behind the desk when the phone rang again. It was Ricksley.

"Worthington, what in the hell are you doing pulling soldiers out of the field and sending them to Kimpo without bona fide emergencies?" he asked.

"Sir, I did what I thought was right. The Red Cross has just verified the emergency," I said.

"It wasn't verified when you sent him to Kimpo," he said.

"Sir, if I'd waited for verification he wouldn't have made today's flight." I found the conversation incredible and Ricksley's thinking a little twisted, if not perverted. If anything, a good leader would be patting me on the back for taking some initiative to help one of our soldiers. As it was I was being dressed down for what I had done.

"You acted without proper authority, purely and simply. Report to me tomorrow morning after PT," he said.

"Yes Sir."

It was quite clear that Ricksley's intention was to harass me. Any officer with common sense would have agreed with what I did. The most Ricksley could do was to attempt to issue an Article 15 to me as nonjudicial punishment. Of course, I'd refuse the Article 15 and demand trial by court martial which I would win easily. He'd end up looking like a fool. At any rate, I was determined not to worry about the situation; in my mind the whole affair was Ricksley's attempt to "get me" as he had faithfully promised that night in front of the club. I could only conclude that he must be rather desperate at this point, because unless I was totally wrong in my thinking, he didn't have a leg to stand on. Anyway, I thought I had better play it smart and get some legal advice as I had been taught to advise soldiers to do. I called a captain, a lawyer whom I had met down at the club one night. He advised me to demand trial by court martial if it came to that. He also told me that he doubted that things would come to such a drastic conclusion, because, in his opinion, Ricksley would be a fool to risk the ire of his superiors by trying to legalize his revenge. The story of the incident in the theater was known throughout the division, ensuring that any attempt at revenge would be quite obvious. In a sense, I could be somewhat confident because Ricksley was too much of a careerist to risk very much for simple revenge. He was also lacking in the type of courage that risking everything called for. I was fairly certain of that.

At any rate, Captain Jenkins called me aside at the PT formation the following morning and informed me that Ricksley would not be able to see me because of an unexpected meeting at division. Our meeting would be rescheduled for a later date. I knew that I'd never hear anything more about the matter.

CHAPTER 18

I signed out of the division on a Friday morning early in September after telling my soldiers good-bye at the morning PT formation. That morning we ran eight miles – the troops had asked that we "run the horn" as a farewell to me. "Running the horn" was going out the southeast gate at Casey, over to Camp Hovey, through Hovey and out Hovey's back gate, through the streets of the village of Toko Ri, across the mountain into south Tongduchon in front of the Lee Inn, up the street to north Tongduchon, into Casey gate, and home to the company. When we halted in the company street, the troops presented me with a plaque engraved with the company nickname, the battalion crest and some heartfelt memorable words on it.

The brigade commander let me use his duty vehicle for the trip to Seoul. My good-byes were all said, and the last person I saw as I left the company was Tom McCarter.

"Keep your ass down, champ."

"See you in October," I said. We shook hands; I climbed into the jeep, and we went down the street past the club, past the Aviation Club and out the main gate, south toward Seoul. I thought about my farewell party the night before; Ricksley had not shown up for it. I was happy about that because I didn't need any of his hypocrisy tainting my send-off. Choe had wept; I knew he'd miss me more than anyone. Koreans are very emotional.

The trip south was pleasant, and the open jeep was cool with the rush of air from the speed of the vehicle. I looked out at the tall rice with its ripe heads bent over, waiting for the impending harvest. Things were still green, but here and there a leaf had already turned, early signs of the approaching fall. Summer is merely a short break between winters in Korea.

I was booked on a flight leaving Kimpo Sunday morning for Tachikawa Air Force Base, Japan. There I would lay over Sunday night and fly on to Saigon by way of Clark Air Force Base, the Philippines. I had reservations at the Naija Hotel for Friday and Saturday nights.

The KATUSA driver turned west at Euijongbu and drove past Camp Red Cloud, across the mountains and approached Seoul from the northwest. The Naija was on that side of Seoul, and he could avoid most of the heavy traffic by taking this approach. As we passed Red Cloud, I thought about it's namesake, Corporal Mitchell Red Cloud. During the Korean war he had held a company sized gap in the lines throughout the night. His company had withdrawn without him as he was mortally wounded and refused to pull back. When the company reoccupied the hill the following morning, Red Cloud was slumped there dead, surrounded by a wide circle of dead Chinese, felled by his Browning Automatic Rifle. The BAR Range at Fort Benning, Georgia, had also been named for him; the wooden sign at the entrance to the range told that he was a Congressional Medal of Honor winner. "Red Cloud's last stand," I thought. It was a good thing that Custer had not had BAR's at the Little Big Horn or Mitchell Red Cloud might not have made it to Korea; he might not have been born. I began to daydream and I could envision the old 7th Cavalrymen in their dusty blue uniforms lying behind their BAR's with a stream of tracers raking the ranks of the Sioux and Cheyenne horsemen. The horses were paints, browns and appaloosas and they screamed as they pitched forward into the masses of dead and wounded mounts and men. Here and there copper-colored men with painted faces ran back and forth firing rifles in the confusion, not knowing whether to break off the attack, fight from behind the dead horses or charge on foot. The BAR's were chopping, chopping, chopping, and the flower of the Sioux nation dying, dying, dying. The barrels of the BAR's were hot, smoking, and the troopers poured canteen water over them to cool them down.

Suddenly I was jolted from my daydream as the tires on the jeep locked and slid. I smelled the rubber burning and heard the squealing of tires on asphalt. An old man had wheeled his oxcart onto the highway at a blind curve; somehow my driver avoided hitting him. The driver got the jeep going again and went around the farmer and his ox. In respect to the farmer's age the KATUSA didn't curse him.

At the Naija I checked in, and was given a room on the third floor above the lounge in the east building. I put my things in the room, bathed and called Kim. She came to the Naija, and we sat in the lounge and talked. She seemed determined to be cheerful; I thought she'd accepted my leaving and knew that it was not the end of things.

We rode up to Nam San and got out beside a small park. We sat on a bench in the sun; there were children playing on the swings and seesaws, while others skipped rope. It was very humid but not quite as bad as early

August had been. Pigeons strutted back and forth over the bare ground, happy to find a grain of popcorn here and there.

After a while we walked up the hill. On the side of the mountain is a large statue of Yu Kwon Soon, a Korean woman patriot who had been martyred in the resistance to the Japanese occupation of Korea. The statue is high and prominent on the slopes of Nam San. Kim's aunt had also been involved in the resistance. She'd been captured and tortured by the Japanese. To talk to people who had suffered so about "live and let live" was quite futile. I thought that the Israelis could perhaps embrace Germans quicker than the Koreans could forgive the Japanese. It was a shame that things were that way, but one had to accept the fact. Kim stared up at the statue, and it was easy to see in her face the fiery idealism that keeps nations hating nations. I wondered how many generations had to pass before Koreans would not hate Japan and the Japanese.

We walked on up Nam San, the road levelled out and wound down past the Crest Hotel. We entered the Crest, went down the steps to the swimming pool, changed, and met by the pool. The water was warm. We swam for a while and then lay in the sun. Later we swam again, and then showered and dressed and went up to the lounge. It was early, but Lee met us there to say good-bye. She had to perform that night until late, so we left her after a couple of drinks.

"James, take care of yourself, and hurry back to Kim."

"I'll be back soon."

We took a cab back to the Naija, ate there and stopped at the cocktail lounge after.

"James, I have to go back home tonight. My aunt is visiting." I could see she did not seem eager to go but had no choice. I was tired of saying good-bye. Everyone who counted knew how I felt. I secretly wished that the flight was leaving the next day, rather than Sunday. Kim waved as the taxi raced off down the street. I had another drink and went to bed.

The following afternoon Kim and I sat in the park at Inchon near the statue of MacArthur and talked quietly. We went down to the beach and had fresh seafood for dinner, with a bottle of wine. After that we walked along the beach. Suddenly the sadness that I'd been dreading washed over me, and I knew I'd be worthless until it was over. Kim sensed my feeling; we stopped and I held her as we looked out to sea. Then it passed, ending suddenly, abrupt from start to finish.

"James, you will come back, won't you?"

"Yes, Kim. I'll be back soon. Kim will you write me?"

"I'm a terrible writer but I will try," she said smiling.

In the room at the Naija Kim opened her purse and handed me a small package, a very expensive Swiss compass. It was a beautiful instrument, and I appreciated the thought behind it more than anything else. I oriented the compass so that the north seeking arrow lined up with the "N" on the compass, and just to the right of the "N" on the northeast side was an engraved "K." I looked up in surprise, and Kim was delighted. She clapped her hands and laughed.

"You understand, James!"

"Yes; how thoughtful." I held her tightly as we kissed, and I hoped that everything would somehow turn out right for us.

I pulled a gift-wrapped package from my bag and handed it to Kim. "Open it."

She carefully unwrapped the gold necklace with its pendant. She was very happy, we kissed, and suddenly I wished that somehow I could have done more. I knew she was happy with the gift. For the moment there was no sadness, and I resolved to sustain the mood until I left. I took her in my arms and our bodies were close and warm and excited for each other. I pulled back the sheets from the bed. Daylight found us holding each other tightly. Now she slept and we both were warmly, happily, sleepily exhausted, but I recalled a line from a Frost poem "And miles to go before I sleep ..." When I came out of the bathroom Kim had packed my bag, and she laughed and showered as I dressed. I went out and got coffee and donuts, and we had these in the room before checking out.

I kissed Kim again at the gate. She sobbed softly as I held her tightly and promised to write. We kissed once more. I left her at the gate and checked in for the flight. The plane was a U.S. Air Force C130, and I went to sleep on takeoff and awoke two hours later as the plane touched down at Tachikawa Air Force Base, Japan.

CHAPTER 19

So that was it, I'd stepped from one chapter of my life into another, the lines drawn between the two chapters. Almost, but not quite; half of me was left in the previous chapter. I processed through Japanese customs, and checked in with the Army ATCO. They confirmed my booking for the following morning and gave me the telephone number of the billeting office. I made a reservation for the night and took a base taxi to the office, where they put me into a decent room with a bath. I left my things there and walked out the main gate to Tachikawa City.

For three years I had lived and worked on Tachikawa Base as a young soldier, prior to being accepted to OCS (Officers Candidate School). There had been only a handful of soldiers in my unit and it had been a strange tour of duty for me. I had worked at the Army ATCO in the air terminal, the same office that had just processed me for my flight the following day. We'd had a lot of free time and not much work; mostly I had played baseball and travelled around Japan with the base team. I'd seen a good deal of Japan and had grown to love the country and the people. It seemed as if I had not joined the Army until I left Tachikawa for Infantry OCS at Fort Benning, Georgia. There were times at Benning when

I wished I'd stayed at Tachikawa, not really in the Army. Truthfully, I'd wanted to be in the Infantry from the day I was drafted.

Tachikawa was much as I had left it, but few of the girls that I had known working in the bars remained. Most of them had married Americans and had gone to live in the States. My favorite bar during the old days had been the Cherry Bar, just off Takamatsu Cho in an alley. I pushed the door open and the middle-aged Japanese lady behind the bar, the owner of the place, yelled at me. "Jamsu-san, when you come back?" she shouted, laughing in delight.

"Today," I said. "How have you been Mama-san?" I asked.

"Good, good. Here Jamsu, beer for you!" she laughed and shoved a tall bottle of Sapporo and a glass at me. "Where you stay now, Jamsu?" she asked.

"I have just come from Korea today, and I'm going to Vietnam tomorrow," I said.

"Oh my, you no go Vietnam Jamsu; takusan dami place; no good Jamsu!" she said seriously.

"OK, I'll stay here!" She laughed; I drank the beer, and she poured. She pulled a long playing record by Frankie Laine from the rack and told the girl at the record player to play it for me. She was proud of herself for remembering that I liked that record.

The bar was half full of Americans, mostly airmen from the base. I thought about the years that Americans had been here in Tachikawa since the occupation began in 1945, following World War II. The Korean War of 1950–1953 brought more Americans here for "rest and recuperation" or just stopping over enroute to Korea or returning to America. Following that war, the stream of Americans had not diminished as the "R and R" program continued; Korea was considered a "hardship" tour, no dependents, no civilian clothes, and no automobiles were allowed. Then Vietnam began to heat up and grew from a flicker to a flame, and more Americans and American cargo transited Tachikawa. In Tachikawa Americans were common – the people had known all kinds of Americans for years. Throughout this entire period Tachikawa Air Force Base had been the "hub of the Far East" for America. Little in the way of American troops or equipment moved in Asia without passing through Tachikawa; the troops rarely got further than Tachikawa because everything they were looking for was just outside the main gate. There was no need to try to puzzle their way through the Japanese railway system to Tokyo, Yokohama, or anywhere else. It was all there in Tachikawa. The city had learned early on to turn the largest profit from this burgeoning industry. From the surrounding countryside, and from as far away as Osaka and Kobe, the girls streamed in with an eye for quick riches, or an American husband; whatever, and it was all there. There may have been more prostitutes per square mile in some other city at some other time, but day in and day out, from the end of World War II to twenty years later, Tachikawa could have held her own with any of them. Probably only God knows how many of those "ladies of the night" married Americans and ended up in the United States. In the majority of cases they proved to be excellent wives and mothers, more reliable than their fickle G.I. husbands. Tachikawa was quite a place.

After a couple of beers at the Cherry Bar I told Mama-san good-bye and stopped at a couple more of the watering holes from the old days. It got rougher and rougher as the alcohol took hold; finally I couldn't stand it any longer, gave up and started back to the base, trying hard to keep from thinking about Kim and unable to do so.

Inside the gate I took the shuttle bus around to the air terminal, bought a cup of coffee and a newspaper at the snack bar and sat at a table and read the paper through. There was an article on Vietnam and the latest casualty figures and names. On the list I recognized the name of a kid from my hometown who was at least five years younger than me. I could remember seeing him on a tricycle when he was a little kid and I was in grammar school. Living in a rural area, we'd caught the same school bus right up until I graduated from high school. This boy's father had been killed in the Korean War, and his mother had raised him as best she could, working in a small supermarket in the town of Canton, North Carolina. She was a member and a strong supporter of our little church. This might have appeared somewhat odd, if not surprising, to those who hadn't known her well, for she was Japanese. She met and married her husband in Tachikawa City where she had worked at the Cherry Bar. And now her boy was dead, and she was left in the southern mountains, half a world from her homeland, to grieve once more.

I wadded the paper into a ball and tossed it into a trash can on my way out.

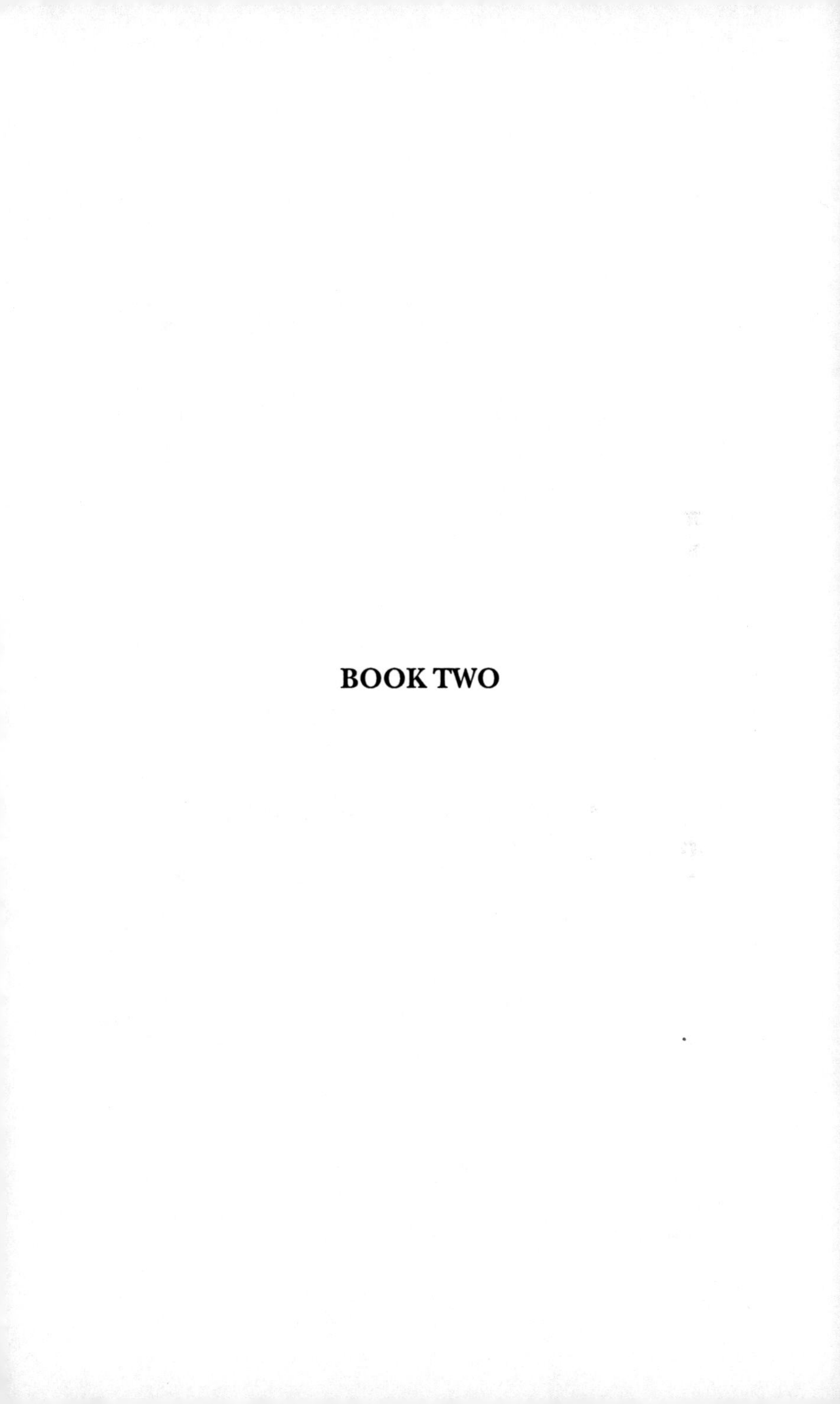

BOOK TWO

CHAPTER 20

The following morning the flight left on schedule. It was another Air Force C-130, a cargo aircraft. When it did haul passengers it was about as comfortable as riding a sled down-hill across a rock pile. "What the hell," I thought, "most people have to walk to war, and here I am flying."

I was asleep before the aircraft was in the air, and I woke when we touched down at Clark Field, Philippines. Everyone was required to offload there, and there was a wait while they loaded the cargo bound for Saigon. I got a haircut in a base barber shop and was back just in time to reboard the plane.

The C-130 droned on into Saigon and touched down at Tan Son Nhut Air Base. The heat was so intense it almost took my breath as we walked across the concrete to the terminal, where we were to pick up our baggage and be given instructions. There were no clouds in the high sky; it was like a sauna bath. There was a smell about Vietnam that I was conscious of for the first time, there at Tan San Nhut. It was not a pleasant smell, and I can describe it only as an odor akin to old body sweat mixed with mildewed clothes and gun oil. At times the odor of diesel oil was part of it also, but that was very understandable because of all the multifuel army vehicles that burned diesel. We became accustomed to the smell but we were always conscious of it.

As we claimed our baggage and were given instructions, I was dripping with sweat and noticed the others from my flight were in the same condition. From school at Fort Benning I remembered a medical subjects class on acclimatization, in which we were told that it would take a couple of weeks to get acclimated. A long wait.

I was assigned to a battalion in the First Infantry Division at Lai Khe about thirty-five miles north of Saigon. I climbed into a deuce and a half truck with several officers also assigned to the First Division, and we trucked to Di An in northeast Saigon; division headquarters was located there.

Saigon, in spite of the war, was a beautiful city with a certain charm; Vietnamese with a blend of French influence. Traffic consisted of military vehicles of all types: small taxis, French automobiles, mostly old Citroens, lambrettas, motorcycles, scooters, bicycles, and ox carts. A very common sight were the attractive Vietnamese girls in ao dais, swept back in the breeze. An ao dai was usually made of silk, often white, with a closed high Chinese neck with long sleeves, tight waist, and a long flowing hem which reached the ankles and was slit up both sides. Under that was worn a pair of ankle length silk pants, usually black. A wide brimmed, conical Chinese rice straw hat, held on by a colored ribbon tied under the chin, protected the woman's complexion from the blazing tropical sun. They were appealing in a special way, with their willowy figures and their easy languid pace, whether they walked down the street or moved about a room. There was a certain charm about a beautiful Vietnamese woman, as if it were unthinkable that she could lose her dignity by getting rushed or hurried into anything.

The streets of the city were lined with large old hardwood trees, always green in the perpetual Indo-Chinese summer. There wasn't a trace of war here, except for the soldiers and military vehicles. There was not a shell hole, no smell of cordite, nor the rattle of small arms and machine guns; only the peaceful buzz of a busy city in the heat of the tropical summer. Policemen in white uniforms, nicknamed "white mice" by the GI's, controlled traffic and walked their beats much as policemen do anywhere.

Our assignments were confirmed at First Division Headquarters, and we were given a briefing that included a brief history of the "Fighting First," or "Big Red One," as the division was called. The division's motto was "No Mission Too Difficult, No Sacrifice Too Great; Duty First!" I was duly impressed by the combat record this division had compiled, particularly in the First and Second World Wars. I spent the next two days at division, and I believe everyone but the chaplain briefed me. I was glad when they finally put me on a helicopter and sent me up to Lai Khe to join my battalion.

At Lai Khe I was met by a lieutenant from the S-1 Section of the battalion. I climbed into a dusty jeep with him and rode down to battalion headquarters. Lai Khe was the division's First Brigade base camp and one of the brigade's four battalions was mine, 1st of the 202nd; and then there was 2nd of the 28th; 2nd of the 2nd; and 1st of the 16th. Along with these four Infantry battalions there were support troops of all types: artillery, engineer, ordnance, and maintenance units and others, as well as one troop of the division's Cavalry Squadron.

Lai Khe was an old French rubber plantation, and a good portion of the base and adjacent territory was covered by rubber trees planted in rows, each with a slash and a bowl under the slash into which the liquid milky rubber dripped. The village of Lai Khe was inside the perimeter, or bunker line, formed in a large circle by the four Infantry battalions, and the Vietnamese of the village resided there. The tan stucco buildings of the plantation houses were in use by the various battalions in whose proximity they lay. Lai Khe was on a slight plateau, which rose above the adjacent terrain. The ground was flat and fell away to a stream on the north and west sides of the perimeter.

Highway 13 bisected the perimeter into an eastern and western half. As the jeep moved along, the lieutenant from S-1 told me about it. This highway was a two-lane pavement, broken in numerous places, running from Saigon north through Phu Cuong, Ben Cat, Lai Khe, and on north past Chon Ton to the Cambodian border. The soldiers called it "Thunder Road," because command detonated mines were blown under U.S. and Vietnamese Army vehicles, destroying them and killing their occupants, on a regular basis along its length. The troops made jokes about the "mad bomber" of Thunder Road. He and his comrades were very good at this game. They planted the explosive, anything ranging from an artillery shell to a five hundred pound bomb. They rigged it for detonation from afar, buried the explosive and the wires from it back to a safe hiding place where the spot of the explosive could be observed, and waited until an appropriate target came along. Later I puzzled over how they decided which truck to destroy; it never seemed to make sense. They would let a truckload of ammunition pass and blow up an empty three-quarter-ton truck, or forego the chance to blow a fuel tanker for the privilege of knocking out a jeep.

The jeep stopped in front of an old French stucco house with a tiled roof which served as part of the battalion headquarters. It was sandbagged for protection against the indirect fire of Viet Cong mortars and rockets. Adjacent to this administrative section was a sand-bagged tactical operations center where the battalion radios were located. This was a twenty-four hour operation with an officer, NCO, and radio operators manning it. I followed the lieutenant into the S-1 section and signed into the battalion. The S-1, a Captain Melton, got up from behind a gray steel desk with a pile of papers on it and came around to shake hands and welcome me to the battalion. He was a black officer, at least thirty-five judging from his graying sideburns. He was slightly stooped, and this made him look smaller than he actually was. His heavy forehead and bushy eyebrows hung out over sunken, surprised looking eyes. Although it was only 1000 hours in the morning I smelled whiskey on his breath.

"Lieutenant, welcome to the Wild Cats!" he said. "Let's talk for a few minutes, and then I'll introduce you to the Colonel."

"Yes, thank you, Sir."

Then followed a disorganized unprofessional briefing which prompted me to ask questions.

"C Company, Captain Sutton will fill you in when you get over there."

"Fine, Sir," I replied.

"Sutton will send a jeep for you as soon as Colonel Crowse has seen you," he said.

There followed ten minutes more of useless information, then I was led across to meet the battalion commander, a Lieutenant-Colonel Lionel Crowse. His quarters which also served as his office was another French plantation house. There was no door to the room in which he sat behind his desk, so I knocked on the wooden door frame outside the entrance.

"Come in, Lieutenant. We've been expecting you," he said.

I entered, came to a military stop in front of his desk, saluted, and reported "Lieutenant Worthington, reporting for duty sir."

He returned my salute, motioning to a metal folding chair beside his desk. I sat down and he talked about the battalion, C Company to which I was assigned, base camp operations here at Lai Khe, and the enemy we faced. He was of medium build with a handsome browned face, faded blue eyes, and black hair flecked with gray; close cropped, parted, and combed neatly. He wore starched jungle fatigues and spit-shined jungle boots; my first impression was that he was a West Point officer and probably a good one. His descriptions, particularly of the enemy, were clear with a brilliance of simplicity which good officers always seemed to have in issuing orders or describing a complicated situation. He spent most of his talk on the enemy, lessons learned, and the "do's" and "don'ts" of operating in this area. Without question, it was clear to me that his words of advice were based on valuable, if limited, experience. The battalion had just come out of the field the day before, and several of the lessons learned came from the experience gained on this operation. He finished and flashed me a broad, reassuring smile as I saluted. I did an about-face and left his office. Outside the sunshine was bright, and it was stifling hot in the noonday calm. Captain Sutton's jeep pulled up in front of the battalion commander's office.

CHAPTER 21

"You the new lieutenant for Charlie Company?" the driver asked.

"Yes," I replied, and tossed my bag into the back seat of the jeep and got in. The driver wheeled the jeep around and down the dirt road through the tall hardwood trees, past an intersection and onto a smaller road through the rubber trees, finally turning off into C Company's headquarters, a sandbagged G.P. (General Purpose) medium tent in a small clearing in the rubber trees. Captain Sutton and First Sergeant Long sat on a blanket sunning bare feet.

"Prevents jungle rot and other things," Sutton pointed to his bare feet. I set my bag on the ground and saluted, reporting to Captain Sutton. He returned my salute without standing up. He was a thin, almost skinny, black officer with a very dark complexion and a handsome face from which two keen eyes fixed me with their searching gaze. His nose flared slightly over thick lips through which his perfect white teeth could be seen as he spoke.

"Sit down and let's chat for a couple of minutes before I take you over to your platoon," he said. I sat down on the ground, and he introduced me to First Sergeant Long, a tall raw-boned, grizzled looking NCO with a pair of horn rimmed glasses that sat across the bridge of his nose a little lower than they should have, causing him to look down at me. His hair had been blond and was now white, with a crew-cut, and he spoke with a broad Alabama drawl. His green eyes sparkled as he talked, and he spoke with a loud nasal twang. After we were introduced he excused himself and went into the headquarters tent.

Captain Sutton looked me over carefully. "How much experience have you had as a platoon leader?"

"Thirteen months in Korea as a rifle platoon leader, Sir."

"Then you must be ready to make first lieutenant."

"If they keep promoting them at eighteen months, Sir."

He then went into some detail on the company, the battalion, and how to operate in the area surrounding us. Finally he took me over to my platoon area and introduced me to Platoon Sergeant Bill Fitzsimmons, whom I instantly liked. Sutton left and Fitzsimmons showed me to the sandbagged tent which was my living quarters just behind the bunker which was the platoon command post. I shoved my bag inside and we stood outside talking. He showed me the six bunkers that were the platoon's responsibility and told me where the mess tent was, then indicated on a blown up map of the Lai Khe camp where the shower point was.

"We've also got some of those Australian Army collapsible shower buckets, so you can take a shower here when you don't have time to go over to the shower point. I'll have your RTO (radio telephone operator) put one in your tent tonight. He and the platoon medic will be back after dark, and I will introduce you then. They had to go to S-1 about pay problems. As for laundry, just throw your dirty clothes in your laundry bag and your RTO can take them to the company CP where they pick laundry up and deliver it. The stuff goes to quarter-master laundry and returns unpressed, sometimes missing buttons, and sometimes not your own clothes, but usually they will fit."

"The alternative is to let one of these old Vietnamese women living within the perimeter do it," he said.

"OK. Thanks. I'd like to meet the men this afternoon after chow."

"OK, Sir. We will do that about 1600 if it's all right." I nodded, and after I got my belongings organized in the tent we went across to the mess tent and ate. Captain Sutton came by the tree that I leaned against as I ate and invited me to eat with him and meet the other platoon leaders. I followed him over to the CP.

Four lieutenants sat on the ground eating their meal, and they rose and shook hands with me as Captain Sutton introduced us. Lieutenant Scott was a first lieutenant and the company executive officer. Second Lieutenant Smathers was the Weapons Platoon Leader, Second Lieutenant Browning was the Third Platoon Leader, and Second Lieutenant Pendleton was the Second Platoon Leader. My platoon was First Platoon. Except for Browning, the lieutenants in Charlie Company looked young, but then I had spent enlisted time before OCS, so I was perhaps three or four years older than the three of them. Scott was a chubby, blue eyed officer with black hair, cropped in what had been a crew cut where he could still get a decent haircut. He had a very slight speech impediment which caused him to speak rapidly to hide it, and this resulted in a slurring of words when he spoke too fast. I got the impression that he was easily excited and could lose control of the situation at hand very quickly. The thought struck me that he probably spent too much time in base camp and too little time in the field; otherwise he would lose that baby fat hanging around his middle.

David Browning was a short stocky man who appeared to be a little older than the other lieutenants. He had a square jaw and a wide mouth, a ruddy complexion, steel-blue eyes and sandy brown hair. I thought that he was about my age, and the other officers looked to be twenty-two or twenty-three. Browning was a man who had confidence in his ability, and his smile and strong handshake transfused some of that confidence; I felt glad to meet him, and instantly decided to seek him out for advice when I needed it.

Smathers had the Weapons Platoon with the company's three 81 millimeter mortars and two 106 millimeter recoilless rifles. The 106's were fairly useless for the war we were engaged in and were always left in garrison. They were designed to knock out tanks, and this enemy had no tanks in the area. The 81's could put out a considerable amount of indirect firepower and could be used for illumination at night when necessary. They could be broken down into their three main parts; barrel, bipod, and base plate, and carried on operations, but the weapons and ammunition were heavy and bulky; a good man in excellent condition could carry no more than two rounds for sustained distances. Later I found that many units considered the 81's to be more trouble than they were worth and simply left them in base camp, or had them brought in by helicopter at night.

Lieutenant Pendleton had the Second Platoon and had just arrived a few days ago. He had replaced an officer who had been evacuated to a general hospital in Tokyo. Pendleton was a skinny kid, with thick glasses and a thatch of red hair.

We finished the meal, and as I left Browning joined me. We walked back to our platoon areas. His platoon was on the left (south) of mine as we faced toward the west on the bunker line in the defense. His platoon CP (Command Post) was practically within shouting distance of mine.

"Drop over tonight and we'll have a drink," he invited.

"Thanks. I'll come by."

At the platoon CP I did some further arranging of my gear and hung the new Australian canvas shower bucket in a tree and took a shower. The water was from an army water can warming in the sun beside my tent. The shower felt good and I dried off in the afternoon sun. I dressed, pulled on a pair of shined jungle boots and put on my steel helmet and web gear. The platoon sergeant came across the clearing and handed me my rifle.

"You'll be needing this, Sir," he smiled as he handed the rifle to me, with a sandbag full of M-26 fragmentation grenades. I took four and snapped them onto the sides of my ammunition pouches and put the sandbag into the tent.

"Is there a designated place to zero (adjust the sights to hit where you aimed) weapons?"

"After you meet the men you can zero down on the bunker line. We have a zero range set up there, and company headquarters clears test firing by simply calling battalion Tactical Operations Center (TOC)."

Fitzsimmons assembled the men in the clearing in the midst of the green rubber trees. They stood in formation, but I had them sit down and make themselves comfortable. They sat on the ground or leaned back against the rubber trees and stumps.

I spoke informally, giving a brief self introduction, and then I covered a few details on tactics and field sanitation. I elaborated on the use of signal cord, a nylon cord carried by each soldier with a loop tied in each end, in the defense or on ambushes. "The purpose of the signal cord is silent communications. When we are waiting in ambush the man who sees the enemy first will tug on his left and right cords, alerting the adjacent positions. In the defense the platoon, to include the listening posts and observation posts, will be linked by signal cords. We will begin using the cord tonight on the bunker line here at Lai Khe."

I then covered a few details on ambushes. "A well laid ambush is a near perfect tactical maneuver, but it requires hard work, particularly in the rehearsal. Here in base camp we will rehearse in the rubber trees the way the ambush will be organized and executed. Questions will be answered, and actions requiring timing will be gone over until you can do it in the dark with your eyes closed. In the field we will also rehearse, and when rehearsals are impossible because of the enemy situation, or lack of time, we will go into the ambushes just like football plays, according to our standard operations procedures. We will have four standard ambushes; A, B, C, and D. We will begin rehearsing these tomorrow morning."

I finished by complimenting the platoon. "Finally, you are a fine looking group of men, and I've heard nothing but good about you. I'll do my best to take good care of you, and together we will do what we were sent here to do. Do you have any questions? OK, that's all." Sergeant Fitzsimmons dismissed the men and joined me at the platoon CP with the squad leaders.

The three squad leaders were young and strong looking and I shook hands with each in turn. All three were sergeant E-5's, although the squad leader slot was a staff sergeant E-6 position by TOE (Table of Organization and Equipment) which detailed the rank and number of personnel as well as the equipment for the unit. Sergeant Rosy McGuire was the First Squad Leader, a sandy blond NCO with bright blue eyes, fair skin and red, round, cherubic cheeks. His short hair, constantly pressed flat by the webbing and sweat band of his steel helmet, still had a hint of curl in it, and I had a vision of him as a child with blond curly hair covering his head and a bright, sunny, blue-eyed smile for everyone as his chubby short legged body tripped around the grass of the front lawn. His nose was only slightly bulbous, but had already taken on a red tint which made him look like a youthful W. C. Fields. The constant twinkle of his blue eyes mirrored the merry heart that beat in his wide chest, and from that day on every time I saw him he looked as if he had just pulled off some enormous practical joke that could only be appreciated by another Irishman and would remain his secret until he met one to whom he could relate it.

Sergeant Willy Rozier was the Third Squad Leader, a black NCO from Philadelphia. He was slow to warm to any white man, regardless of position or relationship with the unit, but had the reputation of being a solidly dependable and courageous sergeant who could be counted on when the chips were down, according to Platoon Sergeant Fitzsimmons. Rozier was a light complexioned man of medium build, an athletic six feet of muscle and bone without an ounce of fat on his trim frame. His light brown eyes evaluated the world unsmilingly, as if there were no jokes, and if there happened to be any they weren't on him. His nose flared widely over thick lips and his brown kinky hair was cropped close on his round head. No matter where I saw Rozier he looked neat, like a drill sergeant who had just stepped out of the barracks to inspect the troops that couldn't hope to match his sharp, clean, creased, shined military appearance. Even with the heat, the exertion and the ever present stress he seemed unruffled.

Sergeant Arch Bigwitch, the Second Squad leader, was a Cherokee Indian from Cherokee, North Carolina. I recognized him instantly as I had known him and his family quite well through high school athletics. I had known his father and uncles through many associations to include athletics, hunting, farm work, and church. Arch was a tall, well built, handsome young man who believed very strongly in the adage that "silence is golden." He was dark, and his occasional smile revealed his perfect white teeth. He had been an outstanding running back as well as a defensive back on his high school football team.

Bigwitch's eyes widened and he smiled that strong Cherokee smile as he warmly shook my hand.

"How are your folks, Arch?" I asked him.

"Fine, Sir. Dad is working for the Road Division on the reservation. Mom is making pottery. They're getting by."

I knew the money for what they were doing was not much. "That's good. I remember seeing you last in a football game at Sylva. You scored three times that night."

"Yeah. We thrashed 'em pretty good that night," he grinned.

His family was living in a cabin back on Wright's Creek in a deep shadowy valley off the road to Soco Gap. I remembered clearly seeing his brothers and him, working in his father's corn field there. One of his uncles had died in World War II in the Battle of the Bulge in the 2nd Infantry Division. Bigwitch's reputation in our company, and indeed the battalion, had grown to legendary proportions through his accomplishments on the battlefield. He had already been decorated three times for valor.

"With talent like this to help me being the platoon leader should be a rocking chair job," I said.

As I left the CP, Sergeant McGuire spoke to me. "Sir, if you have a couple of minutes I would like to introduce you to some of my squad. They are sitting over there by those stumps."

"I'd be happy to meet them Sergeant McGuire." I followed him over to where four soldiers sat cleaning weapons. They stood up as we approached.

"Please sit down and continue what you're doing, men. Sergeant McGuire just brought me over to introduce us."

"Sir, this is Sergeant Murdock, one of my fire team leaders." Murdock was a swarthy looking man of medium build with black crew cut hair. He sat cleaning his rifle.

"Sir, I'm pleased to meet you. How long have you been in country?"

"I just arrived, Sergeant Murdock. How long have you been here?"

"About a month now, but it seems like about a year." He smiled a half smile; a tired, nervous, faint smile which was more politeness than anything else. "Have you ever been to Columbus, Georgia, Sir?"

"I certainly have. I was there at Fort Benning for O.C.S. and later for Airborne School." He smiled a little less guardedly than before, having established some common ground with me.

"I wish to hell I was on my way back there now," he said sincerely. "My little boy is one year old." He showed me a picture of his wife holding the baby.

"Well, we are all going to go back home, Sergeant Murdock. We're going to do this thing right and then get on a 'freedom bird' back to the world," I said with as much conviction as I could muster.

"Sir, I'm a machine-gunner, and I can keep this baby humming; uh, my name is James Hale." Hale sat with his M-60 disassembled before him on a rag, and he was carefully running patches through the barrel and the spare barrel.

"Pleased to meet you, Specialist Hale." I picked up the spare barrel and looked through the bore. It sparkled. "Looks good. Have you ever had a stoppage in a fire fight?"

"Had one, but Howard has had about three," he grinned.

"Howard is Sergeant Bigwitch's machine gunner," McGuire offered.

"Sir, this here's my assistant gunner," Hale pointed at a soldier sitting on the ground beside him, brushing out linked ammunition.

"Yeah Sir, I lug around an extra box of ammunition for his majesty, here! My name is Charlie Long, and I'm from Niceville, Florida."

"Charlie, I'm very pleased to meet you." I shook his greasy hand, and he handed me a dry rag to wipe off with.

"Sorry 'bout that, Sir."

"That's OK. Comes with the job," I smiled.

"Sir, did you go to Ranger School?"

"No, I haven't been yet."

"Oh. Well one part of the course is held in Florida near my home."

"Sir, this is PFC (Private First Class) Branson," Sergeant McGuire introduced the fourth man, an unkept looking soldier, even by Vietnam standards.

"Sir, Howard Branson from The Big Apple!" he announced.

"Well, Branson, how do you think the Yankees will do this year?"

"I hope they lose every game! I'm a Mets fan." His cheeks were smudged with soot, grease or some other black substance, and his ruddy face was sprinkled with a generous dose of acne.

"Well I can't guarantee you a Mets pennant, but I hope you have a good year here. Sergeant McGuire, thanks for the introductions. I have to go zero my rifle now." I patted McGuire on the shoulder and walked across to where Sergeant Fitzsimmons waited by the CP.

"Ready to zero, Sir?"

"Yes, would you call company and let them know?"

"OK, Sir." He rang the company CP on the land line and rang off after he finished. "We are clear to start, Sir."

We walked out through the rubber trees to the bunker line, and I fired for zero, adjusting windage and elevation until I was satisfied. I recorded the zero in my small notebook that I carried in a hip pocket, and we walked back to the perimeter. Fitzsimmons filled me in on the squad and fire team leaders as we walked back through the rubber trees. I asked him for any details he could provide on particularly strong or weak soldiers, and he highlighted the special abilities of the best riflemen, hand grenade throwers, navigators, and the most aggressive fighters. Fitzsimmons left my CP just before dark. I told him I would be at the 2nd Platoon CP for an hour and then would be back at my CP, and wanted him to accompany me on a check of the bunker line when I returned. He said he would be waiting.

Browning's CP was laid out like mine. We sat outside in the darkness on stumps of the rubber trees and talked in the warm night air. The sky was clear, the moon was already up and its dull light bathed the rubber trees and caused shadows in their wake. Mosquitoes attacked aggressively and we sloshed insect repellent all over our hands, faces, and knees, where the jungle fatigues were close to the skin and mosquitoes could penetrate.

"This damn stuff works very well," I said.

"Yes, but it's so goddamned sticky that you have to scrub it off in the mornings with strong soap. James, we are working for a good man. Sutton is smart and he gives a damn about his officers and men," he said.

"He's impressive. Who is that rummy of an S-1 at battalion?"

"Oh, that's old Captain Melton. He's fairly harmless. He has been passed over and is waiting one more passover and the boot. Drinks all the time, but gets the job done fairly well."

"How about Colonel Crowse?"

"Fine officer, but I think he's a bit too much of a gentleman for this war. He takes good care of us, and his tactical head is sound, but he is not aggressive enough for my money."

"How do you mean not aggressive enough?"

"Well, he doesn't patrol aggressively enough, in base camp or in the field, in my opinion. And when we make contact he doesn't try to 'pile on' and make the most of it."

We sipped bourbon and water from our canteen cups; Browning had a bottle of Wild Turkey, which was far too good for the occasion. He laughed and told me he had had that bottle for a month, and now was a good time to make a dent in it. I left after awhile and met Fitzsimmons at the platoon CP.

We made the rounds of the bunker line, talking quietly with the soldiers on position. Things were satisfactory, and they had already implemented the signal cord system. Each bunker had a TA-312 field telephone or a smaller TA-1, a sound powered field telephone, and every position could contact both me and Sergeant Fitzsimmons when necessary. The soldiers were instructed to use the signal cord system until they had to explain the situation, or were called by either Fitzsimmons or myself. My bunker was linked to the third forward bunker by my signal cord so that they could silently alert me along with the forward positions. Fitzsimmons and I were linked by his signal cord. From my CP bunker we were also wired in with Captain Sutton's CP. The PRC-25 radios, the radios we used in the field for all communications, were also located in the bunkers, but would stay cut off until they were actually needed during contact. In defense, the Infantry normally used wire because it is more secure than radio.

Back at my CP bunker Sergeant Fitzsimmons introduced my RTO, PFC Alderman, and the platoon medic, Specialist Fourth Class, or SP4, "Doc" Gill. Alderman was a country kid from somewhere in Florida and was about five feet eight inches tall, broad shouldered, deep chested, and very pleasant and positive, I judged. His twinkling blue eyes took in everything, and I felt that I was being very carefully inspected.

"Private Alderman, do you like your job?" I asked.

"So far, Sir." He measured me.

"Any problems?"

"Well, no, well; sometimes we can't get them damned batteries for the radio when we need them. Other than that I can't think of anything."

"OK. I will check on the battery situation." I turned to the medic. "And how about you, Specialist Gill?"

"None, Sir. I'm the best damned medic in this battalion, and I won't let you down. I was school trained at Fort Sam," he added.

Gill was somewhat more slightly built than Alderman. He was a black soldier from St. Louis and had the reputation of being a top-notch combat medic. He talked and acted like a street-wise kid, but he was also impressed by what he had learned in medics school at Fort Sam Houston, Texas. I wondered silently how long it would be before I saw this young man in action so that I could judge his work myself. From his careful stare I believe he had precisely the same thought about me.

"Sir, there is a GP small tent behind the bunker which is yours. We normally sleep there when we are not on telephone watch," Alderman informed me. "Least we did when Sergeant Fitzsimmons was the platoon leader." He gave me an uncertain look.

"That arrangement's fine with me," I chuckled at his concern, but understood that this was very important to him.

Sergeant Fitzsimmons arranged the telephone watch daily, and besides Alderman and Doc, PFC Lee, the 81 Mortar Section forward observer (FO) attached to the platoon, pulled watch as well as PFC Smithfield who was Fitzsimmons' RTO. The 81 FO and Smithfield shared a hooch with Sergeant Fitzsimmons, not twenty yards from my CP. The telephone watch was pulled in the CP bunker. Actually, Fitzsimmons was not authorized an RTO or a PRC-25 radio, but, as in most rifle platoons in Vietnam, he had both. The firepower was not wasted because in a fire-fight Fitzsimmons and Smithfield attached themselves to the nearest squad and fought with them. When necessary they dug a foxhole on the perimeter with the squads in the field. At least this was Fitzsimmons's explanation to me when we had talked that afternoon. In fact, every rifle squad had a PRC-25 he explained. I didn't want to do anything that would cut down rifle squad strength, but being brand new in the outfit I thought it best to watch for a couple of weeks before making any changes that weren't urgent. Besides, in my estimation at that point in time the platoon seemed to be in pretty good shape, so nothing traumatic needed to be done immediately.

At my GP small tent I lay down with my clothes on, and looped the signal cords around my arms. It was warm so I didn't need my poncho liner or poncho immediately, and I lay them on the ground beside the mattress. The crickets chirped and a gentle breeze arose, and I thought of Kim. When will her first letter get here I wondered. I had written her once from Di An. I fell asleep around midnight.

What awakened me was a sharp tug on my signal cord. I struggled out of the tent and fumbled my way into the bunker. Alderman had just been called on the field phone and he handed it to me. "Yes, what do you have?" I whispered into the telephone.

"Sir, this is bunker one and I have movement to my front," he whispered. "Sounds like one or two dinks, and I want to blow a claymore." He was referring to a claymore antipersonnel mine fired with a hand generator and an electric blasting cap.

"Blow it," I answered.

Instantly the deafening crack of the claymore mine sounded, accompanied by a blinding flash. I called the company CP and gave my report. Bunker one reported that movement ceased, and I instructed him to wait until daylight before checking the area.

The field phone rang from company and it was Captain Sutton.

"What's going on over there?" he asked. He seemed calm enough, but I hoped like hell that we would have a body to show him at daylight. I explained what had happened and what I had done about it, and he simply told me to let him know what the results were when I checked.

At first light the men in bunker one and I went forward through the wire and searched out the area to the front. About two yards from where the claymore mine had been there was a splotch of dried blood on the ground, and a pole charge (an explosive device attached to the end of a pole) lay off to the side. We spread out and moved forward cautiously. We didn't have far to go. In a slight depression about twenty yards in front of the wire the dark sapper lay, his body covered with blood and shrapnel holes. Sappers were demolitions experts who could silently penetrate wire obstacles with considerable skill. We blew the pole charge, buried the sapper where he lay, and turned in his carbine and personal effects. Captain Sutton and the battalion S-2 (Intelligence Officer) dropped by and were sufficiently impressed and passed on their compliments to Sergeant McGuire and his squad.

CHAPTER 22

That morning Captain Sutton was called to battalion to receive the order for an operation that would begin the next day. Before he left he issued instructions to the platoon leaders to prepare the troops for an extended operation of two weeks duration or longer.

At 0900 my platoon began ambush rehearsals, drilling steadily and trying to concentrate on the basics, on through to lunch and again after lunch. The need for noise and light discipline was stressed, and I explained that no one should carry cigarettes out on an ambush since the temptation to light up might overcome a soldier's better judgment under stress. It was better not to have cigarettes out there at all when one violation of light discipline could get an entire ambush killed or captured.

Sergeant Fitzsimmons instructed the platoon on the use of claymores. "Aim your claymores. Aim them. Look through the slot and aim them as I explained to you. Not like that, Sanders. That claymore will kill ants and your other one will kill monkeys. Sergeant Bigwitch, help Sanders aim his claymores!"

We worked until mid-afternoon, and when we knocked off I felt better about our ability to execute an ambush, but we still had a long way to go.

Sergeant Fitzsimmons went back to the platoon area with the troops and turned them over to their squad leaders to get them ready for the operation. They packed what they needed in their rucksacks, drew extra ammunition for the M-79's (shotgun-like weapons that fire 40mm grenades), the machine-guns, and rifles; drew extra claymores, smoke grenades, hand grenades, and LAW's (light anti-tank weapons that were one shot disposable fiber tubes, also good against personnel), and put fresh water in both canteens. Rations for the operation would be issued at the supper meal.

Captain Sutton returned from battalion and called the platoon leaders to the CP for the order. We sat on the ground and took notes as he talked. The mission was a brigade operation into the Michelin Rubber Plantation northwest of Lai Khe out near the Cambodian border. Following a massive prep of the area by air and artillery, three of the brigades's battalions would be inserted by helicopter into their independent areas of operation. The 1st of the 202nd would be inserted first on the west, followed by 1st of the 16th on the east and 2nd of the 28th in the center. Second of the 2nd would remain in Lai Khe, securing the base. Intelligence indicated that the area had long been a safe haven for the large main force regiments that had used the huge plantation as a storage/staging area.

First of the 202nd would combat assault (an assault by helicopter) into three separate LZ's (landing zones) with C Company going into the western LZ; B Company into an LZ two kilometers northeast of C Company; and A Company along with the Recon Platoon, Four Deuce Mortar Platoon, the Battalion Headquarters, and an attached battery of six 105 millimeter howitzers would go in two kilometers southeast of B Company and about two kilometers directly east of C Company. Each company had been given its own area of operation, designated by a "goose egg" on the overlay in the battalion order. Our company AO was partially rubber trees and partially jungle, from the looks of the map.

Captain Sutton had planned to move about five hundred meters west from the LZ and establish a patrol base on a small hill there. From that point the platoons would patrol, primarily by putting out small ambushes on roads and trails in the area where enemy movement was likely. C Company would lift out first before daylight, followed immediately by the other elements of the battalion. The weather for the CA was expected to be fair, so there was little chance of a delay. We would move out of our company area at 0300 and be picked up by the helicopters on the small air strip at the center of the brigade perimeter. Sutton gave individual instructions for the conduct of the operation, asked if there were questions, gave out the password list with the sign and countersign for the next twenty-four hour period and dismissed us.

I walked back toward my CP with Browning, and we stopped at my bunker.

"How long do these normally last?" I asked.

"We will probably be out there around three weeks, but it could last longer if we have any contact. I expect we will make plenty of contact out there," he said. "Are you a little nervous?" he had detected that I was a little tight.

"I guess I have a few butterflies," I admitted.

"Well I guess that's about the most natural feeling any lieutenant in combat can have. I still get that feeling, and probably always will. See you at o-dark-thirty!" He turned and walked on down the trail.

I lay there on the air mattress and thought about home, about Kim, and about tomorrow. Fort Benning could prepare a man well for a lot of things, but when it came time to reach down into yourself for strength and courage it was a very personal thing. I remembered all the grim statistics about the brevity of a lieutenant's life in combat. What was the average? Two minutes? But the responsibility for those men was what counted. That was where it was. All the army doesn't need is some scared lieutenant so badly worried about his own safety that he lets his platoon down. An officer and a gentleman. The pay is different, the uniform is different, the respect is different, but out here you have to earn that respect. Those soldiers don't care where you received your commission. Does the lieutenant have his head together? That's what's important. Can he keep me from getting wasted? That's the thing. Well, we will see. Maybe things will be OK, but starting tomorrow theory would be replaced by clear reality. I drifted off to sleep thinking about it.

At 0230 the radio watch woke me, and I slung my ruck, picked up my rifle, and moved out in the direction of Fitzsimmons' tent. The men were all up and preparing he told me. Shortly the troops filed by in the darkness, and I, my RTO Alderman, an additional RTO named Bentley, Doc Gill, and the FO Lee fell in behind the First Squad and moved up to the company CP.

"First Platoon here, Sir," I reported to Sutton.

"OK. That's everyone. Move out," he whispered to Browning and the other platoon leaders. My platoon fell in behind Browning's and the rest of the company followed.

We waited silently in the rubber trees beside the air strip, and the helicopters were already there sitting silently, waiting to crank at 0400 hours. They had been infiltrated, a few at a time, the day before and throughout the early evening hours of the night before. They sat there in "staggered trail" facing north and looking much like a string of praying mantises, squatting before pouncing on their prey.

At 0400 hours the helicopters cranked and we loaded. The seats were stripped out of the HU-1D "slicks," or troop carriers, and four men sat side by side with their backs against the fire wall, facing the front of the helicopter. Two troops sat with their backs almost against the back of the pilot and co-pilot's bucket seats, facing the four who sat against the fire wall. In small compartments to the rear of the troop cabin, on both sides of the firewall facing out of the helicopter, the door gunners sat on nylon bench seats and manned their mounted M-60 machine-guns. One M-60 on each side of the helicopter comprised the ship's total armament. The gunships that escorted the slicks on an assault carried no troops and were armed with 7.62 mm miniguns, 40mm grenade guns, and 2.75 inch rockets in tubes on both sides of the fuselage.

The birds hovered, gradually moving forward, then gained speed and altitude as they ran along above the runway, and then cleared the rubber trees on the north end of the strip and swung to the northwest toward the Michelin. Gradually the slicks swung to a heading directly west with their gunship escorts above and on both sides looking like fierce mother hawks protecting their fledglings as they learned to fly. By the flight route that had been briefed and the elapsed time I thought that we should be south of the Michelin, almost ready to swing due north in the direction of our LZ. The compass on the dash of the helicopter began to roll around towards the north; at the same time the eastern sky out the right door became dark, rosy, thin layers of light that rapidly spread upward and outward and closed on us at a rapid pace, gradually revealing dark green jungle below.

Far to the north the ground erupted in sound and light as the artillery preparation began to pound the LZ's. The "whump, whump, whump" of the projectiles exploding as they slammed into the trees and tangled foliage surrounding the LZ was one long roll, and the slice of open space in the jungle at the western side of the Michelin was lit up like mid-day by the flashes of the explosions. Suddenly the roaring rasps of 2.75 inch rockets bursting from their pods on each side of the gunships added to the crescendo, and the gunships raced forward, first slamming rockets, then 40mm grenades, and finally streams of minigun bullets, into the areas adjacent to the LZ where waiting enemy might hide. As the gunships finished their passes, the door gunners on the slicks suddenly opened up with their M-60's, plunging fire into the trees and brush on both sides of the LZ. The whole thing had been coordinated to the split second; as the last artillery rounds fell they were white phosphorus rounds signaling the end of the artillery prep. As they burst, the gunship rockets began striking their beaten zone around the LZ, and as the gunships cleared the LZ the door gunners on the slicks picked up the fire where the gunships had left off. When the gunships opened up with their rockets I had been unprepared. The sudden noises fortelling violence startled me, and I'm sure I jumped. I looked quickly around me at the men. Was it still dark enough so they hadn't seen me jerk in surprise? If they had, they were concealing it very well.

The slicks hovered in on short final and we dropped to the ground. As we cleared the helicopters they picked up in a forward rush that had been almost uninterrupted by our exit and roared up and out, clearing the trees and circling back to the southeast towards Lai Khe to pick up other rifle companies. We hit the ground and lay facing out from the center of the LZ. As soon as the helicopters cleared, we were up and running to the edge of the jungle, then hitting the ground again, straining, looking, listening for any signs of the enemy. I could see Captain Sutton and his RTO on my right. I had First Squad push out an LP/OP (Listening Post/Observation Post) of three men about twenty meters forward of the platoon off the LZ. The other platoons put out their security, and Captain Sutton called and confirmed the route and order of march. First Platoon was to lead off on point followed by the remainder of the company.

First Squad took the point, with PFC Branson the point man followed by SP4 Hale with his M-60 machine-gun. I followed the last man in First Squad, along with my RTO. The other two squads followed. We were spread out with eight to ten meters between men. The early morning light was still not totally bright, and the jungle thickness was roofed by double, and in some places triple, canopy under which there was a sort of perpetual gloom because of the absence of light. There was no trail, and had there been one we would not have followed it. I would have preferred a double point, but the dense underbrush, brambles, wait-a-minute vines, and bamboo clusters discouraged it. As we moved out I looked back at the radio antennas behind me that clearly marked me as the platoon leader, although they were all on their short antennas, and even these were folded down. Directly behind me Alderman had his radio on our platoon frequency that was my means of controlling the platoon. Behind him, Bentley had his radio set on the company frequency, and on this radio Captain Sutton and I communicated. The 81 mm mortar FO, Lee, had his radio set on the fire direction net of the 81 mm Mortar Section; he could also switch to the 4.2 Inch Mortar Platoon fire direction net as well as the artillery fire direction net. I would have to see him work before I would believe that a young PFC could handle that much.

The platoon moved forward in silence. Although it was thick, we were moving without using machetes to preserve the noise discipline. Occasionally I caught a glimpse of McGuire up front directing his squad. He was using hand and arm signals to maneuver the point left or right. The jungle was ominously quiet in sharp contrast to the deafening noise of the LZ preparation a short thirty minutes ago. As I struggled to get around a large cluster of bamboo I saw that the man in front of me had halted. McGuire passed the whispered word back for me to come forward. I took Alderman and moved up the column to McGuire. He explained that the point man had encountered a wide, well used trail with fresh footprints. I eased forward to have a look. Branson saw me and waved his rifle left and right, pointing out the trail and its north-south direction. The footprints were no more than an hour old judging from the places where there was a trickle of water and a wet print. I sent security left and right and crossed the trail only after securing the far side also. I called Sutton and explained the holdup.

“Take your time; this is Indian country,” was all he said.

We finished the crossing and our security was relieved by Second Platoon’s security, and we pushed on into the small hill that was our destination and was to be our patrol base. We moved into our assigned sector of defense. The 81mm Mortar Section set up in the center of the perimeter around Captain Sutton’s CP, forming an inner circle or a second circle of defense.

It was impossible to get mass clearance, so no attempt was made to set up the single 81 mortar that they were humping. We would have to depend entirely on the artillery and 4.2 mortars for indirect fire.

We worked hard and as silently as possible to get ourselves into a good defensive posture. We located one LP/OP to the front of one of the M-60 machine-gun positions, around fifty meters forward of the foxhole line. This was a three-man position, and they linked themselves to the M-60 position with signal cord and to my CP by land line, hooking a TA-1 field telephone to their end of the wire. The wire and the signal cord were then carefully concealed all the way back to the foxhole line. The digging and position preparation went on all morning and afternoon, and finally the foxholes were completed with parapets in front of them. The idea was for the men in the foxhole to fire around the ends of the parapet when necessary, using it for frontal protection. Overhead cover was erected and we were even able to get some overhead sandbags in. Then the entire position was camouflaged, and all fresh earth was carted away and concealed. I walked back towards our perimeter from the LP/OP and made note of any improvements the camouflage needed. All signal cords were installed between positions, and the squad leaders ran a cord back to my CP. Fitzsimmons had located his foxhole in the Third Squad area, and he and I were linked by signal cord.

I dug alternately with the RTO's, Doc Gill, and the FO; soon we had a CP trench behind the foxhole line. The foliage was thick and if you looked hard you could see the positions at ten meters at best. I checked the foxhole line and the claymores were in and looked OK except that they needed a little more camouflage; one or two had to be reaimed. Corrections were made and finally I stopped to eat a C-ration of "boned chicken" and some crackers. I used a heat tablet to warm the chicken, and seasoned it with a can of "Type 2 Cheese Spread" and some hot sauce. The cheese melted and ran down into the chicken and was pretty good with the crackers and canteen water.

After eating I walked over to where Sergeant McGuire sat propped against a sapling drinking a C-ration can of coffee. "Your squad did a good job on the point getting us in here," I said as I sat down on the ground beside him.

"Best goddamned squad in the company, Sir," he said with a twinkle in his blue eyes.

"Your point man needs to concentrate more to the front and not check you so often for directions," I said, trying not to overwhelm as much as to hint.

"Sir, I've already talked to Branson about that. I should have given the second man in the column a compass and let him keep the point on our heading, even by going forward to him and physically making contact. We have the problem ironed out." I was completely satisfied with his response.

"Sir, you must know Bigwitch very well. Let me tell you, he's the best there is, bar none. Nobody can ambush and track like him."

"How about you?"

"Well, I do some things better than him, but I can't think of what they are right now!" He chuckled.

"We're going to do just fine, Sergeant McGuire." I walked back to my position with a confidence I hadn't felt before.

CHAPTER 23

Around 1530 Sutton called the platoon leaders to the CP to lay out plans for the night. I left Fitzsimmons in charge and went over to the CP with my FO. Sutton went over the night ambush plan as his artillery FO fired in two DT's (defensive targets) or protective fires. Sutton was not happy with the noise, and he knew that to at least some degree our location would be jeopardized, but it had to be done for survival in case of a strong attack. Anyway, we had been inserted with a prep of the landing zone that morning, so the enemy knew we were in that vicinity anyway.

That night each platoon was to put out two ambushes at locations designated by Captain Sutton on his map. First Platoon was to ambush two trails on the map, about a kilometer to the west and northwest. Browning was to ambush the main trail that we had crossed that morning on the way in. On-call fires from the 4.2 mortars and the artillery were allocated to each ambush. We broke and I headed back to my CP and called Fitzsimmons and the squad leaders over and went over the plan. Sergeant McGuire would execute the ambush to the west, and I would take the one on the northwest.

My ambush included Alderman, Lee, and Branson from First Squad, PFC Howard from Second Squad, and PFC Baroni from Third Squad. I talked with them before we began our ambush rehearsal.

"Lee, what about indirect fires?"

"Sir, I will plot two or three along our route and a couple for the ambush site." He was surprised that I had asked his opinion, and his dark Chinese eyes snapped as he replied.

"Where are you from, Lee?"

"Sir, I'm from Hilo on the Big Island. I mean on Hawaii," he added with a nervous chuckle, realizing that I might not know Hawaii from Oahu. He was slightly built and had a dark handsome smile and white teeth.

"I've been there."

"Oh yeah? Man that's the greatest place on earth!" He seemed to relax as he spoke of home.

"How are things going, Branson?"

"Sir, when this thing's over I'm going to give you a guided tour of The Big Apple. Ever been there?"

"No, but I've always wanted to go. Perhaps you can escort me later."

"You betcha, I'll show you things you ain't never seen!" He was happy to talk of home.

"Sir, you ever been to MoTown?" PFC Howard, the skinny black machine-gunner challenged me.

"No, I can't say that I have, but I've always pulled for the Tigers."

"Best muthafuckin' town in the U.S. of A., and that's it Jack!" he said positively.

"I'm sure it is, Howard. Where are you from, Baroni?"

"Same as Branson, Sir, from The City." Baroni was Italian and proud of it. I later learned that his idol was Joe Dimaggio, reflecting his father's opinion.

"What the hell you mean the city? New York ain't shit compared to MoTown!" Howard shot at Baroni with a twinkle in his bright black eyes.

"OK, let's get down to business." I went over all the details and then rehearsed the ambush we were to set up. McGuire also conducted a rehearsal and then departed just after dark for the ambush site. I left ten minutes later in a different direction.

I walked point going out and was somewhat surprised when the underbrush thinned out along the route I had chosen. I halted the patrol short of our site and Alderman crawled forward. The trail split into a "Y" at our ambush site, and I found that point and watched for ten minutes. Alderman went to bring up the rest of the ambush. I lay there alone, keying on every sight and sound. The rasping noise of dry leaves raking against each other caught my ear. There it was a second time. I glanced left and right but could distinguish nothing that might have caused the sound. The wind was still, so that eliminated one possible cause of the sound. The moon illuminated the ground in front of me through holes in the jungle canopy. Suddenly a small rattle of leaves to my front allowed me to pinpoint the noise. A large cobra raised off the jungle floor not a yard in front of me, its ghostly grayish color magnified the size of the snake, and the hood below its rocking head flared out widely. My only possibility would be to use my rifle as a club, but I seemed paralyzed to act. The fear that surged over me was taking control. I was too terrified to move, and I remember thinking that if I moved the snake would strike. I heard a noise behind me, and I was sure it was Alderman and the rest of the patrol. I wanted to scream out but fear gripped me, and I was unable to utter a sound. Suddenly I felt Alderman's knee jam into my back as he fell forward across me, swinging his machete in a wide flat arc. The blade struck the cobra below the flared area of its hood and went clearly through. Alderman regained his feet and threw the snake off the trail with his machete.

I gradually regained my composure. I was soaking wet with sweat and felt weak. I forced myself up on one knee and began giving directions for the establishment of the ambush. We formed a linear ambush with the end men split out about fifty meters. Each carried two claymores, and they were set up according to plan. The prearranged signal to execute the ambush was the firing of my claymores. We settled in to wait, linking the ambush with signal cord. I was still shaken by the experience.

Around midnight the moon disappeared behind a bank of dark clouds and visibility was less, but there was still a good deal of light from the sky as we were out of the double and triple canopy. The wind stirred through the tree tops, and off to the west a tiger coughed restlessly. Suddenly they were there. I received a sharp tug from the security man on the north and I passed it on by tugging to my right, to the next man. We had set up facing east, and now six men strained; watching, waiting, ready to execute. The Viet Cong point man passed in front of me and paused. Something had told him that things weren't right. He looked left and right and then straight at me. I thought he had seen something, although I knew I was concealed. After what seemed like forever, he moved down the trail followed by other shadowy figures clutching AK-47's. One, two, three, four, five, six, seven, eight, nine I counted, as they moved into the kill zone. The last nervously watched the rear. I thought that he was probably the last man.

It was time to do what we were here for. I squeezed the two hand generators simultaneously sending six volts down the firing wires to the electric blasting caps attached to the two claymore mines at the other end. The two claymores were like a clap of thunder, followed instantly by ten more claymores fired by the rest of the patrol. The fire, smoke and concussion spewed forth into the kill zone along with hundreds of steel pellets, then swirled, reversed and died away, as did the long rolling echoes of the crack of the claymores.

There was some movement to my right front in the kill zone and some moaning further down the trail to my right, but it all stopped quickly. We hugged the ground and waited for daylight while I reported to Sutton, who acknowledged. He didn't play "fifty questions" with me, nor did he give a field manual full of instructions on what to do next. I began to understand that C Company was led by a professional.

At first light we went forward and checked the kill zone. There were nine VC along the length of the ambush, in various hideous poses. In two cases the legs had been completely blown from under the bodies. One Cong's head was missing. I was sick, but I hid it from the men. We retrieved the weapons, rucksacks, and all pocket litter, and I reported that we were on our way back into the perimeter. We passed through the foxhole line, carried the VC gear up to Sutton's CP and dumped it on the ground. Three other ambushes had made contact; two of those had killed a VC each, although the force they ambushed was from eight to ten people. Sutton was not happy about those two actions, and was wringing answers out of Lieutenant Pendleton when I arrived. Browning had sprung the ambush that he personally led on a force of thirteen VC and had managed to kill eleven and capture two, one of whom died before he could be evacuated. The other was not badly wounded and was evacuated that morning, with the rest of the enemy gear.

Captain Sutton informed us that both A and B Companies had made contact during the night although their success was not significant, compared to ours. Both companies had taken casualties, and B Company had suffered two KHA's (killed by hostile action). In one of B Company's ambushes the troops had opened up with small arms fire rather than depending on claymores and hand grenades, and the VC had reacted by throwing grenades at the muzzle flashes killing two B Company soldiers. There was a lesson for the living – don't fire small arms in an ambush at night unless it is absolutely necessary. I made a mental note to rehash this with First Platoon, to emphasize the point.

That day the troops sacked out and rested with the exception of one recon patrol per platoon; I sent Second Squad out to recon two kilometers to our front. The Second Squad Leader, Sergeant Arch Bigwitch, rehearsed his squad in preparation for the mission. It was a long way from the cool shadowy gorges of the Great Smoky Mountains to Vietnam, but Bigwitch had made the transition adequately. He enjoyed his solitude, and did not normally drink or hobnob with the troops, even on stand down. He was an excellent navigator who moved in the jungle with the quiet speed and skill of his ancestors. His squad held him in deep respect, and every member had tried in some way to pattern his own movements or mannerisms after Bigwitch.

I went over the route with him and covered the preplanned fires that he had on call. He would go to the north on the leg of the patrol outbound until he reached the rubber trees of the Michelin and check out a cluster of buildings that showed on the map. From that point he was to circle to the southwest at a distance of approximately two kilometers from the perimeter, crossing a stream enroute, then recross the stream on the way back and finally turn due east and reenter the perimeter.

"How are things going back home?" I changed the conversation from professional to personal.

"Aw, you know, Sir. Nothing ever changes back there. Dad got a new Winchester .308 in Bryson City last week, and he can't wait to get in the woods with it." He seemed not to mind opening up to me, probably because of our common roots.

"Probably saved for a year or so for it. Dad has one and he loves it."

"Yeah, it's good for black bear as well as deer. He ain't ever bought a license!" We laughed because we both knew he had killed more bear than anyone we could name.

"Bigwitch, if you can pick up a prisoner it would be great, but don't jeopardize the patrol unnecessarily." I shifted to business again.

"Sir, there probably won't be any prisoners," he said in a barely audible voice.

The patrol kicked off. His radio was set on the company frequency, but he was reporting to my CP although Captain Sutton's CP monitored every transmission on that frequency. He was not to break radio listening silence unless he made contact. Each hour on the hour we would call him for a situation report, and if everything was OK he would merely break squelch twice, that is, he would mash the "push-to-talk" button on the radio handset, which would cause an interruption in the rushing noise common when the radios are on. Our radio operator monitoring in the patrol base could pick this up easily and understand that all was OK with the patrol.

Bigwitch's patrol departed the perimeter at 0800 hours with a total of eight men. They had tied down all loose items of clothing and equipment and camouflaged all exposed skin. All rifle slings had been removed to prevent the perpetual rattle that every good soldier despised. They carried only one canteen of water because there was plenty of water in the area, and it could be purified with a couple of iodine tablets that each soldier carried. Foliage was stuck in the camouflage covers of their steel pots to break up the egg shaped outline of the helmets and was also worn in the web gear. They carried extra C-4, det cord (explosive cord that could be rigged to fire like any explosive), blasting caps, firing wire and a ten cap blasting machine.

After the patrol left I called Fitzsimmons and the squad leaders over to the CP and issued instructions for the night ambushes. Fitzsimmons would take out one ambush and Sergeant Rozier, Third Squad Leader, would take out another. These patrols would set up their ambushes slightly further out than those of the night before and would go out on different azimuths from the perimeter. Fitzsimmons was to establish one mechanical ambush (MA), on a trail junction about five hundred meters from where his live ambush would be. Rozier would also establish one MA, about four hundred meters from his live ambush, and on an entirely different trail.

"Sergeant Rozier, anything I can arrange to assist your patrol?" I asked.

"We'll get the muthafucker done." He was sullen. I knew there was little anyone could do about that. He would do the job, but I couldn't make him like it.

"Fair enough. Let me know if I can help." He turned away without expression and walked to his squad position.

Following this planning session I racked out on my air mattress under the shade of two ponchos snapped together and strung between two trees, suspended about two feet off the ground.

I slept soundly until mid-afternoon. When I awoke Sergeant Fitzsimmons was standing there with a C-ration can full of coffee, which he handed me with the warning, "Watch it, it's hot."

"Thanks. Any word from Bigwitch?"

"Yes. They made contact just before noon at that cluster of hooches on the map in the rubber trees. Killed three of the bastards and wounded and captured one. Also found quite a few documents in a tunnel under the floor in one of the hooches. They are on their way back on a different route, but they were instructed to come back without doing the rest of the route."

"Good. Anyone hurt or any weapons?"

"One man got a grenade frag in the arm. Didn't hit a bone or artery. First aid dressing did the job OK. They're bringing in an SKS and three AK-47's," he said.

"OK. Let's call a dust off when they get back here. There's a one ship LZ about five hundred meters to the south."

"Sir, we dusted him off from out there," he said.

"That was certainly the right thing to do if he was badly wounded," I thought. If he wasn't badly wounded there was no reason to jeopardize the patrol by having a dust-off called to their location. Every dink in three grid squares knew what a helicopter landing meant, and especially a dust-off with the large red crosses plainly visible on its sides. I opened a can of "Spiced Beef With Sauce."

Sergeant Fitzsimmons stood looking at me, waiting for the obvious question. I asked it. "Who in the hell called for a dust off?"

He seemed relieved that I had asked. "Sir, I had discussed it with Bigwitch and decided on no dust off, but Lieutenant Scott broke into the net and overrode my decision. In fact, he already had a dust off on the way in."

"OK. The XO (Executive Officer) can explain it to me. He's not running this platoon," I said.

I started for the company CP when all hell broke loose out to the northwest. I sat by the radio on the company net and waited. It wasn't long until Sergeant Bigwitch made his call. "Charlie One-Six, this is Charlie One-Two; over."

"This is Charlie One-Six, over."

"This place is crawling with dinks! I've been ambushed and we have at least two dead and another wounded; over."

"Roger; give me a set of coordinates, over."

He read back the grid and requested artillery fire on the south end of the ambush, where most of the enemy could be seen. Someone shook my arm urgently, and I stared into Lee's face. He had the grid and needed an azimuth, he said. I gave him an azimuth by the map and what Bigwitch had told me, and he soon had a fire mission in progress. I was concerned about the possibility of hitting the patrol if the coordinates were not accurate, but the artillery first fired a smoke round, which was a high burst and thus safe.

"How's that first round?" Lee asked Bigwitch.

"Good, but a little too far over. Drop 100." I breathed easier, because Bigwitch's coordinates were obviously correct.

Lee sent the correction to the artillery FDC and soon another smoke round was on the way. "How's that?" Lee asked.

"Right five zero, fire for effect."

"Battery five for effect on the way."

I heard the distant popping of the 105 mm howitzers as each of the six tubes in the battery fired five rounds. Captain Sutton ran up and dropped into my CP trench.

"I've got four gunships on the way to help out. It's not too thick out there where he is, so maybe they'll help."

"What about a relief force?" I asked.

He looked at me sharply and saw that I was dead serious. "No, James. That's what they want. They have every possible route out there covered by ambush. Don't be too quick to rush into the jaws of hell. Let's see what he can do for himself. We could only complicate matters."

"What about air?" I asked.

"A FAC should be on station in minutes," he told me. "The FAC has Bigwitch's callsign and frequency."

"OK, Sir. Thanks."

"Charlie One-Two, this is Charlie One-Six, how was the fire for effect?" There was no answer. The din of small arms had abated considerably. I waited two minutes and called again.

"Charlie One-Six, this is Charlie One-Two, rounds on target, repeat, over," he said.

"Rounds on target, repeat," Lee told the artillery FDC.

The gun ships arrived on station and contacted Bigwitch. "Charlie One-Two, this is Tiger Six, pop smoke and give me an azimuth and distance to the target, over."

"Smoke popped; over," Bigwitch replied.

"Roger, got green, over."

"From the smoke the azimuth is one hundred and ninety degrees and the distance is fifty meters," Bigwitch told him. "All along that heavy tree line."

"Roger, rolling in hot," the gunship lead told him. We could hear the 2.75 inch rockets and 40 mm grenades from where we sat.

"Charlie One-Two, this is Sidewinder Three-One with a flight of jets on station; mark with smoke and give me an azimuth to the enemy, over." The Air Force FAC had arrived.

"Smoke popped, over."

"Roger, I have purple smoke; I see the gunships making passes. Is that where the enemy force is? Over."

"Yes, but the gunships are firing a little too close; over." "Bigwitch was incredibly good under pressure," I thought.

Shortly the jets rolled in, dropping five hundred pound "snake eyes," high drag bombs, and Bigwitch made his report. "All that shit is really taking a toll, and I think I can get out of here," he said.

I called back, but there was no reply. I called every five minutes for the next thirty minutes, then someone yelled from the perimeter, "Hey, we got movement out here!"

"Don't fire!"

In a couple of minutes the brush parted and Bigwitch and four other walking members of the patrol staggered in, carrying the dead bodies of two soldiers. They had managed to bring in all documents from the previous action at the hooches. Bigwitch had a bullet hole in his leg. He was the one that he had reported wounded. All enemy weapons had been abandoned in the urgency of getting the dead out, and breaking contact. Before Bigwitch was dusted off with the two bodies I got his complete account of the patrol. The one thing he was vague about was the prisoner; he would only state that the prisoner died in the ambush. Later, I got PFC Larson's account of what transpired at the ambush site.

"Sir, Sergeant Bigwitch didn't want to bring the prisoner back, but he said you wanted one, so he said he was bringing the prisoner back for the Lieutenant. He was afraid the prisoner would run, so he looped that det cord around his neck, rigged it to fire, and walked along holding the blasting machine. When we got ambushed he fired the det cord and the whole upper half of that dude's body disappeared!" he said.

"Thanks, Larson. You did a great job out there." I reported that the prisoner had died in a burst of enemy small arms fire when the ambush was initiated.

The thing I couldn't figure out was how we had gotten away without losing the entire patrol, and it finally came to me. The VC had not had time to set up the ambush. When the helicopter had gone to pick up the wounded man, one or two VC had rushed to the spot to follow the patrol and determine the route of march. Since the patrol was not following a trail, they could only guess at a route of march and attempt to set up a hasty ambush. The patrol had not gone into a linear kill zone but had bumped into the VC unit, probably a reinforced platoon, as they attempted to lay the trap. The speed of the artillery had not been anticipated, nor had the quick response of the gunships and jets. I had been more than impressed with the response of the supporting arms. I felt guilty as hell that Captain Sutton had had to initiate the calls for gunships and air. When I would have sent a relief force rushing out to assist Bigwitch, Sutton had stepped in to explain how you kept your people alive here. I knew one thing for certain; I would never doubt this company commander, and I was determined to learn all I could from him.

While we were standing around, patting ourselves on the back for having come out of a mess, I thought about the two kids who had died. I had barely known what they looked like; two eighteen year old kids who had been in the army all of six months, now headed south in body bags. Captain Sutton told me we would have a memorial service for them as soon as possible. “That's OK, but it won't bring them back,” I thought.

I called SP4 Dillard aside and told him he was taking over the squad.

“I already have, Sir. Platoon-Sergeant Fitzsimmons told me. We have adjusted the foxhole line to eliminate the one hole we can't fill.”

Dillard's blond hair was cropped close and his green eyes sparkled with enthusiasm as he talked. “Are you sure you can handle the squad, Dillard?”

“Sir, I'm gonna show you how to run a squad. Sergeant Bigwitch has helped me a lot, and I can use that map now.”

“How in the hell can a kid this young in a situation this rotten be so positive?” I wondered. “Well I'm sure you'll do fine. Don't hesitate to see me or Fitzsimmons if you need anything.”

“OK, Sir. Anything else?”

“No.” He left for his position.

I was impressed, and discussed the situation with Fitzsimmons. During the conversation I gave him a little pat on the back.

“Sir, Captain Sutton has got his shit together. I hope like hell we never lose him.”

“You and me both,” I replied. “I still want to know what Lieutenant Scott thinks he is doing, to order that dust off on his own.”

"Sir, don't be hard on him. We had had contact out there, so the dinks knew pretty well where we were, anyway," he said.

"Yes, but not exactly, and that's what the dust off told them. The only reason they didn't wipe out the entire patrol was because the patrol was moving faster than they anticipated."

"You're right, of course, Sir, but don't be too hard on him. Captain Sutton has already ripped his ass. I heard it," he said.

Still, I had to let him know that he wasn't sharing the command of my platoon with me.

CHAPTER 24

Captain Sutton called the platoon leaders to the CP at 1700 hours and told us to put our patrols on hold. "What time's EENT, (end of evening nautical twilight)?" He asked the first sergeant.

"At nineteen thirty-three," the first sergeant examined an extract of the intelligence annex to the operations order.

"OK. At 1945 we move, lock, stock, and barrel. We will set up here." He had marked the map, about eight hundred meters west of our current location. "Keep quiet. I don't want to hear a goddamned thing when we move out of here. When we get to our new location there will be no digging, no noise, no light. We can do that tomorrow. All ambush patrols are canceled for tonight. No one starts packing anything until 1930. Then he covered the order of march and details of platoon assignments at the new location. "Any questions?" There were none.

We packed quickly at 1930; my platoon tagged on behind Weapons Platoon. We silently eased out of the old location, slowly and deliberately, and finally closed into the new location and fumbled around in the dark until we were in the right positions. We set up as Sutton had told us, using the clock system, with twelve o'clock exactly magnetic north on our lensatic compasses. We had barely reached the new location when we heard a dull "thunk, thunk, thunk," somewhere north of us; it was impossible to tell how far away. Before the sounds were repeated a second and third time the thunderous cracking crunch of mortar rounds exploding on the perimeter of the foxholes we had just vacated, blended into one continuous roar. We tried to count the rounds, but after twelve it was impossible. Sutton grabbed Lieutenant Lowell Redd, his artillery FO, and told him to get counter-battery going on a set of coordinates he had picked out. He sat there with Redd, huddled under a poncho with a red-filtered flashlight looking at a space where mortars could set up to correspond to the azimuth he had read on his compass by the sound of the tubes. Redd had the artillery going in five minutes and the mortars ceased to "thunk." Even if the artillery hadn't come near them, it had at least caused a cease fire. I hoped like hell that we had cleaned their ass, but I sincerely doubted that we had come within five hundred meters.

We established the best defense we could set up, with one LP (listening post) in front of each rifle platoon. I went to sleep wondering if Sutton had a cousin on the VC side who kept telling him what the VC were going to do. A few soldiers who had bitched when they were forced to pack up and move in the dark were silent for the time being.

At 0300 I was awakened by the blast of a claymore to our front, followed by two more. The field telephone rang frantically; the three man LP had blown their claymores on a VC force passing parallel to their front, heading west. The LP was a three man crew from Sergeant McGuire's squad, lead by Sergeant Murdock. Murdock was whispering into the telephone, explaining the situation. Even under these circumstances his broad Georgia drawl came through.

"How many do you estimate?" I asked.

"Maybe ten. Should we come back in now?"

"No. Just keep still. They don't know where you are, and they've probably taken casualties. If you get more movement, throw grenades."

"I think we must have killed and wounded several. The movement has stopped. Can we fire that on call artillery target out to my front?"

I hesitated. We had not adjusted those defensive targets in, and I wasn't too keen on firing this DT without knowing exactly where it would be. I rationalized that the artillery would have safe-sided it some. "OK, here it comes. Get down." I ran across to the company CP and told Lieutenant Redd to fire DT 101, which he called back and had on the way immediately. I ran back to the telephone, fifteen meters away, and waited. "Pufft," the white phosphorus check round slammed in.

"Good; fire for effect!" Murdock rasped into the telephone. Shortly, six 105 mm rounds slammed in, followed by twelve more.

Murdock reported that movement to his front had ceased.

I now had an open line to Redd. "How about firing two rounds every fifteen minutes on that target from now until daylight? We can go out and check the results."

"OK, no problem. We will start in five minutes."

I informed Murdock, and in five minutes the first two rounds slammed in.

"Sir, there are screams and groans coming from that area!" Murdock reported.

"OK, we will fire the DT one more time, battery one." I called Redd and soon the six rounds screamed in.

"Great, right on the money," Murdock whispered.

We resumed the two rounds every fifteen minutes and fired until daylight. Just after BMNT (beginning of morning nautical twilight) I had Sergeant McGuire take his squad out to his LP, pick them up, and search the area. There were nine VC dead, killed by claymores and artillery, as well as numerous blood trails. The squad picked up eleven individual weapons, to include four SKS's and seven AK47's, and an RPG7 rocket launcher with seven rounds. There were a number of grenades and some satchel charges, gear, and pocket litter. As I analyzed the action I thought that this element was probably part of a large force that had been sent to attack the old perimeter behind the mortar preparation. After finding nothing there, they had broken into smaller elements and moved back to the west. This element had moved from east to west, just missing the perimeter and passing south of it, in front of First Platoon's LP. We blew the grenades and satchel charges in a hole outside the perimeter and evacuated the weapons, gear, and pocket litter after marking it.

After that we moved again, this time about one kilometer to the north-northeast, where we were almost within sight of the rubber trees of the Michelin. We dug in to the eyeballs; it wasn't too difficult to see that we had stirred up quite a hornet's nest. This area had been a safe haven for four main force Viet Cong regiments and at least one separate battalion for years. Now we were in their midst, so far creating mayhem and confusion on their side.

This time First Platoon was on the northeast from twelve o'clock to four o'clock. There was an open area in the center, so the 81 section was able to set the mortar up, but didn't fire to settle the base plate or register. We also had an LZ just east of the perimeter, in front of my platoon. The platoon leaders gathered at the company

CP at 1500 hours to receive Sutton's instructions for that night's activities. We were to put out two ambushes per rifle platoon, within a kilometer of the perimeter. First Platoon had a trail junction in the jungle to the east and a bridge across a creek on a road up in the rubber trees of the Michelin. I gave the trail junction ambush to Sergeant McGuire and the bridge to Platoon Sergeant Fitzsimmons. In addition, each ambush patrol was to install a mechanical ambush within five hundred meters of the live ambush. McGuire's MA was to be placed on a north-south trail east of the trail junction he was ambushing, and Fitzsimmons was to set his MA on a northsouth road five hundred meters to the northwest of his live ambush. There were dozens of ways to set up a mechanical ambush. The necessary ingredients were firing wire, electric blasting caps, a power source, explosive device, and a trigger mechanism of some type. McGuire was going to install five claymores, daisy chained together with the naked firing wire ends inserted under a strip of copper fastened to the upper jaw of a clothes pin. Another strip of copper tacked to the lower jaw of the clothes pin would hold the naked ends of the wire leading to and attached to a new PRC-25 battery. A plastic C-ration spoon was to be inserted, handle first, between the copper plates on the jaws of the clothes pin. A hole was bored through the mouth end of the spoon. A clear fishing leader tied through the hole would then be stretched across the trail about four inches off the ground and attached to a tree on the far side of the trail, the clothes pin also attached to a tree on the near side of the trail. When someone came down the trail and tripped the fishing leader the spoon would be pulled from between the jaws of the clothes pin, the copper strips would touch completing the circuit, and the claymores would go, wreaking havoc on a long section of trail.

Fitzsimmons was using a similar version of McGuire's MA but with claymores and det cord, the det cord being placed on the trail, running the length of the kill zone and covered by a half inch of dirt. There were a thousand ways to do it and all of them would work with varying degrees of efficiency. It all seemed to be very simple, as long as we held the initiative. If we could always force our terms on the enemy, the advantage was ours in a totally powerful way. But when he held all the cards, when we had to move, and he was doing the ambushing, the shoe was on the other foot. So far, the brilliance exhibited by Captain Sutton had paid great dividends in the two highest commodities the Infantry deals in: keeping our people alive and well, and killing the enemy.

Because of the openness of the rubber plantation, the trees were planted symmetrically with wide lanes between and there was absolutely no underbrush, Fitzsimmons decided to go out later than usual, to allow himself a little more darkness. Both ambushes were out and established before I turned in with the radios, and the man on watch was within arm's length of my air mattress.

Sometime around midnight I was awakened by the rain splattering against the two ponchos strung over me. It began lightly, then increased to a solid downpour. The foxholes filled rapidly and men climbed out of the holes and lay beside them. The sky was totally black, and even the starlight scopes were of marginal use. I pulled the poncho liner tighter around me and thought of Kim. What was she doing tonight? Did she have a date, or was she waiting at home for my letters, not knowing if I would make it back, not really knowing what I would do about her if I did make it back? I dreamed of being entwined by her long arms and legs; we were again on Chosun Beach, under a poncho liner groping, taking each other at the risk of the world seeing us at our lovemaking. It was real. I held her, struggled, gasped, and fought through to ecstasy, and she needed me as much as I needed her. We melted into each other.

"Lieutenant, Lieutenant!" Someone was shaking me, grasping my shoulder, and I couldn't wake up. Slowly, I realized that someone was there with me, and suddenly I sat bolt upright, wide awake, concerned about what I might have said in my sleep. "Lieutenant, sounds like McGuire's in contact!" the RTO whispered. The sound of the claymores blowing and the smaller blasts of hand grenades from the east indicated that McGuire had contact. After what seemed like hours, McGuire called.

"Charlie One-Six, this is Charlie One-One, just blew the ambush on five dinks. No movement in the kill zone. Will give you a full report at first light, over."

"Charlie One-One, this is Charlie One-Six, roger. Stay alert. Out." I finished the transmission quickly, because I wanted him to concentrate on what he was doing and not on me.

Not two minutes later I heard what sounded like Sergeant McGuire's ambush all over again, except that this time there were only claymores firing and no hand grenades.

"Charlie One-Six, this is Charlie One-One, my MA just went. I will check it out in the morning; over."

"This is Charlie One-Six, roger, out."

Around 0400 hours the rain slackened. I was fairly dry except for my arms and ass. Somehow water had gotten to my air mattress and ran down the cracks between the panels, and where my buttocks had flattened the panels I was soaked. I pulled the poncho liner tighter around me and finally went back to sleep. When I awoke it was raining again, and I peeped out at a slate gray sky.

McGuire was on the radio. "Charlie One-Six, this is Charlie One-One, we have four dinks dead in the kill zone and one other who is barely alive. Wait out," he broke off his transmission. I thought I heard a shot from the east of the perimeter, but I couldn't be sure.

"Charlie One-Six, this is Charlie One-One, correction. We have five dead VC and five weapons. There are four AK-47's and one SKS. We are headed out to check out the MA; over."

"This is Charlie One-Six, roger; out."

The MA had killed three VC, with weapons, and McGuire called this in. There were also several blood trails, indicating that there were VC wounded from the MA. The patrol came back about forty-five minutes later, and Fitzsimmon's patrol arrived at about the same time. This ambush had not heard or seen anything and were soaking wet for their trouble, like everyone else. No other company ambushes made contact that night. We were to be resupplied that day, so Sutton decided not to evacuate the enemy gear until the resupply ships came in. That way the resupply ships could back-haul everything.

CHAPTER 25

So far our luck had been consistent, and I was starting to believe that Sutton might be a hell of a lot more capable than I had suspected. For that day's patrols we were to send out one per platoon, and the patrol was to establish a day ambush and set one MA. I would take this patrol out. If I found a good night ambush spot, I was to drop off a stay-behind patrol of three men if it appeared that we hadn't been observed. That ambush and a close in ambush by Second Squad would be First Platoon's two ambushes for the night. I was a little worried about Bigwitch's replacement, because being a good rifleman is a hell of a long ways from being a good squad leader. I asked Lieutenant Redd to work with him that day and teach him as much as possible about calling for and adjusting indirect fire. Also, Dillard was to rehearse his ambush until he could do it anywhere with his eyes closed. I asked the company first-sergeant to drop over during the day and talk to Dillard, giving him as much technical advice and moral support as he could. Long gladly agreed.

My patrol slipped through the perimeter at 0830 and headed northeast into the Michelin. I had seven men with me: Alderman, Bentley, Doc Gill, Lee, and a fire team leader and two riflemen from Third Squad.

Prior to departure I had had an opportunity to talk with the men. Bentley was a curly haired stocky soldier from Athens, Ohio. The thing you could never forget about Bentley was that his face was always dirty; always. He loved grease. If there was anything around with grease or oil on it Bentley had to have his hands, and indeed his nose, in it. The corners of his mouth always looked as if he had been dipping snuff and it had dribbled out the corners of his mouth and downward. In fact, he didn't dip snuff at all. He was never shaved completely clean. Even after he shaved there would always be patches of hair here and there that had escaped his errant razor. The machine gunners loved Bentley because Bentley loved to clean their guns for them. The only problem was that they always had to wipe the gun clean of oil because Bentley would soak it down.

"Sir, I'm ready to go."

"Bentley, your rifle is dripping on the ground. Be sure and wipe all that excess oil off."

"Yes Sir." He applied a rag to his rifle. "Sir, are we going very far?" I had gone over the route with them.

"Look at this route again." I went over the patrol route on the map once more.

"I just wanted to know so I could decide whether to eat heavy or not." Silva was cracking up laughing. Bentley was a clown without any effort on his part to be one.

"Bentley, if you be nice to me I'll let you clean my gun when you get back," Howard wisecracked from his position on the foxhole line.

"Sir, Jacobs and Oliver here, they want to go on R & R to Tokyo when we get back in," Specialist Silva told me.

"Tokyo's a terrible place for R & R. It's too expensive, and the girls aren't that friendly to GI's because they know you don't have a lot of money," I said.

"Well where should we go, Sir?"

"Well Bangkok is outstanding. Sydney is great also. They have those good old big friendly ones there! Where do you want to go, Silva?"

"Me, I'd just as soon go to Saigon, myself." He was a handsome dark faced kid of Italian extraction from Chicago. "I'm trying to save some money to get married when I get back to the world. Gonna have a real old fashioned Italian wedding with all the trimmings. More food and wine than you've ever seen!"

"I'm sure it will be splendid, Specialist Silva."

Our route was a long one, taking us into the rubber trees about two and a half kilometers, then swinging back to the southeast to the jungle, and reentering the perimeter almost directly east of the company. There were clusters of buildings on the map that I hoped to check out enroute. I had enough demolitions to blow any bunkers or tunnels that we encountered. We each carried a LAW. Although designed for anti-tank use this weapon was excellent for firing on troops in bunkers or fortified positions. It had a lightweight, disposable body that could simply be chucked away after firing its one round.

Doc Gill had a light aid bag, so he shouldered Alderman's radio, and Alderman took point. I followed Alderman, with the rest of the patrol strung out behind me, swinging along with long Infantry strides. We had two radios with us-one carried by Doc on the company push and one carried by Lee on the 81 fire direction net. If we dropped off a stay-behind ambush SP4 Silva, the fire team leader from Third Squad, would head it. He would have with him PFC Jacobs and PFC Oliver, also from Third Squad. We had rehearsed them carefully. We would leave Lee's radio with Silva.

The early morning sun's rays warmed the jungle's upper canopy and diffused through to provide faint light to the perpetual gloom underneath the layered mattings of green. Birds twittered in morning excitement as they flitted through the tangles of green and gray. A snake slithered his way across a large knobby hardwood root and glided silently into a bamboo cluster. Insects buzzed in orchestration, lending a certain somnolence to the jungle floor as the point man, Alderman, stepped over the root and circled left around the stand of bamboo. We strung out behind Alderman, separated from each other by several meters as we plodded cautiously along, peering right, left, and ahead to the man in front of us.

It was still early morning, but not a whisper of a breeze stirred, and we perspired freely through our olive drab jungle fatigues. The torpid air smelled of dampness and decay and something else. Alderman signaled for the column to halt, and the patrol relayed the signal back the length of the short sweaty line. We silently crouched at the alert, peering to the flanks. Alderman had been on point for perhaps an hour, and I stiffened at his obvious concern for whatever had alerted him. Indeed, something very curious and somewhat foreboding had cautioned my own keener senses, and I could actually feel the hair on the back of my neck standing up and pressing against the sweaty collar of my fatigue shirt. "I could see Alderman kneeling beside the stand of bamboo with his rifle pointed to the front, as he tested the hot steamy air with sharpened senses. There it was again. A faint cloying odor mixed with a sharp foul smell akin to that of roasting decaying flesh. Had there been a sound mixed with the odor to further heighten my nervous anticipation? Again. There was little question now. Was it the ever so faint gurglings of human laughter? The sound of movement behind me broke my concentration, and I wheeled to face Bentley and Doc. Alderman had slipped back to where I crouched.

"Sir, it smells like dink chow cooking, and I'm not sure but I believe I heard voices in that direction," Alderman whispered as he pointed up a slight rise in the ground behind the bamboo cluster.

"Are you sure of the direction?"

"Well, no. But it seemed to come from over that way."

We proceeded cautiously along, and by my map we should have been nearing the forest edge. The wind was now moving slightly, blowing in our faces, so the odors and murmurs of sounds must have emitted from somewhere to our north, perhaps from out in the rubber trees.

We eventually left the cool, dark cover of the forest and entered the endless lines of rubber trees that stretched as far as the eye could see. I felt completely naked. As much as possible we hugged the line of rubber trees along our route and avoided the middle of the lanes between the lines of trees. The distinct odor of cooking food wafted in to us. Going was very good, in spite of the obvious need for caution, because there was absolutely no underbush. Soon I spotted a cluster of three buildings that were on the map and a target to check, about eight hundred meters to our front. I silently cursed myself for not bringing an M60 machine gun. It would have been perfect for this terrain and vegetation. What the hell, we would just have to make do with what we had. A little voice in my head said "You live and learn," but another said, "You die and don't learn." I sent Silva, Oliver, and Jacobs up some five hundred meters, just southwest of the hooches, to cover us. They crept rapidly through the rubber trees, bent over, and moving at a fast shuffle. I took the rest of the patrol forward hugging the row of rubber trees just south of the hooches. We halted about five hundred meters from the hooches, where I saw a wisp of smoke rising lazily from between the buildings.

A woman in black peasant garb walked from one hooch to the adjacent hooch, carrying a large metal pan. Just behind her a VC with an AK47 exited the building and went across to a third hooch. I glanced across to Silva's position and saw that they were set up, looking at the hooches at a ninety degree angle from the way we were looking at them. That meant that if the VC fled out the opposite side of the hooches from us Silva could still see them clearly and bring fire on them. I spread my four men out in line, and we crept forward. I hated these goddamned open rubber trees and the French who had planted them. We could only hope to get within good rifle range before we were detected. I saw movement from one of the hooches and signaled everyone to freeze. Three VC came from the far hooch and entered the hooch nearest us on the right. I waved the patrol forward until we got within fifty meters of the hooches, then halted them. I crawled over to Bentley, gave him instructions, then moved back to where I had started from. I took my LAW, extended it, stood and braced my shoulder against a rubber tree, and aimed the LAW at the back wall of the stucco type building with the tile roof. I looked across at Bentley, who stood aiming his LAW also. I turned, reaimed, and fired the LAW through the back wall of the house. A split second later, Bentley fired his LAW through what was left of the wall. Fire belched out of the LAW tubes and the rockets made for killing tanks slammed through the wall with a deafening blast as the armor killing rounds penetrated and exploded. The wall and nearest half of the hooch disintegrated. Four dinks ran out of the far hooch to investigate the explosion, not knowing what had happened but probably suspecting that artillery fire had caused the noise. Silva's crew opened up at the same time, and at that range a blind man couldn't have missed. The four VC were cut down in the cross fire without firing a shot. The cracks of the rifle fire reverberated down the long rows of rubber trees and the echoes moved further and further away and then died. No one moved for at least ten minutes.

Finally I took Bentley and Alderman and we spread out and eased forward to check out the hooches. A hooch apiece, I thought. I pointed to Bentley to check out the left near hooch; to Alderman to check out the far hooch. I would check out the hooch we had fired the LAW's into. I motioned that Bentley was to check his hooch first and that Alderman and I would cover him. Bentley crept up to the back wall of the hooch, turned the corner, and rolled a grenade in through the open front door. He turned, ran back to us and hit the ground, which we were already hugging. Smoke, dust and debris boiled out of the open cracks, the door, and one open window of the hooch. We waited for two or three minutes, and Bentley checked the hooch out. Alderman and I checked our hooches, using the same procedure. There was one body, that of the woman we had seen previously, and no equipment in Bentley's hooch. Alderman's hooch yielded quite a few documents and a miniature printing press, as well as several B40 rockets and 82 mm mortar rounds concealed in a tunnel under the floor. My hooch contained five mangled bodies and more documents than we could carry. We checked for tunnels under the floor of the totally wrecked hooch and found one, but found nothing inside the tunnel. We had a total of nine weapons, there were ten dead bodies, and three hundred rounds of ammunition, documents, and the printing press.

I called Captain Sutton with an update on our initial reports and requested two helicopters to evacuate the materials and men. I recommended that we leave the stay-behind ambush concealed in the destroyed hooch, where they would have visibility in all directions and could set up their claymores after dark. He didn't like leaving them there, but reluctantly gave in on the condition that I brief them carefully on the way to run to reach the perimeter. He also insisted that I leave one more man with them. I suggested that I stay but he wouldn't hear of it because of my responsibilities to control the rest of the platoon. I left Lee with them. He told me that there would only be one helicopter, to get a PZ ready, and that the bird would be there in twenty minutes. I wrapped det cord around two rubber trees and primed the cord, ran the firing wire back, and blew the trees off their stumps near the ground. We dragged the trees off the PZ, I concealed Silva and his three man crew amongst the bodies and debris in the bombed out hooch and made sure that they understood where to place their claymores. As an afterthought I primed two coils of det cord in the other two hooches and covered the det cord and firing wire with a half inch of dirt, running the firing wires back to Silva's position and attaching them to the ten cap blasting machine. By this time Silva had more information than he could handle, so I decided against setting up an MA. I explained once more that he had two on-call artillery fires then showed him where they were by having the artillery fire three rounds on each of them. We had been there too long, and although creating noise and then leaving was part of the stay-behind plan, designed to draw the VC, I didn't want to get a helicopter shot down.

The helicopter beat into the PZ, landing on my purple smoke. We loaded the gear and climbed in. The chopper hovered forward, cleared the rubber trees and circled around over the jungle south, and down at C

Company's one ship pad. We climbed out and pulled the gear off for inspection and marking.

Captain Sutton had decided to resupply that afternoon after the helicopter brought in the patrol. The resupply ships had finished and departed when faint explosions, then a spattering of small arms fire could be heard from the north in the direction of Silva's stay-behind. Seconds later, Lee called the CP to fire the DT's that we had put in that morning.

"Charlie One-Six, this is Charlie One-Three-Alpha, over," Silva called.

"This is Charlie One-Six, over."

"This is One-Three-Alpha, four dinks came from the north into the area and were checking out the hooches. We blew the demolitions and fired, killing three, but one was wounded and got away; over."

"Roger, get back in here, ASAP; over."

"Roger, on the way, out."

I called Lieutenant Redd to fire the DT's again. About forty-five minutes later Silva, Lee, Oliver, and Jacobs made their way back into the perimeter, soaking wet with sweat. Captain Sutton walked over to my CP where they had flopped down to get their breath. They each carried an AK47. The wounded VC had dropped his in his haste to escape. The patrol had rifled their pockets for the usual pocket litter and had picked up a sand bag of Chicom friction grenades that one of them had carried. Silva was grinning from ear to ear, and I gave all of them a healthy pat on the back.

Sutton announced that ambushes for that night were canceled. We were to prepare to move ASAP. All patrols were back in, so movement posed no problems. We would drop off two stay-behind ambushes enroute to take care of anyone following. In addition, one MA would be established at the north side of the perimeter and left in place as we departed.

He covered the order of march out. Third Platoon was to drop off two three-man stay-behinds which could get into position and hide as the rest of the company passed by them, thus concealing them in their preparations. They were to set up just off the route of march, one to the left, the other to the right about five hundred meters further south. After an hour they were to fold up and rejoin the company.

We moved out with Browning's platoon in the lead. The prescribed route was off any beaten trails and swung in a two kilometer arc, initially bearing to the south-east, then curving back to the south-west. The going became tougher the further we went, but the coolness of the triple canopy jungle helped. About thirty minutes after we started we heard the sounds of small arms fire to our rear. We continued to move, as I monitored the company net for any word. In a few minutes the first stay-behind from Third Platoon called in that two dinks had walked directly into their ambush and had been blown away. In about thirty minutes that stay-behind pushed past us, enroute to rejoin Third Platoon. One member carried a long bolt action sniper rifle with a scope mounted on it, and another carried an SKS. About twenty-five minutes later the other stay-behind passed, moving toward the head of the column.

We closed into the new location about an hour before dark and began preparing the defensive perimeter in earnest. There had been some mail on the resupply birds, and several members of my platoon received letters. No packages were brought to the field, but were held in the rear for the troops until they returned to Lai Khe.

Darkness settled in, and Sutton called the platoon leaders to the CP.

"We are moving again," he said. He had a red filtered flashlight and we were hidden within Sutton's poncho hooch. This time we were moving five hundred meters west. The news of the move was greeted by tired looks, but no one said anything. Sutton's sense of what had to be done next had been proven precisely correct on too many occasions.

"If I see one cigarette or hear one rifle sling rattle I'll have your ass. We have to work hard out here to stay alive," he said. He covered details of the defense at the next location. "Do I have any questions? As soon as I get my CP location picked out come over. There are a few things we need to hash out. That's all."

We moved out shortly, slowly covering the distance to the new perimeter. After we settled into our defense there, I walked over to Captain Sutton's CP. He had Lieutenant Pendleton by the short hairs, administering a total ass chewing. I suspected that was the rehashing that he had in mind. After the other platoon leaders arrived his poop session did not contain anything very significant. He mentioned to Lieutenant Smathers that we had a pretty good war going on here, and he would just love to see Smathers get interested and involved! I was embarrassed for Smathers, but he probably deserved the criticism. He then announced that we would stand down, send out no patrols and prepare the defensive position tomorrow. There would be ambush patrols, two per platoon tomorrow night. We were happy for the break.

CHAPTER 26

The night passed quietly. I listened for mortar fire on the last position, but it didn't come. "The Viet Cong commander must be confused and frustrated," I thought. The ground was damp but the sky was clear, and there were insect sounds and occasional bird shrills from the night hunters. Once I heard the cough of a tiger and thought of William Blake's poem. It kept running through my memory, "Tiger, tiger, burning bright ..." We were in triple canopy now and practically no light could be seen as I lay on the air mattress.

I thought of Kim and a feeling of emptiness swept over me. I felt tired of the loneliness and wondering if we would ever have what we had had during those golden moments. When would my mail catch up to me? Maybe there would be a letter when we got back. I had written twice and carefully addressed the letters, even checked with the mail clerk at battalion, to be sure the letters would be routed to Korea. I slept fitfully and dreamed of Kim running alongside the Han Tan River to meet me as I carried wood for a fire from the mountainside. She wore a sweater with no bra, and as she ran, her silky raven hair flowed back over her shoulders, and her long legs and high rounded hips moved so gracefully that she seemed to glide across the sand. Her black eyes sparkled, and her full lips were parted in a happy laugh.

I dropped the wood and ran to meet her. We sank down in the sand and made love in the open, and I thought that Korean peasant women were watching us from the hillside. The dream faded, and I was in a smoke filled pool room trying to beat some man who never missed. He ran through rack after rack. Finally I left him and got a sandwich. When I returned he was still shooting, and I never got a shot, and lost money on every game. That faded and the faces changed and I was half awake and able to dream what I wanted to.

Finally it was as close to daylight as it gets in the jungle. Fitzsimmons and I had coffee and a C-ration as we discussed plans for the day. The first order was to adjust the perimeter, dig in, and put together a solid defense. In the meantime a small patrol would sweep out to some three hundred meters in front of the platoon, looking for enemy signs and a stream. That afternoon the platoon could bathe, clean rifles, grenade launchers, and machine-guns. They could then sack out with security rotating, and perhaps get two or three hours of sleep. I would take the far ambush that night and let SP4 Dillard take the near one. I picked out a spot on the map where a prominent trail crossed a stream, about a click (kilometer) and a half from the perimeter. I would set up there. A trail junction, about eight hundred meters to the northwest, looked like the spot for Dillard's ambush. Sutton approved the plan.

"Are you sure Dillard can hack it?" he asked.

"No, but he's had all the instructions we can give him, and everyone has to go through that. If he makes it, we have a good squad leader."

"If he don't we have a dead squad," Sutton looked me dead in the eye. "But what the hell!" he laughed. "I take the same risk every time I send one of you new 'butter bars' out the first time. Speaking of butter bars, you ain't one."

I didn't understand, and had an idea that I had blown something big. "What do you mean, Sir?"

"Just think of all the things you've done wrong in the last four days." As we spoke the other lieutenants had drifted over to Sutton's CP, and Fitzsimmons and the squad leaders had walked up.

"What the hell's going on, Sir?"

"Get your heels together, Lieutenant. Group ten-shut!" Sutton commanded, and the muddy heels of jungle boots popped.

The first-sergeant spoke, "Attention to orders. The following promotions are announced: Second-Lieutenant James Worthington, OF109630, promoted to the grade of First-Lieutenant ..." he read in a quiet, firm voice. Sutton stepped forward and pinned a silver bar on the right side of my jungle fatigue collar; everyone shook hands with me in congratulations.

"Now get that off of there and put it in your pack before you get shot. Otherwise the enemy will never suspect that you are an officer, I guarantee!" Sutton joked. The others laughed, but I had the feeling that no matter how many times I was promoted no other could possibly be as memorable. Sutton had really played it to the hilt.

At my platoon area, we dug in, camouflaged, and consolidated the defense. We worked until noon, and the defense was in pretty good shape when we took a break for a C-ration meal. I went over to Second Squad and ate with them.

"Sir, when will Sergeant Bigwitch be back?" one of the troops asked.

"Well, I don't think we'll see him again out here, but I wouldn't be surprised if he rejoined us when we get back to the rear." They munched thoughtfully as they reflected on that. The conversation shifted to home; the troops wanted to talk about their girls. SP4 Dillard, the squad leader who had replaced Bigwitch, sat quietly.

"Who do you have waiting for you, Dillard?" I asked.

"Sir, I have the most beautiful girl in the world, and her name is Julie. I get three letters a week, and we are going to get married as soon as I get back," he said enthusiastically. "She is working at the bank in town and saving some money each month. I am also saving most of my pay so we can get started right. I'm not even going to take R & R," he said.

"I'll take his and mine both!" said PFC Howard. "Both of them in Bangkok!" The other troops laughed. "Sir, where will you go on R & R?"

"I'll probably go to Korea," I said.

"Korea? Why would you want to go there?" Howard asked. Then the light came on. "Oh, Sir, I see. What does she look like? Let's see a picture!"

I pulled a picture of Kim from my wallet.

"All right! Now I get the picture!" Howard laughed. The others nodded in appreciation.

We finished the C-rations, and resumed our preparations. We had found a stream with plenty of water only fifty meters to the front of the perimeter. The troops carried their steel pots full of water back into the perimeter and took a "whore's bath" with soap, wash rag, and a pot of water.

I spot-checked weapons that afternoon. When I was satisfied, we posted light security and the troops sacked out on their air mattresses except for security. One learned very quickly in the Infantry that a couple of hours sleep snatched here or there might mean the difference in an ambush or engagement, when the time came to separate the quick from the dead.

Late afternoon we rehearsed the two ambushes, then one more time. Dillard appeared to be ready. We never put out night ambushes until after dark, which lessened the possibility that the ambush would get ambushed or mortared. As we slipped through the perimeter and moved off on our azimuth it was pitch dark. Dillard's patrol was tagged on the tail end of mine to be dropped off enroute. That night I had Alderman, Bentley, Doc Gill, and Lee in my patrol. Dillard's patrol included PFC's Howard and Larson and four members of Second Squad.

The going was slow, aggravated by the thickness of the jungle. We slithered over the high roots of the hardwoods, got tangled in vines and creepers, and scratched and cut by the ever present bamboo limbs. Bamboo had to be the toughest thing growing anywhere. I thought that they should make rifle barrels and mortar tubes out of it. I could remember many of the Japanese paintings of bamboo in all forms, brilliant and beautiful in their simplicity. Somehow I didn't believe I would ever find them beautiful again.

We reached Dillard's ambush site and dropped him and his six man squad. I thought about helping him set up but decided against it, for fear of destroying his confidence and leading his squad to doubt his ability. We covered the ground a little more rapidly after we dropped them off. Alderman was on point and we were behind him, closed up tight because of poor visibility and close terrain. We wore soft patrol caps with two vertical luminous strips side by side, each about an inch long, in the back so that the man behind could see. Our hands and faces were blackened, and the sleeves of our jungle fatigues covered the arms for camouflage and protection against brambles. We wore black glove shells on our hands to help in handling the cutting bamboo branches and other thorny vegetation. Everything was tied down tightly, rifles were carried without slings, and the two claymores carried by each man were secured to web gear by olive drab cloth straps. Hand grenades were secured to the sides of the ammo pouches with the strap through the pull ring and snapped. The demolitions and two LAW's were spread among the five patrol members.

We moved as quietly as possible, but occasionally a grunt or a muffled curse could be heard or a bent twig slapping against a patrol member as it was released from the body of the man in front. Alderman was on point, and I followed him with Bentley and the radio behind me; then came Lee, with Doc in the rear. We were still about four hundred meters short of our selected ambush site when Alderman halted abruptly and I bumped into him. Just in front of us was an improved trail about two meters wide. On investigation we discovered the cut brush, some of it fairly freshly chopped that had been cleared from the route. The road, it was more road than trail, was marked by cart, bicycle and footprints. It seemed to be straight, although we only checked for forty meters or so in either direction, and visibility was next to nothing. I used my starlight scope to get a better view. It was a virtual highway and was totally invisible from all prying eyes because it was hidden under triple canopy jungle.

I called Sutton and whispered a description to him. "Charlie-Six, this is Charlie One-Six, request permission to set up exactly four hundred meters east of our selected site. We have a regular red ball running through here, over."

"This is Charlie-Six, roger, set up your skinny (ambush) on that road. Cover as much linear distance as you can safely handle, and be prepared to high-ass out of there in case you latch on to one too big to eat," he said.

"Charlie-Six, this is Charlie One-Six, roger, out," I ended the transmission.

I got the patrol together and we selected a rendezvous point forty meters back; a huge teak tree with several yards clear of underbrush around its base. "It's so goddamned dark that it will even be hard to spot this thing. Here's what we will do. The ambush will not be linked by signal cord, but your cord will be used to guide you back to this spot. Everyone tie your cords to this small sapling, then work your way to your ambush spot on the road. From north to south it will be Doc, Bentley, Me, Lee and Alderman. Bentley, give me your radio. OK. Set up your claymores but don't fire them until I fire mine. I will string the det cord and rig it to fire. It will run down the center of the road, so get back at least ten meters and get behind some substantial cover, like a large tree. No noise. After we pop the ambush, wait five minutes and slip back to this spot. Then we will decide whether to remain or return to base. Is that clear?" There were no questions.

We tied off to the sapling, I slipped on Bentley's radio, and we moved back to the road. I held up about ten meters from the road, shucked off the radio, and secured my demolitions. Doc and I worked our way forward to the edge of the road and were just preparing to move up to where we would start laying the det cord when Doc grabbed my arm. I stopped, frozen in my tracks. From up the trail there was movement in the darkness and an ever so soft squeaking noise. We sank slowly to the ground and eased to a prone position. To be discovered at this stage of establishing an ambush meant serious trouble. If they fired on us as we lay this close to the road they couldn't miss. Worse, a hand grenade's fragments would cover a large area killing or wounding two or three of us. I prayed that the others had also been alerted to the sound of movement.

My heart was pounding rapidly, and I could feel its thumping in my chest against the ground; I tried to flatten out in the low brush and vegetation, and I was aware that my hand and arm were almost out in the trail. Three dark figures moved past in the inky blackness. The VC in the middle was pushing a bicycle, and one of its wheels squeaked slightly under the apparently heavy load lashed atop its frame. I knew they would spot us at roadside when they drew abreast of our hiding place. The thought came to me that if I opened up on them with my rifle on automatic I could probably kill all three. Instantly I rejected that too easy solution as two more silent figures became visible in the inky blackness just behind the original three. The first three with the bicycle slipped past us and continued on down the red ball. As the other two passed it was clear that the man in the rear was dangerously close to our side of the trail. I clutched my rifle in a choke hold and panicked anew. I tried desperately to lie perfectly still but almost began firing as he stepped on the muzzle end of my rifle and went on down the route, soon out of sight in the darkness. I was soaking wet with sweat, and my pulse still pounded in my ears.

We waited another five minutes and then moved out onto the trail, silently and rapidly. I began the det cord north of Doc's position. Doc assisted me by covering the det cord with dirt from the crown of the road, using a bayonet to scratch a small trench for the cord and covering it as he went. It had to be done quickly, and we made too much noise, but it couldn't be helped. I primed the det cord, wired it, and attached the firing wire to the generator at my position. Then I put out my claymores, angling them to fire down the long axis of the road, their fires overlapping just about in front of my position, carefully selecting a defilade position for me and the radio with cover from two hardwoods left and right. I checked the other positions, and when they were ready I went back to my position by the radio. Then began the waiting.

At about 0300 the wind stirred through the branches and I thought I heard noise on the road, but I looked thoroughly up and down the redball and saw nothing. I fought drowsiness and lay without moving more than my eyeballs. I checked the luminous dial of my watch and it was 0350 hours. Noise on the road shocked me wide awake. Through the starlight scope I saw a regular convoy passing through the ambush. A point man passed, followed by two more soldiers and then carts, each pulled by one man and rolling smoothly on their two bicycle wheels. Bicycles with heavy equipment lashed on were interspersed between the carts. I turned the starlight scope to look up the road for the end of the column, but as far as I could see the column continued, well past Doc's position. I looked back down the road to the south and the point man passed Alderman's position. I waited another three second count and fired my claymores. A split second later the eight claymores of the rest of the patrol went. In at least three places along the trail, spectacular secondary explosions ripped the night in great fireballs, throwing gear, wood, debris and human flesh in all directions; I hadn't counted on the secondary explosions and had planned to detonate the det cord later, after the survivors came to check for wounded and salvageable equipment. The carts had probably been loaded with mortar ammunition, grenades, anti-tank rockets, satchel charges, and miscellaneous ammunition. At least three 120 mm mortar tubes had been lashed on the cargo bicycles.

There had been one huge secondary explosion north of Doc Gill's position, caused by his far claymore or the det cord which ran north of his area. VC could be seen north of Doc's position running back and forth across the road in confusion. I called for the artillery target I had plotted north of Doc's position. I had taken too long so I called for a battery five, delay fuse, and moved back to the teak tree where the rest of the patrol waited.

Lee lay on the ground with Doc working over him.

"Sir, he's dead," Doc said as he looked up at me with tears in his eyes.

I was shocked that we had a casualty and couldn't understand it. "Give him mouth to mouth," I said. Doc began mouth to mouth and worked with him a good five minutes.

"Sir, it's no use. He's dead. The femoral artery is severed, and he has a severe chest wound. I don't see how he got back this far," Doc said.

I checked the lifeless body, then we quickly rigged a poncho stretcher between two poles and began the journey back. I had the artillery target fired again to cover the sound of our movement. Daylight was creeping in and I wanted to get back before it was completely light. Apparently a round from one of the ammunition carts had detonated in mid-air, throwing shrapnel in Lee's direction. I agonized over his death but nothing relieved the hurt, and the weight got heavier as I realized that I had suffered three dead and two wounded, in less than a week.

We took a different route back, so we did not pass Dillard's ambush site. Captain Sutton met us at the edge of the perimeter and helped to carry Lee's stretcher. Sutton's headquarters had a helicopter enroute to take

Lee's body back and two more to back haul the enemy gear that Browning's ambush had captured. All three were loaded with a heavy resupply of ammunition, claymores, demolitions, and grenades.

I was told that that night Browning had ambushed a small resupply column, killing four VC and capturing a cart load of 82 mm mortar ammunition and some grenades. No other ambush had made contact.

Ten minutes after our arrival, the helicopters settled onto the pad on the north side of the perimeter. After offloading we gently loaded Lee's body and watched the helicopter take him away. I had turned his weapon, rucksack, and personal gear in at company, where it was marked and sent back to the supply sergeant, on the second bird. The weight on my shoulders seemed much heavier, and I stumbled numbly through the patrol debriefing. Sutton tried to put things into proper perspective for me, but that did not bring Lee back.

CHAPTER 27

A heavy resupply of ammunition of all types had been brought in with the helicopters that morning. I thought it strange because we had just resupplied. We packed and moved about five hundred meters eastward as soon as the last ship cleared. Daylight patrols that had been scheduled were canceled to be rescheduled from our new location.

We had barely cleared the old perimeter when the mortar rounds poured into it. "They are really pissed off now!" Sergeant Fitzsimmons told me. "They are just about desperate enough to do something stupid." I reflected on that.

At the new location we sent out daytime clearing patrols but did little else. There was an old saying that kept ringing through my head – "You've got to eat the elephant a bite at a time!" Apparently Captain Sutton knew how to pace the company. At the new location we had a small clearing in the center of the perimeter for medivac, resupply, and a mortar pit.

Sutton called the platoon leaders together. We sat around him on the ground ready to take notes. "Dig in to the eyeballs and get overhead cover. We will fire in the DT's, and there will be a total of four. In addition, I will send back the data for some air strikes, as early

in the morning as we can get them, and we will divert them if we are in contact. A four deuce mortar defensive target will be plotted and fired to the fronts of all three rifle platoons. Lay three mechanical ambushes in front of each platoon three hundred meters out. You can put those in as soon as the clearing patrols get back. When you put them in keep security out beyond them so you are not observed. I want a heavy LP with at least five men and three claymores apiece, out two hundred meters in front of your positions. They will be your next line of defense after the MA's. After the LP's, or close in ambushes if you prefer, do their jobs and withdraw, you have the artillery and heavy mortar DT's. Of course our own 81 mm mortar will be firing for you. Any questions?"
My God, he is really intense this morning, I thought.

"Sir, how do you know they will attack us in strength tonight?" Browning asked.

"Men, let's put it this way; I'm not cleared for all the intelligence that division and brigade generate, but I reap it's benefits. Other than that I will tell you that common sense says they are pissed off. We have caused some fairly severe problems for a multi-regimental sized Viet Cong unit, with an understrength U.S. rifle company," he said.

"How has the rest of the battalion been doing, Sir?" I asked.

"A and B Companies have had some contact but not anything to compare with what we've had. Apparently we were put down almost on top of a VC headquarters, maybe even Central Office South Vietnam (COSVN), according to intelligence. To us it doesn't matter too much who they are, but we have hurt them significantly. Colonel Crowse told me that the enemy command headquarters for this entire region has put top priority on eliminating C Company, 1st of the 202nd."

"Then why aren't battalion and brigade reinforcing us?" I asked the obvious question.

"I'm getting to that. A and B Companies are to move into a common perimeter, about eleven hundred meters east of us, just after dark, with the mission of relief or reinforcement of C Company if the need arises. The other two battalions of the brigade, east of us, will be lifted into LZ's west of us about two kilometers. The LZ's will be prepared by two thousand pound bombs called 'daisy cutters' and dropped by the U.S. Air Force. Immediately upon insertion each battalion will send its companies eastward into widely spread blocking positions, about one kilometer west of us, forming a linear north-south block in a series of strong points, to destroy the enemy who is attacking us as they withdraw, and to prevent their reinforcing. Intelligence is sure that the greatest concentration of enemy forces in the area is about three kilometers west of this perimeter. Any questions?" There were a few, readily answered. "OK, I'd like Lieutenant Redd to cover the indirect fires for the defense."

"We have priority of air and artillery over the entire III Corps area," he began. "If we are attacked in the strength that we anticipate, we will need all the artillery we can get. There will be our own DT's, fired by the 105's, as well as a target list surrounding this perimeter, to be fired on call by the 155's, 8 inch howitzers, and even the 175 mm guns. I have simplified my target list to four blocks, east, west, south and north. For example, if I call for the west block of targets, every target will be fired automatically, in the number of rounds I request. As for air, I have four "sky spots" to be put in from midnight to 0400 hours. These are computer controlled bombings of pre-planned targets, and are on likely enemy staging areas from which attacks could be launched against this perimeter. At first light there will be no fewer than two flights of jets with an airborne FAC (Air Force Forward Air Controller) on station as an air cap at all times. At 2200 this evening a total of eight B-52 strikes will go in west and northwest of here, the nearest being three kilometers west of us. These are targeted against what intelligence in Saigon believes to be COSVN. In short, we have all the indirect fire we need. Are there any questions?"

We sat there, too stunned to do much more than stare open-mouthed at Redd and Sutton. I half believed that at any moment Sutton would say "April Fool" or something like that, to indicate that he had been putting us on. He was definitely not putting us on. We had the better part of the morning and the rest of the day to prepare, so we began in earnest.

To me, it was obvious that an attack of the magnitude expected would come behind a heavy preparation by indirect fire. The enemy would use 60 mm, 82 mm, and 120 mm mortars, as well as 122 mm rockets, so I emphasized overhead cover. I explained everything I knew to Fitzsimmons and the squad leaders, and was pleased to note the positive reaction on the part of the entire platoon. I had seen them work but never like this. They clearly understood the situation. The frequency and intensity of the enemy contact we had already had lent credence to the intelligence picture that Sutton had painted.

That day I checked and rechecked as never before. Fitzsimmons and the squad leaders did the same. The artillery and 4.2 inch mortar DT's were fired in very early at our request, so that they did not detonate the mechanical ambushes which we put out after the DT's were in. I personally supervised the installation of our three MA's. Finally, the close-in ambush was established by Sergeant McGuire's squad after they had completed their perimeter positions to which they would return upon withdrawl of the close-in ambush. McGuire had a total of himself plus six on the close-in ambush, each man with three claymores.

The entire defense was wired in with signal cord, to include the close-in ambush. The sound powered telephones were hooked in a "hot loop," and a land line was run to McGuire's position in the close-in ambush. I installed a direct line to Redd for artillery and 4.2 mortar coordination. We were told that Lee could not be replaced, so we simply had to make do the best we could with what we had. I had Redd's fire plan, so I knew I could do the job myself, but it might detract from my ability to direct my platoon's efforts. I discussed this with Fitzsimmons; he saw no problem with me doing both as it would require no change of locations; merely reaching for another radio handset would do it. I thought that sounded a bit simplistic, but agreed for lack of a better solution. The problem was solved when we received a replacement FO, the most experienced in the battalion, from the 4.2 Inch Mortar Platoon. Later I found out that Captain Sutton had helped solve my problem. SP4 Creighton arrived, and I went over the fires with him. He was a heads up kid, and his reputation was solid. After we finished he discussed the fires with Lieutenant Redd. Finally the jungle grew darker, and I made a last round of the foxhole line, checking weapons and most particularly the two M60 machine-guns. They were clean as a whistle, and I relaxed and drank a cup of C-ration coffee.

"Well, what do you think?" I quietly asked Fitzsimmons.

"Sir, we are as ready as we are going to get. I'm glad we moved after resupply this morning or we would be short more people than we are now. Our fields of fire here are shit, but if you can cover this much dead space we've done it. I'm glad we haven't had any helicopters come in here, but when we fired in all those DT's I'm sure the VC decided where we were," he said. "There's one other thing, Sir," he hesitated.

"What's that?"

"Do you get the feeling that we are nothing but bait here, Sir? I feel like a hunk of cheese on a rat trap."

"Fitzsimmons, we happen to be the company in the cauldron this time. Those are the breaks," I replied.

"Sir, I'm with you, no matter what the case may be, but I don't like being the bait. Battalion could have reinforced this perimeter today."

It was no time to argue tactics. "We will be OK if the weather holds and all that air is available. Besides, we have half the artillery tubes in division laid on us."

"Well, we're stuck with it one way or the other. Anyway, we've had some success and morale is high. We have never knocked them over like this."

"Did any mail come in on the resupply ships?" I changed the subject.

"Nothing. I figure we will get a couple of sacks on the next resupply."

"How's your family doing at Fort Riley?" I asked.

"Oh, pretty well. They are off post in Junction City. My daughter's a senior in high school and my son's a sophomore. Boy's playing football, and it looks like he may make the first team."

"What position does he play?"

"He's an end on offense and a linebacker on defense."

"Your wife seem happy enough there?"

"Yes, she's got the car, and she can drive anywhere she wants. She's working in the lunch room of a grammar school on post up at Custer Hill," he said.

We broke off, each with our own thoughts. He spoke as if everyone should know Fort Riley, Kansas, like their front yard, and I had never been there. He had been a young rifleman that first winter in the Korean War, and the effects of the frostbite on his toes gave him problems.

I made one more round, checked the close-in ambush and got two breaks in squelch, and lay down on my air mattress to get a couple of hours sleep. I would need it.

CHAPTER 28

At 2200 my eyes flew wide open and I thought the end of time, Armageddon, or some other great calamity had befallen us. The ground shook as if it were being ripped and torn apart, and indeed it was. The complete obliteration of sixteen square kilometers was taking place west of us, as the arc lights (B-52 strikes) went in. There were eight strikes, and one strike literally destroyed everything in a box two kilometers long and one kilometer wide. The B-52's were so high that when they pickled their five hundred pound bombs we couldn't hear the planes. "That ought to give 'em a few headaches," I thought.

I dozed and woke again as the sky spots went in after midnight, much closer than the arc lights had fallen. I hoped that all that ordnance wasn't just killing monkeys and making toothpicks out of teak trees. All night, harassing and interdiction (H&I) fires had been falling on randomly selected targets, picked by map reconnaissance. This occurred every night but not with the regularity that we had tonight.

At about 0200 hours the unmistakable cracks of the claymores in one of the MA's west of us shattered the air. Almost simultaneously another MA on the north went. The perimeter was alerted, every weapon was manned, and squad leaders anxiously searched their fronts with starlight scopes.

I listened carefully but all was still, like the calm in the eye of the hurricane. We didn't have to wait long. The blasting crunch of the first mortar round blinded me temporarily and steel flew in a wide circle around the point of impact. I felt a stinging pain in my right upper arm and a warm trickle ran down past my elbow and into the palm of my hand. Doc tied a bandage around the shrapnel wound, and I slipped my fatigue shirt back on. Suddenly the mortar rounds began to cover the perimeter, one blasting crunch mingling with the next. Then the 122 mm rockets showered in, and when the rounds burst on the trees or in one of the canopies the hot shrapnel showered down from above. One finally understood why the army issued steel pots for head gear. Someone on the perimeter yelled "sappers" and popped a hand flare. At least three VC sappers were visible, running crouched over toward the company CP. Doc fired on the nearest sapper as he passed my CP and the figure in black pajama-like uniform with blackened hands and face did a jackknife and lay where he fell. I fired into the face of another; his head disintegrated, and the body staggered a few steps and crumpled. Someone in the company CP wrestled with the third sapper, choked him into unconsciousness and didn't stop until the job was completely done.

Two more sappers were killed on the foxhole line, and gradually the mortar fire subsided as our artillery put out counter-battery fire at the mortar tube locations. Apparently, we had killed the last of the sappers, but the hand flare had destroyed the night vision of some of the troops who hadn't shielded their eyes.

Claymore blasts from the front indicated that either another MA had been tripped, or our close-in ambush had been sprung. The TA-1 phone rang and Sergeant McGuire whispered in the telephone. "One MA to my left front has just blown, and there is a lot of screaming and groaning in that direction. My immediate front is crawling with VC and I'm blowing the ambush now," he said. McGuire's ambush blew the heavy banks of claymores, and I heard the blasts of several grenades; then McGuire's patrol shouted the password and ran through the perimeter. The troops occupied their foxholes and McGuire ran over and dropped into my CP trench. I started the artillery DT's on the area he had left; SP4 Creighton was working the adjustments.

"Sir, the woods are crawling with VC. When that flare went back here, they knew exactly where the perimeter was located and they bore straight down on us. I don't know how many we got but there was all sorts of screaming and moaning out there. I have one man slightly wounded with a grenade frag; probably one of ours. I think it hit a tree and bounced back."

"OK Doc, look at him." I turned but Doc was not there.

"Sir, he's got casualties on the perimeter he's tending to," Alderman said.

"OK, Sergeant McGuire. He will get your man."

"Sir, I'll rejoin my squad," and he ran hunched over to his position.

I knew we had casualties from the mortar and rocket fire, but I had no idea how many. Doc Gill ran from hole to hole, doing all he could for them. Twice he ran back to a large bag of medical supplies in the CP trench. He tore dressings and morphine from the bag, using a red filtered flashlight.

"How many, Doc?" I asked.

"One serious, two pretty bad but they will make it, and several minor frag wounds. Baroni will probably die. The rest of them are capable of fighting. I have done all I can for Baroni, but he's in shock and has lost too much blood. I have an IV going now, but he is not long for this world, unless I miss my guess. I've given him morphine," he added. "That goddamned tree burst, just over Third Squad, did it."

"Stay with it, Doc. We can't possibly dust anyone off now, and it's going to get worse." As if to underline my last words, enemy small arms fire in heavy fusillades began to rake the perimeter. The troops still hadn't fired their claymores, and I noted that they were pretty cool under fire.

Creighton had the artillery going in, and he had called for "continuous fire." The 105 mm DT's were cracking in with ferocity, and the four deuce mortars were pounding for all they were worth. The troops fired back at muzzle flashes and an occasional exposed VC. It was 0330 hours, and I prayed for daylight, so that the air could get at them better.

Suddenly there was an enemy foray to our left front in the First Squad area, answered by the thunderous blasts of McGuire's claymores. The fire slackened considerably, but right behind the lull charged four VC, and they were into the perimeter line in a flash. One of the VC carried a pole charge and had started to swing it in a wide arc when the squad's M60 machine-gun cut him in half. The other three were killed by rifle fire, but the damned terrain was simply too close. After that incident, I passed the word to fix bayonets.

The artillery continued to pound, and our company 81 mm mortar was dropping rounds a mere fifty meters beyond the foxhole line. There was a lull in the fire and I heard Doc digging into his reserve supplies again.

"Sir, all of them are stable except Baroni, but he's managing to hang on. He might be able to make it under the best of conditions, but I'm not optimistic about his chances." He took a look at my arm. "How's it feel, Sir?"

"Stiff as hell but otherwise OK," I said.

"The others are OK for the time being. Smithers from Third Squad and Smithfield, Sergeant Fitzsimmons' RTO, should be dusted off later, but they can continue to function for the time being. Fitzsimmons has a piece of shrapnel in his left forearm, but it's not serious. If I had enough light I think I could get it without any trouble. It's not deep."

I looked at my watch. It was 0430 and someone was talking on the company net. I grabbed the handset from Alderman. The voice came through loud and clear. "Charlie Six, Charlie Six, this is Sidewinder Three-One, Sidewinder Three-One," the FAC was somewhere in the area!

"Sidewinder Three-One, Charlie Six, over," Sutton answered.

"Charlie Six, Sidewinder Three-One, will have a flight of jets on station in three zero minutes, understand you can use some help?"

"Roger that. It should be light enough to see when they arrive. I'll fire a hand flare up from the center of the perimeter. There are friendlies about forty meters in every direction from the flare. All troops outside our perimeter have returned and are now inside, over."

"Roger, artillery at this time, over?" the FAC asked.

"Roger, artillery going in all around the perimeter from firing positions east and southeast of us, over," Sutton answered.

"Roger, then we will be working from the southwest and breaking to the north. How thick is the canopy, over?"

"It's triple canopy, over."

"Then we will begin with five hundred pound bombs, over."

"This is Charlie Six, roger. When will the next flight arrive, over?"

"They will be here before the first guys finish, over."

"Good, keep'em coming. Negative further, out."

There was a hell of a commotion on the other side of the perimeter in Browning's sector. Small arms fire crackled into a roar, mixed with claymore and grenade blasts. The distinctive sound of AK-47's in great numbers could be heard and the incoming small arms fire blistered the perimeter and beyond. It was getting lighter and I caught myself playing spectator, when I had my own business to attend to. I turned back to our front, where the small arms fire had dwindled to a sporadic crackling. I could distinguish the nearest foxholes now and light was improving by the minute.

The "fizz-pop" of Sutton's marking flare sounded behind me and I could distinguish the roar of Sidewinder's jets as they made dry passes over the perimeter. Sidewinder fired a white smoke rocket after Sutton discussed their first strike, deciding to put it in front of Browning's platoon. The jets rolled in, pickling their high drag bombs, and the earth-shaking explosions were so close they seemed to be in the perimeter with us. Following their five hundred pound bombs, they strafed the area with 20 mm fire then dropped their napalm and departed.

By now it was full daylight and the second flight of jets began their bombing runs in front of my platoon. Between their passes I could hear absolutely no small arms fire. They brought the napalm in even closer than the high drag bombs and 20 mm, and the green jungle canopy crackled and burned and smoked and the heat literally singed eyebrows. The napalm forced the VC in closer to us and the perimeter line opened up with a fusillade of aimed rifle fire as the targets became lucrative. All the while the artillery pounded and whined and shifted back and forth through the trunks and tangles and bamboo, seeking out Charlie Cong, wherever he tried to hide.

A third set of jets put a strike into the south of the perimeter in front of Pendleton's platoon, and after their last passes a strange hush fell over the area as our artillery ceased momentarily, as if to get its breath. I heard Captain Sutton's voice behind me. He was talking on the battalion net, and I listened to his one sided transmission.

"Roger, I need small arms ammunition, grenades and 81 mm mortar HE, over," he said. He paused. "This is Charlie Six, roger, the fire has slackened, but it's not over by any means. Have the resupply ship make a high pass, and if he takes fire he shouldn't try to get in here, over." Pause, and "Roger, I have a one ship pad and can mark with smoke. Those dust offs should be here by the time the resupply ship finishes. Out."

Sutton called me on the land line. "How many do you have to be dusted off?" he asked.

"I have one urgent and two more ambulatory," I said.

"Well, as soon as that resupply bird clears the area start them this way; the two dust offs should be here by the time you get here with them. There are five from Third Platoon and four from Second Platoon. That's a total of twelve but I think they can handle that many," he said.

The "whup-whup-whup" of a slick beating in from the east broke the temporary stillness, and the artillery resumed firing as the HUEY approached. Captain Sutton's purple smoke had been identified by the pilot. Suddenly the enemy small arms fire crackled, and Sutton tried to warn the helicopter off on the company net. The pilot must have received the transmission, but he brought the ship on into the hole in the jungle and hovered down onto the jungle floor. Small arms ripped holes in the ship and a .51 caliber machine-gun opened up from the north, firing directly into the co-pilot's side of the cockpit. The ammunition was kicked and shoved onto the ground, and I saw a tall sergeant and a captain working feverishly to get it off. Both of them were hit repeatedly by small arms. The co-pilot's lifeless head hung and the pilot began to hover the wounded craft out of the crossfire. Somehow it managed to wobble over the trees and turned eastward. We later learned that it crashed and that the charred remains of everyone aboard were accounted for. The Captain had been the Battalion S-4, Captain Gillette, and the sergeant was Sergeant First Class Eglin who worked for Gillette. How in the hell they ended up on a company resupply mission was a mystery to me, but they and the helicopter pilot and co-pilot had known the danger they faced. Later, I learned that they had "rogered" Sutton's call to stop them from landing but came in anyway. I hoped that we could finish the thing so we could get our wounded out, but there was fight left in these bastards.

We continued with the air and artillery, and one air strike knocked out a total of three .51 caliber machine-guns, including the one which had fired on the resupply ship. By 1000 hours A and B Companies had started, and both of the other battalions of the brigade had been lifted into their LZ's west of us to spread out and block the enemy routes of withdrawl. At around noon A and B Companies arrived, and enemy fire had fizzled to nothing. We sent out patrols that met no resistance, so the dust offs were called in and the wounded evacuated. Baroni died in the first dust off, five minutes after it lifted out of the PZ. There were enemy dead everywhere, and small arms and crew-served weapons lay where they had fallen, unlike any battlefield scene any of the old-timers had ever encountered, because the VC were totally fanatic and very successful in recovering their weapons and casualties from the battlefield.

We resupplied after the patrols got back, and Doc Gill never ceased in his efforts to properly dress wounds and care for those who were wounded but not evacuated. I walked over to where he was picking a piece of shrapnel out of Sergeant Fitzsimmons' arm, and I noticed an aid bandage around his thigh on the outside of his bloody fatigue pants. On closer examination he had a clean bullet hole through the thigh and had never mentioned it or requested evacuation. I put him on the fourth dust off that arrived that afternoon.

CHAPTER 29

At 1600 hours a column of main force Viet Cong, reeling from the clobbering they had taken in the fight, ran head-on into a heavy ambush laid by 2nd Battalion, 28th Infantry, and left sixty-five dead members. Remnants of another VC unit ran into 1st Battalion, 16th Infantry and were soundly threshed, leaving twenty-six dead and five wounded, captured. Intelligence later confirmed the destruction of a reinforced VC regiment, in this fighting in the vicinity of Dau Tieng.

I was dog-tired, and my troops looked like they could use about two days of continuous sleep. They were in a mood of silent jubilation, however, fully realizing the enormity of the struggle we had been involved in.

At 1615 hours the brass began to arrive. Colonel Crowse was followed in by the brigade commander, the division commander, and finally General Westmoreland. The helicopters could land only one at a time, so they came in, dropped their passengers, lifted off, and circled off to the east.

Captain Sutton took the entire entourage on a tour of the battlefield, and the death and devastation was sobering, even to these old warriors. When they came back through the perimeter they passed my CP and halted at the company CP. A and B Companies had spread around the outside of our perimeter and set up, and Captain Sutton led the General around to meet the company. Sutton reported a total of seventy-nine members present. There were at least twelve wounded, with field dressings and bandages visible, as the General walked around the perimeter.

The General spoke to the troops and sincerely thanked them for their heroic and highly successful efforts, not only in this victory but throughout the operation. He shook hands with everyone then called for his helicopter. The division and brigade commanders had a few words of praise, then left the battalion to Colonel Crowse. Crowse promptly announced that C Company was being withdrawn to Lai Khe, and that every officer and man would get a three day in-country R and R to Saigon over the next week, fifty percent of the company at a time, and would have no perimeter responsibilities at Lai Khe for a week. The tired, haggard, gray faces listened in wide-eyed wonderment and managed a few weak smiles, and even a few small cheers.

We began extracting to Lai Khe immediately and were all on the ground on the airstrip before dark. We occupied our company area at Lai Khe, being careful to stay out of the way of 2nd Battalion, 2nd Infantry, which was responsible for the defense of Lai Khe for as long as the operation continued.

First-Sergeant Long checked with battalion rear and picked up two sacks of mail for C Company. Fitzsimmons picked up the platoon mail, but there was nothing for me. I mailed a letter I had written in the field, but couldn't understand why at least one letter hadn't caught up with me by now.

The troops went to the shower point, put on fresh fatigues and headed for the "Red Dog Saloon," the battalion club down the road toward battalion headquarters. I went to the brigade clearing station, where they probed a piece of mortar shrapnel out of my upper arm. It hurt like hell; worse than when I had been wounded. The thin, balding doctor who did it was totally impersonal about the whole thing, as if he were dealing with an inanimate object on an assembly line, or a side of beef. I didn't want the son-of-a-bitch to kiss me, but he could have been professional enough to at least smile a couple of times. He gave me some pills to take and painted and dressed the thing. I was glad I didn't have anything more serious, with that impersonal bastard on duty.

"I guess you'll get the Purple Heart for this minor wound," he said, his coldly impersonal blue eyes unsmiling and his thin lips in a straight line.

"Yeah, and I guess you'll get one when I break your snotty nose," I said, and I stood up preparing to do just that. He retreated rapidly through the tent fly, and I never saw him again.

I left the clearing station, returned to the company area and took a bath, using the Australian shower bucket. I dressed in my clean jungle fatigues and walked up the road to the Red Dog Saloon. The First Platoon troops were glad to see me. They were clustered at two tables on the far side of the room, and ushered me to a seat at the head of the table. The other platoons had claimed a couple of tables each, and the place was full. Sergeant Fitzsimmons sat beside me, and Sergeant McGuire was on my left.

"Sir, we decked them mutha fuckas, didn't we?" PFC Howard yelled down the table.

"Like they ain't never been decked before!" I yelled. The troops yelled and cheered like crazy. Crowse is brilliant, I thought. Napoleon had accomplished the same thing with a few pieces of colored ribbon, but the modern day American soldier thrives on free time, his time off from the rigors of whatever.

"Sir, tell us about shooting that sapper!" Sergeant Rozier yelled.

"Yeah, we heard you hit him between the eyes and his head disintegrated!" another troop yelled.

"No, the lieutenant hit him and his dick string flew up through the cavity where his head had been!" another yelled. Everyone laughed, but the best answer I could muster was a broad smile.

We sucked beer down like a camel drinks water. In a short time I could feel the effects of the alcohol.

"Sir, I'm gonna screw my liver loose down there in Saigon!" SP4 Hale yelled at me. Everyone laughed, and then a long discussion ensued about whether your liver had anything to do with screwing.

"Hell, that ain't what your goddamn liver is for!" yelled SP4 Silva.

"Well what the hell's it for?" asked Hale.

"It's a solid brass plug between your gut and your asshole, like the plug between a TV anchorman's ears!" yelled McGuire. Everyone died laughing, and the barmaid brought another round. Fitzsimmons started to recite lines from Kipling's "Gunga Din."

"Man, PSG (Platoon Sergeant) knows some shit, don't he? What battalion was that mufucker Gunga Din in, PSG?" Howard had a beer in each hand and was trying to drink from both cans. His olive drab T-shirt was making a vain attempt to absorb the spillage.

"PSG Fitzsimmons, tell us about 'em hanging Danny Deever," yelled Hale.

"What's the price of corn and hogs, you silly shit?" Silva sloshed beer on his bosom buddy Hale.

I decided it was time to beat a strategic retreat to the bar before I was summarily drowned in beer. I joined Browning there.

"Here's to you, Jimbo!" He pushed a Budweiser at me and raised his.

"And here's to you, my man!"

"Man, that was some kind of ass kicking!" he said.

"Yeah. Are all of them like that?"

"No. Hell, I've never seen anything like that!"

"Captain Sutton is one hell of a commander, huh?"

"He's out of this world. Can you imagine taking a skinny rifle company, setting us down on top of the better part of three VC main force regiments, and not only surviving, but pretty well kicking their ass in the process?"

"It's totally uncanny the way he moved us around. It's easy to understand that you move after helicopters visit your area, but man, that guy has a sixth sense about when to jerk up and move."

"Sure as hell does. You and I can learn a bunch from that guy," he said. The alcohol had had it's effect, and we were talking "troop jargon." We two and Lieutenant Lowell Redd, were going to Saigon the following morning with a contingent of troops. They were "hooking" us down on a CH-47 helicopter. I guess trucks down "thunder road" would have been OK, but after our battle against that kind of odds, it wouldn't go down well to have the "mad bomber" knock us out on the way to R and R.

We left early and walked back through the rubber trees to the company area. I dropped off at my CP and said good night. Browning was a hell of a fine officer, and I was glad I had him on my side. In some ways he reminded me of Nolan Broyles. I slept the sleep of the dead that night.

At 0900 hours the next morning the hook took off for Saigon with Browning, Redd, me, and thirty troops. It seemed we had barely lifted off when we sat down at Tan Son Nhut. There was a bus there that took the troops to the Ambassador Hotel where they could check their weapons in and find almost anything else they were looking for, which in plain language meant a bottle and a woman. There was plenty of both to go around.

Browning, Redd and I were staying at the North Pole BOQ in Cholon. Redd's buddy, who worked in Saigon, put us up there in a couple of empty rooms whose occupants were on R and R. We checked our weapons in and went upstairs to our rooms.

"Hot water, sheets, and the whole bit!" Browning yelled.

"Yeah, and I'm taking a hot bath the first thing!"

I could actually still see the sweat and grime of the jungle running off of me. My arm was stiff and sore, but I wrapped the wound in a sheet of plastic wrap they had given me. I was taking the pills they had given me, so I wasn't too worried about infection.

After bathing, we dressed and walked down into the streets of Cholon. Quite a large Chinese population resided here, and there were Chinese restaurants here and there. After a while we took a cab to the Ambassador Hotel to see what sort of place the troops were staying in. We bumped into Sergeant McGuire, already half looped, with a slinky looking Vietnamese girl practically wrapped around him.

"Hey sir, this is a cousin of mine! We last saw each other at a family reunion in Peoria five years ago!" he yelled.

"Sure McGuire, I can see the family likeness, but aren't you a little nervous about incest?" I laughed.

"Hell, I ain't worried about any of them social diseases!" he said, holding up a box of condoms.

"Don't you dudes be late for that helicopter three days from now," I said as we walked up the steps to the bar.

"Sho nuff, Lieutenant, we ain't forgetting about that!" he yelled.

It was too early but we drank anyway. It really didn't go down very well, but after another everything was OK.

"Where's your home, Lowell?" Browning asked.

"I'm from Dallas. How about you two?"

"I'm from Sevierville, Tennessee, and Worthington's from Canton, North Carolina," he said.

"Wow, sounds like the two hubs of commerce and industry in the east!" Redd laughed.

"What the hell has Dallas got other than bullshitting Texans?" Browning asked.

"Yeah, the only Texans worth a damn died at the Alamo, and most of them were from Tennessee and North Carolina!" I said.

"Hey, whoa! What's this ganging up shit? I should have known better than to go drinking with two grunts from the Smoky Mountains!" he laughed.

"Good old Lowell. You sure smoked their hubcaps out there yesterday," I said.

"Yeah, were you really in control of all that artillery out there? Man you sure were ripping their T-shirts!" Browning laughed.

"The artillery lends dignity to what would otherwise be a vulgar brawl!" yelled Redd, raising his beer in a toast. We all three knew that without artillery in the fight, we wouldn't be sitting here now.

Sometime that afternoon we ordered a hamburger and stumbled out of the place and started making the bars of Tu Do Street. We were sitting in booths with hostesses in one bar, buying them "Saigon tea," sweetened water with no alcohol, when I spotted a tall Chinese hostess with large breasts at the bar. I went over and bought her a drink and ended up upstairs in bed with her. Browning and Redd had already left with two other hostesses.

"Me virgin! Only make love two times before," she said.

"Yeah, to the First Cav and the First Division," I said. "But what the hell. It belongs to you."

She hadn't understood a word I said, and I didn't give a damn about conversation anyway. I left in a couple of hours and made my way back over to Tan Son Nhut where we had landed. They had a nice officers club, and I sat there at the bar and shot the breeze with a couple of pilots until the place closed. Then I caught a cab back to the North Pole BOQ, took a hot shower and went to sleep between those heavenly white sheets.

The next morning I dragged Redd and Browning out of bed and we went over to Tan Son Nhut and had breakfast at the officers club. We toured Saigon that day and ended up at the Caravelle Hotel that afternoon. I couldn't believe how well these troops had it in Saigon. We had a steak in the Caravelle that night that would equal anything we could buy at an officers club in the States. After that we drank and talked. I left around 2200, made it back to Cholon and racked out. I heard them come in around 0100.

The last day in Saigon was spent much like the first. I ended up drunk in some whore's bed and stumbled back to the BOQ late; I didn't bother to check my watch and probably couldn't have read it anyway.

Next morning we hooked out of Tan Son Nhut back to Lai Khe, and the rest of the company began their three day break, hooking to Saigon on the CH-47 that brought us up.

CHAPTER 30

We killed time cleaning gear and orienting new replacements over the next three days. The fourth day the rest of the battalion closed into Lai Khe on foot, our troops hooked in from Saigon, and the battalion was once again in one piece.

The next three weeks we worked our AO (area of operations) in front of the Lai Khe perimeter out to thirty kilometers, and sometimes beyond, patrolling and ambushing day and night. Twice we secured a segment of Highway 13 from Ben Cat, which was immediately south of Lai Khe, as far south as the battalion could extend. Other elements secured other segments of the highway until it was secured all the way to Saigon; then resupply convoys moved safely up the road to Lai Khe, offloaded, and returned to Saigon. The ammunition of all types, both mogas and diesel, medical supplies, repair parts, new weapons, vehicles, clothing, food, drink, etc, had to be kept flowing, to keep the brigade and its attached units operating. I often wondered at the incredible tonnage of supplies and equipment it took to keep a U.S. unit operating. And Victor Charlie (enemy VC) made it on a handful of rice, some nookmam (rotting fish oil), a few grenades, a rifle, and a few cartridges. His shoes were made from discarded automobile tires and inner tubes; the former provided the sole, and the latter the straps to hold them on his feet. He had no socks. Our troops called the sandals "Hanoi racing slicks." His pants and shirt were usually black Vietnamese peasant garb which had been repaired over and over again until they were one solid patch. If he had headgear it was the conical rice straw hat. He fought a pretty good war with those paltry furnishings. Our supplies came from halfway around the world, and his from next door.

The North Vietnamese Army, NVA, Charlie's (the VC) northern cousins, were much like us, in that they were soldiers in uniform with standard equipment and uniforms. The NVA didn't understand Charlie any better than we did. They hated to operate down in the flat lands because that was Charlie's territory, and Charlie's booby traps killed NVA as easily as they killed the "Giac Mi," American soldiers. Charlie saw the NVA as foreigners, and in his opinion he had been fighting a successful war without these fancy dans with their funny accents, who walked in with their superior attitude and tried to dictate the action. The VC were armed with various weapons, but most prominent among them were the U.S. M1 rifle, the U.S. M1 and M2 carbines, the U.S. BAR (Browning Automatic Rifle), and the French MAS36. After those, there were various others to include Chicom submachine-guns, Russian AK47's, and the Russian SKS, but the VC usually did not have the luxury of an AK47. These VC were generally hamlet guerrillas, village guerrillas, and local force guerrillas.

Then there were main force VC units or the elite of the guerrilla army. They were well organized, thoroughly experienced, much better equipped than other VC units, and probably, unit for unit, better soldiers than their NVA counterparts. In and around our area of operations the main force regiments were the Q271, Q272, Q273, and Q274, as well as a highly touted VC battalion known as the Phu Loi Battalion. Depending on which tent you happened to pop into at battalion or brigade you might see that unit plotted in a dozen different places on that many different intelligence maps. The intelligence people cloaked the Phu Loi Battalion in an aura of mystery, and they became legendary in III Corps. I always wondered how much credit that unit had been given when it probably hadn't been anywhere near that particular battle. Sometimes I even wondered if there really was a Phu Loi Battalion or if it had been conjured up by frustrated intelligence officers, to cover their various sins and errors in "order of battle." The troops made jokes about the Phu Loi Battalion. They would point to some grubby sixty year old ragpicker in the streets of Lai Khe and announce that he was a member of the elite Phu Loi Battalion Reconnaissance Platoon. That drew a few chuckles.

One hot, dusty afternoon the company trudged back in through the perimeter and standing there by the wire was a familiar figure. I was further back down the column but the troops in front of me were yelling and pummeling the guy and slapping him on the back. He saluted as I walked up.

"Sir, Sergeant Bigwitch returning to duty."

"Bigwitch! How are you? Are you completely OK?" I asked.

"Sir, you know you can't kill a man from the Smoky Mountains!" he laughed.

"I'll buy you a beer over at the Red Dog tonight," I told him.

That night we had a homecoming. One of our own was back. Howard, Larson, Dillard, two more of the old guys and four new replacements were gathered around Bigwitch and Fitzsimmons, and I sat across the table from him.

"How were those nurses down there at 93rd Evac?" I asked.

Bigwitch grinned. "There was one on the night shift who was great!" he said. "She gave special therapy for my type of wound!"

The troops roared. "How long was you gone?" yelled Howard. "There will probably be more than ten little Indians running around down there at Binh Hoa!"

"Bigwitch was trying to give those nurses a Cherokee history lesson." Larson said, "Lesson three was how he was getting even by screwing the white man!" Larson was a rangy kid from Calhoun, Georgia, and he was one of Bigwitch's greatest admirers.

"Hey Larson, you people from Calhoun are living on the Cherokee capitol and we're gonna take it back!" Bigwitch countered.

"Hey Larson, you ass kisser. Do you think if you kiss a lifer's ass every day you'll get promoted? What's Bigwitch gonna do for you?" P.F.C. Rene Sibler, recently reduced from Sergeant to Private First Class for A.W.O.L. (absent without official leave), had found an audience.

Larson lunged across the table and hit Sibler squarely in the mouth, knocking him backwards over the next table. Sibler grabbed a metal folding chair as he got up and brought it down with a smashing blow to the top of Larson's head. As he raised the chair to deliver the coup de grace Chavez delivered a roundhouse blow to his nose and the blood gushed as he fell backwards, partially supporting himself on the table. Chavez followed with a powerful right uppercut to the stomach, and Sibler rolled groaning to the floor. Gill and Mason picked Sibler up and half dragged, half carried him out of the club. Larson got up and took his seat again as if nothing had happened. We drank a beer toast to Bigwitch, who appeared to have hardly noticed the fisticuffs.

Bigwitch, the quiet one, was glad to be back, and he wasn't so quiet tonight. We drank until around 2000 and made it back to the area. Weapons Platoon had filled in for us, briefly, on the perimeter while we welcomed Bigwitch back. That meant we owed them one, but we would pay them back by helping them with their next ammo detail. It was good to have Bigwitch back; he was a hell of a squad leader.

Next morning we slipped through the wire at 0400 hours and separated into four elements, consisting of the three squads and a fourth comprised of the platoon headquarters patrol, which I led. With me were Fitzsimmons and his new RTO, Bentley, SP4 Hale from First Squad, Alderman, Creighton, and Doc Gill's replacement, PFC Haygood.

Sergeant McGuire was establishing a daytime ambush on a prominent trail junction out ten kilometers from the perimeter near our northern company boundary. Bigwitch's ambush was to be fifteen kilometers out and further south than McGuire's, and Rozier was to conduct a moving patrol, well south of Bigwitch's ambush, but going out about twelve kilometers then circling north and returning to the perimeter. My patrol's mission was to start southwest, head east, and cross Highway 13 between Ben Cat and Lai Khe, passing into and through 1st Battalion, 16th Infantry's area and turning south out of their AO into no man's land southeast of Ben Cat and north of Highway 13. There we were to set up in the woods about three hundred meters north of Highway 13, adjacent to a favorite VC tax collection point on the highway. This had been coordinated with 1st of the

16th before hand. Intelligence had asked battalion to conduct this mission directed at VC infrastructure.

Going was good, and we reached our destination and spread out in the cover of the woods and waited. I put out security to our rear, and Hale set his M60 machine-gun up on the tripod and laid it on the spot on the road where the tax collectors had been stopping civilian buses, trucks, and lambretas and forcing the people on these conveyances to pay tax. We were well above the road, looking down on it, and from our position to the road the ground dipped, so that to reach the road a man would have to go down and then back up again. There was only sparse brush between us and the road, however.

There wasn't a cloud in the sky; the day was hot and humid and not a breeze stirred. We were in the morning hours prior to the dead of the day, 1100 to 1400 hours, which the Vietnamese called "pok" time. No Vietnamese in his right mind, civilian, VC, or ARVN (Army of Vietnam or friendlies), moved during pok time. That was the time to string hammocks up between trees and sleep. I looked at the patrol, and we were well camouflaged. The silent, motionless waiting had to be done perfectly now, for any movement would surely be spotted in the clear light of day. We waited. Noon came and went, and my stomach growled because a can of C-rations at 0330 that morning was all I had eaten. The troops were the same.

The traffic on the highway moved along at a fairly brisk pace. At around 1430 hours the wind began to stir and I was glad for even this tiny respite from the heat. I looked over at Hale, lying behind his gun with the feet of the tripod dug into the clay. The sweat was dripping off his nose onto the traversing and elevating (T and E), mechanism of the machine-gun. Hale was a good machine-gunner, and his ammunition was coiled in layers in the box made to carry it, rather than crossed in bandoleers over his chest Poncho Villa style. No professional would carry machine-gun ammunition that way because the first time he was fired on and had to hit the ground, mud, dirt, and debris stuck on the rounds and lodged in the links that held the belt together. When he tries to feed that through the gun it jams, and the unit is without the major instrument of its firepower.

At around 1500 hours I saw movement in a cluster of hooches on the far side of the highway. I eased my binoculars up and looked. Five VC came up the bank to the road from the cluster of hooches and set up a portable table for one of their members who sat down and opened a ledger. Two of the VC stood beside the table holding their carbines at a loose "port arms." One of the other two went down the road about twenty meters from the table, and the other took his position up the road, about twenty meters. They began to stop traffic and collect "taxes."

The traffic was heavy, but after an hour or so it began to thin out and we made our move. Hale was to cover us as we went down into the dip and up towards the highway. When they tried to flee or to open fire on us, he was to hose them down with the M60, and we would take care of whatever was left over. We slipped forward and into the dip, leaving Haygood, with Hale to cover his back. The VC had stopped a charcoal hauling truck, bound for Saigon, and were taking piaster (South Vietnamese money) notes from the driver. The driver cranked the truck engine and pulled out for Saigon. At that particular moment the highway was clear for a couple of hundred meters in each direction. Two little girls were playing in front of one of the hooches across the road. They must have been four or five years old.

We went into the bottom of the dip, and one of the VC yelled out, having spotted one of us. He fired off a wild burst over our heads, and Hale opened up with his M60. We ran up the embankment toward the road as Hale raked a stream of 7.62 mm rounds over that segment of road. As I topped the embankment it was clear that the three VC at the collection table had done their last good deed for the IRS. The tax collector's pith helmet was split like an eggshell, dyed gold and vermillion by blood, flesh, and brain. His two guardian angels had absorbed more 7.62 rounds than they could stand up under and had buckled and sprawled in the white clay. I ran across the road and caught just a glimpse of one of the other two as he disappeared around the hooches and headed toward the woods. I threw my rifle to my shoulder and then slowly lowered it as the two children ran across the packed dirt in front of the hooches.

We policed up three weapons, all old U.S. M1 carbines, several hand grenades, the tax records, some documents, pocket litter, and a stack of piaster notes. We crossed back to Hale and Haygood and moved back towards Lai Khe to the 1st of the 16th perimeter. There we were challenged, responded properly, and then entered between two bunkers and went up to the company CP behind the bunker line. We used the field telephone and called company for a truck. Shortly we were on the deuce and a half headed back to the company area. We climbed off the truck and were debriefed at Sutton's CP with a battalion S2 representative and a division intelligence spook there to take notes. I turned in everything but the money, which I gave to Fitzsimmons to use for the next platoon party. Our other three patrols had made no contact. I received a call the next day from brigade S2 inquiring about the money, and I explained how the two VC who escaped had taken it with them.

"Why let some REMF (Rear Echelon Mother Fucker) at brigade or division take the money when the troops that risked their ass for it could use it for a platoon party?" I thought.

CHAPTER 31

Fall came on, and we could hardly tell it except that the Vietnamese were harvesting rice again. In some places they actually got three crops annually off the fertile ground in this land of abundant sunshine, heat, and rain. Vietnam without war would have been a paradise, but a frog without warts is a rare animal. They had been fighting here forever, and I couldn't imagine that they would stop until perhaps the peals of Gabriel's trumpet echoed down the universe. Most of the young men and women in Vietnam had never gone through one entire week in their lives without hearing the crackle of small arms fire or the thumping explosions of grenades and mortars. It was a way of life to them. To see a neighbor sprawled dead across the paddy dike, or on the shoulder of the road, with bullet holes tattooed across his body was a normal event. They simply accepted it with perhaps a "sin loi" or an unemotional "sorry about that."

The U.S. troops soon became hardened; apathetic to death and the ever present danger from every direction, just like the Vietnamese. I will never forget the twisted smile on a seventeen year old American soldier's face, who had beaten the brush as an Infantryman for eleven months and seen his share of hell, when we broke into a stucco hooch that we had just hand grenaded and encountered the incredibly torn body of a dead VC who had literally been splattered all over the room. "Sir, this son-of-a-bitch needs a band-aid," he announced. This was a boy become a man, cynical and old before his time. The longer they stayed in the field the more calloused they became. They could move like animals, their instincts became super sharp, and they developed a sixth sense about when and where we would meet the enemy.

If you ever watched a veteran rifle company with a year of combat under its belt it was a thing to behold: after hundreds of miles of walking in the hellish heat, days on end of subsisting on C-rations and dozens of sleepless nights waiting in ambush, or chilled and wet from the cold soaking rain. If you ever saw them form up and move out, marching in formation, then you knew it was a thing of wonder and grim beauty. Lean as greyhounds, hollow cheeked, with large piercing eyes sunken in bony sockets, nostrils flared and efficiently feeding oxygen to strong lungs; accustomed to sprinting, walking great distances for extended periods of time, and generally carrying a load unnatural for modern man when they stepped out, their strides were long and efficient; flowing strides produced by lean strong legs with wiry achilles tendons and long steel-like sinews. God and his handmaiden nature prepared a man for the rigors of war, for the fear, the endurance required to survive through struggle, hunger, thirst, and wounds, and the inhuman and abnormal strain on both mind and body.

The Infantryman in Vietnam coped. He had no other choice. If he chose to drop out on the trail he was picked up by the VC and usually tortured to death and left hanging in a bush with his testicles cut out and stuffed in his mouth. On one operation, when we were securing the engineers as they built a critical road link east of Ben

Cat, a cook in one of their units left the perimeter on a bicycle in the daytime and pedaled into Ben Cat to see his girlfriend. That night he attempted to return on his bicycle over the unsecured section of road between Ben Cat and the perimeter. He was captured by the VC and tortured to death. When we found him he was naked and had long gashes on his thighs and other parts of his body where the VC had opened the cuts with a knife and then pulled barbed wire back and forth through the cuts until he finally died. I hoped that he died quickly but the extent of the torture indicated that he did not.

Such was life and death in "the promised land" as Lieutenant Browning cynically called it. He and I drank a beer together and commiserated when things got really bad.

I had received one letter from Kim about three weeks after I arrived at Lai Khe. It was a short note that talked mostly about the weather. I hadn't received another letter, and it was the middle of October. Something was wrong that I didn't understand, and I didn't know what to do about it. I continued to write but only once every couple of weeks.

Late October came and we ambushed, cordoned, searched and destroyed, combat assaulted in helicopters, and fought the war. Near the end of October I decided to take my R and R around Christmas time and see what had happened to Kim. I was disappointed, but I still hoped that there was some logical explanation for her not writing. I had received a letter from Tom McCarter, indicating that he would arrive in Vietnam near the end of October, after a short leave. I had written him where I was assigned, so if by some stroke of luck he would get assigned to the brigade at Lai Khe maybe he could shed some light on what had happened to Kim. I knew that those were two big maybes.

One afternoon we came back through the wire late and I got a call on the land line at my CP. I could hardly hear the voice on the other end, so I sprinted over to the company switchboard to see if I could hear a little better there. It was Tom McCarter at 2nd Battalion, 28th Infantry, where he had managed to get himself assigned. We arranged to meet in front of brigade headquarters, and I told Captain Sutton where I would be that evening and left Fitzsimmons in charge.

I walked up the dusty red road through the rubber trees and turned right at the crossroads near 2nd of the 28th Headquarters and walked past their S4 tent, past their aid station to the large pink quadrangle. The lights were on in the building and staff officers hurried back and forth. I waited, and in five minutes a familiar figure strode across from the dirt road with a broad boyish grin on his face.

"You took your sweet time getting here!" I grabbed him in a bear hug, then we stepped back and shook hands.

"See you lost your baby fat. Ain't they feeding you over in the Wild Cats?" he laughed.

"Come on, times a wasting. Let's get over to the Brigade Club and have a beer!" I laughed.

We walked down the road I had just come up, passed the 2nd of the 28th Headquarters and on down the road to the west until we came to the two story house that had been transformed into an officers club. It was actually a beautiful house, totally incongruous to the combat constructions and sandbagged bunkers around it. The walls were white and the ceiling high, with a large ceiling fan which didn't work. Steep spiral stairs led to the second floor where there was a bathroom and a couple of bedrooms, with white sheets on the beds. How the hell this had survived and what it was doing there I couldn't understand, but the thought struck me that in the not too distant future, Charlie would level it with mortar fire. Just so it didn't happen tonight.

"Tell me about Korea, Tom. Is it still there?"

"It is indeed, but nothing has changed since you left. We were pretty much on the bottom of the heap, as battalions go, when I left. I came away OK, since Ricksley had his mind on other things and didn't get his licks on me for the rifle range incident or the Aviation club fracas." He looked quickly at me when he mentioned Ricksley.

"Have you seen Kim since I left?"

"Once or twice briefly. Say who's your battalion commander and what the hell do you do for a living?" he changed the subject, too quickly.

"Tom, let's have it. What's going on with Kim?" I was tense.

"James, I hadn't meant to tell you right away, and I guess there never will be a good time to do it, so I'll tell you now. She's been seeing Ricksley." The shock hit me like a bucket of ice water in the face. A concussion grenade would not have stunned me more. I sat shocked, silent. Tom's face couldn't hide the sympathy and hurt he felt.

I caught my breath. "Tom, tell me about it." I could hardly hear my own voice, and my breath came irregularly, catching in my throat. For some reason that day on the Han Tan River came back to me in sharp clear images, and I saw Kim huddled by the fire, trying to stay warm on our crazy mid-winter picnic.

"There's not much to say, James. One weekend Ricksley went to Seoul, and the following Saturday he and Kim walked into the club together. He had her back on one other occasion when there was a Korean show in the club. He missed two commander's availability checks and got his ass chewed by the commanding general. He was usually around in the evenings during the week, but gone on weekends." Tom took a deep breath, sat back in the straight backed chair and stared out the window in the direction of the perimeter. His blue eyes were moist; it had been difficult for him.

"Well, to hell with it all. To hell with her and to hell with Ricksley," I said. "Drink up! Let's have another beer. Do you have any dice in this French cathouse?" I yelled at the bartender. He brought two Buds and the leather dice cup and we played "horse" for the round. Tom won.

"Not my day, Tom," I attempted to laugh, but nothing came out except a slight rasp. "Well, as the troops say 'Sin Loi, motherfucker, sorry about that.' Tom, here's to the best friend I've ever had." We drank up.

"I'd better get back over to the company."

"James, I'm in C Company in the 28th, and my platoon area joins 1st of the 202nd; I guess it's your C Company."

"Yes, in fact I've seen that platoon CP area. I'll drop over tomorrow night."

"OK, James."

We walked back up to the crossroads, shook hands and left in opposite directions. My God, how empty, hopeless, and beaten. And that son-of-a-bitch Ricksley. It could have been anybody else, and it wouldn't have been quite the same. What happened to Kim? Why the change? Had it all been a farce, just play acting? Had we really had nothing at all? No, I couldn't believe that. Kim loved me or at least she had loved me; I was sure of it. Well to hell with it! Gone. Not worth worrying about. Don't mean a thing. Sin Loi.

I finally fell asleep an hour before daylight, and the watch awakened me just as the glowing red clouds in the half light of morning began to wax lighter in color. Another day dawned in the promised land.

CHAPTER 32

In mid-November we combat assaulted into an area six kilometers north of Lai Khe after two false preps and false insertions. The helicopters took fire going into the LZ and coming out. We pushed into the rubber trees north of the LZ and immediately came under heavy small arms fire from the north and east.

The battalion sized operation called for A Company to move up Highway 13 on foot after daylight and turn west between Ap Ben Dong So and Bau Bang, angling toward Lo Ke, a small cluster of buildings on the map that had once been the rubber plantation's French overseer's dwelling. After A Company turned off the highway and moved a few hundred meters, they were to hold up for thirty minutes, then continue in the same direction. Intelligence had indicated that a VC regiment had been located the night before, in the direction of Lo Ke. The plan was to move A Company up the highway, in broad daylight, where they were sure to be seen and reported to the VC regiment. The regiment would probably poise for action, and when A Company left the highway and began moving west it was likely that the VC would attempt to ambush them one or two kilometers west. After A Company took the thirty minutes halt, giving the VC time to shift around to face them in preparation for the ambush, B and C Companies would combat assault into Lo Ke after false insertions north of Lo Ke. The false insertions were done in the hope that the VC would reorient part of their forces to face the fake heliborne threat from the north, and thus expose their rear to B and C Companies as they were landed at Lo Ke.

As C company cleared the LZ we went on line facing north and B Company went on line side by side C Company and to our right. Our Third Platoon on the west flank faced west, closing the flank. Colonel Crowse called for the preplanned artillery fires north, northwest, and northeast of us, and the gunships began to work the VC regiment over with rockets, 40 mm, and miniguns. Air arrived and the jets began passes, dropping five hundred pound bombs, followed by napalm passes, then CBU (cluster bomblet unit) passes, and then strafing over the whole area. A Company eased forward on line from the east and almost immediately made contact, not in the column that the VC expected but in a line of fighting riflemen that stretched out wider than the mouth of the horseshoe ambush the VC would have had them enter. Still, the VC regiment was a battle hardened veteran unit of main force guerrillas that weren't about to be pushed over by a battalion without a fight.

I looked to my front; the smoke and fire was intense, and it was difficult to see the enemy. I started to pick up the muzzle flashes, and finally the picture became clear, and the lines of muzzle flashes came from ground level. It was obvious that the enemy was firing from a trench that ran east-west, about three hundred meters to our north. I crawled across to Captain Sutton and explained the situation as I saw it. Browning's platoon and mine were facing north, returning the enemy fire, along with B Company on our right. Lieutenant Pendleton's platoon was facing west, stretched on a line north and south, enfiladed to the frontal fire of the VC regiment, and he was taking casualties. Sutton understood the problem immediately; as I talked he requested more air, specifically napalm. In addition, he called to Pendleton to work his platoon south, out of the fire. I didn't know what he had in mind, but it became clear when he again called Pendleton and told him to move southwest, then north and then east into the flank of the VC unit.

"When you have flanked them get those machine-guns up there and smoke their ass. If you can enfilade that trench we will be in great shape. Don't move north until the air is finished. By that time you should have a turkey shoot." I had my doubts about Pendleton's ability to comprehend what Sutton had told him, much less carry it out.

We waited, trading fire with a tough unit, superior in size to ours. I heard the jets roaring in the near distance and the radio crackled.

"Sidewinder Three-One this is Charlie Six, forward elements marking with smoke, over," Sutton said.

"Roger, got green," Sidewinder Three-One came back.

"Roger, go to work on 'em. They're about three hundred meters north of the green smoke, spread east to west in a trench. Recommend napalm, over," Sutton said.

"Roger, firing marker now, over." He fired a white smoke rocket almost directly into the trench where the VC were.

"This is Charlie Six, that's perfect, make some crispy critters, over," Sutton told him.

"Roger, rollin in, out."

The jets pickled napalm canisters and plastered the area. A few VC attempted to flee and the M60's hammered them down. The jets passed until their ordnance was expended, and the fire from the trench had slackened to a trickle. Sutton had Pendleton move around to the flank of the trench and bring it under fire. It was the best thing that Pendleton would ever do in his life, and he did it perfectly. When Sutton called to warn him that the rest of the company was assaulting the trench, the platoon-sergeant answered that Pendleton was hit badly.

"Can he make it?" Sutton asked.

"No way. He's KHA now. Out."

We charged the trench and orange flashes and pops from the enemy line continued, although greatly diminished. I ran like hell for a couple of muzzle flashes that I could, see, firing on the run, but I couldn't get a well aimed shot off. Suddenly I felt something slam into my left shoulder, and I was thrown onto my back. I got to my feet only to get slammed in the area of my collar bone on the right side. I reached up to see what had happened to me and the blood was pouring freely from both wounds. When I attempted to rise, a hand grenade blast put the lights out completely, and I was soaring, soaring in an individual flight, in a device developed by the army, which enabled me to fly by flapping my arms and guiding my body by instinct. I felt the primordial urge and ability to fly and somehow I sensed that once the creatures that I was descended from may have flown, or at least a flicker of the God given ability to fly coursed through the human sinews and bone and brain. I was slipping away and I tried to stop. I kept telling myself that I had to survive, and I knew in that instant that it was really up to me. I could give it up and sleep the deep long sleep of eternity, or struggle and live on. My mind told me to struggle and my body said give it up, give it up, let it go, float away into everlasting peace and painless repose where all the cares of the world are a thing of the happily forgotten, dead past. I struggled and struggled, but I began to plunge into a long black tunnel, and I was so very, very tired. Eventually the darkness completely closed in. I thought I was probably dead, and that at long last the great mystery of the hereafter would now be revealed to me. Any religious questions I had ever had would be answered. Then I slept the deep dark sleep of eternity in my mind, and there were wires and plastic tubes and needles, and hands cool and hurried, and steel and snipping and cutting and clamping and bags of clear liquid and dark red and more blackness.

Voices became distinct. "There is shrapnel pressing here, and he is stable so we can evacuate him to Japan," and I slipped back into my dreams.

There was more soaring. I again flew through the clouds and then low through the wires of the power lines and I worried about a "wire strike" that I had heard the helicopter pilots speak of, with fear and dread in their voices. Then there were more wires and needles and tubes and deep black sleep. After an eternity the cold blast engulfed me. I thought that maybe I was in Dante's hell, on a ring where I would be perpetually frozen for the cold, unfeeling sins I had committed on earth.

The voices I heard were speaking Japanese, and I was at once aware that I had lost my rifle. I tried to feel around for it, but there was pain as I tried to stretch out my arms. I opened my eyes and I was in a white room in a bed with white sheets. Two Japanese maids were cleaning the room. I could feel that I was bandaged like a mummy, and there were at least three tubes inserted into me. The place smelled of alcohol, and I could see through the door into the hall outside. I saw green uniformed attendants, nurses, and doctors passing back and forth. Three more patients occupied beds in the room, two in the rear near the window and one opposite me, on the other side of the entrance.

"What hospital is this?" I asked one of the Japanese cleaning ladies. She smiled broadly, but did not understand.

"Kono byoin no namaewa nandeska?" I asked in the best Japanese I could manage.

The two ladies giggled in surprise and pleasure, and after that I couldn't shut them up. I learned that this was a general hospital at Camp Zama, Japan, and that I had been there a week. They also told me to lie very still and not to move or I would disturb the flow of fluids. I could see very well now, but I knew that my head was heavily bandaged. As if in answer to my thoughts one of the Japanese ladies held up a mirror, and I saw that my head was completely bandaged, both arms were slung across my chest, and my left shoulder was bandaged heavily as was the area of my collar bone on the right side.

The Japanese maids wore name tags indicating that they were "Yamada" and "Suzuki." They left the room, and I looked around at the other patients. All three had intravenous fluids dripping into them, and were heavily bandaged. I heard a radio playing music in English somewhere down the hall. It was set on FEN, the Far East Network, an American station run by the military in Tokyo.

I wasn't in pain but I was weak. I slept day and night; time had no meaning, and soon I lost track of the date. I had no idea of, nor cared to know, what month it was until FEN began playing Christmas music. Then they pulled the tubes out of me, and I was able to walk up and down the hall, bathe myself and go down to the cafeteria to eat.

On Christmas Eve American school children from the dependents' school on post came and sang Christmas carols. I thought of Kim and our last year's Christmas and New Year's Eve, and the hurt was deeper than that of the wounds.

CHAPTER 33

In mid-January I was discharged from the hospital for convalescent leave and reassignment to the G-3 (Operations and Training) Section of U.S. Army Japan Headquarters, at Camp Zama. I had requested the assignment to Japan because I thought that reassignment to Vietnam might be easier from there, and I was determined to go back. I took an extra long leave of sixty days, and hadn't spent any money in months, so I could afford it.

I signed out of the hospital and caught the train to Tachikawa where I registered for space available air transportation to Korea. I was told to be back at 0500 hours the following morning. I checked into a room at post billeting and showered. The hot water felt good. My wounds were healed, and except for the scars where the rounds had entered and exited and the scars on my head there was little evidence of damage. I felt good that there was no permanent bone damage or anything that impaired motion.

I went to the officers club, ate a light dinner, and afterwards sat at the bar and drank. A letter from Browning had finally caught up with me about a week ago, and I read it again. The fight in which I was wounded had pretty well shredded a main force regiment, and they were no longer considered combat effective. The body count was close to three hundred dead VC, with about the same number of weapons captured. The battalion had suffered six killed and thirty-nine wounded. C Company had lost two lieutenants in the fight, along with two enlisted members killed and fifteen wounded. Fitzsimmons had written a letter detailing platoon losses: we had seven wounded other than me, but none killed. He also mailed some personal items that I had left scattered around the CP.

I nursed the drink and thought about Kim. Since Tom had brought the news to me I had come to accept what had happened, but I still couldn't understand it. Accepting it didn't ease the pain any. I finished the drink, went back to the billets and slept fitfully.

Next morning I made the space available call and caught the prop driven passenger plane for Korea. Korea was cold, with six inches of snow on the ground. January was always the coldest month of the year, and the ground froze hard to depths below a yard. There was fine snow blowing as I stepped out on the street and caught a Korean cab for the Naija Hotel.

I sat at the bar of the Naija and drank and chatted with the bartender. It was as if I had never left. News travels fast in the Orient, and he had somehow heard that I had been wounded. He had a thousand questions about my wounds and then about Vietnam. It was good to hear the pleasant sounds of the Korean language again and to feel the genuine warmth of Korean friendliness. They were to me the most curious people in the world, and if you did not understand that about them you could easily become angry at their curiosity. But that was simply their nature. They had to know everything about everything. One could not be standoffish with them. They were aggressive in all things, as if they had decided as a group to pry out of life whatever was withheld from them.

The place began to fill up as the afternoon waned. Finally I went out to the pay telephone and called the bank where Kim worked. The lady who answered spoke good English, and she recognized my voice because she had sometimes answered the phone when I had called for Kim.

"Is it Mr. Worthington?" she asked.

"Yes, I'm surprised you remember," I said.

"Mr. Worthington, Kim is not with the bank anymore," she said.

"Is that right? When did she quit?" I asked.

"She quit last week to get married," she said.

I hung up the telephone and went back to the bar. The shock was complete now. Somehow I had survived the first jolt when Tom arrived in Vietnam, so this time it wasn't as bad. There was a mixture of dull hopelessness and violent anger this time; more anger than anything else.

I sat there and threw down scotch the rest of the afternoon and stumbled out of the post cab and into my room at billeting just before curfew. "Ricksley, you son-of-a-bitch, your time is coming," I thought. I imagined the one thousand ways I would like to kill him, all of them slowly, like the cook from the engineer unit had been killed, with the barbed wire tearing back and forth through his bloody gashes until he finally died screaming for his mother, God, or anyone. Next morning I went to Camp Casey. I wasn't sure what I was going to do, but I was sure I was going to do it. At Casey I went to my old battalion area and stopped at the club.

Choe was sitting at a table in the lounge drinking coffee and reading the newspaper. He was alone. He sprang up, grabbed me and hugged me, and we talked. It was really good to see him. Then he told me the full story. Ricksley had come out on orders for Vietnam and was due to leave in February, so he had turned the battalion over to his successor, married Kim, and they had gone to Hawaii on their honeymoon. Somehow they had worked out the visa requirements, and he had left her in Wahiawa near Schofield Barracks, west of Honolulu. He had secured an assignment to Schofield Barracks to follow the year's tour in Vietnam. Kim was to wait there for him.

"Why, Choesi?" I asked. "Why did she do it?"

Choe looked at me with tears in his eyes, and I could remember that time on the beach at Kang Nung. "James, she was a kid, and she was infatuated with his rank and the immediate prospect of marriage and security. She probably had pressure from her mother also. That's what I think." The tears ran down the puffy cheeks of his round face. He was truly saddened by the whole thing because he knew very well how I felt.

We talked a while longer. I said good-bye and at my old battalion area visited C Company and spoke to a few of the troops who were in the company area. The battalion was in the field, so I finally gave it up and went back to Seoul.

I stayed in Seoul a week drinking. In the evenings I went out to the cabarets, danced with the hostesses and tried to put myself back together. Finally things started to come right again.

On Saturday I called the Kanko Ferry in Pusan and booked passage for Shimonoseki on the ferry leaving Monday morning. That afternoon I drank in Itaewon and took a short stocky hostess to her apartment and spent the rest of the afternoon in bed with her. I left her before dark and walked down the street to the large intersection, past General Coulter's statue and on down the hill to Yongsan.

The Eighth Army Officers Club was lively that night. A Korean band played good music and sang popular American songs. The more scotch I poured down the better I felt and the more I enjoyed the music.

The following day in Pusan I arranged to stay at Haileah Compound for the night. I was hung over all day, finally felt a little better that evening, and at Chosun Beach sat in the little park where Kim and I had fed the pigeons. I looked out at the cold gray ocean, then at the golden strand of beach, and could see Kim standing there with her sunny smile and her long black hair swept sideways by the ocean breeze. "My God, why?" I thought. I drank until midnight.

The following day the ferry crossing to Shimonoseki was pleasant. In Japan I stayed at Hakata Station. A week's sojourn in Kyushu gave me time to get some exercise and do some running. I found that the exercise helped me to forget much better than the alcohol. I resolved to continue running and to play handball, basketball, or swim at least three times a week.

While in Hakata I made one trip on the train up to Mount Aso, a volcanic mountain that was still active and a great tourist attraction in Kyushu. The train wound through the countryside, then began to climb steadily south up past Kumamoto, up and around the rugged mountainside, eventually stopping at the tiny station of Akamizu. I stopped in a small osoba, or noodle, shop and ate a bowl of hot ramen. It was really good, and it warmed me from the windy chill of the winter air and the altitude.

Up the mountainside the road wound around and over the rim of the huge bowl formed by the circle of volcanic mountains. At one overview point it was possible to view the magnificent panorama of nature's handiwork. This was the largest volcanic caldera in the world. It was a ring of volcanic mountains in a perfect circle, with a break at its northern side. According to Japanese legends the break was caused by a giant's stepping on that part of the caldera rim. Through that break ran the highway, a river, and the railroad that I had come in on. The caldera was thirty-three kilometers across, from one side of the bowl to the other, according to a sign at the overlook. Near the crater of Aso, I walked up a little path past a line of commercial shops, through the crowd of tourists and groups of uniformed school children. There vendors sold bags of yellow sulphur powder from the crater, which was reputed to be therapeutic when used in the bath.

The lip of the crater fell sharply, down several hundred meters to the smoking, steaming crack in the center. Yellow sulphur caked the edges of the crack. The putrid smell of sulphur permeated the air. There was water in the crater, probably from recent rainfalls. I looked down into the yawning pit, and after a while I retraced my steps back down past the shops, and on back down the mountains. I paid the driver and tried to tip him, and he thought I had misunderstood the price and insisted on returning the tip. I didn't feel like trying to explain the western custom of tipping to him, so I took the money back, thanked him sincerely and left him wondering whether Americans could count or not. It was well after dark when I got back to Hakata, and I took a hot bath and slept soundly for the first time in two weeks.

The next morning at the personnel section of the small army intelligence detachment at Hakata Station I picked up an "Officers Preference Statement." I carefully filled out the statement, requesting immediate reassignment to Vietnam. In the limited space available on the form, I indicated that my initial tour had been cut short at about three months when I had been superficially wounded and evacuated to Japan. I stated that I was completely whole again and had been given a clean bill of health by the doctors at Camp Zama. Then I mailed the Preference Statement to Infantry Branch in Washington.

Sunday afternoon in Hiroshima I wandered around Peace Park and went through the museum. Hundreds of uniformed school children with their teachers as guides trooped around the park and were told what had happened here near the conclusion of World War II. Their cherubic rosy cheeks and upturned faces drank in every word their teachers/guides were saying. One could only hope that the human race would see the end of war.

Across town I got a room at a small hotel near the station. I sat in a small yakitori shop that night drinking sake when a group of Koreans came in and sat down at the small bar. They saw me and attempted to converse with me in English.

I replied in Korean and they were delighted. In five minutes I determined they were North Koreans. I threw the money I owed down on the bar and left without another word.

I spent the following night in Osaka and on Tuesday morning took the train north, around the eastern shore of Lake Biwa and north to the coast of the Sea of Japan. I chatted with a Japanese couple and their young son who sat across from me. At one stop the man dashed off the train and bought sake, and we sipped on that until I had a pleasant glow on, and the trip became more interesting by the hour.

I said good-bye and got off at Kanazawa and stashed my bag in a room in a small hotel. The water was hot, and I took a long shower and then fell on the futon and slept for an hour. My wounds were healed, but I still didn't have my physical strength back. I knew that more than anything else I needed exercise and a routine.

Late that afternoon at the cliffs by the sea at To Jimbo I sat on a bench overlooking the vertical fingers of rock that fell away to the ocean far below. This was a place of death. The Japanese had committed suicide here for years on end by leaping from the top of the stone spires to other rocks far below. As I sat there the police were diving in search of a couple that had leaped into eternity earlier that afternoon. The idea did not appeal to me in the least. I had other things to do before that day arrived, before the pale horse came.

Leaving the beach, I walked down the street and drank in the carnival-like atmosphere. In one shop I sat on a bar stool and ate a broiled squid with a type of barbecue sauce on it and drank a tall bottle of Sapporo beer. Four college students invited me to join them at their table in the corner. They insisted on buying me another beer. There were two men and two girls, who seemed to be like college students anywhere. We had a grand time for the better part of an hour until they learned that I was a soldier just returned from Vietnam. They cooled immediately, so I bought them a round of drinks and moved on up the street and caught a bus to my hotel.

I left Kanazawa the following morning and travelled up the coast to the northeast. I spent a week going around Noto Peninsula and seeing the "snow country" of Toyama, Niigata, and Sadoga Shima Island. The area was covered by six feet of snow. Finally I turned south past Nagaoka, the home of Yamamoto Isoroku, Japan's famous admiral of World War II. I crossed the Japanese Alps and journeyed down the Pacific slopes, past the tourist hotels and ski runs to the foothills near Takasaki and then on into the Kanto Plains and eventually Tokyo.

At Zama I checked by the office where I was assigned to see if I had any mail. There were two letters from Infantry Branch; the first one I opened notified me that they were in receipt of my preference statement, and the second one postmarked a week later was a copy of a request for orders to send me to Vietnam with a report date of the 20th of March. That was five days after I would return from leave, so that made it about right. That meant I would never work a day at Camp Zama with that REMF headquarters, which suited me just fine. I checked at AG (Adjutant General or Personnel), and they cut the orders that day and handed me a port call for a flight out of Yokota on 18 March.

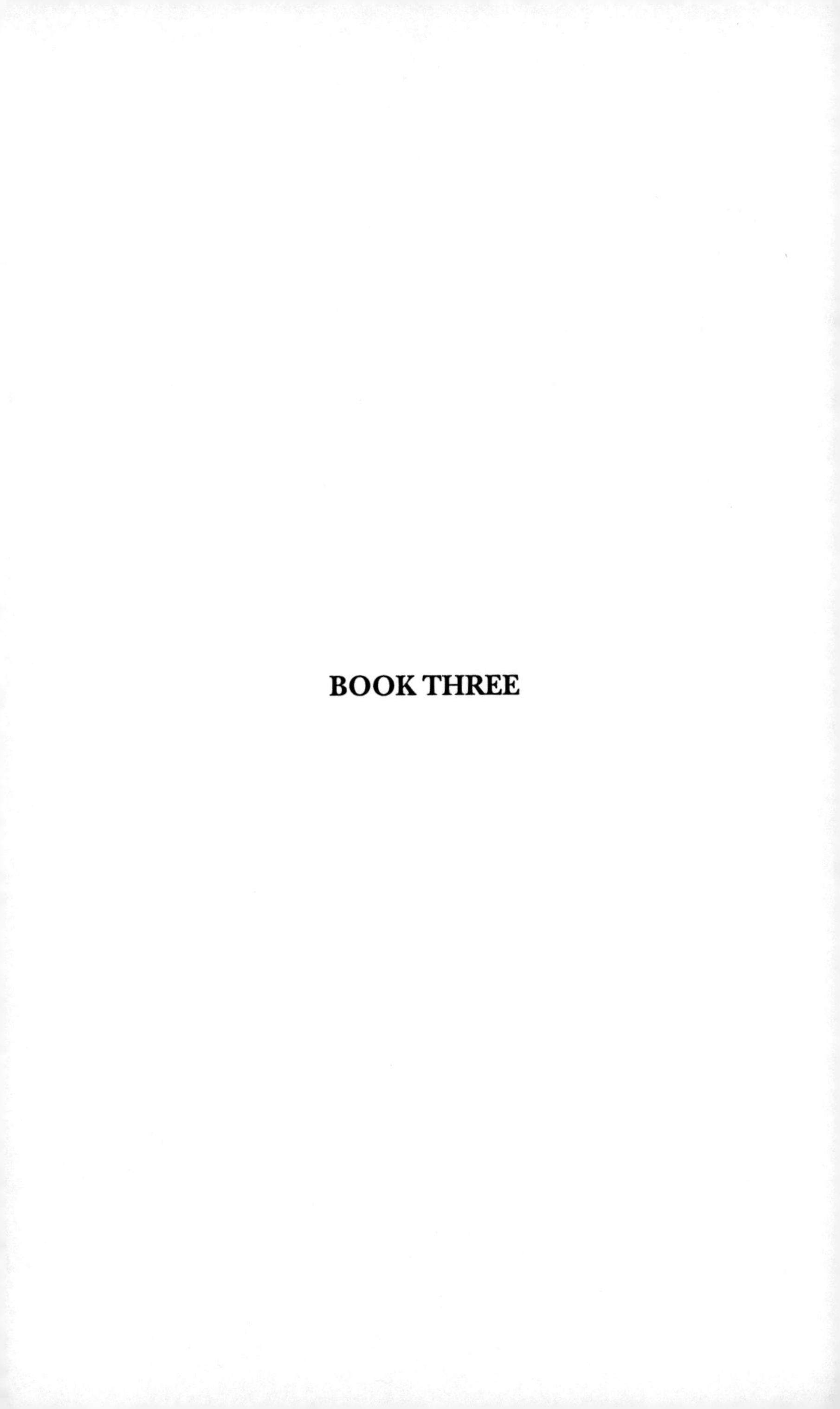

BOOK THREE

CHAPTER 34

As we landed at Saigon's Tan Son Nhut Air Base, I was reminded of a frustrating dream in which you do the same thing over and over again without success or without ever satisfactorily finishing, and woke up only to dream the same dream again the next night. We were processed through by Army ATCO and sent to Long Binh for further processing and assignment.

Long Binh was the typical bureaucratic mess that report depots normally are. I had hated report depots ever since my first week in the Army at Fort Jackson, South Carolina. Three days after I got to Long Binh I was assigned to the 1st Infantry Division again, and once again, after I had requested it, I was assigned to 1st Battalion, 202nd Infantry in the brigade at Lai Khe. I reported into LTC Crowse's office as a replacement. The Executive Officer, Major Roy King, was sitting at Colonel Crowse's desk. I knew Colonel Crowse wasn't due to rotate for another couple of months so I assumed he was on R and R.

"You were in the battalion before, wounded and evacuated to Japan in November. Is that correct, Lieutenant Worthington?" Major King asked.

"Yes, the middle of November, Sir," I said.

"Lieutenant, I know you knew Colonel Crowse. I hate to tell you that he was killed yesterday near Dau Tieng. A sniper picked him out in a crowd, probably because of the rank on his collar. Actually he lived through the worst part but died last night at 93rd Evacuation Hospital in Bien Hoa."

I was stunned. He was a fine, decent man that everyone respected. "Sir, I'm terribly sorry to hear that. He was a fine man and a fine commander."

"Yes, I guess the best ones tend to get it first," he said. "I will be temporarily commanding the battalion. I came here from Second Brigade soon after you were wounded, and my tour is about up. I considered extending to keep the battalion, but I knew they would just ship a lieutenant-colonel in here on top of me to take over, so I'm leaving in two weeks. By the way, how would you feel about taking a company?"

"I'd like to command a company," I said.

"Well, Captain Sutton was also hit yesterday and has been evacuated. He will not be back, so you're the new C Company Commander. He will make it OK, but when he recovers he will be reassigned stateside," he added, as he noted my concern.

"But isn't Lieutenant Browning still there, Sir?"

"Yes, but you rank him by a few days. We considered giving the company to Lieutenant Scott, the XO, but quite frankly, he couldn't handle it. Anyway, he only has four and a half months left, and we want a long term commander," he said.

"OK, Sir. I'm your man," I said. I saluted, was dismissed, and took a battalion jeep down to C Company. I went over to the CP, where the supply sergeant, Sergeant Grossman, reported to me, grinning.

"Sir, welcome back. The company will close in here in about an hour. You OK, Sir? We heard you really were hit badly."

"I'm OK. Tell me who is left in the company."

Sergeant Grossman went into the CP tent and brought out a manning roster. I looked it over carefully, pleased to find that nearly all of my old platoon members were still here. A Lieutenant Sutherland now commanded them, and Grossman said that Sutherland had a good reputation. Third Platoon had been taken over by a Lieutenant Fowler shortly after Pendleton was killed, and he was still there. Lieutenant Smathers still had the Weapons Platoon. It was good to see that many of the men I remembered had been promoted. Bigwitch was now a Staff Sergeant, Dillard had made Sergeant, McGuire was a Staff Sergeant, and Hale was a Sergeant, among others.

As we talked Lieutenant Scott came out of the CP tent, rubbing his eyes and yawning.

"Oh, you're back, James. We don't have a platoon open now," he smiled as if he thought this was a game of musical chairs, or "kitty wants a corner."

"That's OK. I have a job. I'm your new company commander." The shock and dismay registered on his face. He must have thought of the run-ins we had had before, particularly when he had been in the field on that one Michelin operation, and he had forced a dust off on me when I hadn't wanted it.

"Why didn't you go to the field and take the company when Sutton was wounded?" I asked. We might as well clear the air right now, I thought.

"Well, uh, well. They were coming back in today so I couldn't see any use."

"Have you checked to see if the shower point is operational?"

"Uh, no, uh, it usually is."

"Is there a hot meal ready for them?" I asked.

"No, they have one more C-ration left."

"Are there clean clothes in supply right now?"

"I'm not sure. Sergeant Grossman! Are there clean clothes over there?" he yelled.

"I want hot soup and coffee when they get here and a hot supper for tonight. Then check on the shower point and the clean clothes," I said.

He spun sharply and ran for the cook's tent. There was a lot of yelling, then the mess sergeant and two cooks came hustling out, buttoning their shirts and heading for the mess tent. I walked across to the mess tent after about ten minutes.

"Sergeant Bowman, what the hell's going on here? Do you have to wait around and be told to have something hot ready when the troops come from the field?" I asked.

"Sir, my men are hard pushed, and we don't have time to do that sort of thing." I could smell alcohol on his breath.

"Sergeant Bowman, you're relieved as mess sergeant of this company. Report to First Platoon for duty when they get back in." He turned a chalky color and attempted to set things right.

"Sir, I didn't understand, uh, that is, I'm willing to do anything you say. It's just that Captain Sutton never expected this sort of thing."

"Well, I expect it, and that's why you're fired. Drinking before 1700 hours will not be tolerated in this company." The other cooks stood openmouthed and stared. "Sergeant Smith, you are now the company mess sergeant. I trust you understand that your mission is to feed these troops in the best way you know how."

"Sir, I'll do my best," he said.

"You're a good man, Sergeant Smith. Get this mess straight as soon as possible. Let me know if you hit any snags, and we will take care of whatever problems you have. Just use your common sense and straighten this mess out." He saluted, and I've never seen cooks hustle like I saw in the next thirty minutes.

The company arrived on deuce and a halves, and it was a regular family reunion. First Platoon tried to tell me all the news at one time, but I told them to hold it for tonight. We had no perimeter duties that night, so I was determined to let them blow it all out at the Red Dog. Before anything else, I thought I would tell them in formation what was going on.

They formed up in front of the CP, and I announced that I had been made company commander and that I needed all the support they could give me. I let them loose quickly without antagonizing a battle-hardened unit that had just returned from the field. There was hot chow, clean clothes, and the shower point was operational. I asked the lieutenants to stay after the formation.

After the formation broke, Browning ran over and gave me a bear hug. "James, I never would have believed I'd see you back here. You must have asked for it!" he laughed.

"Yes, I did. How have you been, pal? You really look great."

"By the way," he grinned, "Sutton was the most knowledgeable officer I have ever known. You have a big pair of shoes to fill, James!"

"Yes, and I don't pretend to be able to fill them. I'll do the best I can, and with help from you guys we will make it."

"James, this is Larry Sutherland and Sam Fowler," Browning introduced the two lieutenants who had arrived after I left. We shook hands and sat down for a chat. Lowell Redd had stopped by his battery, so he walked in late. We laughed and shook hands. Lieutenant Smathers walked over and stood behind Browning. After that we went over some basics, emphasizing the importance of the ambush, noise and light discipline, the use of indirect fire, and the need for constant professionalism. I also discussed the use of signal cord. The session broke up, and Browning and I walked down the road towards Tom McCarter's area.

McCarter was sitting on a chair in front of his tent and leaped up and grabbed me. "James, I knew damn well you would be back! How the hell did you manage to get back to your old unit?" he laughed aloud. I explained how it happened, and we sat down on the ground and popped a Budweiser that Tom offered us. Browning had met Tom just before I was evacuated, and his opinion of Tom was as high as mine. "Too bad I didn't have Tom with us," I thought.

"James, I have heard about the marriage. I'm sorry," Tom said simply.

"Thanks Tom. Please forget it. Don't mean a thing."

We talked until dark. I went back to the company and talked for a while with Fitzsimmons, then with First-Sergeant Long. Long had gone to pick up mail when the troops arrived, so this was the first time I had seen him. They were both shocked at the loss of Captain Sutton. I asked them how it happened. They had been mortared, and his legs were knocked from under him by one of the first rounds to hit the low ridge line they were crossing. Fortunately, the company was at a halt and he hadn't had the RTO's clustered around him. He was off the side of the ridge, trying to see through the foliage with his binoculars. The femur was broken on the left side, but miraculously, the chunk of shrapnel that broke his leg had missed the femoral artery. Otherwise he probably would have been dead. There aren't any good places to get hit, but the number of men who survived after having the femoral artery severed could be counted an elite group. I didn't know one.

"First Sergeant, why did you have to go pick up mail when you got back here?" I asked.

"Well, Lieutenant Scott has never signed the form over there so that he could pick it up. The mail clerk normally picks up mail but we are without one now, and making do the best we can," he said.

"I'll look into it," I said. I saw Fitzsimmons wink at Long; they both knew that Scott's VIP tour was over.

We left the CP, went through the rubber trees and down the road to the Red Dog. The place was packed and First Platoon was there in force. A few people from A and B Companies occupied a table in the far corner of the room. Smoke filled the room and music played loudly from a record player behind the bar. I sat with First Platoon and soon we were talking warmly about old times.

Doc Gill had been promoted to Sergeant and was now the company aid man, in charge of the other medics out in platoons. Creighton, the mortar FO, also had been promoted to Sergeant. Bigwitch, Dillard, Howard, McGuire, Hale, Rozier, Silva, Alderman, Bentley, and Doc Haygood were sitting at the table in high spirits.

"Sir, you going to make these mutha-fuckers learn how to use signal cord?" Howard yelled down the table.

I nodded and laughed. First Platoon knew they were different. There were things that set them apart, such as the signal cord. It couldn't be confirmed, but there were rumors that Bigwitch had garroted a VC with his signal cord while on patrol. Stories like that, especially about good units that had had some well known battles, grew and snowballed with every telling, getting even larger with the passage of time.

"Sir, tell us about those Japanese women. Is it sideways or straight up and down?" Dillard yelled. Everyone laughed, but a new man, SP4 Suzuki, stood and yelled at Dillard.

"Hey you son-of-a-bitch, do you think I was born sideways?"

"No, but you may have been dropped on your head in the bus station!" Howard yelled. Suzuki looked at Howards's black mischievous smile and the tension was broken. Howard could do that; being black, he was very conscious of race, prejudice, and unfeeling bias. Somewhere along the line he had declared a personal cease fire while we were banded together in the Nam, for a common cause, and mutual support and survival. It was like that with many blacks. Sergeant Rozier had put it quite succinctly.

"Man, I need you here, but when we get back on the block, you the enemy. You got your big fat fucking foot on my windpipe, and it hurts, mauthafucka. Somebody gotta pay for a couple of hundred years of raping, robbing, and degradation of the black man." Rozier was professional and he took care of the troops; all the troops. But you knew where he stood; black, unforgiving, and uncompromising.

"Sir, Sergeant Bigwitch screwed a Montanyard in Ben Cat last week," Bentley yelled.

"Yeah, did you ever see a Cherokee Montanyard?" Alderman asked. "That's what you call a Great Smoky Montanyard!" he laughed. Bigwitch twitched with discomfort and flushed as red in the face as a full-blooded Cherokee Indian can get.

"Alderman, you're from Florida but don't have one drop of Seminole in you; maybe a drop of semihole cause you are kinda half-assed!" Bigwitch said. The troops were rolling on the floor laughing; that was more than Bigwitch normally said in a month.

We had a great reunion but it was time I slipped over to talk to the other platoons. I started with "Browning's Bombers" who were eager to explain that they were the best in the whole damned division. They may have been, too. Browning had them convinced that they were the best and that's important. I spent some time with them and then got around to Third Platoon and Weapons Platoon.

The Red Dog closed at 2300 that night, so I stopped by Tom McCarter's CP on the way back. We talked and sipped a beer but he had to go out early the next morning, so I didn't stay long.

"James, I know how much Kim meant to you. I'm really sorry things turned out this way." He stared into the darkness. Somewhere to the southwest we could hear artillery thudding, and the eerie glow of illumination rounds in that same area marked a battle in progress. They swung back and forth on their parachutes, and the light in the sky swayed left and right.

I said good night and went back down the dusty road, through the rubber trees in the darkness. There was a night breeze blowing, which cooled the hot air, and there was a promise of rain. A few dark clouds drifted across the starry sky, making it darker, and a drop of rain struck my face. The Southern Cross was clearly visible through the rubber trees, reminding me of Van Gogh's muted canvas as the "starry night" shone. Then the long stratified layers of rain clouds covered even the southern sky. As I entered the dark CP tent and lay down on my air mattress, the rain began to fall on the walls and roof. I thought of that rainy night in Pusan when Kim and I went back to the Beach Hotel from Haileah in the rain.

I pulled the poncho liner up around my neck, reached into the darkness, pulled my poncho from my ruck-sack and spread it over the poncho liner. Sometime in the morning darkness, I shook the despair and fell asleep, as the rain beat harder on the rubber trees and the wall of the tent.

The next morning I checked the mess operation at breakfast. There was still a lot to be desired in sanitation, although Sergeant Smith had had the cooks scrubbing most of the night.

"Sergeant Smith, what cleaning materials do you need in here?"

"Sir, we need brushes, brillo pads, soap powder, lysol, degreaser, and a whole list of other things. I would love to paint the floor with some gray rubberized paint. A couple of coats of that and a good scrubbing with Texize and hot water every night would really improve the place," he said.

"OK, take the money out of that can in the CP. You can make a run to Saigon on the next convoy and load up. Get some more silverware and plates, and some new salt and pepper shakers and napkins. Get whatever you can through normal channels and whatever else you need get it any way you can. Use your imagination."

"Sir, is that unit fund money in the CP in that number ten can?"

"No. That money is a contribution from the VC. Every time we deal with them the money in their pockets goes into that bucket. Use what you need from there."

He laughed and saluted, and I moved across to the supply tent. Grossman saluted, reported and offered to show me the company supply. It was immaculate.

"Sergeant Grossman, you've done a great job here. Just think in terms of service to the troops. Do everything you possibly can for them in the way of clean clothes and supplies. You should consider it a personal insult if one soldier runs out of mosquito repellent."

"Yes, Sir. I understand. I won't let the company down, Sir." He saluted; I patted him on the back and left for my CP (command post).

I rang Captain Melton at S-1. "Captain Melton? This is Lieutenant Worthington. How are you? Got back yesterday and Major King gave me C Company."

"Welcome back. We thought we would never see you again. You must have lost a gallon of blood." I didn't particularly need to be reminded.

"Say, do you have any special authorizations for E-6? I have two men I want to promote who don't have enough time in grade."

"OK, go ahead and promote them. I have six special authorizations, as a matter of fact."

I gave him the names and line numbers of Grossman and Smith, and that afternoon in company formation I promoted both of them. In the same formation we gave out twelve Purple Hearts, six Bronze Stars, and two Silver Stars, all of which were awards that should have been given a couple of months earlier. Captain Sutton was the finest combat commander in the army, but some things in garrison got overlooked simply because the priorities were on combat operations. I was determined to do the best I could because I well knew the sacrifices the troops made, on a daily basis. The comfort items were there for the asking.

That afternoon I had a meeting with the officers and the first sergeant. "In garrison, Scott and Smathers will lead ambush and recon patrols, along with the rifle platoon leaders. The Weapons Platoon will start doing patrols as long as we can leave enough people in the perimeter to man two mortars." Smathers scowled and Scott turned a shade paler. The 81 mm mortars rarely fired because of the availability and skill of the artillery and 4.2 inch mortars, so I saw nothing wrong with having Weapons Platoon share garrison patrolling responsibilities. I didn't want them to completely miss the war. I didn't want Scott to miss the war either. Some day, he would probably have a rifle company. He ought to know what to do, based on hard experience rather than a field manual, and I had decided he would get it.

"Lieutenant Scott."

"Yes, Sir," he said.

"Get over and fill out a card so you can pick up the mail. And find us a mail clerk. Get someone who is wounded but can do that kind of work and train him. You and the first sergeant will start alternating field duty. Next trip, the first sergeant goes, and the following one you will take, etc. Any questions?" Five minutes after the meeting I was called to battalion for the receipt of an operations order.

CHAPTER 35

I took my jeep down to battalion and got acquainted with PFC Collins, my driver and one of my RTO's, on the way. Lieutenants Redd and Smathers followed in another jeep. The jeep was immaculate and the engine purred like a kitten. I looked at the dash; the gas tank was full, all the instruments were working. I was impressed with Collins.

"Where do you call home, Collins?"

"Chester, South Carolina, Sir." His blue eyed smile was infectious.

"Will you go back there when you get out?"

"Yes Sir. Me and my brother have built a stock car, and I drive it in the races. My dream is to race at Darlington some day."

I was impressed. "How did you come to choose car racing as a profession?"

"Aw, you know, Sir. Cale and Leroy Yarborough were the heroes of every kid in South Carolina. We just sort of gravitated in that direction, I guess."

"Well, I'm sure you'll do great in it."

I turned to the radio, took the handset and made a communications check with battalion.

"Thunder Three-three, this is Charlie Six, commo check, over," I said.

"Charlie Six, this is Thunder Three-three, roger out."

I then checked my own CP, and no one answered. I made a note to tighten the headquarters on such matters. I had to have commo with the company when I was away, and someone was asleep at the switch.

My driver stopped at the dismount point, and I went into the TOC with Redd and Smathers. Major King met us, shook hands and introduced me to the other company commanders, the S-3, and the S-2. Captain Rick Ballard had A Company, Captain Glenn Cunningham commanded B Company, Captain Cliff Willis had Headquarters Company, Captain Bob Patterson was the S-2 and Major Furman Hickey was the S-3. We shook hands and sat in the gray steel chairs. It was stifling under the lights, and tent flaps were down for security.

Major King opened the meeting; clearly an important mission was in the offing. Southwest of Lai Khe was a large jungle area in the shape of a triangle, with its northeastern corner just touching Ben Cat. The northwestern corner was directly west of Ben Cat, so that the northern edge ran east to west. The distance across was in excess of twenty kilometers. Commonly known as "the Iron Triangle," at this stage of the war it was a safe haven for the VC. Strategically, it was too close to Saigon and could be used to harbor any number of troops and tons of supplies and equipment for a push on Saigon. The South Vietnamese government was particularly worried about it. On one foray into the triangle, the 173rd Airborne Brigade had made heavy contact and had successfully fought against great odds, but not without a price in friendly dead and wounded. The thinking at government level was that the 173rd operation had certainly been successful, but had merely scratched the surface. Consequently, we were to mount a large operation into the triangle and remain for an indefinite period, to thoroughly search for enemy stocks and to evacuate or destroy them according to the decisions made at the time. It was hoped that the VC main force regiments operating in that area could be brought to bay and killed, or depleted to combat ineffectiveness.

A brigade of the 101st Airborne Division would participate with our brigade, along with an ARVN (Vietnamese Army) division. The plan called for the ARVN to take the southern half of the triangle, the brigade from the 101st would take the northwestern corner, and the brigade from the 1st Infantry Division, ours, would take the northeastern chunk. On a map reconnaissance it didn't look like a big piece of ground, but an Infantryman knew what plodding through triple canopy jungle, expecting contact at any moment, could be like. He understood that there was more ground there than many units could hope to cover.

Too many G-3's and S-3's who planned these operations had no idea what moving and fighting on a piece of ground like that could be like. A few broad ten kilometer strokes of a grease pencil over an acetate overlay with time phased lines reading "first day," "second day," etc. and the plan would be quite clear, they thought. One or two kilometers of movement per day in that terrain, given the enemy situation, was as much as a rifle company could be expected to cover, more, in some cases. Ignorant operations officers drew stupid plans and passed them on to equally gullible brigade and battalion commanders, who accepted them without intelligent comment. Those who suffered were those who did all the actual work; the walking, trapping, ambushing, and sweeping; the killing, the bleeding, and the dying. If just one time a brigade command and staff could be formed into a rifle platoon; with the colonel, lieutenant-colonel, majors, captains, and their operations NCO's pressed into the roles of riflemen, grenadiers and machine-gunners; and if they survived one operation the subsequent orders would be profound in their understanding and expectations.

I remembered quite clearly one operation that Ricksley had drawn up as S-3 of the battalion in Korea. The plan called for our company to begin movement just before daylight over a route defined in his plan and to occupy a blocking position south of the main objective by 0900 hours. A Company was to block on the north by 0900 hours, tying in with us on the west, then B Company was to attack into the objective coming from the east and attacking to the west. A and C Companies would block any escape of the guerrillas in the objective area. The route he drew on the map went over a two hundred meter rock cliff and no amount of pleading on Captain Laird's part could make him diverge from his unworkable plan. The following morning, when we moved to the blocking position, Laird purposely took us over a route that would allow us to arrive at the blocking position in time. He deliberately disobeyed orders so that battalion would succeed in its attack. It was an annual training test, and had the battalion failed Colonel Ziegler could have been relieved. I remember Ricksley on the radio, furious because Laird had not taken his prescribed route. "Sometimes, we have to save the dumb bastards from themselves," I thought. I resolved then and there that if it came to making that kind of decision to provide mission success and the safety of the men, I would do it without blinking an eye.

The brigade plan called for 2nd of the 28th to move by helicopter into LZ's blown by "daisy cutters" on the south; we would move into the center sector on foot, at night, the day before 2nd of the 28th's combat assault, followed by the daylight movement of 1st Battalion,

16th Infantry, into the northern sector. 2nd of the 2nd would occupy the perimeter at Lai Khe.

Within the battalion, C Company would lead out and move into our area of operations in the south of the battalion's assigned portion, followed by B Company, battalion headquarters and the 4.2 Inch Mortar Platoon to occupy the center sector. Finally, A Company and the Recon Platoon would trail in the march, halting and operating in the northern sector. This meant that we would have to emphasize security, because we were leading the battalion. Navigation, noise and light discipline, and frontal and flank security would be vital to our success. Redd and Smathers would work up a fire plan for the entire route. I began to formulate my plan as Collins drove me through the rubber trees to the company area. The operation was to kick off the night of the following day at 2100 hours; we would move out in total darkness for security reasons. "I will issue my order as soon as we get back to the CP, to give the platoons the maximum amount of time to prepare," I thought. It was now 1600 hours, so there was plenty of daylight left.

The orders group was waiting at the CP. We sat on the ground outside the CP while I issued the order. As I talked the first sergeant made overlays of the route of march, into the area of operations, and of the assigned sectors, then passed them out to everyone.

"The start point for the march is at our wire, just in front of First Platoon's bunkers. The battalion order of march is C, B plus battalion headquarters and the 4.2 Inch Mortar Platoon, and A plus Recon. The 4.2 Inch Mortar Platoon will be humping two 81 mm mortars, as this is a foot mobile operation and the heavy mortars are too heavy to carry. Our company AO is the southernmost of the three AO's the battalion has assigned, as shown on my map here. South of us will be 2nd of the 28th's A Company, and west of us will be elements of the 101st Airborne Division."

"Our company order of march will be: First, company headquarters, Second, Weapons, and Third. We will move directly out of our bunkers so that there will be no bunching up at the wire. First Platoon's point man will step through the wire at 2100 hours sharp. You all know the route well, down to a point past Ben Cat, but after we enter the jungle of the Iron Triangle, navigation will be critical in the darkness. When we reach our area of operations, First Platoon will occupy the perimeter from four to eight o'clock, Second from eight to twelve, and Third from twelve to four. Weapons will occupy a second smaller perimeter within the larger one around company headquarters and their single 81 mm mortar. There will be no digging until daylight. Noise and light discipline will be rigidly observed."

"During movement, take your time and secure both sides before crossing roads, trails, streams, and open areas. First Platoon, get your point squad out in front as far as possible, to maintain contact with starlights. Remember, they are on the point for the entire battalion."

"Day after tomorrow morning, 2nd of the 28th will CA into LZ's south of us, following a heavy prep. This could flush VC north into us, especially since we moved into that area the night before during darkness. Hopefully, they won't know we are there, so get your security out and be prepared. I want mechanical ambushes and heavy LP's in front of every platoon. First of the 16th will move into an area north of us, by foot, during daylight the first day. Second of the 2nd will defend Lai Khe."

"Carry five days of C-rations with you as we will not resupply on the fourth day but will resupply on the fifth day."

"Here are the pass words for the next two days and the current SOI (Signal Operating Instructions) is in effect. What are your questions?" I answered questions for ten minutes.

"OK. Finish preparing in the morning. In the afternoon I want ambush rehearsal on your four standard ambushes, A, B, C, and D. We have new men, so go over employment of claymores and mechanical ambushes. In addition, Lieutenant Redd will give a class on calling indirect fire and directing helicopter gunship fire and air strikes. We have a hell of a lot of work to do, so let's get started."

We broke up, and the platoon leaders went back and issued their orders. A heads-up, razor sharp outfit can reduce the planning and issuance of orders to ten or fifteen minutes, depending on the complexity of the operation and the completeness of their unit tactical SOP (Standard Operating Procedures) and the time available. Good units rapidly formulate simple sound plans, issue verbal orders with an operations overlay, and execute aggressively. There is an old saying that goes something like "A poor plan well executed beats the hell out of a great plan poorly executed."

I felt comfortable with command at the company level, and I rather looked forward to the operation. I didn't know very much about Major King, but having worked for Ricksley I couldn't imagine he would be nearly as difficult to work for.

That night I tried reading to keep my mind off Kim. After a while I tossed the book aside and had Collins take me over to the brigade club. Major King was there and invited me to have a beer. We drank and talked for about an hour and a half. I decided that he had his head screwed on right. Anyway, I would know for certain, beginning tomorrow night.

CHAPTER 36

Darkness had fallen; the stars twinkled in the tropical sky, and the denizens of the evening, in swarms or individually, attempted to take their repast through our fatigue shirts and pants as the battalion prepared to move. Here and there an unknowing, uncaring, or lazy soldier who had failed to apply mosquito repellent to his exposed skin would be found, and literally legions could feast there.

It was 2030 hours. I watched Sergeant Arch Bigwitch slip through the wire of the perimeter with First Squad of First Platoon strung out behind him. To his immediate rear was SP4 Howard, cradling an M60 machine-gun. He was followed by PFC Larson, and Sergeant Dillard, then four more squad members. Their faces, hands and arms were blackened with charcoal, and burlap and yetti nets with foliage stuck into them broke up the outlines of steel helmets and upper bodies. They moved along like shadows, unhurriedly picking their way across ground that they had walked over in daylight and darkness a hundred times. There was enough natural light to allow ease of movement but they moved bent forward from the waist, every nerve functioning, to see, smell, and to feel the enemy's presence. Mason brought up the rear. A rifle squad's normal strength was ten men, to include the squad leader, a four man fire team, and a five man fire team, but Bigwitch was short personnel, which was usually the case. This squad normally did not have an M60 attached, but Howard was an excellent machinegunner, and Bigwitch had taken the M60 for additional fire power because of the nature of his mission. Sergeant Mason carried a starlight scope in the rear, to gain and maintain contact with the main body of troops after they had moved through the wire at 2100 hours.

The point squad covered ground rapidly, and by the time the main body stepped off at 2100, Bigwitch was nearing Ben Cat, according to his coded push-to-talk message. Sergeant Mason had hung back, looking over the open ground through his starlight. Eventually the lead elements of the main body of the company picked him up through starlight scope as we worked our way south.

Bigwitch soon reached the stream just southwest of Ben Cat. I knew his location by five breaks of squelch on Collins' radio, Bigwitch's code for that check point. I held up the column. Crossing danger areas was time consuming, and I didn't want the company to bunch up at the crossing. At the halt the troops spread out a few additional yards and lay on the ground, alternate members facing right and left.

Going was slow, and when Bigwitch signaled that he had reached the heavy foliage of the northeast corner of the Iron Triangle we really slowed down. I had anticipated contact at that point. It seemed logical that if there had been any breaches of security prior to the operation, that that would be a perfect place for the VC to establish a heavy ambush, catch us astride the stream, in column, and relatively in the open. My pulse pounded harder; the sweat trickled down my nose and cheeks and across my lips, as I listened for the sounds of contact. I sent security teams forward to the left and right before entering the jungle, behind Bigwitch's squad. We closed the gap between the main body and Bigwitch until the point was a couple of yards behind Sergeant Mason. We moved on into the jungle and I breathed easier. There was safety in the cover and concealment of the jungle if you were kind to the jungle. If we were considerate and did not violate the sanctity of the dark silence of the living lushness by beaming a harsh light, or flickering matches or cigarette lighters, making sounds, or breaking the tangled branches and vines, we would be afforded the full protection this great mother jungle could offer. But violate those rules, and the jungle would turn her favor to the enemy.

We plodded on. The going was slow and difficult, but we took our time, and around 0400 hours we closed into our perimeter. The other elements of the battalion had dropped off into their AO's and formed their own perimeters as we reached their assigned areas. We had the greatest distance to travel, being the southernmost element. We had a little time left before daylight, so we busied ourselves with security and the positioning of weapons.

As daylight came we began to dig in. We established strong LP/OP's in front of each platoon. I had each platoon send a squad sized clearing patrol out five hundred meters from the perimeter, to make a check of the platoon front, and return. The platoons had the clearing patrols put out two mechanical ambushes. Lowell Redd plotted fires for the defense of the perimeter and didn't fire them in. Normally he would have had the artillery fire and would have adjusted until he had the rounds striking where he wanted. I had decided not to fire them in until later, well after 2nd of the 28th made their combat assault south of us. That would enhance our chances of contact with VC elements fleeing north from the area of the preparation and heliborne assault. The artillery FDC worked up all the data for these fires, but we would wait to adjust them in.

The clearing patrols made no contact but discovered numerous indications of recent enemy activity, including well used trails, with fresh footprints, cart tracks, and bicycle tracks. The mechanical ambushes had been placed on these trails, some of which ran north-south and others east–west. Not long after the last clearing patrol got into the perimeter the preparation of 2nd of the 28th LZ's began with thunderous blasts of the "daisy cutters," followed by artillery and gunship preparations. Shortly, I heard the armada of helicopters beating into their LZ's south of us, the whooshing of the gunship rockets followed by loud cracks as they struck the earth. Then the endless staccato of the machine-guns of the slicks could be heard, as the troops were landed. The LZ's appeared to be about three kilometers south of us. I checked my map with its operations overlay; the LZ's were exactly three and one half kilometers to our south.

My troops were tense and waiting. I made a last round, checking my positions, and paused by Sergeant Bigwitch's foxhole. He looked up without smiling. "Sir, I hope the bastards surround us; then we'll know where they are." I walked back to the CP.

We had gone to a hundred percent alert posture when the LZ preparation began. About twenty minutes went by, and the claymores in one of the mechanical ambushes to our south, in front of the First Platoon, went off with loud blasts. Not five minutes later, the other First Platoon MA went, and their OP opened up with small arms and claymores a few minutes later. The small arms fire of the OP was answered with a fusillade from almost on top of the OP, and Lieutenant Sutherland called to say that the OP was on its way in with two wounded. I saw them running through the perimeter, and sent Doc Gill to give them a hand. Lieutenant Redd began to adjust artillery fire on the area where the OP had been set up. Before he got it back onto the ground where he wanted it, several VC ran straight into the camouflaged foxhole line and were cut down with small arms fire. The troops were firing at more VC, further back in the trees to the south. Having seen their fleeing comrades cut down up front they turned to the west, hoping the change of direction would take them to safe ground. In two minutes the ringing blast of claymores to Second Platoon's front indicated that one of their MA's had been tripped. At this point, I was fairly certain that the VC unit was thoroughly confused. The artillery fell closer and closer behind them as Redd adjusted it in tighter, and they had met with disaster to their front from a hidden enemy, firing claymores and small arms.

The artillery looked pretty good, so Redd had them fire a battery five for effect. The 105 mm shells with delay fuses punched through the triple canopy without exploding and then went off at ground level. I had him cease fire and mark that concentration, shift around in front of Second Platoon on the west, and fire into the area where the VC had moved. They fired for effect on that target and marked the concentration. We had not had contact for ten or fifteen minutes, and the Second Platoon OP reported all movement had ceased to their front. I waited another thirty minutes, then had the platoons send squad sized patrols forward to check for enemy dead, wounded, weapons, and anything of intelligence value.

In front of First Platoon there were a total of thirty-three enemy dead, including those killed by the two mechanical ambushes. Sergeant Rozier's squad picked up a total of twenty-five weapons, mostly AK-47's, one RPD (Russian light machine-gun), and 2 RPG 7 rocket launchers. The biggest prize was a lightly wounded prisoner, who was sitting on the ground with his back resting against a teak tree, staring glassily at nothing. Doc Gill treated him for shock and bandaged his wound. We fed him after an hour and he eventually came around. I had no LZ to evacuate him from, but already battalion was putting pressure on us to get him out. I explained that we were going to move, and they would just have to wait. Our two wounded from the OP were minor and did not need evacuation.

On Second Platoon's front there were twenty-one dead VC, and we picked up fifteen weapons. We were later to learn from intelligence that 2nd of the 28th had combat assaulted in on top of a regimental CP and that the prep and assault had killed fifty-eight VC. The remnants of the VC regiment had fled north and west, and a battalion had bumped into us, fleeing the shock and confusion of the preparation bombing, artillery, and helicopter gunship fire. We had caught them cold. Battalion kept calling about the prisoner, whereupon I decided to evacuate him to battalion with a squad sized patrol. Battalion was about two kilometers to the north, with B Company, so we moved our perimeter a kilometer to the north just after dark. Then a squad from Browning's platoon would take the prisoner north for another kilometer, just after first light.

We maintained tight security throughout the rest of the day, and I attempted an interrogation of the prisoner, which got nowhere because of the language barrier. I made a note to request a permanent interpreter from battalion, but then discarded the idea knowing full well that they would never assign an interpreter down to company level.

As soon as it started to get dark we moved, picking our way slowly north and holding up on a low rise to form our new perimeter, with the platoons occupying the same portion of the perimeter as they had in the previous one. We did no digging and tried to observe noise and light discipline. Still, at one point after our occupation of the new perimeter, I saw the flare of a match on Second Platoon's perimeter line. I walked across to Lieutenant Fowler's CP but he was checking the line with the platoon sergeant. As I stood there I heard a loud slap from the direction of the perimeter, and this sound was followed by muffled cursing. Lieutenant Fowler arrived back at his CP.

"Sam, who the hell struck that match over here?"

"Sir, it was that goddamned Boykin. He has screwed up about four times since we left Lai Khe."

"What was that scuffle over there?"

"Sergeant Redlegs slapped Boykin for back-talking when Redlegs chewed his ass for striking the match."

"Sam, this is not the old army. Redlegs is a fine platoon sergeant, but he can end up losing everything, slapping soldiers around in this day and time."

"Sir, that son-of-a-bitch Boykin is going to get someone killed. Last night he made more noise during movement than the rest of the platoon altogether."

I reflected. If noise discipline had been compromised, and we had been hit during movement, we could have had troops killed and wounded through the negligent behavior of one bad soldier. I totally sympathized with Sergeant Redlegs, but if Boykin went to the IG (Inspector General), Redlegs would be in trouble. Aaron Redlegs was a Sioux Indian from South Dakota, a career soldier with seventeen years of service under his belt. He had fought through the Korean War and had walked away as a highly decorated Infantryman. He was now a senior

E-7 and would make E-8 any day. I knew he would be a good first sergeant, but unless he learned his lesson about physically abusing soldiers he would never make it.

"Sam, I want to see Sergeant Redlegs at my CP."

"Yes, Sir."

I walked back to my CP and checked the radio watch. Four RTO's shared the duties. There were always two radios operational, one on the company net on which I talked to the platoon leaders, and one on the battalion net on which I talked with the battalion commander, his S-3 and S-2, and anyone else I needed to communicate with in the net. In addition, Lowell Redd's artillery RTO kept his radio set on the FDC net of artillery. My four RTO's alternated on the radios and manned a constant twenty-four hour a day watch, so I needed four because of the intensity of the work and its vital importance. They controlled our link to every kind of help we needed from outside. In addition, they patrolled and fought as Infantrymen.

Suddenly I became aware of Sergeant Redlegs before me.

"Sit down, Sergeant Redlegs. I need to talk to you."

"Yes, Sir." He was a huge man with a dark complexion and wide face, pock marked with the scars of childhood diseases and teen-age acne. His coal black hair was cropped close to his head.

"Sergeant Redlegs, you're a fine NCO, and I look forward to promoting you to the rank of First Sergeant. There is one problem that I see at this time. The days are long past when you disciplined bad soldiers by taking them behind the barracks and beating the hell out of them."

Redlegs' eyes measured me and after a long moment he spoke. "Sir, if Boykin fucks up and gets one of my men killed I will kill him," he said.

Well, here it was; a direct challenge to authority. Either I was being tested, and if so it was the best bluff I had ever seen, or I had an NCO whose old ways could not be changed.

"Redlegs, I respect you totally, and consider myself lucky to have you in Charlie Company. But I need your help, too. If you care at all about this company, and my authority, you will understand what I'm telling you. Striking troops is against the law, absolutely. Some things are different because of the combat situation, but the force of law and authority is not."

He sat motionless and I could imagine the dark expressionless face and the massive flat cheeks pushing up against the piercing stare of the sparkling black eyes, fierce as the gaze of a prairie rattler coiled to strike.

"OK, Sir. I'll help you." was all he said. I could interpret that any way I wanted to. It might mean that he had committed himself to a temporary truce with my position, but would continue to lead his own way when we parted ways. It might mean that his interpretation of "helping" me meant doing away with Boykin and thus purging the unit.

"Sergeant Redlegs, don't strike any more troops," I said quietly.

"Yes, Sir." He stood, saluted, and disappeared in the direction of Second Platoon.

About fifteen minutes later a mortar barrage, fierce and intense, ripped the jungle stillness about a kilometer to our south, on our old position.

CHAPTER 37

Browning's First Squad left at daylight with the prisoner, and we began to dig in. The ground was spongy, with small roots under the surface and larger ones throughout. Digging was slow laborious work. Collins handed me a C-ration can of coffee, and I made a breakfast of crackers, peanut butter, and the black coffee. By 1300 hours we had the place looking halfway decent, but the holes needed a little more depth.

The squad from Third Platoon returned to the perimeter, and a few minutes later Browning brought me a sealed envelope from Major King. It was a recent intelligence report, that there was a suspected regimental headquarters in our AO (Area of Operations), about two kilometers to the southwest. The intelligence came from "a usually reliable source," and it was hoped that C Company would be able to check that location today or tonight.

"James, there were numerous signs of recent enemy activity between here and battalion," Browning said. "There's a trail junction, about here, that would be a great spot for an ambush," pointing to a spot on his map.

"Good. Tonight we will put one ambush up there from Weapons Platoon. They can't possibly fire their mortar from here because of the overhead canopy, so their tube is useless. Wait here a minute, Dave."

Collins called the orders group to the CP. While we were waiting I gave Browning the intelligence that battalion had sent. I had decided to have him take a patrol to check out the suspected area of the VC regimental headquarters. The platoon leaders and their FO's gathered around the CP.

"Tonight Third Platoon will do a reconnaissance in this area for a suspected regimental headquarters," I said. "Weapons Platoon will establish an ambush on this trail junction, about five hundred meters to our north. First and Second Platoons will put out two ambushes each, well off Browning's patrol route, because that patrol isn't likely to return until around midnight or early morning. Dave, if the situation permits, hold up outside the perimeter and come in after daylight tomorrow morning. Doc Gill is going with you to give you another aid man. This canopy is thick, so if you have to dust off anyone they will have to drop a basket litter through to you. Smoke from the ground will dissipate in the canopies before it gets above the foliage, so someone may have to climb a tree to pop smoke. Lowell, I want artillery plotted along their route in and out, as well as on the suspected enemy headquarters. Get with Dave after we break up. Dave, you will recon and report on what is there, but if the opportunity presents itself we will bury them with artillery." We broke up to begin our preparations.

Browning's patrol slipped through the perimeter at 1630 hours. Browning had broken them into teams for the various missions. He would personally head the four man reconnaissance team, travelling light without any claymores. The patrol was in soft caps, and their blackened faces, arms, and hands, their weapons carried without the slings, their tied down clothing and equipment, and their body and head camouflage was a reflection of Browning's professionalism. "The greatest thing that patrol has going for it," I reflected as they passed the CP on the way out, "is superb leadership." Browning was good. As the troops put it he "had his shit together, all wrapped up into one little ball." He gave me a thumbs up as he passed. They moved slowly, bent forward at the waist with heads up, soaking up sights, sounds, and smells.

Just after dark the ambushes went out at ten minute intervals. As the Weapons Platoon patrol passed through the perimeter I stood by their point of exit and looked them over as they filed by. They looked good, but I was mildly surprised when the patrol leader passed me. It was Kim rather than Smathers. I had expected Smathers to take his own patrol. "Why would he send Kim rather than run the ambush himself?" I wondered. Kim was a tough, capable Korean-American from Los Angeles, so the patrol was in excellent hands. Maybe Smathers doubted his own ability. At any rate I would speak to him tomorrow and perhaps do some training if he didn't know how to set up an ambush.

"Long, how goes it?" I asked. Sergeant Long sat on his air mattress, propped his back against a tree and was deep in thought.

"Sir, what is Browning going to do if he finds a regimental headquarters on that spot?" he asked.

"He will tell me and I will inform battalion and get further instructions. We may strike it with air, or possibly with artillery only. Or, we might try to get an arc light in on it."

"But a VC regimental headquarters is a mobile thing," he said. "In fact, they may be gone already."

"You're right, Top. But this is a regimental sized headquarters. It may not be an Infantry regimental headquarters. They have been there for at least two weeks."

"Then it must be some kind of depot for supplies and equipment transfer," he said.

"It may well be. At any rate, that's why brigade and division want it checked out. We can make decisions on how to deal with it after we know what it is."

"But if it is a large depot type complex sprawled over two kilometers or more will an arc light (B-52 strike) take it out?" he asked.

"Most definitely."

We sat and listened to the sounds of night. Two or three times we heard the throaty coughs of tigers, and I wondered what they were stalking and how skillfully they were hunting. They were like us in many ways, except that they ran no risk of running into an equal.

Sometime around midnight my eyes flew wide open; there were multiple explosions boom-booming from the northeast. Every claymore in Sergeant Kim's ambush went, followed by the thuds of M-26 fragmentation grenades. After ten minutes or so he called to say he was staying put until daylight, the enemy in his ambush numbered four or five, and there was no movement or sound in the kill zone.

Five minutes later one of First Platoon's ambushes went. McGuire had ambushed a carrying party of around twenty-five, some with bicycles and a couple of carts, heading along the well used trail from west to east. There was no movement in the kill zone now but he chose to remain there until daylight.

There had been nothing from Browning except negative, or "no change," situation reports on the hour. In that case no news was good news. I went back to sleep and woke about daylight. There had been no further contact during the night. I was squatted with a C ration can of black coffee, waiting, when Sergeant Kim's patrol came back into the perimeter with four AK47's and some pocket litter. A few minutes later the other ambushes returned to the perimeter with the exception of McGuire's. Larry Sutherland walked over to my CP.

"Sir, McGuire's got more than he can carry. I want to send some men out to help him."

"OK, go ahead but watch your security. There may be live enemy lying low out there that escaped the kill zone."

Forty-five minutes later McGuire's patrol came back into the perimeter pushing six new bicycles and dragging two carts of ammunition, most of it 82 mm mortar rounds. There was one 82 mm mortar tube, with base plate and bipod among the equipment. Altogether, they had picked up fifteen rifles including three SKS's and twelve AK 47's. There was one RPD machine-gun and one RPG 7 rocket launcher. There had been twenty-one dead VC in the kill zone and several blood trails leading into the jungle. In addition to the weapons, there were several bags of rice, plastic bags of monosodium glutamate, some candy, and two bags of medical supplies, including penicillin and syringes. There was quite a collection of pocket litter and several documents.

"How the hell do you ambush that many people with a squad, McGuire?" I asked him. McGuire's bag of tricks could produce amazing contrivances on occasion. He had extended the kill zone with a mechanical ambush, a technique he had learned very well.

"Sir, we're just country boys," McGuire said. Thirty minutes later Browning's patrol returned.

"James, that area's crawling with VC, but as far as a headquarters is concerned I couldn't see a specific location, nor did we locate any storage areas. While my recon element was in that area we observed from several different locations, and one time we counted a column of fifteen VC with bicycles and carts moving from the northwest toward the southeast. Three and four men groups moved through the area all night. I dropped my ambushes off at the ORP (Objective Rally Point) and they moved out and took up positions about four hundred meters from the ORP but made no contact. I was sure they would have contact but nothing came their way," he said,

"Maybe we didn't get in far enough. I will see if battalion has any kind of update on that area. The intelligence reports could have been off a few hundred meters."

CHAPTER 38

"I feel bad that we didn't come up with anything," Browning said.

"Don't give it a thought. If it's not there, it's not there. Anyway, we have to evacuate the loot from the two ambushes that hit, so we will resupply at the same time. Then we will move about fifteen hundred meters in the direction your patrol went. At worst, we may get a prisoner who can give information on that area."

I called battalion and made a complete report on Browning's patrol. I also requested the resupply and evacuation of the enemy supplies and equipment and had First Platoon blow an LZ near the perimeter. We resupplied and evacuated the enemy gear and then moved about a click (kilometer) and a half in the direction that the VC headquarters was suspected to be. We put out security, dug in, and rested most of the day. The men slept and cleaned up, and weapons were cleaned. In the environment we were operating in, survival demanded that everything be in smooth working order. The machine-gunners brushed out their 7.62 link belt ammunition. I picked up the barrel of Hale's machine-gun, turned it upside down and listened to the gas piston slide to its stopping place.

"Clean as a whistle, Sir!" he said.

"Right you are, Hale!"

That night each platoon was to put out two ambushes. I explained that we were on top of something significant and that enemy activity in the area was high so security had to be tight. If possible we were to try to capture a prisoner.

The ambushes were to go out after dark, as usual. I thought about how things were going, and knew something was wrong. Over and over I stared at my map sheet, studying every detail. Suddenly it jumped out at me as I stared at a bend in the river to our west. I thought about the events of the last two days and today in particular. We had resupplied this morning and had had significant contact near that perimeter last night. Then we picked up as an entire company and moved in broad daylight in the direction of the enemy, if intelligence reports were correct. I called the platoon leaders.

"All ambushes for tonight are canceled. We are moving again as soon as it gets dark. Inform your men and report back here."

"OK. We are moving a kilometer to the south." I pointed out the location of our new perimeter on the map.

"It looks as if the stream on the map, about five hundred meters from our new perimeter, is a significant obstacle to movement. Notice how it bends into the horseshoe at the widest point." The stream formed a large horseshoe about a kilometer northwest of our proposed perimeter, the toe of the horseshoe pointing south and the heel, with its narrow neck of land between the bends of the river, formed a land bridge to the high ground inside the horseshoe. The ground inside was significantly higher than the surrounding terrain, and the horseshoe was barely a kilometer west of us. I had a hunch; more than a hunch. Browning had checked the area five hundred meters west of our present location without significant results. The hill within the horseshoe was a mere five hundred meters west of the area Browning had checked. The center of enemy activity could be based on, even under, the high ground within the horseshoe.

"Movement to the new location will have to be better than we have ever done; noise and light discipline perfect. We are most certainly right on top of the enemy, and they don't seem to be making any moves to avoid us. When we reach the new location, put out a squad sized ambush three hundred meters in front of each platoon. No digging tonight. Dig in after daylight, but keep the noise to an absolute minimum. We have enough ammunition, C's, and batteries to last five days, but we will resupply sooner if we have to have a helicopter in for any reason. We have thirty minutes of daylight left, but don't prepare for movement until dark. We may be under surveillance, so when we leave here we will drop off an ambush behind us, about three hundred meters from here. The order of movement will be: Three, company headquarters, Two, Weapons, and One. First Platoon, drop an ambush about three hundred meters after we move. Lowell, I want a concentration for the center of this perimeter. The ambush will likely have contact unless I miss my guess, so have them go heavy on the claymores, and get artillery information for them, Larry. I want two perishable mechanical ambushes (ambushes that would eventually blow themselves thus requiring no one to disarm them) left behind us. Second and Third, put one MA each in your areas prior to movement." Then I went over details of our organization for defense of the new perimeter.

"Sir, do you want my stay behind ambush to rejoin us tonight?" Sutherland asked.

"Not unless they have contact and think they are compromised. Even if they do have contact if no small arms have to be fired they can stay put. The artillery concentration on this perimeter should be called only if necessary, because it will blow those two MA's. If one or both of the MA's go off fire the artillery concentration. Anything else?" I coded our plans to battalion.

We moved after it was pitch dark. The jungle was thick with underbrush, so movement was at a snail's pace. I didn't care if it took all night; security took priority over speed. We had not even dropped the ambush off when the blasts of the claymores in one of the mechanical ambushes exploded like a thunderclap at the old perimeter. I called First Platoon to see how far from the perimeter they were.

"Charlie Six, Charlie One-Six, we are about to execute," Sutherland told me, meaning he was ready to drop off his stay behind ambush. "Shall we go back and check that MA? Over," he asked.

"This is Charlie Six. Negative. Also, let's hold that concentration for now. We may really need it later, over."

"This is Charlie One-Six. Roger, out."

The other MA went about five minutes after the first. "They had been there and were observing, so they knew when we left and moved in," I thought. There had to be dead and wounded, and wounded had to be taken care of, so they must have their hands full. The stay behind called for the artillery concentration, and I recognized the voice. Bigwitch was doing what he did best – the ambush. The artillery rounds whistled in, plowed through the canopy and blasted the old perimeter.

We plodded on, changing course one time for the second leg of the trip. We never went the distance in a straight line; if an observer could determine the azimuth we were moving on, he could find us later. I kept an ear to the rear, waiting for Bigwitch's ambush to go. It never did.

Sometime around midnight it started to rain, rapidly turning from a drizzle to a downpour. We finally reached our new location and stumbled around in the inky thickness, trying to get into position. Third and First Platoons had trouble tying in; they had to waste the better part of thirty minutes trying to find each other. I knew we were highly vulnerable at that time, and worried that we might get mortared as we milled around, but I guess God looks after fools and Infantrymen. I made a mental note to have Fitzsimmons show Sutherland how to tie in when we formed a new perimeter.

Dripping daylight finally arrived, and I went around with the platoon leaders adjusting the perimeter in the dim morning light. The soldiers moved sluggishly, soaked and chilled from the rain. No matter how skillfully we used our ponchos to shield us from the rain, we ended up soaked. Bigwitch slipped into the perimeter about an hour after daylight. There was a commotion in First Platoon area. I walked over to warn them about noise discipline when I saw what they were excited about.

Sergeant Bigwitch and Lieutenant Sutherland were approaching with Bigwitch prodding a bound and blindfolded VC along with his rifle. He handed me the prisoner's AK 47.

"Ran right into us as we were setting up. He was running from the direction of the old perimeter after that second mechanical ambush went."

I checked him carefully, but he didn't appear to be wounded. He had on a fatigue shirt and pants, a pair of automobile tire sandals, and a sweat rag tied around his neck. He had worn an AK 47 ammunition belt across his chest with four magazines of ammunition when he was captured. There was another magazine in his weapon, and he had carried two friction grenades.

"Hold him in your platoon area," I told Sutherland. "I'll let you know when and how we will evacuate him."

Back at my CP, my four RTO's, Collins, Singletary, Chavez, and Lockhart, were digging the CP trench. First Sergeant Long carefully assessed their work looking over his glasses, his gaunt frame bent at the waist and his long bony hands on his knobby knees supporting his upper body. He looked much like a modern Ichabod Crane who was about to launch into his pedagogic mode and assemble these radio operators for a class in math.

"Top, that prisoner poses a problem for us."

"I wish we had never caught the son-of-a-bitch. Now when we evac him Charlie will know exactly where we are when that bird lands. We busted our ass to get in here unnoticed. Look at the work we've done on this position."

"Well, what are the alternatives?"

"Sir, I'll give you an alternative. Have you ever heard of the Pancho Villa course in care and feeding of prisoners?" Chavez had tossed his D-handled shovel out of the hole and was proceeding to get out of it. He brushed the dirt off his fatigues and looked up at Sergeant Long and then to me.

"Tell me about it, Chavez."

"The first rule is, if the bastard is causing you problems, kill him." Chavez was a Texas Mexican whose father worked on the King Ranch. He was a tough kid who had learned early the value of hard work, doing ranch chores under his father's rough tutelage. He was an athletic six footer whose dark brown face and sparkling black eyes were roofed by a thatch of black hair swept to the left side, Hitler style. He was about as no-nonsense as a kid could become by eighteen years of age.

Since we were discussing this prisoner's fate, Lockhart, a short black soldier from Jackson, Mississippi, decided he would get his two cents in. "Man, you can't do shit like that, Ramon. They put your ass in LBJ (Long Binh Jail) for that. Ain't you read that card in your pocket about 'The Enemy In Your Hands'?"

Singletary sided with Lockhart. They were inseparable buddies, one black and one white, who had grown up together in Mississippi and come into the army together. They had never been separated since enlistment. "Ramon, you can't kill no prisoner. Didn't you listen to none of them classes they gave us?"

The first sergeant prevailed with wiser counsel. "Sir, we need to stay here and find whatever Charlie is hiding in the horseshoe. Let a patrol take him out a good ways from the perimeter to evacuate him. You have to tell battalion about him."

"OK, that sounds good. I know Major King will use common sense in his decision on how to get this guy back there."

I called battalion and explained the situation to King, requesting permission to hold the prisoner until tomorrow. Before he called back to say no, I had First Platoon readying a squad sized patrol to take the prisoner to the east some six hundred meters, blow a PZ (pickup zone), and evacuate him. King understood, but he had to get the prisoner out as soon as possible. In fifteen minutes, Sergeant Rozier's squad left the perimeter with the prisoner.

At about 0800 hours the rain stopped, and in an hour the sun was beating down on the jungle canopy. The foxhole line started to shape up, and soldiers dug into their rucksacks for dry socks and foot powder. Those who wore underwear changed it. My dry undershirt felt like a million dollars. I hung the wet fatigue shirt on a bamboo branch to dry and sat on my poncho with my boots off, hoping the air and foot powder would dry my wrinkled feet.

The loud explosions from the east were followed by Rozier's radio communication that the PZ was ready. The helicopter came in and landed on Rozier's purple smoke, lifted the prisoner out, and the squad moved south from the PZ about four hundred meters until they struck a trail. At that point they set up an ambush. The plan was to ambush there until after dark, then to return to the perimeter.

I laid my plans for the coming night deliberately. Our job was to locate and report on whatever enemy activity there was within the area first, then to destroy them with whatever means possible in conjunction with any plans that battalion might have. I called the platoon leaders and the orders group.

"Second Platoon, I want a reconnaissance of the area within that horseshoe. Find out as much as possible about the enemy in and around the horseshoe. Let me know the condition of that stream, the best crossing sites and the danger areas. Record any trails in the area on your map or make a good sketch of them."

"Lowell, plot artillery concentrations on the horseshoe area and up to a kilometer beyond. Let's plan a couple of airstrikes on the high ground and within the horseshoe for tomorrow morning at first light. We can divert them if we have new targets at that time or turn them back to battalion in case anyone else needs them."

"Sam, get in and see what the hell is there, and come back and tell me. If you can make a full report on the radio from that site, do it. Use the company SOP code."

"We are very likely to be hit in this area, although our movement in was good. They know we're here but maybe not exactly where. Rozier blew that LZ east of us for evacuation, so you can be sure they will check that area out. Tonight, put squad sized close-in ambushes to your front, out two hundred meters or so, depending on the ground. Dig in as well as possible and get some overhead cover. Check your weapons today and let's get ready."

"Oh. One more thing. Battalion is moving this morning to a point about a kilometer east of where they are now." I pointed out the new location on the map. "That will put them near the eastern edge of the triangle and they will have open ground for LZ's, etc. OK. Let's do it!"

I sat there thinking that battalion had not moved since we had begun the operation and they had been mortared twice and taken casualties both times. "So much for my high estimation of Major King," I thought. There was absolutely no doubt that Charlie knew where they were sitting, and he had to be observing them. If they tipped off their direction of movement they would stand a good chance of getting ambushed. "Aw, what the hell. B Company is with them, and they will screen the route and provide security. Besides, 1st of the 16th is north of us, and 2nd of the 28th is south with that brigade of the 101st to our west. Charlie has his hands full all over the place. But in my heart I knew I was alibiing for battalion's lack of security. Hell, they would be better off sitting where they are than moving in daylight. "Well, Worthington, you had best watch your own company's ass and quit playing colonel," I thought.

The jungle was quiet except for the "chuck, chuck, chuck" of entrenching tools plying the earth. It grew hotter, and above the canopy in the turquoise sky the red tropical sun showered scorching rays in all directions. Not a breeze stirred, and even under the deep insulation of the perpetual green thickness it was hot and humid as a sauna. The soldiers worked without shirts, and were dripping wet. A black soldier in Third Platoon was bent over, digging with his backside to me. The crotch of his fatigues was soaking wet. As he stood up, his straight muscular back glistened with sweat. He stepped out of the hole, and a white kid with thick rust red hair and freckled face and arms dropped into the hole and stabbed at the black dirt with his entrenching tool. Dirty rivulets of sweat ran over his shoulders and back where an occasional tiny errant clod of the black dirt stuck, melted and ran into his fatigue pants at the waist.

I wondered where Kim was and what she was doing. Was she getting settled into Wahiawa, and how would she like being treated like a whore when the good citizens of the community found out she was a Korean, married to a soldier? "Everybody has to hate somebody," I thought, and the Hawaiians hated. Behind the "aloha" at the international airport in Honolulu, along with the colored scented leis and the smiling white teeth, and out on the red baked hills, beyond the pineapple, cane fields and jungles of the Koo Laus; down on Beretania Street lay the real Hawaii, where you were a "goddamned haole" if you were not from the islands. And they would equate Kim to the drink hustlers and prostitutes in the Korean bars in Honolulu. Not your problem now, James. Stop thinking about it. "Don't mean a goddamned thing," I said, and I got up and checked the work on the perimeter.

Before noon I cut the tops out of cans of "White Bread," "Spiced Beef with Sauce," and "Type Two

Cheese Spread." I cut a hole in the center of the white bread, stuffed the spiced beef into it and topped it with the cheese spread, and took an empty can, cut holes in it, bent three sides of the lip of the can inward, dropped a heat tablet into the can, struck a match to it, and toasted my Vietnam cheeseburger. After two bites the radio on the battalion net crackled. It was a one-sided conversation between the battalion Tactical Operations Center, the TOC, and B Company. I could hear the TOC but not B Company, and the picture was all too clear. They had been ambushed, had heavy casualties, and the fight was still going on. As I listened, jets streaked overhead and I could hear the bombs thudding into the jungle to the northeast.

As soon as the air cleared I called the TOC. Major Furman Hickey, the S-3, answered.

"Thunder Three, this is Thunder Charlie Six, should we move to assist you? Over."

"This is Thunder Three, negative. Stay put. We have fought through it and have reached our new area. The air and artillery are doing a good job. Out."

In about fifteen minutes the TOC called back and read a coded message. The first sergeant decoded the message, in grim silence.

"Sir, Major King was killed in the ambush, and Major Hickey has temporarily assumed command of the battalion. They had fifteen killed and forty-two wounded in that mess!" he said.

"My God! Has brigade gotten involved yet?"

"Yes, according to the message a new commander will arrive to take command tomorrow morning."

"Have they gotten all the wounded out?"

"No, they are still dusting people off, but the VC have broken contact. Apparently the air saved their ass," he said.

I called the orders group and gave them the message. There was a shocked silence. It is better to tell it like it is because if you don't, rumors start, snowball and finally run totally out of control. The morale of the unit is shot to shreds.

"Hell, we're OK. If the new colonel is a good one we will be better off than before as a unit," I explained. We discussed it, and the group finally agreed that it really didn't have too great an effect on us directly. Major Hickey was in charge, he knew what had to be done; the new colonel would arrive tomorrow, and things would slowly get back to normal as other replacements trickled in. I wished that I believed it. The worst thing I could do was to seem too concerned, so I adopted a "business as usual" attitude. It seemed to work, but I knew that these young leaders and their troops were looking at the world through different eyes than they had that morning.

CHAPTER 39

Darkness fell, and Sergeant Rozier's squad returned without having made contact. Second Platoon's patrol went out, a tall thick man leading them. His ancestors had formed to make their mounted assault, firing repeating rifles, over the open ground and up the rise that the 7th Cavalry defended under Custer at the Little Big Horn that day. Now Sergeant Redlegs fought in a strange hot jungle so alien to one whose very existence was tied to the buttes and plains, sparkling streams and snowy icy winters where once the buffalo roamed in great herds and sustained his people.

Four men back in the column was a short, stocky black man, whose ancestors were brought to America's shores in chains, in the galley of a slave ship. He had a sneer on his face, although it couldn't be seen, but it was there because it was always there. Boykin's belligerence had been kept in check by the system, but not always. Even the "hammer of Thor," as the troops in Second Platoon referred to Sergeant Redleg's club-like right arm and fist, had only fanned the hatred and resentment in Boykin's breast. The army had outlawed Redlegs' style of military justice long ago, but the residual remains of "behind the barracks" discipline still existed here and there in the platoons and squads of the Infantry units.

Complicating matters was the half-hearted abdicating of command of Second Platoon by a new lieutenant, to the battle hardened, physically tough and universally respected Redlegs. Sam Fowler had grown up in the red clay hills of northern Georgia. He should have been one hell of a fine Infantry officer. Maybe he was and his time to blossom forth and participate in the rites of the samurai had not yet arrived. But his platoon had never been given a more important mission than tonight's patrol, and he sat sulking by his CP, as Achilles had by the Greek ships on the shores of Troy.

"Sam, when are you going to take command of your platoon?" I asked softly, as I stood beside him.

He looked up with a start. He hadn't heard me because he had been lost in thought, mostly about the subject I had just raised, I suspected.

"Sir, Sergeant Redlegs can do the job much better than I can, and this is an important job. He commands the respect of these men and did before I arrived."

"Sam, do you think you are the first green lieutenant ever to step into a platoon that had an experienced platoon sergeant? That happens in every army in the world, practically every day."

"But my situation is different. Redlegs is simply too good for me to compete with."

"You've just told me what the problem is. You're not in competition with him for anything. He is the platoon sergeant, you are the platoon leader. Your roles are separate and distinct, and the stronger and more prepared he is the better off you are. Use him, don't compete with him."

"But, uh, well," he stammered.

"Sam, take hold of that platoon. I don't ever want to see you abdicate your role as platoon leader again. You should be leading that patrol tonight, and the troops, the company, and I know it." I turned away.

The situation reports from Redlegs were "negative," meaning nothing significant to report, right up to midnight, and I dozed off sitting on my poncho beside the CP trench, leaning against a tree. At 0100 hours the radio watch, PFC Singletary, awakened me.

"Sir, Sergeant Redlegs wants to speak to you," he said.

"This is Charlie Six," I answered his call.

He was whispering. "This is Charlie Two Six Papa. This place is crawling with dinks. They cross the water of the horseshoe in boats and there are carts and bicycles everywhere," he said. "They are hauling ammunition, food, medical supplies and other stuff I can't identify. There is definitely a depot or transfer point, most likely under the hill in the horseshoe, over."

"This is Charlie Six. What about the open end of the horseshoe? Over."

"This is Two Six. It's barricaded with bunkers and wire. The water of the stream is deep, flowing fairly swiftly and it's about thirty meters wide, over."

"This is Six. OK. Can you get back out of there? Over."

"This is Two Six. Fire the concentrations on the horseshoe and north of it to distract them, and I'll move while the artillery is going in, over," he whispered.

"This is Six, Roger. Fire will commence in about five minutes. Out."

Lowell called for the concentrations and the rounds started raining in to our northwest. I was surprised when Redlegs called back.

"Charlie Six, Charlie Two Six. Right 300. That would be pretty well on the money. Over."

"Charlie Six. Roger. Get your ass out of there. We need the info. Out."

About 0330 Collins awakened me. "Sir, the patrol is in contact and has two casualties." I listened to the small arms fire not far outside the perimeter.

"Charlie Six, Charlie Two Six, over."

"Charlie Six, over."

"Two Six. We have run into the back of a VC unit moving in your direction. I have one KHA and one WHA. We are on our way through, so don't shoot us up. Out."

I alerted the perimeter and we went quickly to one hundred percent alert. Redleg's patrol came through, carrying a soldier, and a second man hobbled along with his arm around the shoulders of another. The patrol came by for debriefing, which I completed quickly and passed the information to battalion. It looked as if we were going to get hit.

"Who did you lose, Sergeant Redlegs?" I asked.

He looked at me in the darkness, and I could imagine the expressionless mask of the face with the pockmarks and high flat cheekbones.

"Boykin, Sir. Smithers also took a round through the calf of his leg. He will have to be evacuated."

"Does anybody have anything else to report?" They looked at me without speaking.

"OK. That's it. Get ready because they're headed this way," I said. Redlegs had described the VC element he had encountered as about company sized. The patrol had killed four VC in that element for sure, and there had to be wounded.

"Lowell, prepare to fire those DT's beyond the close in ambushes. In fact, go ahead and fire the ones in front of Second Platoon." As I spoke firing broke out from the northwest and shortly after that to the northeast. The close in ambushes in front of Second and First Platoons had blown their claymores and now engaged the enemy with small arms. Both squads requested permission to withdraw; granted. They barely got into the perimeter when the mortar rounds started to pound in. The attacking VC were somewhat confused by the action with Redlegs' patrol and by having met stiff resistance from the squads' close in ambushes. They had deployed to attack but were still not close to the perimeter.

By radio, I diverted to our defense the air strikes planned for the horseshoe. Lieutenant Redd had the artillery going on the DT (defensive target) in front of Second Platoon. Third Platoon's close in ambush had not yet made contact, so the fight was shaping up like a two-pronged attack; one from the northwest and the other from the northeast. I prayed that the airstrikes would get here in time, hoping like hell to hear the sound of the jets. I also requested more air if possible and was told that there was one more preplanned strike which could be diverted to us, but it was scheduled for 0600 hours. We took it, although I worried that it might be late. As it turned out, the timing couldn't have been better.

The attack on the northwest against Second Platoon's area began to build, and the small arms on that side of the perimeter rose to a crescendo. The sky was growing lighter when I caught the faint roar of aircraft to the south.

"Charlie Six, Sidewinder Three-One. Good morning!" I was never happier to hear an anticipated voice than at that moment. In spite of the casual way they approached the job the FAC's that we worked with were professionals. They could deliver when the chips were down.

"This is Charlie Six. We need air on two sides of the perimeter; northwest and northeast, over."

"Roger, please mark, over."

Each platoon had three smoke grenades tied in trees over their perimeter areas and above the canopy. I gave the word for Second and First Platoon to mark.

"Roger, I have a green smoke on the northwest and a purple smoke on the northeast."

"This is Charlie Six. Right now the biggest trouble is from the northwest, over."

"Roger, rolling in to mark." The white smoke rocket fired by the FAC from his flimsy little OV1 aircraft made a hissing roar and burst in front of Second Platoon.

"Sam, how is that?"

"Sounds OK, but maybe a little too close in," Second Platoon Leader yelled. I could hardly hear him for the small arms fire.

"That's where we need it; close in!" I yelled.

"Sidewinder Three-One, Charlie Six, that's good. Go to work, over."

"Roger, passes beginning now." We had not cut the artillery, so the FAC was in contact with the battalion artillery liaison officer, and knew where the artillery was coming from and what maximum ordinate they were firing. He had to know, or an artillery round could bring down one of his fast movers; it had happened before. The jets rolled in and pickled their five hundred pound bombs, damned close in front of Second Platoon. The rattle of small arms fire ceased on that side of the perimeter, and I had visions of VC scrambling madly to clear. The FAC put the second flight of jets on the First Platoon side after marking the area with a smoke rocket. After the high drag bombs came the napalm, where the bombs had made holes that helped the napalm get through the foliage. All the while the artillery pounded away. The jets made their final passes, strafing long strips of jungle in front of Second and First Platoons. The VC fire from those areas had dried up to a fizzle, and the jungle burned and smoked from the napalm, that stuck to everything it had touched.

There was firing from the south now; Third Platoon's squad ambush blew their claymores and fought back with small arms. Redd had the artillery shifted to that side and began to fire south of the squad ambush. Browning had not called about withdrawing his squad, so I called him.

"How are they doing out there?"

"OK. They are still in control of the situation, so I'm leaving the ambush there for the time being."

"OK. Bring them in at your discretion, and let me know when you do. We have another air strike that we can put in at 0600 hours."

"Right."

Not five minutes later the Third Platoon squad ambush had a man wounded and came under intense automatic weapons fire. As Browning started withdrawing the ambush another man was hit badly; he was dead before they reached the perimeter.

The FAC came back. "Charlie Six, Sidewinder Three-One with more ordnance. Where would you like it? Over."

"Charlie Six, marking now. Hit south of the smoke, over." Browning pulled the cord on one of his smoke grenades.

"Roger, got goofy grape, over."

"This is Charlie Six. Affirm, over."

"And Sidewinder Three-One marking now," the FAC said, as casually as if he were switching on the television set in his living room in Podunk, Iowa. He rolled in and fired his smoke rocket. Browning said it was perfect.

"Sidewinder Three-One, this is Charlie Six, that's good, over."

"Roger, going to work."

The jets pounded the area in front of Third Platoon. Large saplings flew as the blast, concussion, and steel of the five hundred pound "snake eyes" lashed the jungle. The smell of cordite and smoke permeated the area. Then the napalm passes began and the jellied, thickened fuel burning at great intensity sucked the oxygen from the air around it. VC firing from that side of the perimeter ceased, but as the jets began their passes bursts of .51 caliber fire could be heard west of the perimeter. The FAC's voice came over the net more excitedly than normal, and I knew immediately that something was wrong.

"Charlie Six, Sidewinder Three-One, they have hit one of the fast movers, over!"

"This is Charlie Six, roger. Bail out in the open ground to the northeast. We have friendlies there in Ben Cat and Lai Khe, over."

"Sidewinder Three-One, roger. He's heading that way, out."

I called battalion to pass the word to brigade to let the ARVN in Ben Cat know what was happening. He was able to bail out over Lai Khe and came down on the runway. We received word that he had been checked out at brigade clearing station and was OK. The million dollar airplane crashed and burned in the jungle northeast of Lai Khe; shot down by bullets from a rusty .51 caliber machine-gun, sighted by Charlie through a bamboo section bent into a circle, with a straight cross formed by two pieces of bamboo in the center. That weapon and others like it were gleaned from the battlefield.

The artillery continued to pound the area west of the perimeter, and a spatter of VC small arms fire continued. I heard yelling from Browning's position. A dazed and wounded VC, standing straight up, walked directly toward the foxhole line. He had a head wound and it looked as if he had taken some shrapnel in his back. He was stunned, his ragged fatigue shirt was blood soaked, and he was unarmed. Browning led him into the perimeter and put him on a poncho behind the line. They tied his hands and feet and roped him to a sapling. Browning's medic did what he could for him, after their own wounded were cared for.

By 0830 hours a silence fell on the battlefield, and we pushed out to check the results of the fighting. The air and artillery had been devastating. In counting the enemy dead I saw no more than twenty that I could say positively were killed by small arms. There were a total of one hundred and seventy-three VC bodies around the perimeter. We picked up three more wounded prisoners. There was a collection of one hundred and fifty weapons stacked up at the CP including some .51 caliber machine-guns, and three RPG anti-tank rocket launchers, as well as a poncho full of both American and Chicom grenades and small arms ammunition. All web gear, pocket litter, and a few documents were marked, dated, and tied in bundles for evacuation. We blew the grenades and ammunition in a shell hole outside the perimeter, and I walked back to my CP.

I walked past Second Platoon where two poncho covered bodies lay by a large hardwood tree. One was huge, and the large bleached white jungle boots stuck out from under the poncho. The other was smaller and lay alongside the larger one, much like father and son. I pulled back the poncho of the larger figure, and the dark countenance was as stern in death as it had been in life. The other body was that of Boykin. He had been hit in the back of the head by a rifle round.

"Sir, Sergeant Redlegs was killed when those first mortar rounds came in," Lieutenant Fowler said.

"OK. Let's get everything cleaned up and ship shape. We will resupply after they finish those dust offs and evacuate this gear."

I walked back to the CP.

"Sir, they will take the bodies out now. We have dusted off thirteen men and that's all. There are four dead," Doc Gill said.

"OK Doc. Thanks, buddy; I saw you working during this thing. You're a real pro."

"Thank you, Sir."

We resupplied, and as each ship was unloaded we loaded the enemy weapons and equipment. We had four prisoners tied and tagged, and evacuated them with the equipment.

I gave battalion an update in code, and when I finished they sent me a coded message. Top had it decoded by the time they finished transmitting.

"Sir, division commander and brigade commander send their congratulations to Charlie Company for one hell of a job. Major Hickey, acting battalion commander, sends his thanks. He and the new commander will be here around 1300 hours."

"OK. Let's get the supplies distributed. Hell, they may hit us again. The damned war isn't over. Let's get back to normal as soon as possible. Readjust your foxhole lines and eliminate any holes you can't fill with riflemen. Get your OP's out as soon as possible. Refurbish your camouflage, and get new claymores out. I will know at 1300, when the new battalion commander gets here, what we are going to do about that complex up in the horseshoe."

"Sir, are we going to move?" Lieutenant Fowler asked.

"Yes, but I would prefer to hold the details until I talk to the battalion commander. At any rate the move will be after dark; most likely a short one, probably around six hundred meters," I said.

"Then do we get the poop just after the new battalion commander leaves?" Browning asked. I had the feeling that he was trying to help me fill the gaps.

"Yes. I'll give you the poop as soon as they clear the area. Don't make any preparations for the new commander. Just do your jobs. He may want to meet you and shake a few hands so stand by the CP when he arrives, OK? If there's nothing else, let's go to work." They got up to leave, but Lieutenant Fowler came to me.

"Sir, can I have a word with you?"

"Of course, Sam. What's on your mind?"

"Sir, what should we do about this Redlegs and Boykin thing?" His lips shook.

"Sam, what are you talking about?" I knew very well what he was talking about.

"Well, uh, you mean you don't draw any conclusions from the way Boykin died?"

"None. What conclusions do you draw?"

"Well, he was, uh, hit in the back of the head by one round."

"Sam, if you're asking me to bring charges against a dead man, without witnesses or evidence, then my answer is no. That doesn't mean that you can't bring charges."

"Yes, Sir," he said.

"Well, Worthington, you don't want to play God," I thought. "Punishment by men, governments, and institutions, can only be inflicted upon the living. Who would be punished if anything happened to reduce his pay? His wife and children, no doubt, and what good purpose would that serve? They were probably huddled somewhere on a reservation, hoping that Redlegs will get home," I thought. "Well, he will. He will be home soon. And if Fowler is so concerned that justice be done, who is going to punish Fowler? If he had done his job he would have been on that patrol, rather than Redlegs. Who the hell knows if Redlegs did it anyway? What the hell? He's dead. Let the poor bastard sleep the big sleep. And now Fowler will get his chance to really be a platoon leader."

CHAPTER 40

I heard the helicopters beating in the distance.

"Charlie Six, this is Thunder Three, in bound in two birds, pop smoke, over."

"This is Charlie Six, smoke popped, over."

"This is Thunder Three, I have green smoke, over."

"This is Charlie Six, affirmative. There's room for two ships in there, but you should land to the north, over."

"This is Thunder Three, roger, out."

Why were there two birds? I knew they might have a gunship escort; those were certainly not going to land. Who else was inbound with them?

Two helicopters hovered into the hole in the jungle and landed. From the lead ship a tall, graying man in crisp starched jungle fatigues, spit shined boots, and soft cap with four stars bounded off the helicopter. His chest was out, he walked erectly, and a sort of perpetual smile displayed even white teeth. An aide followed him. I moved across the edge of the LZ.

"Sir, Lieutenant Worthington reports," I saluted.

"Good afternoon, Lieutenant! It hasn't been long since I visited this company on an occasion just like this one, except that time you were a platoon leader!" General Westmoreland remarked.

"Sir, please step over to my CP, and I'll introduce you to my officers and first sergeant. Sir, this is Lieutenant Dave Browning."

"Lieutenant Browning, I haven't seen you in quite a while. How have things been going?"

"Just fine, Sir." Browning answered.

General Westmoreland was fond of having soldiers know that he remembered them, if he had ever met them. He met each officer, remembered Lieutenant Scott from somewhere and reminded Scott of it. Then he turned to Long.

"First Sergeant Long, how nice to see you again. Where was it we last met?"

"Beats me, Sir, I never seed you before you got off that helicopter!" Long answered with true Alabama honesty. The General was somewhat taken aback, but recovered quickly.

"Worthington, can I see some of the enemy dead?"

"Yes, Sir. Right this way, Sir." I led him through Third Platoon's perimeter, with my RTO's providing security. We swung through the area where the air and artillery had taken its toll then circled around in front of Second and then First Platoons. I looked back at the tail of the entourage and could not have been more shocked if Ho Chi Minh strolled along with us. There, at the tail end of the small group, was Major Hickey and behind him was Lieutenant Colonel William Ricksley! I just couldn't make the connection that Ricksley was the new battalion commander. I turned back to what I was doing. A VC body, torn in two, hung on the stump of a hardwood tree that had been blown down during an air strike. The head was rolled back at a crazy angle and the eyes were open. We swung back into the perimeter through First Platoon's foxhole line, where the General spoke to some of the men and shook their hands. We walked back across the perimeter to his helicopter.

"Worthington, this is one of the finest, most professional, perimeter defenses I have ever seen executed. You and all your men are to be congratulated," as he shook my hand. His genuine sincerity came through.

I saluted, he shook hands with Major Hickey and Lieutenant Colonel Ricksley, boarded his helicopter and strapped in. They cranked, hovered out of the LZ, and disappeared toward Saigon.

I turned to face Hickey and Ricksley, and Hickey attempted to make introductions. I had an overwhelming urge to raise the rifle I carried and fire a complete magazine into Ricksley. He saw it in my face, and I caught him twitching. He was still somewhat shaken by the battlefield scene he had just witnessed, which was his first. Seeing me standing there with my rifle at the ready and considering what he had just done to me, he had no trouble imagining the possibilities.

"Major Hickey, Lieutenant Worthington and I are old friends. We served together in Korea in the same battalion," he said. He extended his hand, and I saluted slowly, deliberately; refusing his hand shake. He returned my salute.

"James, we had a great battalion in Korea and it continued in that same fine tradition after you left. Mr. Choe at the club sends his best as do your other friends around Casey," he said.

It suddenly dawned on me that he had no idea that I had returned to Korea just after he left. Indeed, he seemed to think I knew nothing of his marriage to Kim. I decided to play my little game with him now.

"Colonel, did you see my fiancee Kim Hae Ja, after I left? We are planning to get married when I return, and

I haven't heard from her lately." The fiancee part was for effect. He was stunned and caught short for words. I could see behind those eyes and the twisted smile, and I saw the puzzle he wrestled with. Did I know or not know, and how should he answer?

"Uh, well let's discuss those matters later. Right now we need to go over plans for this complex you say you've found," he changed the subject. "Now exactly what is there in the highground within the horseshoe?" he asked.

I covered the exact information that I had transmitted to battalion that morning. He sat on the ground and rubbed his chin pensively as I went over the information given by Redlegs and the patrol.

"Is that all, Worthington?"

"That's all, Colonel," I said coldly. The son-of-a-bitch. He hadn't been in Vietnam a week; Redlegs had just executed a near perfect recon patrol under impossible conditions, and he wanted to know if that was all, as if we had not done our job. "Easy James," I told myself. "What's done is done; he never was a competent officer, and now the army has dumped the sorry bastard on your head. But just keep cool and suffer through, and his day will come."

"Well, it sounds like little more than a job for a good combat patrol," I couldn't believe what he was saying. I stared at him in disbelief.

"Colonel, that jungled hill within the horseshoe is a kilometer long and eight hundred meters wide at its widest point. We have no pin point objective located within that area, so I'd like to know what a combat patrol's objective would be," I said. "Why can't we hit it with an arc light and go in with the entire battalion, or better still, the entire brigade?" I asked.

"Sir, he's exactly right in my opinion. A combat patrol would do no more than get eaten alive. They are alert and aware of our presence, and I can guarantee that we are under surveillance now," Major Hickey said.

Ricksley glared coldly at Hickey. "Major, I'm commanding this battalion now, and I don't need any advice on how to do the job, especially from lieutenant company commanders!"

I knew that maintaining the survival of C Company would be one hell of a task now. "Well, what do you want done?"

"I want a combat patrol run tonight against the enemy activity you say is there," he said, and I knew that sneer because I had seen it on this face many times before. There it was again; the inference that we might be lying about what we reported from Redlegs's patrol.

"Will that be all, Colonel?" I looked Ricksley dead in the eyes, and he stared back with the contempt one would normally reserve for a bum raiding a garbage can.

"One more thing. I hope you don't think you can send a sergeant in there to lead the patrol. In fact, your platoon leaders are green by my records. I want you in charge of that patrol, and I want you on the radio so I can talk to you," he smiled his twisted smile, and his purple lips and glassy eyes wrinkled in the same look he had given Captain Laird on the range that day in Korea, so long ago.

A blind rage swept over me, and I had trouble controlling the urge to spring on the arrogant, rotten egomaniac. He sucked on his Meershaum pipe and the camouflaged silk scarf was tied neatly around his throat. I tried to view the ridiculous situation from a distance, to determine how really bad it was. A rifle company had just accomplished a reconnaissance patrol against a major enemy activity with near complete success, and soon after had fought a major battle that a battalion would have had difficulty in winning and had walked away with a victory which was personally praised by General Westmoreland himself. I failed to see any logic whatsoever in the discussion with Ricksley; however, there was logic there. The cunning reason of a pack of starving timber wolves stalking a moose lay under the surface of Ricksley's words and contemptuous sneer. What had taken place here on the battlefield had nothing at all to do with it. I looked at Ricksley without replying.

"Well, Worthington, do you understand the mission or not?" With the sarcastic, cutting edge in his voice that I knew well.

"Completely. Absolutely in every way, and most of all your reasons for doing it this way," I said in an even tone of voice. I was in control again.

He understood me. "Well, that's settled. Major Hickey, let's get on back to the CP and fight the war," as he rose and strode toward the helicopter knocking out his pipe. I didn't bother to go with him, nor did I stand at the edge of the LZ to salute as they hovered up and out of the jungle, into the hot blue afternoon sky.

CHAPTER 41

The orders group waited at the CP. My job was a difficult one.

"Worthington, you have to walk back there like we have just won the war and are preparing to celebrate except for one small mopping up job," I thought. To convey the sarcasm, cynicism, and negativism of Ricksley down to my subordinates would have been criminal, to put it mildly. When a superior commander is dead wrong, and any fool in ten surrounding counties can readily recognize it, then the thing to do is protect the men from him and his plans, and if one has a little common sense, and luck, the mission can be satisfactorily accomplished, the men saved to fight another day, and the imbecile commander pleased with the results, thinking that his plan has been carried out, while in actuality nothing near what he envisioned was even undertaken. That was my task as I stepped over the creepers and wait-a-minute vines and around wall to wall bamboo to the command post. Incredibly, my spirits soared; I knew I had done my job, and that at some particular juncture in history, justice would come to Ricksley like the sure hand of God. I couldn't wait.

I explained the mission, then explained my plan to accomplish it. Immediately after dark the company would move to the south, six hundred meters and harbor for the night with no digging, good security, and hopefully, with perfect noise and light discipline. I showed the orders group the exact spot where we were to establish the new perimeter. From where we were presently dug in, in the old perimeter, Second Platoon was to patrol to the north about eight hundred meters and hold up in a hasty ambush. I would take my patrol out to the west from the new location, cross the stream, swing north, pass the horseshoe on its northwest side, and come in on the horseshoe from its open end on the north. When I called Second Platoon, they were to break their hasty ambush and move to the west toward the horseshoe. They were to make contact and deliver a heavy volume of small arms and machine-gun fire, as well as fire several artillery concentrations on the horseshoe, and then withdraw rapidly back to the main perimeter.

For the patrol, I would use Bigwitch's squad of seven men from First Platoon and two of my RTO's, Collins and Chavez. This was no ordinary combat patrol, but the actual requirement was not for a patrol at all, but for far more. In addition, when the patrol left the new perimeter, one squad from Third Platoon would go out with us and drop off behind as an ambush, four hundred meters outside the perimeter, to ensure that we were not being followed.

As for specific actions at the objective I had no detailed plan. My idea was quite simply to break the patrol down into a security element and a combat element. Leaving the security element to cover us, I would take the combat element into the complex and try to destroy the most significant target I could locate and return with as many men alive as possible.

That afternoon I rehearsed the patrol over and over in the perimeter. Extra demolitions were brought in, along with three flame throwers in a one ship resupply that afternoon. Just before dark I had a little time to myself, and sat on the ground with my back resting against a tree and my poncho spread out in front of me, broke down my rifle, and cleaned it carefully. I used the metal chamber brush on the chamber until I was sure there was no carbon there. Reflecting on the day's events, it seemed to me to be the beginning of a long nightmare, with death or total oblivion at the far end of the dark vortex into which I was being sucked. It was easy to rehearse an ambush but not quite that simple to rehearse dying. Why, in the name of fate, coincidence, or God, had Ricksley turned up here, in the same battalion that I was assigned to? I was sure it couldn't have been by his own design. Yet here he was, his evil, disloyal, self seeking ego, trying his best to get me eliminated from the face of the earth. There was absolutely no doubt in my mind as to his intentions. The one thing that I couldn't let happen was to have the men in my company placed in harm's way because of his desire to have me leave "quartermaster style" in a body bag. But what options were there? I was commanding C Company, and shouldering the responsibility for those soldiers. There were less than honorable ways out, of course. I could simply seek medical evacuation because of old wounds, malaria, injury, or whatever. I had seen enough of shamming soldiers to know every trick in the book, but I intended to be able to look myself in the face when I shaved in the morning, and be damned if I would choose that way out. I could request reassignment and have some poor green captain, or worse, a lieutenant, come in cold and take the company down to oblivion with him because of obedience and blind trust in

Ricksley's flawed judgment. Not only had he decided to make me his personal Uriah, but his tactical judgment was not solid. He had no feel for how to meet and successfully defeat the enemy. I recalled some of the faulty plans he had concocted for the battalion in Korea – the frontal assaults when an exposed flank, better still an exposed rear, existed. His lack of knowledge of the use of fire support was appalling. One of his favorite terms was "put some fire balls on their heads." That would have been wonderful had he understood how to do it. Tactically, he was like a musician who was forever slightly off key, "sharping when he should have been flatting" as Sergeant Long would later put it.

The worst part of the problem lay in me. I had been reared with a workable set of morals, but I hated Ricksley passionately for what he had done to me and to others, most of all because of Kim. I did not trust him in even the smallest of matters and to protect the men from him, and do my job as a leader in combat, would be a tight-rope act of the first magnitude.

The other option, which I couldn't resist considering, was simply to kill the rotten bastard. Could that be done and paid for in the eyes of God and man by serving a prison sentence, being executed, or suffering whatever other form of justice the courts would mete out? Yes, but for what? For Ricksley? Better to stuff a banded krait in his pocket and let him take his two steps and die, I thought.

"Sir, we should be moving," Long interrupted my thoughts. It had grown dark as I sat there, absorbed in contemplating the possibilities.

"OK Top, let's move them."

Second Platoon moved out of the perimeter heading north, and the rest of the company began to move toward the south and the new location, about ten minutes later. Someone struck a match in Third Platoon's column. I heard a loud slap and the light was suddenly extinguished. We had been moving for about ten minutes when the rain began to beat down on the jungle canopy. At first we just heard the rain, but after perhaps fifteen minutes it increased in intensity and dropped on us from the leaves,limbs and bamboo tangles, and we were soon soaked. A few men pulled their ponchos from their rucksacks and slipped them on. Ponchos helped, but soon they sweated from the inside and were probably wetter than on the outside.

I stared through the inky darkness at the two vertical luminous strips on the helmet of the man in front of me. The column was closed up tightly, and the men were separated by perhaps a yard's distance. My fatigues were stuffed into the tops of my jungle boots and bloused, and soon my feet were soaking wet because the fatigues acted as a conduit for the water to pass through the wool socks to my feet. The blessed thing about rain was that it completely covered the sound of movement, but in the total absence of light under the jungle canopy, great care had to be taken to prevent breaks in the column. Veteran units had trouble with this, but green units literally fell apart. At one time, the column broke within the Weapons Platoon, and it took thirty minutes to reestablish contact between the two halves.

The Third Platoon's stay behind ambush dropped off in the rain as we went by. I thought they had dropped off a little later than planned, but it didn't matter that much because the job could still be accomplished. Maybe they had "cheated" about one hundred meters so their unaccompanied movement wouldn't be so far, when they broke their ambush and moved to rejoin us. I made a mental note to check on it later. The rain slacked, then stopped, before we completed the movement.

CHAPTER 42

We closed into the new location, and I gathered my patrol for a check before we began movement. Bigwitch had his squad psyched up for the mission. No one wanted to carry the flame throwers but I insisted, so they were changed off frequently because of their bulk and weight. We moved out with the squad from Third Platoon tagged on to our rear. Bigwitch personally took point, and his squad moved out, closed up tightly behind him. I followed his last man with Chavez and Collins behind me.

We dropped off the covering squad where they were to establish their ambush. They made too much noise, and I held up the column long enough to chew the squad leader's ass. We halted short of the stream, and observed our proposed crossing site and the ground around it through our starlight scopes, for perhaps fifteen minutes. I secured the rope firmly to a sapling on the near bank, and Chavez dropped his heavy gear and boots and swam to the other side with the rope in hand. After Chavez had secured the rope two security men crossed and took up their posts, left and right of the crossing site. We made the crossing, using two poncho rafts to carry the flame throwers and radios. The last man crossed with the end of the rope; we reorganized and swung out on the selected azimuth to bring us to a point northwest of the open end of the horseshoe.

The rain had started to beat down again around 2300 hours, slacked and finally stopped sometime around midnight. We could still move without fear of making noise because of the wet spongy ground. I checked the azimuth frequently and had two pace men keeping track of the distance. I had just checked to determine how near to our rally point we were, when the man in front of me turned and grabbed me with a hushed whispered "Enemy!" We dropped silently to the ground, and I crawled forward to the point and observed through a starlight scope. A trail which was more like a road crossed our line of movement at a right angle. VC moved back and forth as if along the sidewalks of any busy city in America. I counted over fifty VC in twenty minutes.

I judged that we were just short of our proposed rally point, and decided on the spot to withdraw about one hundred meters from the road's edge, to establish the rally point there, rather than where we had originally planned. Before moving back I marked our location on the side of the road with two stones laid side by side, just off the road. We moved back to the rally point and dropped our heavy gear, including the radios and flame throwers. I made a report to battalion and Ricksley came on.

"Charlie Six, this is Thunder Six. I want details, goddamn it! These abbreviated reports are of no use to me!" I reached down, cut the set off, and called the first sergeant on the company net.

"Charlie Six Papa, this is Charlie Six, over."

"This is Six Papa, over."

"This is Six. From now on make my reports to higher after I make the reports to you. I am not going to talk directly to higher until I choose to do so, over."

"This is Six Papa, roger out."

I had no intention of jeopardizing the patrol to keep that fool informed. He would just have to get by with the relayed information. I knew this would rub him raw. "Fuck him," I thought. "Fuck the son-of-a-bitch."

Dillard was left in charge in the ORP. I took Bigwitch, Howard, and Chavez, and we moved out to make our reconnaissance. We took one radio, which Chavez carried, as well as our demolitions and rifles. Bigwitch was on point, and I followed him, with Chavez behind me and Howard in the rear. We moved as quietly as possible, halting at the road, observing for five minutes, then crossing on line, side by side at the same time, to reduce the time of exposure. As Bigwitch took the point again and we fell back into single file he stopped abruptly and I bumped into him. Bigwitch lashed out savagely with his knife with an overhead to downward motion, striking the VC who had stumbled into our patrol in the side of the neck. He wrestled the surprised VC soldier to the ground with a throat lock from behind and desperately clapped the open palm of his other hand over his mouth. I fell on the VC's waist and held him flat as Bigwitch wrestled with the desperately writhing figure. Blood spewed from the VC's neck, and one of my sleeves was soaked.

Gradually the struggling ceased. We paused briefly to see if the commotion had alerted other VC, and Bigwitch stood and waved us forward. Fifty meters beyond the road we turned south and soon came to a partial clearing, where the underbush was cleaned out. We held up while I searched the cleared area with my starlight scope. I could hear the stream washing between its banks. If our navigation was accurate, we should have been near the open end of the horseshoe, at the north end of the complex. We crawled forward a few more meters, and almost stopped on top of the heavily bunkered barricade. The open end of the horseshoe was closed off by a double apron barbed wire fence, with heavy bunkers of logs, sod, and natural camouflage behind the wire. At least five sentries manned the barricade. Near the center of the barricade there was a gate and a two-man guard post. A wide trail ran into the complex through the gate. The wire in front of the gate was a movable section of double apron barbed wire which could be dragged aside to allow passage when the gate was opened.

As I watched, a cart and bicycle convoy approached the gate from inside the complex. The two VC guards pulled the barrier aside and the convoy came through the gate and moved up the trail to the west. When the barrier was pulled aside I could see inside, where there was a series of storage bunkers beginning just inside the wire.

After the supply train passed I crawled over to Bigwitch and we discussed how best to get inside the complex and do some damage. Leaving Howard to observe, Bigwitch, Chavez, and I worked our way back, crossed the road and reached the ORP, rapidly. I drew a diagram of the barricade. My plan was to have Dillard take the patrol back to the barricade with Chavez guiding them, then set up and wait. I would take Bigwitch, Larson, and Mason, go around to the south side of the horseshoe and cross there. We would have to cross the stream, then recross it, where it curled into the horseshoe. We would pick our targets after we got inside. When we were ready, we would call Second Platoon, have them move up and open fire from the east, as well as call the artillery concentrations we had plotted within the horseshoe. After we finished inside I would call Dillard and have him open up at the barrier. We would attempt to go out the barricade where the supply convoy had gone through. We finished the hasty plan and moved out.

In my segment of the patrol we were loaded down with gear, and the going was very slow. I carried the radio and the demolitions and Bigwitch, Larson, and Mason each lugged one of the flame throwers. As we approached the water, we halted to observe. The far bank of the bend in the horseshoe was clear at the moment. Bigwitch swam across to where the VC boats were tied, selected one, and returned with it. We quickly loaded the gear and crossed the narrow stretch to the far bank. We tied the boat where Bigwitch had found it, and hugging the vegetation, moved toward the high ground within the complex.

There were major trails crisscrossing the complex, and near the highest point of the hill I heard movement approaching us on one of the trails leading from the summit of the hill. We hugged the ground; five armed VC came abreast of where we lay, and halted. After a long pause they moved on. We were almost ready to begin movement again when three VC came up the trail from the opposite direction and moved toward the high point of the hill. As I observed through the starlight scope they moved aside some brush, then rolled back a slab of canvas and entered the hill. I crawled forward to get a better view. Several antennas protruded from the crest, and I began to hear voices just in front of me somewhere. I eased forward and the voices grew louder but were still muted, much like a hive of bees. I crawled on a few more feet and discovered the underground installation was directly in front of me. I listened. The sound of many voices hummed from the vent to an underground room, and judging from the antennas and the location, here on the highest point of the hill, it could well be the headquarters of the complex. The sounds of activity emitting from the air shaft were clear and I could hear laughing, talking, and shouts. I brought Bigwitch forward, and we took his flame thrower and dumped the jellied thickened fuel down the air vent, followed by the fuel from Mason's flame thrower. Then we set up four claymores in and around the entrance, scooped out holes around the entrance and placed and primed the demolitions. I called Second Platoon and told them to begin. When I heard the crack of their rifles and machine-guns to the east I fired a blast from Larson's flame thrower at the air vent and the bowels of the mountain erupted with the muffled explosion of the napalm inferno we had leaked into their sanctuary. We discarded the flame throwers and waited. Momentarily a rush of the VC able to attempt escape poured from the mountain at the entrance. We blew the claymores and demolitions sending arms, legs, and heads flying in separate directions and caving in the mouth of the entrance. I felt something wet and sticky splatter on my cheek, and reaching up I raked away blood and viscera.

I called Dillard and told him to open up at the barricade. Immediately I heard the sounds of his grenades to the north a few hundred meters, followed by the chatter of small arms. Flashes lit up the night sky as we ran toward the barricade, and met trouble. Five VC ran down the trail from the north, and it was a classical meeting engagement. Bigwitch fired first and then the VC opened up. I felt something tear through my thigh, and I was knocked flat by the shocking power of the AK 47 round. We shot our way through, but I saw Larson stumble and fall. He tried to crawl, and he was moaning. I grabbed one arm and Bigwitch grabbed the other. We were now in a stumbling foot race toward the barrier. The sounds and flashes of Dillard's fight at the barrier grew in intensity as we moved onward in that direction. Larson died somewhere short of the barrier, and became easier to carry. My leg was a shower of blinding pain and I had to stop. I ripped the fatigue leg open and applied a first aid bandage, then tried to catch up. Mason came into view about ten yards ahead, with Larson hanging over his shoulders. It was getting light, dictating the urgent need to press on before we lost the cover of darkness. The fire at the barrier ceased before we reached it. A wounded VC fired on us from the barrier, and Mason went down with Larson sprawled on top of him. Bigwitch fired a single round taking the top of the VC's head off. Mason was dead when I reached him. I shouldered Larson, and Bigwitch dragged Mason through the barrier as Dillard and Chavez pulled it aside. As we went through the wire three VC ran out of the brush to the left, outside the barrier, firing as they ran. Chavez fired from the shoulder at them until a round struck him in the throat and knocked him to the ground on his back, with the bright red blood spewing onto his fatigue shirt. The three VC were down, and PFC Goodrich fired into them as one tried to regain his feet. Bigwitch stopped, dropped Mason, and put a bandage on Chavez's throat, but it was only cosmetic. The round had ripped a gaping, ragged hole through the soft part of his neck and had splintered the top of his spinal column on the way out. Goodrich had been wounded below the knee in the earlier fighting at the barrier.

We shouldered our three dead comrades and retraced our route to the ORP. I called for the artillery concentrations. At the ORP we halted to make three poncho litters for the dead and to reorganize. I made a complete report to company; then as an afterthought I switched on the radio set on battalion's push and gave my report. We moved over our return route, which was more direct and certainly easier in the daylight than our route out had been.

At the stream we halted and observed for perhaps twenty minutes, and then Bigwitch swam the rope across and secured it on the far side. Sergeant Dillard and PFC Jones then crossed and set up security on the far side, and we poncho rafted the radios and bodies across, securing the loads with a safety rope. Twenty minutes later we made it back into the perimeter. My leg was bleeding again and my head was light. I looked down and my boot was soaked with fresh blood, warm and slick and squishy between my toes. Doc Gill was all over Goodrich and me, quickly had IV's going, cleaning the wounds as best he could. Suddenly I felt tired; the sweet black curtain of oblivion covered me, and I was back in the Smoky Mountains of western North Carolina in early spring, on the bank of a swift, clear, cold mountain stream. I lay in a bed of wild flowers beside a Cherokee girl, but there was something very familiar about her as if I had known her for a long time.

I awoke in the helicopter. Goodrich was there on the stretcher beside me, and the medic told me we were headed for the Evacuation Hospital at Bien Hoa. We were hustled from the dust off pad into the hospital, and soon I lay on clean sheets with whole blood going into me as well as the clear glucose that Doc Gill had started. That AK 47 round was like all the rest we had felt, seen, and tested in Vietnam. It had a cylindrical rod core and a soft metal jacket the color of copper. When the round hit, somewhere in its fleshy, bloody, bony path it separated, the rod staying intact and going on to sever and maim until it finally spent its energy and stopped or exited out the other side. The other part of the round, the soft metallic coat, split off the rod and flattened into a ragged, rending piece of shrapnel an inch across, which stopped sooner than the rod because of its size.

There was an Australian soldier in the bed across the room, and we talked briefly before I lapsed into blessed sleep.

CHAPTER 43

When I awoke the sun was shining through the window, and they wheeled in breakfast. I ate it and drank the black coffee and waves of anger started to wash over me as I thought about the patrol into the horseshoe. Mason, Chavez, and Larson, dead. "OK Ricksley, your time is approaching," I thought.

The Stars and Stripes carried a full account of 1st of the 202nd's destruction of a major enemy headquarters in the Iron Triangle and read in part "...Lieutenant-Colonel William Ricksley's courageous assault on a major Viet Cong headquarters, reputed to control all enemy units in the Iron Triangle just northwest of Saigon, may have been the most important action in the war in this Corps area to date. The unit, personally led by Ricksley, stormed the communist stronghold in the morning hours of darkness Thursday, Vietnam time. In a personal interview with Ricksley who was wounded during the fighting..." I turned over and retched into a towel. He was the most completely rotten species of animal that inhabited the earth; a jackal and hyena hybrid perhaps. And Kim had married him.

Three days later, I convinced the doctors at Bien Hoa to let me return to my unit. They didn't protest very much. My wound was clean and healing, and besides, they needed the bed.

On the way to Lai Khe I found out that the operation in the Iron Triangle was continuing, but that 1st Infantry Division troops had been pulled out to prepare for another mission. Hell, they're already back at Lai Khe, I thought.

From the pad at Lai Khe I called the company, and a jeep picked me up shortly. It was Collins, and he was really surprised to see me.

"Sir, we didn't do very much after you left. They pulled us back to guard battalion headquarters. We were there two days, and the battalion returned to Lai Khe yesterday," he said.

"Did we take any more casualties after I left?" I asked.

"We had one soldier in Third Platoon, Watkins, who fell in a punji pit and had to be evacuated," he said. "That happened on the move back to Lai Khe."

"Have any of you seen anything in the newspapers about our combat patrol into the horseshoe?" I asked.

"No, we were getting the Stars and Stripes but they stopped them about a week ago," he said.

I didn't say anything, but I wondered where the paper had gotten the story I had read in the hospital. We stopped at battalion, and I checked in with the S-1 to let him know I was back to duty. The clerk barely nodded as I signed in, climbed into the jeep and went on down to C Company.

"Sir, I thought we had a new replacement! If I had known it was you I would have met you!" Long yelled as he ran out to grab my bag.

"Hey, hey, that's OK Top! I'm fit as a fiddle," I laughed. He insisted on carrying my bag over to my tent.

"Sir, Colonel Ricksley announced that you wouldn't be back, at battalion formation yesterday," Top said.

"Well, I guess that shows you how much he knows!" I laughed. "Goodrich will be back in about two weeks," I added.

"Sir, here's your rifle and gear," the first sergeant handed me the rifle and web gear.

I went around and spoke to the officers to let them know I was back. Browning told me that they had arc-lighted (put in a B-52 strike on) the horseshoe area two days after our patrol. Second of the 28th had been sent in to check the area and had located a huge depot complex with numerous weapons, ammunition, and food stocks. In addition, they checked the headquarters area that we had used the flame throwers on and reported that there was not much left except the charred remains. The bodies had been buried, and the documents and equipment evacuated.

So there it was. Our sister battalion ended up with the task we should have been given, and apparently Ricksley hadn't said a word in protest. It was really difficult to believe that after all that we had accomplished at a great price in blood, our battalion gladly relinquished any claim to that ground and the enemy spoils we had discovered. "Well Worthington, who the hell ever said this would make any sense, anyway?" But it did make sense. Without debating tactics, I knew those men died in Ricksley's attempt to send me south in a bag.

I went over to supply and drew fresh gear to replace the combat losses we had suffered on the patrol. Sergeant Grossman rushed around helping me any way he could.

That afternoon I had an officer's call at the Red Dog and caught up on the news, as well as made up lost beer drinking time. Bigwitch came over and we shook hands and talked for a long time. He was genuinely concerned for me and my personal safety, as well as the safety of his men.

PFC Lockhart interrupted me with a message that the battalion commander had called for me to report to him at his headquarters. I left the Red Dog and walked up the dusty road to the headquarters and reported to him.

"Lieutenant Worthington reporting as ordered," I said as I entered without saluting. He was sitting behind a red hardwood commercial desk that I had never seen in the headquarters. The large carved teakwood name board, inlaid with ivory, spelled out "Ricksley" and occupied a good deal of space on the desk. It sat there as if to bully more than to inform. Everyone knew his name as he was the battalion commander, and if a visitor didn't know it he could read his name tape. He sat pulling on his Meerschaum with his straight black hair wet and combed back and his lips in their perpetual sneer. He blew smoke across the desk at me and finally spoke.

"Worthington, why didn't you report to me when you returned?" he asked.

"I signed in at S-1," I said.

"That's not what I asked you, Lieutenant," he said.

"Well since you put it that way, I had nothing I wanted to say to you and nothing I wanted to hear from you," I said, staring straight through him.

"Damnit Lieutenant, I am your commander!" he exploded. "Don't you think you owed me the courtesy of telling me personally that you were back?"

"Not at all."

"Damn you Worthington, I'm going to get you! You may be able to cut your radio off on some commanders, but you won't get by with that with me!" he screamed.

"You have taken the only thing from me that ever meant anything. Now you've tried to kill me, and you demand my respect? Surely you're joking?" He was shocked by my bluntness, by the frontal assault, which apparently was totally unexpected. He sputtered in confused rage.

"Those are strong accusations, Lieutenant. You had better be prepared to back them up with facts!" he stammered.

I was sick of the son-of-a-bitch. "Will that be all, Colonel?"

"Get out of here, and get out of my sight, Worthington!" His face was crimson, and he had completely lost control. I turned and left without saluting.

"Salute me, goddamn it!" he screamed at my back. I climbed into my jeep, slumped comfortably down in the seat and propped my right knee against the dash.

"Back to the company area, Lockhart."

The battalion had not yet assumed responsibility for the perimeter, so that night at the Red Dog it was one hell of an evening. Tom McCarter came and joined us at my invitation. His unit had just returned from the field that day. We drank to our fallen comrades and then to the success of the operation. At some point, we went over to the bar and I told him how things stood in the battalion between Ricksley and me.

"Damn, I knew he was a rotten bastard, but he's even worse than I thought," he said.

"This can't continue, Tom."

"Hell no! In fact, maybe it's time you took the whole matter to the brigade commander," he said.

"What good would that do, Tom? At best I would be transferred out of the company, leaving these poor guys to be made cannon fodder by that stupid ass. As long as I'm here I can at least shield them from him."

"James, he will get you killed, and then the company will be without you, anyway," he said.

"Well, there is an option," and I looked straight into the keen blue eyes of the best friend I had. I needed advice, and he was the best possible source at the present time.

"Killing the son-of-a-bitch will not help things, James. You would just go to jail, or worse, and eventually your conscience would haunt you," he said.

"Conscience hell! I could kill him ten times and never lose a night's sleep over it." He looked at me strangely, his eyes displaying mild surprise.

"We need to talk, James. I didn't realize how far this thing had gone," he said. Dave Browning walked up at that moment, and we dropped the Ricksley matter and turned to happier thoughts.

"Tom, James is trying to win the war by himself!" Browning laughed. "Smoking up Charlie's underground bungalows and that kind of action!"

"It's about time you got over here. I thought you had quit drinking or something drastic!"

"You know I'm no quitter!" he laughed. For a while I was reminded of the old days in Korea when Nolan and Tom and I would get together and commiserate about Ricksley. But it was different now. The man was trying to kill me, after betraying the special trust between a senior officer in the chain and his subordinate; not once but twice. As my battalion commander, he had moved in on Kim before I had hardly reached Japan. No officer at that level that I had known would have stooped so low. He had deliberately plotted my death, along with the rest of that patrol. That's the way I interpreted the course of events. Having been deceived by Ricksley once, I would never trust him again, under any circumstances.

"Three Budweisers! Give us the dice cup!" Tom yelled at the bartender. We took one dice apiece and "peeweed" for who would roll first. I won with a six and started the dice with two sixes. Tom rolled two fives and Dave had three sixes and was out. I battled with Tom until we had a "horse" each and then lost with four sixes after he stayed with four deuces and was able to roll a fifth.

"Well you've still got that horseshoe up your ass!" I laughed. We touched cans and drank to each other. Out of the corner of my eye I saw someone approaching us. I turned to face the dark countenance from the shadows of Soco Gap and the reflections of the Oconaluftee River.

"Sir, welcome back," Bigwitch said with a smile. There was a respect near to kinship between us because of our common birthplace, but more, as a result of the dangers we had overcome together, and especially because of the patrol into the horseshoe. I bought him a beer, and we talked quietly for a while. Tom and Dave joined the troops and left Bigwitch and me at the bar.

"I wondered if you had slipped a screw when you took those heavy goddamned flame throwers with us," he laughed quietly. "I didn't know you were going to make a cookout out of it!"

"Bigwitch, what do you hear from home?" I asked.

"No big news, Sir. My brother got a Cherokee scholarship and will go to the University of Tennessee this fall."

"Hey, that's great. Does he know what he will study yet?"

"No, he wants to get his first year general subjects out of the way while he decides," he said. "Two of my classmates went up to Western Carolina University at Cullowhee last fall, and they really like it," he said.

"What does Cullowhee mean in Cherokee?" I asked.

"It means 'valley of the lillies'," he said. "Sir, can I ask you a question?"

"Shoot."

"What's between you and Colonel Ricksley?" he asked. Well, here it was. You learn never to fraternize in any officers school, whether it's OCS, ROTC, or West Point, and this was the precise reason. Anyway, if something happened to me, and I didn't make it back from the promised land maybe Bigwitch would. He could at least give the people at home some idea about me. I decided to tell him at least a portion of the story. "Why do you ask?" I said.

"Well, Lockhart drove you up there today, and he was sitting outside the headquarters waiting on you. Sir, there are no doors on that house." Good old Lockhart. I would have a talk with him about the special duties of a company commander's driver/radio telephone operator.

"We had a serious run-in before, in Korea." He looked at me with those dark inquisitive Cherokee eyes, and I knew I had to tell him more. "He married my girl after I left Korea," I said.

"You mean the one whose picture you showed the squad when we were up in the Michelin?"

"Yes." And then he understood everything.

"Goddamn, Sir, I'm sorry."

"Please keep that to yourself."

"I will, Sir. That son-of-a-bitch."

"I'll drink to that." We ordered another Budweiser, and I looked up to see Ricksley coming in the door. "Bigwitch, you better drink them both. I'm leaving," and I brushed past the tables and out the doors and walked on back down the road toward C Company. The sky was dark and cloudy, and it started to rain. I didn't hurry. My leg ached, and suddenly I felt very old and very much without any purpose. "What was the use of anything?" I thought. "Nothing, nothing, nothing." The rain picked up in intensity, and I was soaked by the time I reached the tent. I sat down on my air mattress and reached into my rucksack for a bottle of scotch I had stashed there. I poured scotch into a canteen cup and opened a canteen and poured warm water into the scotch and began drinking it. She wouldn't go away, and we were there on the beach at Kang Nung together, holding each other tightly, wishing it would never end. "Well it's ended, James. It's finished." I turned up the bottle of scotch and drank straight from it. "It's over. Except for one little detail."

I woke about 0200, shivering in wet fatigues. I changed into dry clothes and went back to the air mattress. It was wet, so I turned it over and covered it with a poncho and lay down and pulled the poncho liner over me. The rain beat steadily against the tent walls, and there was a chill in the air. I couldn't sleep, and my leg hurt like hell. I lay and thought, finally slugged down a couple of inches of the scotch, and then it was all right, and after a while I slept.

The rain stopped some time before dawn, and the sky was clear at daylight. That day we cleaned weapons, then the rest of our gear. I inspected the LAW's and hand grenades, and we turned in some old LAW's and drew new ones to replace them. Mid-morning the first sergeant went to battalion, picked up some replacements and parceled them out to the rifle platoons, except for two 11C, mortarmen, who went to the Weapons Platoon. That afternoon we did ambush training. Just before the evening meal Lieutenant Redd conducted a class for all the platoon and squad leaders on how to call indirect fire. He was a damned fine instructor, understood the problems of trying to call indirect fire and could explain the process in simple language that the soldiers understood. Sergeant Creighton assisted him, and it was probably better than any class I had received in OCS on that subject.

First Sergeant Long had left mid-morning, with a convoy going for resupply at Di An in Saigon. He said he was going to pick up beer and soda for the troops rather than wait on brigade to do it for us. He took C7, one of the Weapons Platoon three-quarter-ton trucks, a tactical vehicle that normally carried a mortar squad with 81mm mortar. He, the driver, and the truck went up in a bang and a puff of smoke at the Cao Dinh Bridge. The mad bomber blew a five hundred pound bomb under C7, and there wasn't enough junk left to bring two dollars on the World War II scrap metal drive. Fortunately the bodies could be identified, saving the trauma of a "missing in action" report; I got Top's things together the following morning and took care of getting them sent home to his wife in Alabama. Since Redlegs was dead, Fitzsimmons was the ranking E-7 in the company, and took over as first sergeant. Bigwitch took over as platoon sergeant of First Platoon, as he outranked both McGuire and Rozier, and Sergeant Dillard became squad leader when Bigwitch moved up. I sat around for a couple of days trying to dream up ways to get the mad bomber, but I finally gave it up. You could ambush every night from now on, and you might get him by accident your fiftieth time out. That was not productive. At any rate, we held a memorial service two days later for all of our dead. I would miss Long terribly. He had been a trusted subordinate as well as a close friend. I would never forget the day he had nonplussed General Westmoreland.

CHAPTER 44

We assumed that the battalion had been pulled out of the operation in the Iron Triangle to prepare for another commitment, but several days passed with no operations order. We patrolled around Lai Khe day and night and waited for the next shoe to drop. Ricksley tried to act as if nothing had happened between us, and I saw very little of him, to my peace of mind. I tried to use the valuable time we had available in training the company. The troops learned quickly; in that environment motivation was no problem.

Then one morning we were called to battalion for an order. I took Lockhart and my jeep, with Lieutenants Redd and Smathers. We sat in the rear of a tent with a wooden floor and gray metal chairs. Major Furman Hickey, the S-3, briefed the operation. I could clearly see by the posted map he was preparing to brief from, that we were going back to the Michelin. I was not surprised in the least. With the operation in the Iron Triangle still in full swing and another operation northwest of Saigon, west of the Iron Triangle, and north of Cu Chi by the 25th Infantry Division, the 173rd Airborne Brigade, and an ARVN (Vietnamese) division, it was logical that Viet Cong units would relocate farther north for safe haven. When the heat was off they could move back into their old sanctuaries. Their tactics were to choose where they fought. When we attacked them in strength, if the advantage was in our favor, they would vanish, to hit us at a weak point later when they chose to do so.

We would be combat assaulted into company LZ's, much as we had the last time into the Michelin. This time it was a single battalion operation, rather than the whole brigade going in. We would be east of where we were on the previous Michelin operation. C Company would go in on the east of the battalion, with B Company in the center, A Company, battalion headquarters, the 4.2 Inch Mortar Platoon, the Recon Platoon, and a battery of 105mm howitzers in the west. The operation would kick off at 0400 hours day after tomorrow, Major Hickey told us.

The S-2 briefed that an enemy regiment had moved into the area where we would operate, having come up from the Iron Triangle early on in our previous operation. In addition, the Phu Loi Battalion was currently based in that area.

The artillery liaison officer covered the fire support for the combat assault, and the preparation looked less than impressive. "What the hell? We are getting spoiled with all this firepower," I thought. At any rate the artillery would fire a light prep on the LZ's. He explained that the two larger operations in III Corps had priority over us on the artillery and air. Well, that would be great unless we landed on top of more than we could handle. In that case it would be wonderful to be spoiled by more firepower.

Then Ricksley gave us his version of an inspirational Patton-like speech, except that it was so phony and riddled with outworn cliches that we wanted to gag or go outside and barf, more than fight the enemy. I was glad when he finally shut up.

We made our way out of the briefing tent and took the jeep back down through the rubber trees to the company area. I passed the word that my order would be issued at 1400 that afternoon. That gave the platoons and squads the rest of the day and the next to issue their own orders and prepare. Also, Lieutenant Scott and Fitzsimmons would have plenty of time to arrange logistic support for the operation. This time Scott would be going out on the operation, and Fitzsimmons would be staying in the rear at Lai Khe, running resupply from there. That would be the first field duty Fitzsimmons had ever missed, he told me. I was not surprised, but I felt pretty good that a guy like Fitzsimmons, who had always had his neck stuck out, was finally getting a little break. Scott didn't look too happy, but he prepared the supply list with more enthusiasm than I'd ever seen him muster.

That afternoon I issued my order for the airmobile assault, movement to, and occupation of our initial perimeter. We would depart the company area on foot at 0300 hours the morning of the operation. At the airstrip we would load the slicks and move at 0400 hours. Our field strength for the operation was ninety-nine men. The Weapons Platoon was taking one 81mm mortar for the operation. The company needed seventeen helicopters to lift it, but there were only nine available, so we would go in two lifts; the first lift would form 360° security of the LZ for the second lift, and after everyone was on the ground we would move west five hundred meters and establish our initial company perimeter. We would carry five days of rations per man, and each rifleman would carry in three claymores and a LAW. The company would carry the normal amount of small arms rounds, grenades, and demolitions. I went over the terrain on the map until I was satisfied they knew it.

"Do your new men have signal cord?" They all answered in the affirmative except Sutherland.

"Well, when will you issue it to them?"

"Sir, I feel that signal cord idea is pretty much a waste of time."

"Well Larry, when you are running this company you can do away with it. I'll be around to inspect for that item and the knowledge of how to use it before dark," I said. Browning glared at Sutherland, and I knew that they would have a little lieutenant to lieutenant chat after the meeting broke up. Redd's fire support briefing and Fitzsimmons' resupply information followed, and then everyone departed the CP to begin preparation for the operation.

That evening I checked by Sutherland's Platoon and he was out on the perimeter. Bigwitch met me at the platoon CP and assured me that Sutherland had taught a class on signal cord after issuing it to the new men. I was satisfied. I looked over the other rifle platoons, then checked Weapons Platoon. I called a couple of practice fire missions as if I were an FO, and checked the time it took the fire direction center to compute the data and the gun crews to apply the data to their weapons. They were very quick, well within acceptable limits.

"Sir, you know you won't catch me short!" Sergeant Kim said.

"I know, Kim, but I like to check once in a while for my own peace of mind!" I laughed. Lieutenant Smathers stood beside Kim, smiling nervously. "He was not a bad officer if he would only screw up his confidence a notch or two," I thought.

I walked back to the CP and checked my communications with battalion and with the platoons. After a while Fitzsimmons and I walked over to the mess tent and ate. Sergeant Smith asked me how the chow was. It was “chili-mac,” a favorite of the army. I had never liked it, but if it could be made tasty, this was a fine attempt.

“Tastes great, Sergeant Smith. Any problems?”

“No, Sir, the mess is running very well.”

“Good. Keep up the good work.”

We left the mess tent, and Fitzsimmons went to the CP for a short meeting with the platoon sergeants. I walked over to Browning’s CP and caught him cleaning his rifle.

“Going hunting, are you?”

He laughed. “Looks that way, and there are plenty of critters in that section of woods if I remember correctly.”

“Yeah, we will have our hands full, I’m afraid.”

“James, what’s happened to you, pal? You really seem down.”

I was surprised. I hadn’t known that my feelings were that transparent. I guess when a man knows you as well as Browning knew me it becomes hard to conceal your emotions. “Oh, nothing big. Things aren’t going quite right back home. By the way, you’re down to two months, aren’t you?”

“Yes, and I’m going back to Benning for the Advanced Course. I’m really looking forward to it. I like that Columbus, Georgia, area, and I can go up to Atlanta once in a while on weekends.” he said. “They got them big old good ones up there with healthy boobs!” he laughed.

“Well save some of it for me. I will probably be back there before you leave.”

We sat and talked until I went back to my CP. It gets dark quickly in Vietnam. It seemed that one minute I was sitting at the CP looking at the bunker line and the next minute I couldn’t see the bunkers. The stars shone brightly in a clear sky. A gentle evening breeze blew through the rubber trees, taking the hot edge off the tropical summer night. I rubbed insect repellent on my hands, arms, face, and knees to ward off the evening denizens. A snake crossed in front of me, clearly visible against the white sand in the moonlight. He made his way into the rubber trees and disappeared. "Why had she done it?" I wondered. Maybe Choe was right. She was young and impressionable, and in a country where everyone knew everything about the military, a lieutenant-colonel was a very important person. The security of marriage to an already successful man must have been attractive. Then I thought about the times that Kim and I had made love. I wondered what their lovemaking was like, and was suddenly angry and clearly jealous. The anger subsided quickly, as I sat there in the evening breeze, listening to the sounds of the night. A dog barked beyond the wire in some Vietnamese village, and a night hunting bird's shrill cry broke the stillness. I crawled into the tent, onto the air mattress and slept.

The next day the platoons and squads rehearsed ambushes, and there were classes on claymores, LAW's, grenades, and demolitions. Some officers thought that once they were in combat the training was over. Hell, that's when they really needed to train, more than at any other time. With the rapid turnover of troops, one day we could have a tough battle-hardened, experienced unit, and the next we would be giving orders to green replacements who couldn't even arm a claymore mine. In combat, we had quickly found, boredom is the norm; the actual time spent fighting is a fraction of the total. The best way to use the dead time is in training. Troops who are confident in their ability to do their job become quick and professional, and their chances of making it back home increase with their proficiency. A glance would reveal the professionals and the amateurs. The veterans had everything snugged down tight, from the camouflage covers on their steel pots to their rucksacks. Their rifles had no slings and their web gear fitted perfectly with no loose straps. Their boots were tied tightly and generally bleached white after all the dye disappeared in the paddies, streams, and scrapings against rocks and jungle vegetation. They might have a jungle fatigue shirt on, or nothing more than an olive drab T-shirt. The "newbies" had new jungle fatigues and boots, and the camouflage covers on their helmets were loose and somehow amateurish. The rucksacks had loose straps and flaps and unbalanced loads and looked as if they might fall apart at any moment. You could see it in their white faces rather than in the wind and sunburned complexions of the vets. More than anything else there was a stark difference in their bodies – the lean, hardened, hollow-cheeked combat veterans, alongside young bodies with round, ruddy cheeks and soft fatty middles, arms, and thighs.

I went around and checked the training, the initial loads the men would carry, the radios and telephones, the things everyone had to have in good working order to survive and do the job. Things looked OK, and late afternoon I went over to see Tom McCarter. His battalion, 2nd of the 28th, had the Lai Khe perimeter security, and 2nd of the 2nd Infantry had gone down into the Iron Triangle and begun participation in that operation. He pulled out a bottle of scotch, and we sat on the ground drinking it with water out of canteen cups.

"James, I never got to finish what I was saying to you the other night in the Red Dog. Please don't do anything crazy," he said.

"Tom, I got you. Thanks for the advice," I said. He knew that was a very noncommittal answer, but he also knew that this was too important, too serious, to mitigate with words.

"James, I just want to be sure you know what you are doing in terms of forever, rather than next week," in the soft, even voice of an old friend who understood me, perhaps better than I understood myself. But he also understood the festering hate under the surface, that couldn't be hidden or explained away. I could detect the dejection and frustration of a righteous crusader, who knew his cause was lost.

"Tom, where was Nolan Broyles killed?" He seemed happy to finish his impossible task of counselling me on the Ricksley matter, and his expression shifted, reflecting a lighter, if somber mood.

"He was killed on an operation in the Iron Triangle with the 173rd Airborne Brigade. They went in there alone and did a great job before any other major American units really got their feet on the ground," he said.

"He was a fine officer and a great guy. Do you remember that sorry-assed Ricksley trying to make his death a negative example for the battalion?"

"Yeah, that was when you stood up and called him a son-of-a-bitch in front of the entire battalion!" We chuckled at that, but I knew that the game was not over between Ricksley and me. There were still a few innings to be played.

We finished the scotch and water, and I left him, took a few steps, stopped, and walked back to him. I reached into my pocket and pulled out an excellent Swiss compass with a "K" engraved on its rim on the northeast side when I oriented the compass to north.

"See if you can make use of this, Tom," I pressed the compass into his hand. There was moisture in his clear blue eyes as our eyes met, then I turned and moved through the rubber trees and out onto the red dirt road and back to C Company, 1st of the 202nd Infantry.

CHAPTER 45

The helicopters beat northward into the red glow of dawn. The jungle was still dark below us. I held my map flat on my lap and kept up with our progress as best I could. We were in the lead ship, and I sat against the fire wall on the outside looking forward out of the left side of the HUEY. I looked to the left oblique and saw Bigwitch in the next ship, with six of his men. It was chilly that morning, so the helicopters were able to lift seven men rather than six. They had burned off part of their fuel load prior to picking us up. They had shown up with only seven ships, but we were able to make it in two lifts, and anticipated no trouble unless one went down for some reason.

I saw the artillery flashing on our LZ; the gunships roared forward and began throwing 2.75 inch rockets into the periphery of the LZ even before the artillery was cut. Eventually the door gunners opened up with their M60's, hosing down the woods around the LZ. The lift ships hovered in, and we jumped out and flattened face down on the ground. The wash from the helicopter blades threw dust and debris all over us on the open LZ. The LZ was cold (there was no fire), and we ran to its edges to set up security for the next lift in. The second lift landed without event, and we moved out to the west toward our initial position.

Third Platoon had not cleared the LZ when I heard the "thunk, thunk, thunk" of mortar rounds hitting the bottom of their tubes, prior to screaming upwards in their long high arcs.

"Mortars, mortars!" I yelled. Troops dived into depressions, shell holes, or any place that offered a little cover. The rounds crashed in, and exploded with the blasting crunch so hated and feared by the troops. There were six rounds altogether, and they fell across the LZ with perfect precision.

Someone was screaming back in the vicinity of the LZ. Lieutenant Browning came onto the radio.

"Charlie Six, this is Charlie Three Six, I have two KHA's and three WHA's. Request immediate dust off, over."

"This is Charlie Six, roger. Get clear of the LZ and bring in the dust off south of the LZ at the first suitable clearing, over."

"This is Charlie Three-Six, roger, out."

I called the dust off and he was there in twenty minutes. Browning directed him into a hole about seventy-five meters south of the LZ. When the helicopter started down I heard the mortars fire again, and I could only pray that they were firing on the same data as before, assuming that we would dust the wounded off from the same LZ we had landed on. The tubes thumped a second time as we waited in agony for the first rounds to land. "Whump, whump, whump" they exploded harmlessly on the LZ we had gone into, and three more rounds crashed in. The dust off lifted up and out of the small hole in the jungle, swung around and raced south just over the top of the jungle.

We immediately moved out to the west and coiled into a perimeter around a low rise in the jungle. Each platoon sent out a clearing patrol to its front, about three hundred meters and back, and established LP/OP's of three men each, about one hundred meters to their platoon fronts. Everyone dug in earnest. Half of the men dug, while the other half manned their weapons. The machine-guns were always manned and laid in before any preparations began, other than placing out security.

I walked across to Browning's CP.

"Dave, I'm sorry, buddy."

"They were good men, James. I'm afraid Allison will die, also."

"I'll get a report on their condition as soon as I can." I walked back to the CP, where Singletary, Lockhart, and Collins were digging along with Doc Gill and Redd's recon sergeant and RTO. The trench was taking shape rapidly with all the experienced hands involved.

I called brigade to check on our casualties. Sergeant Allison had died in the helicopter. The other two would make it, although both were serious enough to be evacuated, and we would likely never see them again. I walked over to Browning's CP and told him. He looked at me with tears in his eyes, and he didn't speak. What was there to say?

That night we sent one ambush per platoon out to about one kilometer from the perimeter. At about 2300 hours, Browning's ambush triggered on a squad sized VC element, killing an estimated seven or eight. We would know exactly how many at daylight. His ambush was north of the perimeter as his portion of the defense was from ten o'clock to two o'clock. First Platoon had six to ten, and Second Platoon had two to six.

At 0200 hours Fowler's Platoon's LP reported movement to its front, and ten minutes later they blew their claymores and threw hand grenades. Lieutenant Fowler requested permission to withdraw.

"What's the situation there now, Sam?"

"No sound or movement at the present time."

"Then leave them there for the time being."

Thirty minutes later the LP opened up with small arms fire. "Sir, I think we should withdraw them now."

"Bring them in." He reported when they reached the perimeter, and I walked over and talked to Sergeant Bangs, Second Squad Leader, and two of his squad members.

"Sir, the woods are full of them. I counted at least thirty through the starlight scope, before and after we blew the claymores," Bangs said. "They were milling around as if they were trying to find us."

Reports from the foxhole line indicated movement to the front. "OK, Sam. Let's fire the DT on your side of the perimeter." I told Lieutenant Redd to fire, and it came crashing in with a vengeance a few minutes later. Several foxholes saw VC to their front after the DT was fired. and they blew their claymores. No small arms were fired, a mark of professionalism that I hadn't expected. "Perhaps Fowler is beginning to understand what this is all about," I thought.

There was no further contact that night. The next morning Browning's patrol reported seven dead VC and brought in seven AK 47's and some pocket litter, none of which had any particular intelligence value. There were six bodies and nine weapons discovered at Fowler's Platoon's front as well as several blood trails. The bastards were probing to try to locate us, and they probably had not pinpointed us yet. That action may have given our position away, however, because of the artillery defensive target we had fired.

As soon as all three night ambushes returned I issued the order to move north a kilometer. The move was to be made as carefully as possible, and we sent a patrol from Browning's platoon north to the new area to secure the perimeter. We moved slowly and deliberately, but I had the feeling that we were being watched. I sent the word back down the column for Scott to come forward to talk to me. About five minutes later he caught up and I instructed him to take the company on up to the new location and establish the perimeter. I would drop off with the company headquarters and set up an ambush.

I filled the headquarters group in, and we dropped off and set a wide ambush, blocking anyone following the main body. The column was moving at a snail's pace for security, and we were concealed and had our claymores set up before the tail end of the column passed through us. It was a hasty ambush, but it looked pretty good because we were dispersed, down, the claymores were set, and the signal cord was in place. We waited.

Five minutes passed, and a VC broke through the brush following the column. He paused, looked around, and waved his hand underhanded in the oriental fashion to indicate that others should follow. Six VC popped through the underbrush and followed the point man with weapons at the ready. They carried AK 47's with the curved magazine locked and ugly muzzles pointing forward. I waited until I thought the point man was going to step on me, and when he was past my claymore I blew the mine with him directly behind it. The rest of the mines went, almost like sympathetic detonations. I leaped on the point man who was writhing on the ground clutching the backs of his legs. I thought about trying to save him as a prisoner, but the blood spewed from the femoral artery on the left side, and he went limp and died while I still held him. The others were dead also, Collins told me. I pushed the body away; we recovered the weapons and stripped anything of military or intelligence value from them and moved out rapidly to overtake the column, just as they reached the new perimeter area.

We pushed security patrols in front of each platoon and began to establish the perimeter. Before we could dig a shovel full the "thunk, thunk, thunk" of mortars sounded, and incredibly they couldn't have been more than a hundred meters away. I ran across to Bigwitch and told him to go for them. Sutherland was standing with his mouth open, shaking his head when Bigwitch and his old squad sprinted out of the perimeter. The mortar rounds impacted back in the area of the perimeter we had just left. The tubes fired again, and then explosions of a different kind could be heard in rapid succession from the area of the tubes, and then the staccato hammering of Howard's M60 joined the fray. Bigwitch's rifles opened fire and then a few AK 47 shots were fired. Then more of Howard's M60 fire hammered at some target we could not see but could well imagine. Half of the squad came lugging in an 82mm mortar and two AK 47's. Lieutenant Sutherland sent McGuire and his squad back with them and soon two more 82mm mortars, ten AK 47's, as well as a large number of 82 mortar rounds were carried into the center of the perimeter, along with documents and pocket litter from the dead.

"Sir, we caught them cold," Bigwitch told me. "There was one VC standing security, and the first hand grenade nailed his ass. The rest was easy, with them bunched up around the mortars," he said.

"Good job, Bigwitch. I'd better go over and console Sutherland a bit. I really shouldn't have done that the way I did," I said.

"Don't worry about it, Sir. We got 'em, didn't we?" Bigwitch grinned.

I walked over to First Platoon CP, and Sutherland met me. "Don't say it, Sir. I understand completely. You did it because of the urgency of the situation," he said earnestly. "Sir, I'm not cut out for this. I should have done exactly what you did, but I was standing there wondering what to do next," he said dejectedly. I knew I had a rebuilding job to do, but for the first time I really felt that Lieutenant Larry Sutherland was going to make it. We sat down and had an open talk. I promised him I wouldn't interfere with his command of the platoon, but I counselled him on aggressiveness. He and I parted, understanding each other more completely than ever before.

The perimeter was taking shape rapidly. I called the platoon leaders to the CP along with the rest of the orders group. The "chuck, chuck, chuck" of entrenching tools digging in the black jungle earth broke the dim, hazy green stillness.

"OK. For today we prepare the defense. Tonight we go to work. I want two ambushes per platoon, and a mechanical ambush put out by each live ambush." I pointed out their ambush sites on the map. Charlie had to be somewhat confused at this point, especially when we successfully eliminated his squad of watchers who were reporting our location, and his 82mm mortar section which in effect was his artillery. I thought about moving that night, but I scrapped the idea. The VC would probably attribute the loss of the mortar section to a moving patrol's chance encounter and aggressive action. Nevertheless, they would check.

"Lieutenant Sutherland, go out now and establish two mechanical ambushes on the northern edge of the mortar position we just eliminated. They will be in there to check that out, probably this afternoon. Any questions?" There were none, and we broke to get to work.

I had made the decision not to evacuate the enemy gear because that would give away our position. Lieutenant Smathers approached me at the CP.

"Sir, one more tree out of here and we will be able to fire," he said.

I was surprised at this unusual demonstration of even mild aggressiveness on his part. "Well, saw it down, but be very quiet in the process." He stood around for a few seconds and I could see he had something else on his mind. "What else do you have for me?"

"Sir, let's use those 82mm mortars for close in defense. I know we have no firing data for them but for close in defense they would be great, and no data would be necessary."

I didn't care much for the idea, but I wasn't worried about the safety of it because firing two or three hundred meters from the tubes could be done easily. Besides, I hated to kill the spark of initiative I saw in Smathers. "Go ahead. I don't see any problems." I smiled and thought he could feel the approval I felt for this positive attitude. He turned and left, and his platoon began digging in their three new mortars. He found out pretty quickly that the one tree he thought he needed to cut so he could get mass clearance wouldn't do it. Six trees later he had it.

I watched the Weapons Platoon saw down their last tree. The rifle platoons were using the trees and their limbs for overhead cover, and the position looked better by the hour, although I was afraid we had made too much noise establishing it.

Ricksley had been strangely silent so far, and I wondered what his next little game would be. I wasn't naive enough to believe that he had backed off his plans for me. The most likely course of action would be to follow the events as they unfolded and seize an opportunity when he saw it. B Company had contact the night before, after their combat assault. Their casualties had been significant; there were five killed and fifteen wounded. That action was probably taking up much of his time. He probably had the brigade commander breathing down his neck. I had monitored one transmission this morning, that indicated that the brigade commander had flown in to talk to Ricksley personally. What most amazed me was the fact that Captain Cunningham had let Ricksley convince him not to move after they were mortared and had suffered a ground attack. I listened to another radio transmission in the early afternoon, in which Ricksley personally coached Cunningham on his defense plans for the coming night.

"Bravo Six, this is Thunder Six, over."

"This is Bravo Six, over."

"This is Thunder Six. I want you dug in to the eyeballs with overhead cover. Do you have overhead cover? Over."

"This is Bravo Six. Negative, over."

"This is Thunder Six. Then spend the rest of today on that. In addition, I want you to put in extra defensive targets around your position, over."

"This is Bravo Six. I already have a total of four artillery DT's around us now. I don't need any more, over."

"This is Thunder Six. I'm telling you to double that number, and I want them all fired in! Over." I detected the irritation in Ricksley's voice, and knew he would soon lose control of himself. Any discussion of one of his ideas was considered an affront. At any rate, Cunningham was digging himself a hole he couldn't get out of, literally. I thought about switching over to his company net and advising him to move just after dark, but I knew Ricksley selectively monitored company nets. His attention was riveted on Cunningham, so he would be monitoring B Company's net. I gave up the idea.

"This is Bravo Six. Roger, over." The conversation continued. It was not uncommon for Ricksley to tie up a tactical net for thirty minutes explaining one of his schemes. Poor Cunningham. Poor B Company.

"This is Thunder Six. Don't put out any ambushes tonight. That will mean you can fire your artillery without waiting on patrols to come back in." By denying Cunningham the ability to ambush he was taking away all early warning, other than the very close-in listening posts. The ambush, if properly executed, could be a tremendous advantage in the defense because it acted as a "spoiling attack" and delayed and disorganized the attacker and caused confusion as to where the actual defensive perimeter was located. Then while he was temporarily halted, trying to regroup to continue the attack, we had the opportunity to effectively employ our artillery because we would know exactly where he was. That further disorganized his attack and demoralized his troops, whittling down his ability and enthusiasm to attack.

Ricksley's guidance went on for ten minutes. I finally left the radio, forsaking Cunningham to his fate, and wondering what ours would be.

Mid-afternoon a breeze stirred, but had it been a gale we would have barely felt it. I checked the perimeter. Digging had ceased and the last touches of camouflage were being applied. I went back to the CP and Collins made coffee for us. I cracked a can of "Ham and Lima Beans," scraped off as much of the white grease as I could and threw it on the ground. Then I doused the Ham and Lima Beans in hot sauce and heated it over a heat tablet. I guess the only thing that I have ever eaten in my life that gave me indigestion one hundred percent of the time was Ham and Lima Beans. We couldn't even give it away to the Vietnamese kids on the side of the trail as we passed by, and if we tried we were duly impressed with their ability to speak English appropriate to the occasion. Like "Hey muthafucka, Ham and Lima Beans number ten! Sao Lam, mai sao!" I ate Ham and Lima Beans throwing off more grease as I ate the meal with crackers and warm canteen water. The crackers and warm canteen water tasted OK.

The patrols prepared to go out. Final ambush rehearsals were going on all over the perimeter. The morale seemed to be high, and it was pleasant to watch professionals prepare for a job. I patted a few backs and offered a word of encouragement here and there. As I passed by First Platoon I saw Bigwitch showing two new soldiers how to set up a claymore mine. He was down behind the mine demonstrating how to sight it. I saw him take a straw and show them how to sight it in the dark. He looked up and smiled, flashing his white teeth. I spoke and passed on.

At the CP Collins had coffee, and was passing the assignments for radio watch for the night. Lockhart was restringing our poncho hootch to lower the profile a little. The sky was clear above the canopy, and it didn't look like rain that night.

"Any problems, Scott?" I asked.

"No, Sir, but we need to resupply tomorrow if we have any significant contact tonight," he said.

"We can resupply right here if we have to. A couple more trees and we will have it just in front of First Platoon."

"Sir, we already have a good pad picked out in front of Third Platoon which won't require any cutting."

"Good. We will use that if we have to." He knew what his job was, and I appreciated his initiative. There was a spark of pride that I hadn't noted in Scott before.

"How are things going back home?"

"Really well, Sir. They are anxious to see me. I leave in two months," he said.

"Let me guess. You and Browning came in on the same day."

"The very same day. We rode in in the same helicopter."

"How do we stand on batteries?"

"Sir, there is one extra per radio."

"Good. Check on the starlights (night vision scopes), also."

"Yes, Sir."

Darkness fell and the ambushes filed out of the perimeter at intervals. The platoons and squads had learned a lot in the Iron Triangle, and it showed in the way they did everything, from keeping quiet to applying camouflage. Of course there were the newbies, but they were learning rapidly.

Fitzsimmons and I had discussed assimilation of replacements into the company before this operation. "Top, we have to insure that new men are properly met and taken care of when they first arrive."

"Yes, and keeping them away from bad troops like Boykin and Sibler is important."

"Yeah Fitz, but what is so important about that? They will eventually meet the bad eggs anyway."

"Yes, but that goddamned Sibler is a leader; a negative leader. He has his own little following. There is a certain charisma there; yes, a negative type of charisma that attracts men. They tend to listen to Sibler, for whatever reason."

"But how do we deal with it?"

He turned and looked me dead in the eyes and his serious tone did not escape me. "We get rid of the Siblers, one way or the other. The reason Sibler has survived is that you officers have spent too much time trying to exercise leadership on him. He's a worthless piece of shit and a waste of our precious time."

"But that's the system, Top."

"System hell, get rid of the sorry bastard. The first time he bats an eye bring charges and kick him out of the unit; either jail his ass or kick him out of the army. He will destroy more morale than you can ever build. He's a bad influence on every soldier in the unit."

There was little sense in continuing the discussion because Fitzsimmons was emotionally involved, but more than that, he was probably right. I had changed the subject because he had made his point.

I sat on the ground listening to the company and battalion tactical nets. All patrols were out and the company net was quiet. "So far, so good," I thought. The ambush patrols were now in the most critical phase of the job. Setting up was always a nervous task as security had to be excellent, while quick and sure hands prepared the kill zone. While troops were arming claymores they were most vulnerable. During this time of unpreparedness, if an enemy patrol should blunder into them, the resulting action would be a point-blank shootout, with no odds in the patrol's favor. Security during that phase of an ambush needed rehearsal, perhaps more than any other phase of security. After an hour I started to breathe easier.

Off to the west, explosions suddenly broke the stillness of the jungle night. At first I thought it was one of our ambushes, then I recognized the characteristic crunch of mortar rounds impacting. The battalion net crackled; it was B Company telling battalion they were getting mortared. I counted eighteen mortar rounds bursting, and Cunningham yelled excitedly into the radio about a number of casualties and needing at least three dust offs. Ricksley came on the battalion net and between him and Cunningham confusion reigned supreme for a good thirty minutes. To complicate things the VC rolled a ground attack against them, led by sappers. I couldn't keep up with the garbled communications from B Company, but I could hear Ricksley. "The smartest thing Cunningham could do would be to cut his radio off and fight the battle," I thought.

I heard a transmission from the battalion Recon Platoon indicating they had been ambushed and had taken casualties. They must have been on their way out to establish an ambush when they got hit. Ambush patrols are vulnerable when they leave a perimeter that the VC are watching, for they can be seen moving out, hit by a superior force, and annihilated before they can set up. The trick was to keep the VC from knowing where the perimeter was, and to move the ambush out after dark so it couldn't be easily seen and tracked.

"Charlie Six this is Thunder Six, over!" Ricksley called.

"This is Charlie Six, over."

"This is Thunder Six, what is your present disposition? Over."

"This is Charlie Six. All elements are in position according to plan, over." I knew the son-of-a-bitch had not looked at my patrol plan. He thought that we were sitting huddled in one knot in the perimeter. That was far from the case, with two ambushes out per platoon. There was a long pause; I could imagine Ricksley fumbling around, trying to see where my company was. Fortunately, it was posted on the map board at his elbow, so he finally understood that we were in no position to run a relief mission.

"This is Thunder Six, roger, out." He had been ready to send us helter skelter through the dark jungle to aid B Company, never thinking that the VC were experts at sucking units to a point and ambushing them enroute. I could hear him talking to Captain Ballard, the A Company commander, but I could hear only Ricksley's side of the conversation. "Ballard must be in the same perimeter with Ricksley, so why doesn't he walk over ten meters or so and talk to him?" I wondered. "What an incredibly stupid asshole. He ties up the unsecured command net with tactical plans, when he could tell Ballard face to face. Goddamned imbecile. He might as well go tell the VC what we're doing," I thought. Communications security on our battalion command net must be a standing joke with the VC. At any rate, it sounded as if most of A Company was in the perimeter, and Ricksley's grand scheme was to send A Company plunging off to relieve B Company. I didn't know whether I could listen to the rest. Ricksley now prescribed the route, a prominent trail on the map, which A Company should take enroute to B Company, because of the necessity for speed.

A Company reported their departure and thirty minutes later, at around 2300 hours, was ambushed on the trail. It sounded bad on the radio, but apparently they finally fought their way through the ambush. They suffered ten dead and twenty wounded in that fiasco, and by the time they reached B Company the fighting was over. B Company had seven dead and twenty-five wounded. The two companies formed a common perimeter for the rest of the night. I could hear traffic that indicated they were evacuating their wounded and dead.

Recon Platoon finally made it back to the perimeter. They had suffered three killed and seven wounded when they were ambushed. The battalion headquarters was now being secured by Recon Platoon, the 4.2 Inch Mortar Platoon, the artillery personnel of the 105mm battery, and the headquarters personnel.

"What a goddamned mess," I thought. "That fucking Ricksley has just about destroyed this battalion, and if the VC hit that headquarters location now, they can overrun it." I made up my mind that I was not going to let him destroy C Company as long as I was in command. At 0200 hours, one of Third Platoon's ambushes blew, and ten minutes later one of First Platoon's ambushes cracked down on something. The initial reports came in that the ambushes had hit fairly large VC columns coming from west to east; indicating that they were possibly the same units that had hit A and B Companies. A few minutes later, two mechanical ambushes blew. From the direction of the explosions I judged that both had belonged to First Platoon. Assuming that the VC we had made contact with were the same elements that had hit A and B Companies, their pattern of movement seemed to be to the northeast, passing north of our perimeter. I got Lowell Redd to fire two concentrations of artillery fire to our north, hoping that we would get lucky and hit the bastards as they passed us. "Where were the VC going?" I wondered. I looked at my map with a red filtered flashlight but no obvious pattern developed when I studied the contour lines, and the natural lines of drift. "Hell, they could be going anywhere," I thought. But if they continued in the present direction they could hit Highway 13 near Chon Thon around daylight. I called this observation in to the battalion TOC and requested that someone notify the Special Forces detachment at

Chon Thon. Maybe they could put out a few ambushes and hit a column or two of the VC.

Ricksley answered the radio and ordered me to personally lead a recon patrol out at first light to try and locate the VC. "Do you have that Lieutenant? You lead that patrol." I understood his motive. Well, maybe they would hold up to reorganize, because I was sure Third Platoon and First Platoon's ambushes had hurt them, and undoubtedly they had taken casualties in their contacts with A and B Companies and the Recon Platoon. I alerted Sergeant Bigwitch to have a squad ready to leave around daylight. Lieutenant Sutherland was out on ambush.

Well, here it was. Another opportunity for Ricksley to finish his little plan. How many times would it take before he succeeded? Then I started to feel a twinge of guilt. What was so unusual about the task he had demanded that I accomplish? But then it became very personal when he dictated "You lead that patrol." I knew we would be able to pick up their trail. They surely had wounded and they would be confused, and thus careless. There would be blood trails. I knew Bigwitch could follow them in darkness, so in the light of day it would be a snap. That old dragon called fear crept through my consciousness and drove the more honorable emotion of guilt away. Suddenly I felt a chill and drew the poncho liner tight around my shoulders. My stomach started to flutter with butterflies; not clean butterflies of anticipation that you have when you step to bat before a huge crowd. No, these butterflies were of the gut wrenching species better known as fear. Then I thought of Kim, and a strange mixture of fear and anger overcame me. My body shook until the anger dominated the fear. "To succeed we must plan, and to survive we must execute violently," rang in my ears as it had congealed in my thoughts about what absolute truth was in combat. I clung to that phrase and became calm and purposeful. With resolution I reached for the handset to the radio.

I called battalion and asked for two airstrikes northeast of the perimeter for the following day at noon, giving false information on the targets so that the strikes would be approved. Bigwitch selected his old squad to do this mission, and I wasn't surprised at his choice. I let everyone sleep until thirty minutes before daylight. The patrol route and other information were called in to battalion. The rest of the company would rest and prepare to ambush again that night. I went back to my thoughts. For a small patrol to track a clearly superior force was suicide. I was afraid, but at least now I had a plan.

Just at daylight, we left the perimeter in a northeasterly direction. The weather was good, and holding, so signs of the VC were still fresh. Singletary, Lockhart, Collins, and Doc Gill were there from company headquarters. Bigwitch had brought Dillard, Howard, Jones and three more members of Second Squad, for a total of twelve. I had considered bringing Lieutenant Redd with me, but he would be urgently needed in the perimeter if it got hit while we were out. I had planned some on-call artillery concentrations along our route, passed them to him, and he called the FDC and had them work them up.

Bigwitch took the point himself with Howard following with his M60 machine-gun. The rest of the squad followed, and I tagged at the end behind PFC Jones, a black soldier from Mississippi. Behind me were Collins and Lockhart carrying the radios, followed by Doc Gill, with Singletary as rear security. We had enough demolitions to take care of any tasks that might arise, and each man carried a LAW and four hand grenades.

Complete daylight came quickly, and we made contact by radio with First Platoon's two ambushes before we reached them. We passed both ambushes and made certain of the location of their mechanical ambushes as we talked with them. There were numerous VC dead in the second ambush, and the patrol was just beginning to search the ambush kill zone as we passed. The ambush that had blown on the VC column was Sutherland's. It was plain to see that they had done a superb job. I patted Sutherland on the back and got all the information I could on the VC direction of movement. Clearly, they were moving to the northeast and there were enough blood trails, debris, and other signs of movement for Bigwitch to follow. The trail led directly into the first mechanical ambush that had blown, so the same VC unit had been hit twice; once by Sutherland's live ambush and once by the mechanical. There were seven dead VC in the mechanical ambush and more blood trails, indicating that some VC had escaped the second trap as well as the first. "They have to be the luckiest bastards alive," I thought. I held up the column, while Bigwitch and I moved three hundred meters to the north to check the other MA. There were at least ten bodies, sprawled at crazy angles on the small jungle trail and off its side. Again there was a blood trail. We followed it for a few meters, but it soon gave out. The Charlie who had left it lay across the trail where he had died, about twenty meters out of the kill zone. His left arm hung by little more than the skin.

We made our way back to the patrol and moved out on the well marked trail of the surviving VC. In their haste and confusion there had been no attempt to do anything but flee the ambush site. A blind man could have followed them for a kilometer. Finally the blood trails gave out or we lost them, but there were still enough signs of movement for Bigwitch to follow. The jungle was breaking up. The area we were passing through grew light, then the jungle gave out completely.

I slipped forward to where Bigwitch waited. "Damn, just when we were making progress."

Bigwitch pointed to the ground. "The blood trails start again here."

"I don't like these goddamned open rubber trees."

"But if they continue in the direction they are going they will reenter the jungle in about four hundred meters," he pointed to the map. It was easy to see that they were travelling in a straight line, with little thought of covering the trail.

"OK. Let's put a double point in front of you, then you drop back as far as you can without losing sight of them. We will spread the column wide and keep well separated, with twenty meters between men," I said.

"Sir, let's plot some artillery on the edge of the jungle where they will probably reenter, if they keep travelling in the direction they're going now. I'd hate to get caught in these damned rubber trees if they're waiting in the edge of the thick stuff for us."

I gave Lieutenant Redd the coordinates where we wanted the artillery concentration plotted. He took the data, and as an afterthought he told me that all patrols were back in the perimeter.

"Any problems on the two air strikes we requested last night?"

"No, they're too confused at battalion right now to nix anything."

"This is Charlie Six, roger, out."

The double point moved out. After they got well into the rubber, Bigwitch moved out on the blood trail, which dried up in about one hundred meters. We continued in the direction we had been moving, then Bigwitch picked up the blood trail again, after another hundred meters. We caught sight of the jungle where they had reentered. We held up while the double point advanced and entered the jungle, but the VC trail played out completely.

Bigwitch searched back and forth through the trees and finally picked up splotches of blood on a hardwood root indicating that they were still going in the same direction. I kept up with our location exactly on the map, and we moved forward again. The excitement in the air was electric. I felt like a rabbit about to corner a fox, but I knew that if we could get those two air strikes diverted to the right place, and the artillery was responsive, we could at least dent them.

Suddenly Bigwitch held up his hand. "Damn," I cursed to myself. I heard a stream running, and I knew we had reached it. It was a small freshet, not on the map, but strangely the trail stopped completely at its edge. The water was shallow and the banks almost non-existent. They had probably continued, walking in the water from this point. "But which way?" I wondered. Ten meters to the northeast the small rivulet entered thick brush. Bigwitch grabbed my shoulder, and held a finger over his lips. There were sing song voices speaking in Vietnamese, somewhere behind the brush from which the small stream flowed.

We spread the patrol out and concealed them, then Bigwitch and I pushed through the brush, cautiously. It thinned out shortly, and we peered through at a sprawling base camp running through the jungle on both sides of the stream as far as we could see. There were VC all over the area and rice straw hootches could be seen twenty meters into the complex. There were also some wooden structures further down.

At least fifteen wounded VC lay in front of us on rice straw mats, the center of attention in the camp. Several bodies lay to the side with mats over their faces.

"Well, here it is. The whole thing."

"Yeah, let's get out of here before someone leaves or comes, because we are dead into their main gate," Bigwitch said.

We made our way back to the patrol, then withdrew to a dense bamboo cluster about three hundred meters away. I called Redd and told him what we had and to gear up every tube of artillery he could get laid on it. Also, I requested that both airstrikes be diverted to the coordinates of the hootches in the center of the camp. I looked at my watch. It was 1145 hours.

"Charlie Six this is Sidewinder Three-Three, over," the FAC was approaching from the south and I could hear his little fixed wing aircraft humming in our direction.

"This is Charlie Six. We've located an occupied regimental sized base camp, and we can use your two strikes and everything else you can divert to it, over."

"Roger, wait out."

He called back in five minutes. "We have two more strikes in addition to those you requested, and they should be checking in in about five minutes, over."

"This is Charlie Six. Roger. At this time there is no artillery. We will begin the artillery when your fast movers begin, over."

"This is Sidewinder Three-Three, roger, I have the artillery located, so no problem. Where are you? Over."

"This is Charlie Six. I can't mark now but we are almost directly under you, over." I vectored him to a spot directly over us and confirmed our location.

"And Sidewinder Three-Three. Roger, I have you plotted. The hired help has arrived, and I'm marking now, over." I heard the smoke rocket go in, in the direction of the base camp. We spread out in a hasty ambush, because it was very likely the VC would spill out of the base camp in every direction once the air strikes and artillery hit them. I called Redd and told him to start the artillery.

CHAPTER 46

The ground rumbled and shook as strike after strike of five hundred pound bombs ripped the jungle canopy and tore into the VC camp. The artillery pounded away at the target, while the smell of cordite and smoke wafted through the jungle. Eight inch howitzer rounds and 175 mm rounds were mixed with the 105 mm rounds that cracked and crunched and sent shrapnel whining and pinging in every direction. Four or five VC tore past the bamboo cluster where we were hidden, in a foot race to escape the death from the sky. The jets followed the five hundred pounders with napalm. The jungle blazed, and secondary explosions began to pop off.

We hugged the ground and waited. Another air strike began as soon as the first one finished, and altogether four flights of jets expended ordnance on the camp. Just when I thought they were finished, another flight rolled in and began hammering. Shrapnel whined and slashed all around our position and leaves from the canopy above our heads showered down as they were severed from the trees. Pieces of steel as big as dinner plates spilled over into our position. I looked at a jagged smoking piece of shrapnel that had fallen to the ground beside my right boot.

I glanced at the tense faces of the men as they hugged the ground, trying to climb completely into their steel helmets. There was no more movement in our direction by the VC.

"Charlie Six, this is Sidewinder Three-Three, I'm going to have to break station and refuel. We have finished. Can you assess? Over."

"This is Charlie Six. I'll attempt to and call in through channels, over."

"This is Sidewinder Three-Three, roger. I saw a number of hootches go up in flames, and there were multiple secondary explosions along that little stream. Good to do business with you; see you later! Out."

The artillery was still working over the area, and the symphony of singing, whirring, pinging shrapnel was shrill and close. I got the patrol up, and we eased forward as far as we could move without getting our heads torn off by the whacking, exploding shells. The artillery ceased, and I confirmed this with Redd on the radio. He informed me that there was more when we needed it and urgently requested an assessment. I promised him we would try.

We pushed forward cautiously, and the screaming of the high pitched, excited voices in Vietnamese reached our ears. Through the underbrush I could see them coming out of holes, while several little knots of them milled around in confusion. There were bodies lying everywhere. Some of the living were trying to take care of the wounded. Others were wounded themselves, some seriously. The hootches I had spotted earlier were burned to the ground.

"Let's get 'em Sir!" Bigwitch was at my elbow.

"Why not?" I passed the word for everyone to get on line and fire LAW's first, and then use small arms and grenades. We did the best we could to spread out, in the tightness of the area, without being detected. When the men appeared to be reasonably settled I gave the signal;

we extended the LAW tubes and sighted. I fired into a knot of eight or ten VC and they flew like tenpins in a bowling alley. The rest of the patrol fired their LAW's, and we began to rake them with small arms fire. There was no attempt to return fire, and I could see VC fleeing through the underbrush as far as visibility permitted. Finally a few shots of return fire began to pepper in from unseen enemy positions. This built steadily in volume until finally I decided we had better leave while we still had the option. We ran stumbling through the jungle thickness, back to the bamboo cluster that we had selected as our rally point. I counted heads; we were missing one.

"Who's missing?" I asked.

"Sir, it must be Jones. He was right beside me when we started," Dillard said.

"OK. Let's go back and get him."

We went back some 75 meters and found Jones dead, with the back of his head shattered, apparently by a rifle round. We picked him up and moved back toward the rubber trees. We hadn't moved a hundred meters before we received a burst of fire from our left front from three or four weapons. Dillard went down and PFC Pickering was hit in the thigh. We returned fire, while Bigwitch crawled around to the right for about twenty meters and threw a grenade into the ambush. He sprinted in behind it firing his rifle. We left Pickering and Dillard with Doc Gill and moved forward. A VC broke through the underbrush in front of us, apparently fleeing from Bigwitch's assault. My first round hit him in the chest and the second caught him in the throat. He went over backwards, leaving a crimson spray in the air. We quickly checked the area from which they had ambushed us. Three VC were killed by Bigwitch's grenade and rifle fire.

Doc Gill had taken care of Dillard and Pickering but neither one could move on his own. I decided to get two helicopters to extract us. We could blow two or three trees down and make a decent PZ. Bigwitch and Howard went out with the det cord and blew the PZ while I was on the horn calling for the ships to lift us out. Ricksley answered my call and gave me a "wait out." Then he called back.

"Charlie Six, this is Thunder Six, over."

"This is Charlie Six, over."

"This is Thunder Six. I will be there to personally assess your situation in ten minutes, over."

"This is Charlie Six, roger, out."

"What in the hell was there to assess? I had one dead and two wounded and was in the middle of the remnants of an enemy regiment. To me that was fairly simple. There had to be more to it. Why does he want to fly in here? If he's trying to prove something it may be a bigger risk than he has bargained for," I thought.

Bigwitch, Collins, with his radio, and I started for the LZ/PZ that Bigwitch and Howard had blown. I heard Ricksley's helicopter beating toward us from the southwest. We broke out of the jungle into the rubber, where I pulled the pin on a smoke grenade and threw it into the LZ. The grenade popped; purple smoke boiled out of it and rose into the blue afternoon sky. There was a slight breeze stirring which started to dissipate the smoke but not before Ricksley saw and identified it. He was still two minutes out.

Suddenly two VC burst from the rubber trees and came running directly across the LZ. Collins and Bigwitch dropped them just off the pad, and one of them pitched forward and rolled almost to my feet. The other fell against the trunk of a rubber tree with blood gushing from his upper arm, some into the bowl used to collect rubber and the rest down the trunk and onto the white sandy soil. He gradually slid down the rubber tree trunk, rolled over, and lay looking up into the tree's branches with sightless eyes.

The helicopter pulled out of its descent, banked and rolled out into a wide circle.

"Charlie Six, this is Thunder Six. Do you have contact at this time? Over."

"This is Charlie Six. We did have but there is no contact now, over."

Ricksley didn't answer. The helicopter banked and descended, hovering into the LZ. Ricksley jumped out, and the helicopter lifted off and went into a wide circular pattern to our southwest. Ricksley strode past the two VC and picked up the AK 47 that lay at the feet of the dead guerrilla in front of me. He looked at Bigwitch and Collins.

"Sergeant, take the RTO and check with your rear perimeter to see if they have any contact," he said. The radio Collins carried was on the battalion frequency, and for some reason he wanted us to check with our rear area on our company net. I started to switch the set Collins carried to the company frequency, but then there would be no radio on battalion's frequency and the commander was on the ground with me.

Sergeant Bigwitch shot me a deliberate glance. I nodded for him to go. "Yes, Sir," he replied to Ricksley, as he followed Collins into the jungle. I assumed that Ricksley wanted to talk with me privately; that explained his sending Bigwitch and Collins on ahead.

I pushed into the thickness of the jungle. We walked about ten steps in the direction of my patrol perimeter. They were well in, about two hundred and fifty meters further.

"Worthington, drop that rifle and turn around." Ricksley's voice sounded hollow and slightly quivering, but the impact of his intentions still had not clearly grabbed me as I let my rifle slide to the mossy jungle floor and turned to face him. Calmly, slowly, he pointed the muzzle of the AK 47, snugging the stock into his shoulder and aligning the weapon on me. He was unsmiling and deliberate, and his twisted purple lips parted to speak.

"I was relieved of command one hour ago, Worthington, and it was because of you and those other two dunces commanding my companies. I would have been a general," he said "I have Kim," he said snarling. "And that damn bitch married me and is still in love with you. Can you believe that? She has me and she is still in love with a nobody."

He ground his teeth between his purple lips, and the sweat rolled down his cheeks. "How did you get commissioned? You could never have gotten into West Point. And that stupid Korean bitch still loves you, a nobody's nobody."

As he leveled the AK 47 at the center of my chest I knew that my chances were slim. I tried to time my movement as I watched his facial expression and his hands. I saw his finger begin to tighten on the trigger and I dived for a bamboo cluster to my left. The sharp blast of the weapon rang in my ears, and I felt instant pain in my chest. As I rolled over and over I felt the jarring impact as I slammed into the bamboo. My eyes were bleary and I could not see. I forcibly jerked my head to the side and my eyes began to focus. I lay on my back as Ricksley walked into view, leveling the rifle at my face. He was unsmiling and deliberate as he walked almost onto me. I tried to struggle but nothing worked, and I found myself listening for the explosion of the next round into my face. I stared into his eyes and listened for the last sound I would ever hear. As my eyes locked with his, his lips parted to speak.

"Here's to the execution of a nobody. You don't deserve to live another heartbeat."

Suddenly the blast came, and I jerked as I prepared for whatever eternity had waiting for me. Ricksley's head exploded and splattered me with blood and viscera. The body pitched forward across my legs and twitched before lying still with half the hideous grin of the purple lips still visible on the twisted face.

Bigwitch walked deliberately into view, holding an AK 47 at the ready. He delivered a savage kick into Ricksley's midsection, sending a fresh spray of gore as the body rolled off my legs. Bigwitch bent over me, but I could hardly see or hear him. The sky rocked and became black, and I was back on the river beach of the Han Tan. A beautiful tall girl with long silky hair ran across the sand spit in my direction, flashing perfect white teeth and the most beautiful smile I had ever seen. I reached for her, and then the image faded. She was going away, fading into the eternal darkness, and I couldn't reach her. Then the darkness closed.

I could remember Bigwitch loading me into the dust off but could recall nothing else until my eyes opened at the brigade clearing station. I was staring up from a stretcher at the two packets of fluid suspended from a wire and plugged into me. One was dark red and the other a clear liquid.

"You're a mighty lucky young man," the surgeon was saying, "With a wound like this there is usually serious damage. We are evacuating you to Japan. It's a lovely place. Have you ever been there?"

THE END

Made in the USA